REVIEWS

"A VERY ENJOYABLE read. If you like an authentically written historical novel that captures the essence of time, this is a book you will enjoy. If you like a good mystery with lots of plot twists, you will enjoy this book. If you like a book with well-developed characters that grow and mature over a period of time, you will like this book. In short, this story contains a wonderful blend of many elements that will appeal to a broad audience."

Book Review from "Window to My World"

"This book, although fiction, weaved historical facts and detail throughout. It captured my attention from the start. I hated to put it down when I had something to do or somewhere to go. The storyline is captivating and draws in the reader quickly. Mr. Cline writes in a way that I found easy to read. I loved this book, and I highly recommend it to others."

Book Review by Sandie from "Pages I Turn"

THE LAST CONFEDERATE BATTLE

A Novel

BY
JOHN J CLINE

OTHER WORKS BY
JOHN J. CLINE

Books

"Sea Stories & Navy Tales" "Toby and the Wooden Flute"

Short Stories

"Decoration Day" (April 2011)
"The Master of the House is Gone" (March 2011)
"The Old Man and the Football Team" (November 2010)
"The Santa Legacy: A Christmas Essay" (November 2012)
"The Girl Who Touched Me" (May 2011)
"The Flower" (May 2013)

Music

Song of Idaho
American Bridal Waltz
Sunset in the Harbor

ISBN: 0578127245
ISBN-13: 9780578127248

Library of Congress Number: 2009911140
CreateSpace Independent Publishing Platform
North Charleston, South Carolina

Cover created by Photo-Artist Marc Auth www.authphoto.com

Printed in the United States of America

Fifth Printing Corpus Editus Books
http://idahoauthor.com

DEDICATION

This book is dedicated to my family and friends who continually make my life more fun and exciting.

Forward

HISTORY RECORDS THAT the last battle of the Civil War was fought on the red clay soil of the Rio Grande River at Palmito Ranch, near Brownsville, Texas. That battle took place in mid-May 1865, more than a month following General Lee's surrender at Appomattox, Virginia. There are factual accounts of skirmishes that took place long after Lee's surrender. This fictional story details the lives and occurrences that led up to the Last Confederate Battle; a fight that took place several years after the battle at Palmito Ranch.

PROLOGUE

Near midnight, July 6, 1865

DISILLUSIONED BY NEARLY four years of fighting in the War of Northern Aggression, Captain Andrew Jefferson Davis (Andy to family and friends) sat alone in the dark by a small campfire in what had once been his Georgia plantation's expansive front yard. Uncharacteristically, he was sobbing uncontrollably. During the war, he had seen unbelievable carnage and death, yet tears had never come. It was only after he finally got home that tears flowed. His wife Abigail and their son Toby had been tortured and murdered during Sherman's march to the sea.

A squad of foraging Union soldiers had set fire to the Davis plantation's barns and fields. When Negro field hands confronted the soldiers, the soldiers had said that they were there to set them free. The field hands had tried to stop the marauding soldiers, saying that they were already free, but the sergeant disregarded them and ordered them to hurry and catch up with the main force of Union soldiers who had left Madison earlier in the day.

"You will be cared for," the sergeant said.

Then he set fire to their quarters and the rest of the plantation's out-buildings. With no homes and no possessions, the darkies did as they were told, hurriedly walking to catch the main force of Union soldiers.

As the squad had made their way to the plantation-house, they caught Abigail trying to escape with her young son. Subsequently, members of the squad slaked their lusty thirst by taking turns with Abigail by order of rank and position. A fat, grubby corporal filled his perverted desires with Toby before snuffing out the life of the child by choking him to death, thereby silencing the boy's screams. When the squad had finished with Abigail, a soldier fired a single forty-four caliber bullet into her head. The squad doused the bodies and the mattress with kerosene before setting the house on fire to hide their shameful misdeeds. The flames had been so intense that there were no bodies to bury. The grand plantation-house lay in cold gray ashes with only the chimneys of two brick fireplaces standing somewhat intact at opposite ends of the burned-out structure.

Even though it had been nearly a year since his family had been raped, tortured, and finally murdered then burned, it was his first trip back home following the end of hostilities and his release from incarceration as a prisoner of war. Officials at the prison had taken delight in telling him the ghastly details of his family's demise. When he finally got home, he discovered that the stories were horrifyingly true. Not even rage and near starvation could intrude on his sobbing at the campfire. He had lost everything that he valued most—his family and his home. And they had been taken in the vilest way.

But life had not always been so hard. In the early years, the Southern lifestyle had been very kind to Andy and his older brothers, Dwayne and Everett.

Chapter One

March 4, 1857

THERE WERE TWO years between the three boys, meaning that Dwayne was two years older than Everett and four years older than Andy. The boys were the fifth generation to occupy the Davis plantation. Their great- great grandfather received the original parcel of land in a grant from Georgia's Legislature because of his service during the American Revolutionary War. He built a small cabin and temporary slave quarters and successfully planted and harvested cotton. Upon his death, Andy's great grandfather took over the property and, over time, bought many of the land grants from surrounding farms, establishing a plantation of nearly ten thousand acres— extremely large even by plantation standards.

He built the original plantation-house, barns, a smoke-house, and permanent slave quarters. Fields of cotton stretched as far as anyone on the second story of the plantation-house could see. Fifty or so slaves maintained the fields and the plantation-house under the watchful eyes of a paid overseer.

When their great grandfather died, their grandfather remodeled the plantation house into a fine antebellum mansion with four large white columns decorating the front. There was a long driveway leading from the main road to the columned entryway of the plantation house. The U-shaped driveway was surrounded by expansive well-manicured lawns, large magnolia trees, and slave-tended flower beds. And when he died, their father, Augustus Davis, by nature a very conservative man, took over the management of the plantation, which continued to prosper

Their mother, Elizabeth, a local girl known to everyone as Beth, managed their home and the children. She also personally maintained a small flower garden on the side of the house that collected the morning sun, the products of which she took to the Methodist Church in Madison early each Sunday morning for the glorification of God. Life for the young boys was generally unhurried.

Because the boys were close in age, they wrestled, fought, played, and worked in the field's along-side slaves. Together the boys grew stronger each year. Being the youngest of the three, Andy was constantly bedeviled by his older brothers, but he developed into an easy-going young man with a fast smile who was slow to anger. While all three of the boys were tall and ruggedly built, Andy was clearly the handsomest of the three, which later drew the attention of blossoming Madison girls.

Augustus Davis concerned himself with teaching the boys how to work with their hands. Beth saw to it that they learned how to use their brains—an uncommon accomplishment for privileged plantation-raised children. The boys attended school ten miles to the east in Madison. Each weekday morning just before dawn, Chiggers, a fifteen-year-old Negro slave, would hitch up two draft horses and drive the boys to school in a wagon, picking up the children of other families along the way. When the boys turned twelve, they each received a horse of their choice on which to ride to school and to visit friends at neighboring plantations. When Andy turned twelve, there was no longer a need for Chiggers to make the trip to and from the schoolhouse, so he was diverted to other duties.

Beth tested the boys each evening to ensure that they had learned their lessons from school. She would also open her Bible and read to the boys. She knew that it would only be a short time before they would age sufficiently to warrant their own horses, after which they would likely to be gone more than they were at home, especially in the early evening hours. During harvest season, there was no school because students, both boys and girls, remained at home to harvest the fields and can vegetables, jams, jellies, and other edibles for the winter. They had only enough cows for milk, and steers, pigs, and sheep to feed both masters and slaves and to produce new food-stock for the following years.

For three or four weeks each fall, Augustus Davis took his sons to the mountains, where he maintained a small rustic cabin that he used while hunting. The trip took four days each way. By plantation standards, the cabin, located on the Appalachian Trail in the Chattahoochee Forest, was just a crude shack. But it was only used as a male getaway; a place to rest while hunting larger game that was not normally available in the farmlands of the central plains of Georgia. There were no roads to the cabin high in the mountains. Access was limited to walking or horseback. The hunting days were fun, but they were also learning experiences. Andy killed his first deer at eight and his first bear at twelve. He was an excellent shot with both rifle and sidearm, and he had exceptional hunting instincts. Being the better hunter, he often bested his older brothers on Blood Mountain.

At age sixteen, Andy followed Dwayne's path by entering William and Mary College at Williamsburg, Virginia. Both Augustus and Beth would have preferred that he attend a local college as Everett had, especially since the City of Madison was well known for its private colleges. However, the schools in Georgia had not yet developed into grand institutions on an equal level with William and Mary. Moreover, if the truth were to be known, Andy just wanted to get away—to see different parts of the country, well away from plantations and the Deep South. Although he studied law, he decided early on that he would not likely apprentice for lawyers in Virginia or Georgia. Unlike his older brothers, he was more attracted to the business of agriculture. Therefore, while he pursued his studies in law, he also ventured to farms along the eastern seaboard where cotton was not king. He learned different techniques for fertilizing and watering the land. He fully accepted the idea of crop rotation, an idea that was foreign and easily dismissed by his father, brothers, and cotton-producing neighbors. He was also interested in the practical application of science—everything from John Deere's wrought iron "grasshopper plow" with a steel share, to the sulky riding plow with several plowshares attached to make one rolling apparatus on which the plowman could ride behind a team of draft horses.

He was fascinated by the telegraph, so much so that he begged the telegrapher in Williamsburg to unlock the mysteries of using the telegraph key. After a few weeks of training, Andy volunteered to work the Saturday midnight shift, without pay, so he could learn the telegraph business and improve his proficiency as a telegrapher. When he wasn't busy sending or receiving telegrams, he would spend the dark early morning hours studying for classes by the yellow light of two desk- mounted kerosene lanterns.

After receiving his law degree at age twenty, Andy took a year to travel rather than to clerk for a lawyer or judge. Everywhere he went, he made notes and sketched diagrams depicting agricultural methods foreign to the cotton fields of Georgia. He was especially interested in preventing disease in animals and plants, for he had seen how the Boll weevil could devastate vast acreages of cotton and bring ruin to even enormous plantations. While he was in Europe, he observed an outbreak of Hoof and Mouth Disease. He watched as the disease spread from farm to farm in a matter of days, requiring hundreds of animals to be slaughtered and barns to be burned to prevent the further spread of the disease. Andy traveled to Ireland to view the physical and economic results of the potato famine. He asked a myriad of questions and made a great many notes, all of which he kept in a leather- bound portfolio. Ironically, it was disease that caused him to return home earlier than scheduled.

A letter from his oldest brother had taken three months to catch up with him in England. The Atlantic crossing took nearly a month, and the letter remained in a box in the office of the British Maritime Agent who handled much of the supplies ordered by and for the Davis Plantation. When Andy returned to England, two months after the letter's arrival, he learned that his mother and father, Beth and Augustus, had died of Small Pox, along with half of the slaves. Many other families in Morgan County had also experienced pox-related deaths. Dwayne had written, saying that Andy was urgently needed at home.

It was late fall when Andy finally read the letter. Booking passage on a ship with a master that was willing to brave a dangerous winter crossing was nearly impossible, but he found such a ship two weeks later, and arrived safely in New York in late December. It took another seven days of steady travel by coach to Atlanta, where he bought a horse and tack for the trip to Madison so that he would not have to wait on the local coach that travelled only weekly to the smaller cities in the region.

Andy's brothers, Dwayne and Everett, both of whom now lived in Madison rather than on the plantation, had established different lifestyles. Dwayne had become a lawyer of some distinction. Although he practiced his profession in Madison, he was often called upon to defend the well-to-do in Atlanta, Augusta, Athens, Eatonton, and even in Milledgeville, the capitol of Georgia. He traveled to Milledgeville often, as he had been elected to represent Morgan County in the State Senate. Ev, as the brothers came to call Everett, had married a local Madison girl, and had started a hardware store, branching out to include canned goods, bolts of cloth for handmade dresses, and work-clothes from factories in the north. Like Dwayne's law practice, the store was very profitable, so neither brother was at all interested in running the Davis plantation.

On Andy's arrival in Madison, the brothers discussed the matter of running the plantation over dinner at Everett's home. Ev's wife, Barbara, plied them with thick slabs of beef, vegetables that had been canned months earlier, and Spanish Madera. It was the best meal that Andy had eaten since leaving Europe; shipboard fare having been meager, and roadhouse meals very expensive and generally bland. By midnight, the three brothers reached an agreement that each felt was equitable.

Dwayne, as the oldest of the brothers, had inherited the plantation outright. It was decided that Dwayne would deed the plantation to Andy, with Everett's written approval and dissolution of any future claim on the land in the event of Dwayne's death. In return, Dwayne and Everett would each receive ten percent of the plantation's annual earnings. Dwayne drew up the legal paperwork the very next morning. Each of the brothers signed the documents and wished Andy success as the new plantation owner. Riding to the Davis plantation, Andy was struck by the enormous responsibilities he would now be facing.

Arriving at the plantation, he found the overseer passed out drunk in the parlor; his muddy boots propped up on the fine fabric of Beth's favorite imported ottoman. Andy dragged the drunken overseer out of the house, dumping him in a water trough near the entryway. The sopping wet overseer leaped out of the water coughing and gagging. Looking through blurry eyes he yelled, "What the hell do you think you are doing?" "Who are you, anyhow?"

"I'm Andrew Davis, the owner of this plantation."

"I don't give a damn who you are. Nobody treats me like a darky and gets away with it."

The overseer swung a haymaker, but Andy easily sidestepped, grabbed the overseer, and again dumped his head to the bottom of the water trough, while his legs flailed in the air outside the edges of the trough. The overseer came out of the watering trough with a knife, striking wildly. Andy kicked the overseer's left knee with a sideways kick, knocking the overseer to the ground. Andy disarmed the overseer by stepping on the overseer's wrist and removing the knife from the overseer's struggling hand. Then Andy ordered the drunk off the property.

"I'll kill you," said the overseer, as he lunged for Andy.

Andy, who stood a full six inches taller than the swarthy overseer, jabbed with his left, bloodying the overseer's nose, and then he hit him with a murderous right cross to the mouth, drawing blood and a couple of teeth.

"Get your gear and get out, you don't work here anymore."

"What about the pay that's due me?" the overseer whined.

"How much are you owed?"

"Three months at a hundred a month."

"I'll write you a check. You can cash it at the bank in Madison."

The overseer nodded his head and slowly headed toward the Overseers House to pack his gear and then to the barn to get his horse.

Andy went inside the plantation house and sat behind his father's huge oak desk, pausing a few moments before opening the center drawer to withdraw the family checkbook. He checked recent records to ensure that the overseer was in fact due the amount stated. Andy wrote a check and took it outside where the overseer was walking toward the plantation-house.

"Don't ever come back to this plantation," Andy said. The overseer just nodded his head and walked his horse down the long driveway, wiping the telltale signs of blood from his mouth and nose.

Andy sat on the front steps to the plantation-house pondering his predicament. He had no overseer, so he would have to manage the plantation personally. Several of the slaves who worked in and around the plantation- house stood several feet away in wide-eyed fear. Although they had known Andy from his birth, they were none-the-less afraid of him. He had been gone a long time, and he was after all, their master. And he had just beaten a man with his fists, a white man at that, to a bloody pulp. Andy stood and approached the slaves, all of whom backed away except for Chiggers, who stood his ground. Andy smiled and called each one by name as he shook hands with the males and greeted females. He had grown up with them and considered them more as friends than slaves. The feeling was not altogether mutual. They were after all, slaves.

It was the noon hour and the slaves were coming in for dinner. Breakfast was a light meal, followed by a heavy dinner, usually a two-hour affair, which included an hour or so of rest. Supper was eaten in the evening. The word "lunch" had no meaning in southern circles. Lila, the plantation house cook summoned Andy to the table as she had for years. He ate sparingly, his mind occupied with the operation of the plantation. The slaves ate ravenously and the talk at the table was all about Andy's beating up and dismissing the overseer. The feeling, both in the plantation-house and among the slaves, was greatly unsettled and speculative.

Andy called Chiggers to the study. "Have a seat, Chiggers."

Chiggers' eyes widened in disbelief. Slaves were never allowed to sit in the plantation-house, especially not in the company of the master. Chiggers furtively looked left and right. No one was watching, so he cautiously sat on the edge of the chair in front of the big oak desk.

"Chiggers, which of the men know the most about what needs to be done around the plantation during the winter months?" Andy asked.

"That would be Otis. He been in the fields for nigh on twenty years."

"Tell Otis that he is in charge of the field workers until I can come up with a plan for running this plantation. Have him report to me each evening before supper with an accounting as to what has been done during the day."

"Yessa, Massa."

"Chiggers, you practically raised me. You took me to and from school and we used to sneak off and fish together each spring. Call me Andy, as you always have."

"Yessa, Massa—ah Massa Andy."

Chiggers left the plantation-house to go find Otis.

Andy spent the next two days and nights studying papers that dealt with the business of the plantation. On the third and fourth days, he inspected the plantation, stopping periodically in each field to examine the earth, making notes in his journal along the way. On the morning of the fifth day, he rode back to Madison to meet with his brothers. His message would be devastating.

Arriving in Madison at mid-day, Andy met first with Dwayne. The two argued loudly; anger boiled up in Dwayne. But in the end, Dwayne acquiesced and said that the plantation was Andy's to manage as he saw fit. Although he vehemently disagreed with Andy's plan, it was up to Andy to decide on how the plantation was to be run.

Everett was shocked when told of Andy's plans for running the plantation. Ev thought that Andy would surely turn the townspeople and neighboring plantation- owners against him, and maybe even against the two brothers. In the end, however, Everett realized that since his was the only hardware store in Madison, he could probably weather the firestorm that would surely come.

To Andy, the facts were simple. The plantation's earth was showing signs of serious mineral depletion. For generations, only cotton had been grown. He had made the decision to continue to grow cotton on one half of the farmland, but he wanted to begin a rotation of crops including wheat, alfalfa, soybean, corn, sorghum, and barley on the other half. He also wanted to experiment with a plant from the legume family of plants that was grown in South America, and which he had first seen while visiting a farm in South Carolina. He wanted to grow peanuts for food value, both for animals and humans, and for vegetable oil. Andy would be the first to grow peanuts in the central plains. However, it was not his choice of crops that would turn neighbors and townspeople against him.

Andy's analysis of the plantation's books revealed that the plantation was not grossing the profits that it once had. He was convinced that part of the loss was due to soil depletion; the soil was not producing as well as it had in the past. Also, the price of seed and fertilizer had greatly increased. Lastly, most of the slaves who had died during the previous year's outbreak of small pox were field hands. It would cost between twenty-five and fifty thousand dollars to replace them; money that would result in diminishing returns over the years as slaves became too old to work in the fields. Replacing the lost slaves would cost nearly every cent that the plantation had saved for operations. So, Andy wanted to try something different. He wanted to spend the money on new technology and new farming practices instead of slaves.

Returning to the plantation, Andy asked Chiggers to have the slaves assemble in the barn at 7:00 a.m. so that he could talk with all of them, men and women, at the same time. He had spent the night writing twenty-seven letters. It was well after midnight when he finally fell across the mattress of his massive four-poster bed. He didn't bother to undress.

Waking early, Andy splashed cold water on his face from a plain white porcelain washbasin that was situated on a massive oak dresser.

He shivered as the winter air gushed into the bedroom from a partially open window; the fire in the bedroom fireplace had burned out while he slept. He privately admitted that he was shivering in part because of what he was about to do that morning.

"Massa Andy," Chiggers called from the bottom landing.

"I'm upstairs, Chiggers"

"Everyone except Lila is in the barn, Massa Andy."

"Find Lila and escort her to the barn. I'll be there in a few minutes."

"Yessa Massa Andy," Chiggers said.

Chiggers turned to face Lila who was standing with her hands on her ample hips in the hallway.

"I told you woman—you had to go too. Come along, now."

Lila grabbed Chiggers arm and he could feel her shivering, but it wasn't from the cold winter air. They walked in silence to the barn.

Andy arrived in the barn noticing that families stood together, single men stood as a group, and single women huddled together at the back of the gathering. Some of the children were running and yelling playfully while their mothers tried to quiet them. As soon as the children saw Andy, they immediately became quiet and ran to hide behind their mother's skirts.

"This plantation is losing money," Andy started. The slaves shrunk back a step or two.

"But it's not your fault," Andy continued.

"The land is tired. We need to change the way we farm if we are going to realize our full potential. We need to learn new methods of farming and to use new tools. That means you will have to learn new ways too."

The look of fear was clearly evident on the faces of every man and woman.

"However, I think it is important that each of you have a reason for learning those new skills. I also think it's important that you be motivated to work even harder than you have in the past. And I intend on giving you that motivation; not through beatings, but through freedom."

The slaves looked at Andy and each other, not comprehending what he was saying.

"I have here a letter for each one of you. The letter says that as of today, you are free men and women. You are free to leave, but I hope you will stay—as paid field hands and house staff, not as slaves. I will pay you ten dollars a month to stay and work the land. That's half what a white field hand makes in many places up north, but I will continue to provide quarters and food, just as it has always been. Field hands up north don't get that. Otis and Chiggers will be paid a little more, because they will be your supervisors. Otis will be in charge of field operations, and Chiggers will be in charge of domestic operations including the plantation house, food storage, meal preparation, and for other domestic issues such as seeing that there is sufficient wood for the winter and clothes for you and your families. If you chose to leave, I would suggest that you quickly go up north. You will not be well regarded here in the South; not even with this letter."

Murmuring became louder and louder as Andy talked. One woman fainted and another yelled, "Halleluiah, freedom."

Andy continued by saying, "any man who stays and works the land for ten years will receive ten acres of land. The land will be deeded to him. He will have to pay taxes from his earnings to the county, but it will be his land. We will help him build a house on that land, and he can raise animals and vegetables to feed his family."

"Together, we will work the fields and make this plantation profitable for you and for me and my brothers. There will be no work today. Think about what I have said, and make your decision to stay or to leave. Pick up your freedom letter from Chiggers and let him know what you decide."

Andy left them standing in the barn and returned to the plantation-house. It was a huge gamble, but what had just happened would be nothing when compared to what his neighbors and the Madison townspeople would say when told about Andy freeing his slaves.

Andy went into the study and sat behind the big oak desk. Freeing the slaves was not the only gamble. He was about to spend the entire plantation's capital buying six pairs of draft horses and riding plows.

Although he didn't know how many of his former slaves would stay, he had to be able to work the land come spring. He worked at the desk for several hours.

"Andy, come eat your supper," Lila said.

"Lila, you were not supposed to work today. I can make my own supper."

"I been cooking meals for the Massa's family on this plantation since I was a young girl. I'm not stopping now."

"Does that mean you are going to stay?" Andy asked. "Yes, I got my freedom letter from Chiggers, but what do you think freedom means to a female slave who has no relatives and nowhere to go? This is my home too."

"Well Lila, I'm glad you are staying. I would miss your rhubarb pie," Andy said as he grinned.

"No rhubarb pie for you if you don't eat your supper, even if you are the Massa."

"I'm not the master any more, Lila. Now I'm just your employer."

"No sir, you are my family, now git yourself to the table."

"Yes'em," Andy said contritely, but with a grin.

After supper, Andy returned to the study where Chiggers was waiting to report those who would leave, and those who would remain.

"Massa Andy, everyone has their freedom letters, but only one young buck, Calhoun, wants to leave. He said that he would leave in the morning."

"Make sure the cooks prepare some food for his trip, and give him a change of clothes. There's an old suitcase in the storage shed that he can have to carry his belongings. I wish him well,"

"Yessa, I'll let him know."

"Tell everyone that I am glad they are staying. I'll see them in the morning. Ask Otis to come by. I want to go over plans for winter work."

"Yessa, I'll go fetch him now."

And except for Calhoun being found dead a few days later hanging from a tree with his freedom letter stapled to his chest with a hunting knife, the days and months went by without incident.

Crops were planted in the spring using the new draft horses and riding plows. They planted cotton in half the time and the yield was nearly twice what it had been in years gone by. The new crops fared well, but he had to sell them in Atlanta and other cities, as no stores in Madison would buy from Andy, with the exception of his brother, Everett. His neighbors and the Madison people had been outraged by him freeing his slaves, so they shunned him. But something that they wouldn't be able to ignore was the fact that the Davis plantation fared so much better than neighboring plantations. Even after reducing the number of cotton fields by half, the yield on those reduced acreages equaled many of Andy's neighbors who produced cotton on far more land.

The first harvest, since freeing his slaves, yielded much more than he expected. As the days turned cooler, the crops were sold, and it was time to take the substantial cash receipts to the bank in Madison. And after a growing season of hard work, it would be good to see his brothers, who themselves had been too busy to make the trip to the plantation; especially since they were still peeved over Andy's business decisions.

At midmorning, Andy saddled his restless black stallion for the trip to Madison. He attached two saddle holstered forty-four caliber Colt Dragoons and sheathed a double barrel ten-gauge shotgun in the rifle scabbard. He wasn't expecting trouble, but his saddlebags were bulging with cash from the crop sales, and he wasn't about to take chances with the plantation's money. Andy bid good day to Chiggers as his tall stallion pranced down the plantation's long driveway. Reaching the road, Andy turned east to Madison and allowed the stallion to run for about a mile at full gallop. He slowed the blowing horse to a slow walk for the rest of the trip, allowing the horse to cool long before they reached their destination at the Madison Bank.

Andy dismounted and tied both reins in a half hitch on the rail. The stallion didn't like standing in one place and was prone to walking off whenever he got the chance, especially if there was a hearty patch of green grass nearby. Andy untied the saddlebags and threw them over his left shoulder. He left the Colts in their saddle holsters, but took the heavy ten-gauge shotgun—again, just in case.

The accountant met Andy at the door and ushered him into the banker's office. Like most plantation owners, Andy seldom did business at the teller's window. As he entered the banker's office, he shifted the shotgun to his left hand, extending his right hand to shake hands with Mr. Bennett, the banker and a longtime family friend. Before he could say anything, a female voice from the other side of the room asked, "Have you become so notorious as to need a shotgun to do business, or are you now a bank robber?" Andy turned, and had the briefest moment of difficulty recognizing the young woman.

"Why Abigail, you're..."

The woman crossed the room in three quick steps, raising her parasol in a threatening manner.

"I'm what, Andrew Davis?"

Andy's right hand involuntarily shot up to his left cheek where he touched a one inch scar—a scar that was left by this same young woman a few years earlier when she hit him with her riding crop.

"Beautiful," he said in a whisper.

The woman looked into his eyes, and then her gaze shot to the floor. She blushed slightly.

"I see you two remember each other," the banker said smiling.

He had watched his daughter and this young man grow up. He had listened to his teenage daughter's continual grousing over Andy's incessant teasing and about him constantly pulling her pigtails. The last time Andy had pulled her pigtails, Abigail spun around, whipping Andy in the face with a riding crop, drawing blood and leaving the scar. He never pulled her pigtails again. And in truth, it was only a short time later that she stopped wearing pigtails altogether.

"I almost didn't recognize her, Mr. Bennett. She's... grown up."

"You both have," the banker said smiling broadly. "Now Abigail, you get yourself home. Young Mr. Davis and I have business to attend to."

"Oh father, Mr. Davis isn't going anywhere," Abigail said smiling as she moved toward the door.

Andy held the door for Abigail and asked, "When can I see you?"

"Why Mr. Davis, why ever would you want to see me? I have no pigtails for you to pull," she said as she smiled smugly and left the office.

Andy turned to face the banker. He tried to hide his feelings, but the banker noted the silly grin on Andy's face.

"Andy, why don't you join us for supper this evening; say about six?"

"That's very gracious of you, Mr. Bennett. I'll be there."

"Well, I guess we better take care of business then," the banker said.

Andy was looking at the door again; his mind obviously not on business.

"Oh yes, of course," he said as he turned his attention to the banker.

Andy placed the saddlebags on the banker's desk saying, "I would like to make a deposit, but I also need a couple of drafts made out to my brothers in the amount of $10,000 each."

"Looks like you had an exceptionally good year, Andy."

"Yes the new equipment is working well; so much more efficient than planting by hand."

"The townspeople have given you a hard time, but it looks to me like you have had a better yield than any other plantation in the area," Mr. Bennett observed. "That's not going to make you any more popular with your neighbors, Andy."

"Yes, Mr. Bennett, my neighbors and the townspeople have been acting in a very un-Christian manner, but I am convinced that we have to change with the times. New equipment will eventually replace slave labor, and farming will actually become more profitable. Northerners don't realize the cost of owning slaves. They think it's free labor. It's not free."

"You're preaching to the choir, Andy."

"Sorry, Mr. Bennett, you have always been a good friend of the Davis family."

"That's okay, Andy, but you're still going to be in for a hard time. People are afraid of change."

"I know."

After counting the cash, Mr. Bennett penned a receipt saying, "I'll have your drafts in a few minutes."

"Thank you, Mr. Bennett. I'll wait out front."

Within a quarter-hour, the banker handed the two bank drafts to Andy.

"We'll see you at six then," the banker said.

"Thanks again, for all your help. See you at six," said Andy as the two men shook hands.

Andy left the bank and headed over to Dwayne's office up the block. Entering the office, Andy smiled and called out, "Hello brother! Congratulations on your re- election."

Dwayne looked up and asked, "What brings you to town, Andy?"

Andy pulled a draft from his shirt pocket and said, "This."

Dwayne looked at the draft and whistled lowly. "Wow, is this ten percent?

"Yes."

"You've had a good year."

"Yes, the new equipment is working very well," Andy said again.

Dwayne looked at Andy with hard eyes, wondering if he was being impertinent since Dwayne had been vehemently against the changes that Andy had made.

"Well, if you can turn this kind of profit each year, you will have convinced me," said Dwayne.

Andy just smiled.

"So, how have you been?" asked Andy as he flopped down on the leather couch.

"I'm doing well, but I've been travelling too much. Re-election caused me to be on the road meeting constituents. Now that the election is over, I should be home so that I can practice law and make a living. I don't know if I can afford to be a state senator," Dwayne said smiling.

"Do you need money?"

"No, not really—I'm making out better than I make it sound, especially with this draft. I'm fine."

"Well congratulations again, Dwayne. I had better get over and see Ev and give him his share."

"He'll be just as surprised as I am; you have obviously done very well, Andy."

"Thanks, I'm glad that you think so. See you later."

Andy walked up the street and entered the hardware turned general store where Barbara and Everett were stocking shelves.

"Hey Andy," Everett greeted. "You can't possibly need supplies so soon. Chiggers got a whole wagon load last week."

"No, we're good as far as supplies are concerned. I just stopped by to give you this," said Andy as he held out the bank draft.

Everett's eyes widened as he noted the numbers on the bank draft.

"You can't be serious; this can't be ten percent." "Exactly ten percent," Andy replied.

"Wow! You did really well."

"We did very well; better than even I expected," Andy replied smiling.

Everett showed the bank draft to Barbara who congratulated Andy on a good crop year.

"Why not have dinner with us, Andy, and stay the night?" Everett asked.

"I would Ev, but I've been invited to dinner with the Bennett family, and I'll stay at Dwayne's house, returning to the plantation early tomorrow."

"I saw Abigail Bennett walking home from the bank. She has turned into quite a beautiful woman," said Barbara. "As I remember, you two were quite close before you left to attend different colleges."

"Yes, she is beautiful," Andy admitted, while trying to hide the fact that he was blushing.

Everett started singing, "Andy and Abigail, sitting in a tree…"

"Oh hush up Ev," Barbara chided while smiling, remembering that she and Everett had been targeted by that same childish song just a few years earlier.

"Gotta go now, Ev. I've got some bills to pay." "Okay, Andy, have a good evening," said Everett with a sly smile on his face.

Andy blushed again and hurriedly left, closing the door behind him with a louder than necessary bang.

Inside the store, Everett and Barbara laughed knowingly as they reached out to touch each other. Everett started singing again, "Andy and Abigail, sitting in a tree…"

"Oh hush now Ev, and get back to work." They both laughed out loud, remembering their own romance that had eventually led to their wedding.

Andy left the store feeling vindicated—by his brothers, anyway. Finishing his business in town, Andy waited anxiously for the six o'clock hour.

At dinner, Andy couldn't take his eyes off of Abigail. He courted her all the following winter, every chance that he could get away from the plantation, which was most every weekend. In the spring, Abigail consented to be his wife. Almost a year later, a son they named Toby came into the world—a world that looked very much as if it was without limit.

Chapter Two

March 4, 1857

WINSTON HARRISON WAS an angry man who had secrets. He believed that life owed him riches and position, and he chose politics as a way of getting both. His secrets kept him from seeking elected office, lest his secrets be made public. Therefore, in 1850, he accepted a staff position in the office of Aaron Hill, the Whig Party Senator from New York, who had a few secrets of his own.

Within a few years, Harrison rose to the position of Chief of Staff. Although he treated subordinates mainly with disdain, he had a talent for charming the rich and powerful including the Congressional leadership of the Free Soil, Independent Democratic, Independent Whig, States Rights, Unionist, and the Democratic parties. Harrison had the reputation of being a debonair and resourceful man who got things done when other legislative staffers failed.

As a lawyer, Harrison learned to craft legislation that few people understood, not even the legislators. The bills he wrote were usually self-serving, but they had titles that legislators and the public could passionately support, even when the body of the bill said the exact opposite of the title. Legislators rarely got beyond the title and the first few paragraphs of any draft legislation, so Harrison's bills tended to be several pages long with flowery paragraphs headlining the proposed legislation.

Senator Hill almost never read bills, not even those that he sponsored. He relied entirely on his chief of staff to tell him when and how to vote on any bill that came up before his committees and on the floor of the Senate.

Harrison knew that most Congressional delegates didn't bother to read bills either, so the position of chief of staff for a Congressman or Senator was extremely powerful and influential, well above and beyond any governance of the U.S. Constitution. They were in effect the unelected dictators of legislation, and they were invisible to all except legislators and the special interest groups that they served. Harrison had developed a network of staff chiefs who would support him, without question, if they wanted to get their bills through Senator Hill's committees.

Aaron Hill, the once appointed and twice elected Senator from upstate New York, was not dumb. Rather, he regarded the legal language in most legislation to be minutiae that he was more than willing to leave to Harrison. As a successful farmer, Hill had initially been appointed to the Senate by New York's Governor William Bouck, himself a farmer, after the previously elected Senator unexpectedly died. Even though he was a life-long Whig, Hill was popular with the delegates of the several other political parties that made up the state legislature. The state legislature, not the public, elected New York's two U.S. Senators. Also, it didn't hurt that he had the political support and financial backing of his district's largest farmers, and that he knew which legislative hands to grease. All-in-all, Senator Hill was generally regarded as a likeable gentleman farmer and a successful Capitol Hill legislator.

In 1855, Senator Hill switched from the dissolved Whig Party to the newly organized Republican Party. The dissolution strained relations between former Whigs who felt compelled to join different political parties. Such was the case with his long time friend, Judah P. Benjamin, the Senator from Louisiana and former classmate at Yale University. The two men had been roommates while studying the law, although Judah had not completed his studies there.

Even after switching parties, Hill easily won re-election in 1856. With the convening of the 35th U.S. Congress in March 1857, Senator

Aaron Hill and Winston Harrison sat in the Senator's office late at night under the glow of a single gas lamp. Both men wore their heavy overcoats, as the capitol building was cold. "Congratulations on your reelection, Senator."

"Thank you, Winston. You played a large part in my reelection, and I offer you my most profound thanks. Perhaps you should take off a few days, with pay of course, before we get into the business of new legislation."

"That's a very generous and tempting offer, Senator; however as you know, Minnesota and Oregon were recently admitted to the Union, and their Congressional delegates have just arrived in Washington. I have agreed to help them find office space and to get their new staffs situated."

"Smart move, Winston, we may need their votes on the Senate floor. Helping them get situated now is a good way to get their help later. Let me know if I can be of assistance."

"You might swing by and greet the new senators when you have time. By the way, have you met the new president?"

"Buchanan? Yes, I met him briefly before he was sworn in."

"Did you know him before he was elected to the presidency?"

"Not very well. He was a senior senator and I was a very junior senator in the thirties and early forties."

"Well, Senator, I expected that it would be tough getting bills through a Democratic Congress this year, but now with the Democrats also controlling the Executive Branch, we may have an extremely lean year."

"Personally, I thought our candidate, Fremont, could beat Buchanan, but I didn't count on former President Fillmore and his damned Know Nothing Party swinging their voters to Buchanan. Imagine that! The Democrats control both the executive and the legislative branches. Yes, it's going to be a tough few years. Fortunately, I can still work bills through committee by working with my good friend, Judah Benjamin, the Democratic Senator from Louisiana, who is now the committee chairman."

Senator Hill changed the subject by saying, "Well Winston, I have a roll call at ten o'clock in the morning, so we better call it a day.

Can I offer you a ride home? I have a carriage waiting in front of the north wing."

"Well I won't turn down a ride, especially with snow on the ground."

"I'll have the driver drop me off and then take you home."

"Thank you Senator. You go on ahead, and I'll turn down the gas lamps in the other offices."

The two men rode in silence as the carriage made its way down the three and a half miles of Pennsylvania Avenue to M Street in Georgetown. The steady clip-clop of the horse's hooves lulled the two tired men to sleep. Senator Hill woke with a start as the carriage stopped in front of his large Georgetown house.

"See you in the morning, Winston," said Senator Hill as he stepped out of the carriage and paid the full fare.

"Goodnight, Senator," Harrison called from inside the coach.

The driver pulled the extra-large collar of his Coachman's Cloak over his ears as he turned north into the wind and snow for the forty five minute, two and a half mile trip, to the house on Adams Mill Road.

Although both houses were located in the northwest section of Washington D.C., the general location was the only thing that the two houses had in common. Where the senator's house was a grand three story brownstone on a congested cobblestone street near the Potomac River, Harrison's house was a two bedroom clapboard house in a nearly undeveloped area of the city, just off Adams Mill Road, a dirt road that was deeply rutted by wagon wheels. Harrison could easily afford better, but isolation from the rest of the city better fit his need for privacy. The isolated hilltop house was ideal for containing the screams of his victims. It was also ideal in that the densely wooded area surrounding three sides of the house prevented prying eyes from observing him as he dragged dead victims to their final resting place in the wooded valley below. Harrison was a man with very dark secrets.

The driver had difficulty maneuvering up the deeply rutted road in the light snow, but he eventually made it to the long driveway leading to the house with dark gray peeling paint. Harrison stepped out of the carriage, then turned, almost as an afterthought, and gave the driver a dollar tip.

"Thank you, sir," the driver said in a flat voice, "Have a good evening."

"You're welcome," said Harrison, who smiled as he thought about what awaited him inside.

The driver turned the carriage out of the driveway and headed down hill for the trip back to center city. Harrison entered the dark cold house and lit a kerosene lantern. Gas pipes had not yet been installed in this sparsely developed area. He lit a fire in the fireplace, and then walked over to the heavy oak closet door with a wrought iron deadbolt. He slammed the meaty part of his fist on the center of the door and smiled when he heard a faint whimper from within.

Harrison went to the barn where he fed and watered his horse. He seldom rode his horse to the capitol, as he had nowhere to keep it while he conducted the business of government. He carefully placed a blanket on the back of his sorrel mare, tying rope-ends around her belly so that she would not shake off the blanket during the night. It would be another cold night. Then he went inside the house and started a fire in the wood stove in the small kitchen where he cooked a meal, both for his victim guest and for himself.

He roughly pulled the cold, naked girl out of the closet by grabbing a handful of her long, dark hair. She wasn't able to move very fast because her ankles had been hobbled with rope, much the way he would hobble his horse when there wasn't any other way to ensure the horse wouldn't run off. The gag, taped over her mouth prevented her from screaming. Her hands had been tied to her trim waist. The tape and gag were removed, and one hand was untied so that she could eat, which she did ravenously. It was the only meal that she had eaten all day. Harrison filled a large metal tub with icy cold well- water and lifted her into the tub. When she refused to sit, he punched her in the stomach, doubling her up in pain, thereby forcing her to sit in the cold water. He washed the trembling girl with perfumed soap, caressing her private parts. She trembled even more at his coarse touch. Harrison liked girls of fifteen or sixteen best because they had the firm body of a young woman and the brain of a child. He enjoyed dominating them. Usually, his young victims succumbed within a day, but this girl, Shannon, was strong-willed and had lasted for three full days before she finally gave in to all of his physical demands. Harrison took the shivering girl to the living room fireplace where he dried her, again caressing her. Then he led her to the bedroom... It would be a cold night, but Shannon would keep him warm.

Just before dawn, Harrison put Shannon out of her misery. He dressed her in the street clothes she had worn to the house and placed a brass button in her hand, which he made into a fist—suggesting that she had somehow ripped it from the uniform of a soldier. Her grave in the deep valley below had been dug days earlier. He wrapped her in an army blanket and dragged her down the hillside to her final resting place. He unceremoniously dumped the body in a four-foot deep grave and then placed rocks of decomposed granite over her so that no part of her body or the blanket was exposed. The rocks prevented the soil from compressing into the grave, and if stray dogs dug up the ground, they would eventually be faced with the sharp-edged rocks that would tear the pads of their feet and prevent them from digging further. But there were few dogs in the hills along Adams Mill Road. He topped off the grave with three feet of dirt and leaves so that it looked like the rest of the forested area.

Senate office workers noted that Harrison seemed to be just a little more pleasant that morning. He actually smiled at them and said "good morning." He *was* smiling. He felt exceptionally good, and he had made it to the Senate gallery in time for roll call. He sat in the gallery reminiscing about the previous night's activities. He felt alive!

Over the next four years, Harrison's craving to feel so alive increased. The wooded canyon below the house with the dark gray peeling paint was becoming a substantial graveyard to young female victims. But nobody seemed to care that they were gone.

Friday, March 1, 1861

"Good morning, Senator. How was your trip?"

Good morning, Winston. The trip was long but I think that Lincoln is finally ready for his inauguration on Monday. A plot to assassinate him was uncovered in Baltimore, but the Pinkerton men who were with him got us to Washington without incident. How are things here?" "Well, the staff has been getting ready for the special session on Tuesday, but there is a great deal of concern over the secession of Southern states. Many of the Southern legislators have already resigned, and the rest will likely be dumped from the congressional rolls later this week. I believe that Virginia, Arkansas, North Carolina, and Tennessee will soon follow. God only knows how many other states will join them."

"Winston, as you know, the Congress does not recognize secession. And I can tell you privately, neither does Lincoln. He thinks that secession is illegal, and he is willing to use force to preserve the Union. We may actually go to war in order to preserve this Union."

"Your friend, Senator Judah Benjamin, resigned on February 4th. He left you a note," said Harrison. Senator Hill opened the folded paper and read, "Let not the close bonds of personal friendship be put asunder by political and geographic differences." It was signed simply, "Judah."

Harrison continued by saying, "Senator Benjamin was appointed as the Confederacy's Attorney General the day after he resigned from the Senate."

"Also, Senator Joshua Hill of Georgia resigned after his state seceded in January. He only recently moved his belongings, saying that he is returning to his home in Madison. He wanted to personally say goodbye to you. I told him that you were still on the campaign trail. He thinks we will be at war in a very few weeks. Senator Hill said that he argued against secession, both in his statehouse, and with the citizens in his district. But he also said that his position is that a state that signed the Declaration of Independence, fought in the Revolutionary War, and voluntarily ratified the U.S. Constitution should have the legal right to withdraw from the Union. As he put it, "They voluntarily entered the Union, so they should be able to voluntarily leave the Union." He also indicated that he believed that the Southern states should have taken the secession argument before the U.S. Supreme Court for a determination."

"Joshua is a good man, however, if the Southern states were like-minded, they should have petitioned the court before they seceded. We're going to war I tell you, Winston, and soon."

"Too bad we can't consult with the courts first though," Winston said.

"Too bad indeed, Winston."

On Monday, Lincoln was inaugurated as the sixteenth President of the United States. Hannibal Hamlin was sworn in as Vice President. Both the Senate and the House chambers gained a Republican majority. Senator Hill again became chairman of several very powerful Senate committees. Just over a month later, on April 12th, hostilities opened the Civil War.

When war first broke out, Harrison, who had just turned thirty, saw the conflict as a way to achieve the riches he desired. Senator Aaron Hill, as Chairman of the Committee for Military Logistics and Supplies, controlled most of the funding for weapons and ammunition that the Union Army so desperately needed. He also sat on the powerful Ways and Means Committee that acted on legislation that funded literally everything in the Federal government. And because the army was so desperate for war-making materials, it was relatively easy for Harrison to coerce army buying agents into awarding contracts to those vendors that he recommended, vendors who would kick back a portion of each sale to Harrison and subsequently to Senator Hill.

Not only did he take money from vendors, but he received a portion of each shipment of arms and ammunition, which was diverted to a farm in Maryland where they would be sold on the black market. The diverted weapons were listed simply as "lost in transit." Nobody ever questioned the losses. Senator Hill knew nothing about the kick-backs or the diverted supplies. The money he received from his chief of staff always came through a private non-profit political organization labeled for the Senator's reelection, money the Senator eagerly accepted.

Harrison took pleasure in the knowledge that many of the military weapons and supplies that he sold on the black market were being purchased by agents of the Confederacy, thereby prolonging the war, while simultaneously adding to his personal wealth. He silently hoped the war would last for at least ten years. He couldn't care less that Union soldiers were being killed with the weapons and ammunition that he sold on the black market. Their deaths were merely a means to an end—that being to increase his personal wealth.

Chapter Three

April 1861

STATE SENATOR DWAYNE Davis was at the statehouse in Milledgeville, Georgia, when the Legislature received word by telegraph that General Beauregard of the Confederate Army had attacked Fort Sumter at Charleston Harbor in South Carolina, on April 13th. Dwayne felt that it was ironic because a Senate committee, of which he was a member, was trying to determine how to separate the State of Georgia from the Union. Although Georgia had seceded from the Union on January 19th, Union officials were still collecting taxes for the United States from ships arriving in Savannah Harbor.

Other U.S. officials were still at their jobs in Georgia. The attack on Fort Sumter ended all that. Union tax collectors and other Federal officials were recalled to the north within days.

Although diplomacy had clearly failed, the bombardment of Fort Sumter resulted in no one being killed or wounded; that is until the commanding officer, surrendered the fort. He ordered the firing of a final salute during the Union evacuation, whereupon a canon misfired, killing one Federal soldier and seriously wounding three others. Had both sides been willing, war could have been prevented, even after the shelling of Fort Sumter.

Early in May, with all-out war clearly on the verge, Dwayne submitted a request to President Davis for a commission in the Confederate cavalry. In late June, he received a commission as a Colonel and was ordered not to the cavalry, but rather to the Attorney General's office in Richmond, Virginia, the new capitol of the Confederate States. Dwayne resigned from the state senate, returned home to set his affairs in order, said goodbye to his brothers, and then left for Richmond, where he reported to the Attorney General, Judah Benjamin.

At first, his duties revolved mainly around reading and writing legal papers. But then early in August, Dwayne received new orders appointing him as military attaché to Great Britain and France. Dwayne had no time to let his brothers know where he was going. He covertly shipped out on a sloop for the Bahamas, where he boarded a British merchant ship and sailed to London, arriving in late September. Dwayne's first duties were to secure accommodations in London for two Confederate envoys who were empowered to draft treaties with England and France, and who were scheduled to arrive late in November.

John Slidell, along with his wife and children, boarded the *Theodora,* in the dead of night at Charleston Harbor on October 11, 1861. He was to be an envoy in France. James Mason, who was to be posted in England, was accompanied by two paid male secretaries. Both he and Mason carried documents identifying them as envoys and diplomats of the Confederate government. The *Theodora,* a ship leased by a Southern businessman to haul cargo, was the ship of choice because it had a shallow draft. It was that shallow draft that allowed it to sail well away from the harbor's main channel, the mouth of which was guarded by Union warships.

Leaving the next day at one in the morning, the captain of the *Theodora* navigated the shallow byways and managed to make it to the open sea unnoticed by the Union flotilla. Once on the open ocean, the ship was capable of speeds in excess of twelve knots, faster than that of the Union ships guarding the entryway to the harbor. The two envoys felt relatively safe.

The two day trip to Nassau went by uneventfully. During the day, the skies were blue with big puffy white clouds, and the trade winds reduced the discomfort of increasingly hot and humid temperatures. John Slidell and his wife felt at ease as they strolled along the wooden decks. Upon docking at Nassau, they learned that they had missed the British steamer that would have taken them to St. Thomas, the primary port for British ships that were homeward bound. The group decided to stay onboard the *Theodora*, sailing on to Cuba where a British mail ship was scheduled to depart Havana for London in a few weeks. Again, the seas were calm and the weather most satisfactory.

The stay in Cuba was also pleasant. Slidell's children played in the plaza and swam in the shallow waters of the local beach under their mother's intensely watchful eye. By the time of their next sailing, the children were as brown as berries and the family was both relaxed and ready for the next leg of their long ocean voyage.

Slidell, a lawyer and former U.S. Senator representing Louisiana, and James Mason, a Virginia lawyer and U.S. Senator until the outbreak of the Civil War, talked excitedly about their common European missions. They looked forward to the opportunities that awaited them. They were in exceptionally good spirits as they found adequate steerage on the British mail ship, *RMS Trent*.

The mail ship left Cuba on time, heading out to sea through the deepwater channel that would take them to London. The trip was no secret. Not only did the Federal intelligence service know of their leaving, the trip between Cuba and London was printed in Cuban newspapers; the editors of which treated the two envoys as minor celebrities who had stopped in Cuba on the way to their final destinations in Europe.

The group spent much of the first day at sea settling into their quarters and becoming familiar with the ship. British officers treated the two envoys with the respect that their positions demanded. Again the seas and the weather were cooperative. The journey was off to a good start.

Following lunch the next day, the Slidell's returned to their cabin to put the children down for an afternoon nap. John Slidell was reading when he heard the unmistakable sound of cannon-fire. He exited his cabin and ran down the passageway, heading for the pilot house. James Mason was only a few steps behind. A second shot could be heard as they neared the hatch that lead to the main deck.

"John, do you have any idea what is going on?" asked Mason.

"No, but it can't be good."

The two men made it to the main deck where they observed an officer from a Union warship standing on the quarterdeck. The *Trent's* master made his way to the quarterdeck where he met the Union officer saying, "By what right do you have to fire on a ship of Her Royal Majesty's government?"

Lt. Fairfax introduced himself as the Executive Officer of the *USS San Jacinto.* He demanded that the British Master turn over a list of passengers. The ship's master refused. He also refused to allow the Union officer to search his vessel for contraband. Slidell and Mason, who had arrived on the quarterdeck, identified themselves as diplomats.

"Mr. Slidell and Mr. Mason, I request that you and your entourage voluntarily come with me to the *USS San Jacinto,*" the lieutenant said.

Both men refused.

Two boatloads of armed sailors and Marines boarded the *Trent.*

The lieutenant went on by saying, "In that case, I am seizing you and those travelling with you, including your luggage, possessions, papers, and dispatches as contraband."

"By what authority?" Slidell asked.

"By the authority of my Commanding Officer, Captain Charles Wilkes," the lieutenant responded with a sly smile.

"Then your captain must be the son of an ox. We are not contraband. We are duly empowered diplomats and envoys of the Confederate States of America, sir."

The lieutenant answered, "Well sir, now you are contraband."

The *Trent's* master objected vociferously, but to no avail.

Armed U.S. sailors and Marines lined the passageways while the envoys and their entourage packed their belongings at the point of bayonets. Mrs. Slidell and the children were terrified. The Southerners were led away to waiting small boats where they were ferried to the *USS San Jacinto*. Once onboard the Union warship, they were treated as prisoners rather than envoys. Guards watched their every move.

Mason whispered, "Did they get the dispatch bag?" "No," responded Slidell. "I left the dispatches in the custody of an officer on the *Trent*. He will deliver them to a Confederate official in London."

"Well some good came out of this, I guess,"

The *USS San Jacinto* sailed to Boston where the two envoys and their secretaries were imprisoned at Fort Warren. Mrs. Slidell and the children found housing and awaited the outcome of the seizure and a coming trial. President Lincoln, as were most citizens in the United States, was deliriously happy with the seizure. Newspapers spread the happy news and Congress rewarded Captain Wilkes with a gold medal. However, over time, the president listened to those more learned in maritime law. He came to realize that the seizure of the envoys was actually a violation of maritime law. By December, the tone of the papers and the public had reversed itself, and the envoys and their entourage were released and allowed to continue on their journey to London.

As a military attaché, Dwayne was responsible for obtaining weapons and ammunition, which the French and the British were willing to provide as long as the Confederacy could pay. Millions of bales of cotton that the British wanted, and which likely would have been more than enough to equip Confederate forces with weapons and ammunition for much of the war, sat in warehouses and on southern piers. There were those who thought that if they withheld the cotton, the British would enter the war on the side of the Confederacy. Southern leaders anticipated that the British would break the Union's blockade to get the cotton they needed to make products to sell on the world's markets. *They were wrong*. Within a year, the Union produced a more effective naval blockade, which the British refused to break.

Without diplomatic recognition, neither England nor France were willing to provide the Confederacy with either a line of credit or weapons, except those that were paid for with cash—pounds, francs, gold, or silver. They wouldn't accept Confederate dollars. As the war progressed, Southerners began sending their jewelry to pay for weapons. And because they were paying with jewelry, they only got about ten cents on the dollar. Dwayne resorted to melting the jewelry for gold and selling the gem stones separately. But even then, they only got about forty cents on the dollar. President Davis was so sure that England and France would side with the Confederacy because of their need for cotton. But in the end, both England and France drained Confederate cash reserves and left the Southerners abandoned. Dwayne had asked other European countries for weapons and help. They too were willing to supply weapons and ammunition—for cash.

Dwayne asked to be transferred to the cavalry and to be given a battlefield command, but his requests were always denied. Judah Benjamin, who in September of 1861 was appointed Secretary of War, said that Dwayne was more valuable in Europe. But Dwayne surmised that it was more likely that the administration just didn't want to spend the money to send another officer to Europe in order to bring Dwayne back to the war at home.

WHEN DWAYNE HAD left for Richmond in June, Everett and Andy rode south to the Georgia capitol to see Governor Joe Brown. Arriving in Milledgeville after a three day ride, it took another week to finally get to see him. Even then, it was only because the Governor fondly remembered Dwayne that he agreed to meet with the two brothers at all.

To Andy, Governor Brown appeared to be a dour old man with a long white beard who was not particularly fond of plantation owners. The Governor had made his money in coal and iron mining and in real estate. However, he talked fondly of knowing Dwayne, remembering that it was Dwayne who had urged the state legislature to resist secession, asking instead that the lawmakers direct the state

Attorney General to take the case for secession to the U.S. Supreme Court. But the Governor smiled and shook his head, his long white beard swaying from side to side; pointing out that by then it was too late for a judicial answer. Even though no bullets had yet been fired in Georgia, the fact was that the South was already at war.

The two brothers requested commissions in the Georgia Militia, a request that Governor Brown granted, thereby appointing them as Georgia Militia Captains. Then he said something that surprised them both.

The Governor looked at Andy and said, "I'm told that you have been planting vegetables and growing food products on at least half of your plantation. Is that true?"

Andy nodded his head in the affirmative.

The Governor continued by saying, "Then, by God, you are either a visionary or a damn fool. Right now, it's getting harder to ship cotton, both because of Union blockades and because our Southern government has decided to withhold cotton from the world market to force England and other European countries to join the Southern cause. We have cotton stacked in warehouses ready to ship so that we can buy weapons and ammunition, but we have to run the blockades to get our cotton to friendly ports in the Caribbean to load on British ships. It is cotton we have, but its food we will need. And I am old enough to have known privation. We can't eat cotton. And as the war wears on, we will endure a shortage of food, both for soldiers and for the civilian population. There is plenty of time for you to go to war. What we need now is for you to return to your plantation and plant food to feed our troops. When it's time, I'll send you to war. I also need you to convince the other landowners to grow food."

Andy told the Governor that the other growers wouldn't listen to him.

Governor Brown said, "You've got to convince them. We have to feed the army and eventually, we will need to feed the civilian popu-lation. Will you do that, Andy?"

Andy answered that he would try his best.

Then the Governor turned to Everett and said, "I'm also told that you run a general store in Madison. Is that right?"

"Yes, sir" Everett answered.

"Then I believe that you too should return to Madison. Set up a supply line with the store owners from surrounding towns so that we can ship food and supplies by wagon from plantation fields and small towns to the warehouses in Atlanta."

"Will you do that for me?" he asked. "Yes, sir."

The Governor ended the meeting by saying, "There will be plenty of time for you two to get your fool heads shot off, hopefully on some remote battlefield and not actually defending your homes. This war is going to last a lot longer than people around here think. Go with God. I'll send you a dispatch when you two need to join the battle."

With that, the Davis brothers were dismissed. They returned home and set to work performing the tasks that they were assigned. They took a lot of criticism from the townspeople who thought that the younger Davis brothers were shirking their duty by not going to war. It would have been easier to have gone to the battlefield. But for the next few months, they did as they had been ordered by their Commander in Chief, the Governor.

Andy tried to talk the other plantation owners into growing food instead of cotton. They steadfastly refused. Cotton was still putting money in their wallets.

Everett set up a schedule for wagon trains to take food from Madison and the surrounding towns to army warehouses in Atlanta following the end of the growing season. As they traveled through the towns, people brought out food that they had canned. Some families gave up livestock to feed the troops. The food trains were slow moving to Atlanta.

Meanwhile, young men in Madison and surrounding towns joined either the Confederate Army or the militia. Those who joined the army were shipped off immediately to Richmond. Those who joined the Georgia Militia paraded around in new uniforms, drilling while waiting for orders to travel north to go to war.

Townspeople and plantation owners continued to shun Andy for freeing his slaves. Some of the shunning spilled over to Everett. However, both townspeople and plantation owners needed the products and services that Everett provided, so they continued to use his store to fill their needs. Madison's social environment was uncomfortable, both for the brothers and for the townspeople who dealt with them. It was, however, Everett's wife Barbara and Andy's wife Abigail who felt the community shunning the most."

Chapter Four

Monday, August 5, 1861

AT SIX-FOOT-FOUR-INCHES AND 250 pounds, Chief of Detectives, Franklin Stone stood out in a crowd everywhere he went. He started his police career as a uniformed police officer, working in some of the roughest neighborhoods in New York City. He was known as a tough, ham-fisted officer who usually functioned as the tip of the police spear anytime the department conducted a raid. And because he was the tip of the spear, he had twice been shot; once in the leg, and once in the chest. The last shooting nearly took his life.

After six years as a uniformed police officer, he had successfully passed the departmental test for detective. He gained a reputation for solving the really difficult cases that no one else seemed to be able to break. After seven years of working cases, he was promoted to Chief of Detectives. During his five years heading up New York City's detective bureau, Stone had built a professional investigative organization that closed more major cases in one year than had been solved in the previous ten years. On that August Monday evening, Stone waited in the hot empty hallway on the third floor of City Hall. Chief Detective Stone had no idea why Commissioner Kennedy had summoned him.

John Alexander Kennedy was the leader of the Police Commission; a group of six people who together actually ran the New York City Police Department. Commissioner Kennedy stepped into the hallway and greeted Stone with a strong handshake, inviting Stone to enter the spacious office.

"I'm sorry for the short notice, Chief Stone," said Kennedy as he pointed to a chair.

"No trouble at all, Commissioner," Stone responded as he took a seat.

"You are aware that then President-elect Lincoln was here in New York City last February."

"Yes sir, he caused quite a stir in Manhattan."

"Yes he did. However, what you may not know is that I met with him unofficially for well over an hour. I found him to be a strong and affable man; a straight shooter."

"That's high praise, coming from you, Commissioner," said Stone, wondering where this was going.

"Yes it is, Chief. But I want to impress upon you what kind of man I believe our new president is—especially now that our country is at war. I believe that he is a man that you can trust."

Chief Stone said nothing, waiting for Kennedy to drop the first shoe, so to speak.

"One of the first issues that the new president took on when he got to Washington D.C. was the formation of a police department. After the war started in April, Washington D.C. filled with all manner of scoundrels, all looking to make a fast buck. In a few days, he will formally announce the establishment of the Washington D.C. Metropolitan Police Department."

Stone remained silent, waiting for the other shoe to drop.

"I'm sending you to Washington D.C. for at least a year, and maybe for the duration of the war."

"What will I be doing in Washington, sir?"

"First, you will meet with the president at 10:00 a.m. on Wednesday, the day after tomorrow. He will explain what you will do. You will still be a member of the New York City Police Department. You will still draw Chief Detective's pay, but you will work in Washington D.C. and you will report only to the president."

"Why me, Commissioner?"

"Because I believe that you are the best man for the job, and because you're not married. You don't have a wife and kids to care for. This could be a very dangerous assignment, Frank."

"But I take it that you're not going to say what the assignment entails, Commissioner."

"No, other than it is important to our president, and therefore, it's important to our nation."

Commissioner Kennedy handed Stone a single sheet of parchment.

"This letter, signed by the president, commissions you as a Colonel in the U. S. Army. It should be all the identification that you need to get around in the northern states. If you have to go into the Confederacy, there is nothing that I can give you that will ensure your safe passage. You will be on your own."

"Will I be going into Confederate States, Commissioner?"

"I don't know, Frank. You may. Either way, I wish you good luck," said Commissioner Kennedy as he opened the door.

Clearly, the meeting was over. Stone had many questions but realized that he would get no answers. He shook hands with the Commissioner and walked out of the office without saying good-bye. In the hallway, he stopped and looked at his commission again. Murmuring to himself he said, "Amazing! I've just been drafted into an Army in a nation that doesn't have a draft." Shaking his head, he walked out of City Hall and headed home to pack.

Stone caught a midnight troop train filled with New York Militia, who like him, were headed to Washington. The civilian ticketing agent looked at him with an air of boredom and said, "No civilians—troops only."

Stone produced his commissioning letter, whereupon the ticket-ing agent stood a little straighter and said," Sorry, Colonel. Without a uniform, I didn't know," as he handed Stone a boarding ticket. Stone thanked him and headed for the track.

He went around the long line of troopers, showed his ticket at the gate, and made his way to a car that hadn't yet filled. He found an unoccupied seat in the front of the rail car, stowed his luggage, and sitting, placed his hat over his eyes in an attempt to grab a few hours of sleep.

"Who the hell do you think you are, occupying a seat that's reserved for officers of fighting men?" a young lieutenant asked indignantly.

Stone ignored the boorish officer. Knocking the hat from Stone's head, the officer started to berate Stone again, but he only got two words out when he found himself lying on the train's floor with Stone's foot on his throat. Stone stood towering above the struggling officer.

"The only fighting you've ever seen was in a schoolyard, junior." Stone looked at the troops and asked, "Is this your leader?"

"No!" the troopers yelled in a rousing chorus.

The train started moving. Keeping his foot on the officer's throat, Stone opened the window, then reached down, and in one motion, threw the lieutenant out of the window. The soldier's sword clattered against the window frame as he departed head first out of the moving car.

"Hoorah!" yelled cheering troopers.

Stone retrieved his wide-brimmed hat and returned to his seat. He was undisturbed for the rest of the trip.

It was early Tuesday morning when Stone walked onto the streets of the nation's capitol. It was his first trip to Washington. Compared to New York City, Washington appeared to be cleaner, although the traffic was just as congested. Stone caught a carriage in front of the railway station and rode the few blocks to the Willard Hotel. Although crowded to capacity, the staff of the Executive Mansion had placed a reservation, and the hotel staff hurriedly escorted Stone to his room. He spent most of the day walking the streets, familiarizing himself with the downtown area in preparation for his new assignment and for the next morning's meeting with the president.

An early riser, Stone bought a paper and had a leisurely breakfast in the Willard's luxurious restaurant, paying three times the price for a similar breakfast in any one of a dozen restaurants that he had passed during his familiarization tour of the downtown area. At the appropriate time, Chief Stone left the hotel for his meeting with the president at the Executive Mansion.

Pennsylvania Avenue was heavily congested with horse-drawn wagons and carriages. Even a little rain was sufficient to make the avenue a muddy rutted quagmire. He carefully picked his way across the muddy street and stood in the driveway leading to the front door of the President's House, what some people had come to call— "The White House." He was amazed that even in war, there was no guard at the gate. He walked up the unprotected driveway and knocked on the door, noting that there was no number or address on the building. He correctly assumed that most everyone in the District of Columbia knew the location of the Executive Mansion.

A staff member opened the door. Stone displayed his commission and stated that he had a scheduled meeting with the president, whereupon the staff member escorted Stone upstairs to the president's private offices. The unnamed staff member introduced Stone to one of three presidential secretaries who checked Stone's name on an appointment list and then asked Stone to follow him down the crowded hallway.

"Who are all these people?" Stone asked.

"People who want something from the president," the secretary responded without emotion.

"There sure are a lot of people," Stone marveled.

People lined the downstairs area, the stairwell, and the hallway leading the president's private living area.

"Are there always this many people?" Stone asked. "Always," the secretary answered, again without any sign of emotion.

The two men entered a small office where the secretary crossed the room and opened a glass-paneled door leading to the roof of the west terrace.

"The president is waiting for you in the greenhouse," the secretary said pointing to a wooden structure in the middle of the terrace roof.

Stone walked to the greenhouse door and noticed that the president was talking with another man who seemed vaguely familiar.

Knocking on the door frame, Stone waited until the president motioned for Stone to enter as he kept talking with the other man.

"Chief Stone?"

"Yes, Mr. President."

"Chief Stone, I would like to introduce you to Allan Pinkerton," the president said.

"I know you by reputation, Mr. Pinkerton." "As do I know you, Chief Stone."

"Allan saved my life a few months ago by uncovering an assassination plot in Baltimore during my travels to Washington, just prior to the inauguration. He and his agency have since been hired to provide the military and me with war-time intelligence. He has developed valuable surveillance techniques, and his men are particularly adept at infiltrating enemy outposts, which brings me to why I need you here in Washington, Chief."

Stone, who was the same height as the president, looked the Commander in Chief in the eye and said, "Mr. President, I am the Chief of Detectives in New York City. Here in Washington, I'm just Frank."

"Frank," the president responded, Allan tells me that this city is indeed filled with spies. We are less than a mile away from the Confederacy in both Maryland and Virginia. In fact, our national capitol is a mere hundred miles from the Confederate capitol. There may even be spies here in the Executive Mansion. Although Allan and his men are handling intelligence, I need an independent investigator to look into the information that Allan and his men develop. That includes information about murders, the theft of war-making supplies intended for Union troops, but which are ending up in enemy hands, and other high crimes and treasons."

"Will I report to Mr. Pinkerton?"

"No, you will report only to me. But you and Allan must collaborate for the common good."

The president paused. "Let me put it another way, Frank. Will you be my detective?"

"Yes, Mr. President, but I do have a number of questions."

"Such as?"

"Mr. President, I'm worried about your safety."

"So is Allan, however, I cannot allow myself to become imprisoned by the job of president. I must be able to come and go as necessary so that I may participate in the management of this war. Also, I must be able to meet with the people. They expect to meet with me. I cannot become a prisoner, Mr. Stone."

"No, Mr. President, you can't. But if I am to report to you, I need to know that you will be alive to receive my reports."

"Well Frank, please be at ease. If I travel outside the District of Columbia, Pinkerton men are my escorts and my protection."

"Well that's something, sir."

"Now Frank, I have some questions. Have you given any thought as to where you will live while you are in Washington?"

"No sir, I haven't."

"I understand that Commissioner Kennedy will continue to pay you as Chief of Detectives."

"Yes, Mr. President, he did indicate that before I left." "Good. That's important because although you will be paid as a colonel in the army, I will not be able to pay your expenses. If I put your expenses in the budget, everyone will immediately know who you are and what you're doing. It is important that you report only to me, without the knowledge of the Congress and official Washington. Do you agree to those terms?"

Stone understood that the Congress had not declared war. The secession of states was a civil insurrection, not unlike the Whiskey Rebellion that George Washington had put down as president. Stone answered by saying, "Yes, Mr. President. I am basically a frugal man and my needs are simple. I will make do."

"Good. Now as to where you will live, you need to be able to come and go without prying eyes. Also, Mr. Pinkerton will need to meet with you periodically without people taking note."

"That makes good sense to me, Mr. President."

"Mrs. Kaitlin Jenkins, who was widowed a few months ago when her late husband, Colonel Ben Jenkins, was shot and killed on the road to Washington, has offered the use of her home in rural Maryland. It's an hour or so away on horseback, but the home is spacious and has some unique characteristics that I think you will find useful. She will provide you with a bedroom and her dead husband's library, which you can use as an office. She will not intrude on your privacy, I assure you. She is a good woman and a patriot, and she can use the extra money that your rent will provide. Allan knows the way as he has visited the home of the colonel several times, and has already come to terms with Mrs. Jenkins on your behalf. By the way chief, coming from the big city like you do, can you ride?"

Stone laughed. "Yes Mr. President, I ride."

"Good, good. Allan will find a good non-military horse and proper tack for you. Unless you have more questions, I really should get back inside."

"Just one more question, Mr. President." "Yes?"

"How and when will I report to you?"

"Good questions. Every Tuesday evening, Mrs. Lincoln and I play host to the good people of the district for two and a half hours starting at about 7:00 p.m. and again on Saturday afternoon. Come to either or both of those public functions, and no one will question why you are here. When you have caught my eye, proceed to the basement where I will meet you as soon as I can break away. We can exit the building and talk in the privacy of the garden. Allan will show you the way as you leave this morning. If there is urgency to our meeting, come and tell the staff that you have an urgent message. The staff is used to waking me with bad news. You can also pass information through Mr. Pinkerton."

"Thank you, Mr. President."

"No, thank you, Chief Stone. I think the three of us will make a good team."

The president left Stone and Pinkerton standing in the greenhouse while he returned to the interior of the Executive Mansion to meet with the plethora of people who wanted his time.

"So Chief, what do you think?" asked Pinkerton.

"I guess if we are going to work together, you had better get used to calling me Frank," said the grinning Stone.

"Frank it is. Please call me Allan. Let me show you to the basement and to the garden, and then we will get you checked out of the Willard and head over to your new quarters in Maryland."

Stone checked out of the Willard Hotel and waited a little over an hour for Pinkerton who showed up driving a carriage with a saddled horse tethered to the rear of the carriage.

"I thought a carriage would be better suited to hauling your luggage, Frank."

"Good thinking," said Stone as he easily loaded a trunk and suitcase in the carriage.

"The horse and tack are yours, Frank. A man of your size needs a tall horse, so it took a little looking to find an adequate animal. He's strong willed and strong in stature, so I believe he will meet your needs."

"How much do I owe you for the horse and tack?" "Nothing. Mr. Lincoln was very clear that you were to have the best horse and tack that I could find on such short notice. Unlike you, however, the Pinkerton Agency can recover costs associated with intelligence work and for protecting the president."

The two men rode in silence until they exited the city. Once in the countryside, Pinkerton said, "By the way, Frank, Mrs. Jenkins will provide breakfast and dinner, and she's a good cook. That's included in the fifty dollars a month rent. Your first month's rent has already been paid. In case anyone asks, she will say that you are the cousin of her dead husband and that you are helping her with the property, which includes several hundred acres of farmland that is worked by day laborers. I think it will meet your needs. Any questions?"

"Yes. Is it always so damned quiet out here?" Stone asked, looking around the countryside. "I'm used to the noise of the city."

Pinkerton laughed, "Yes Frank, it is quiet unless there's a storm—or unless Johnny's artillery starts a barrage. We've seen no Confederate troops here yet. But you must always remember that

Maryland people are partial to the South. That is important for your cover. If you have to talk with Southerners, you can say that you live in Maryland, and they may be more cooperative, believing that you too are a Southern sympathizer. No need to tell Northerners where you live. You can tell them that you are staying in one of the many Washington army camps, if necessary."

The two men rode the rest of the way in silence, each reflecting on the war and the roles that they were required to play.

Kaitlin Jenkins was much younger than Frank Stone expected of a colonel's wife. Also, she was trim and attractive with dark haired ringlets gracing her round shoulders. He felt a stirring that he immediately tried to put out of his mind. She offered her hand, which he took as he would any lady, lightly grasping only her fingers. But Kaitlin surprised him by reaching deeper into his hand, shaking it with a manlier grip. Her skin was soft and smooth, but there was strength in her hand. Clearly there was more to this woman than her youth and loveliness would suggest. A slight Irish lilt in her voice added to her charm.

"Good morning, Mr. Stone. Mr. Lincoln told me that he places great faith in you. You are most welcome in my home."

"I do hope that my being here will not be awkward for you, Mrs. Jenkins."

"War brings with it certain necessities that might not be appropriate in peace time. As my dead husband's cousin, few people will consider it unusual for you being here. Oh, otherwise bored wives may privately wag their tongues, but that will come to nothing. Let me show you to your rooms."

Frank Stone and Allan Pinkerton followed Kaitlin up creaking wooden steps to the master bedroom. She had earlier moved to a smaller bedroom following the death of her husband.

"I trust this will adequately meet your needs, Mr. Stone?"

"It's much more than I expected or deserve, Mrs. Jenkins," he answered, noting the large four poster feather bed and a dresser that was next to a door that he supposed was a closet. A small desk with a candle was positioned against a wall opposite of the closet, next to a floor-to-ceiling bookcase.

"You are supposed to be family, Mr. Stone. Please call me Kaitlin unless we are in the company of strangers or neighbors. The day workers will notice if you continue to address me so formally."

"Then I hope you will feel free to call me Frank, Kaitlin."

"Thank you, I will be very comfortable calling you by your first name."

Kaitlin continued her orientation by saying, "The colonel built this house to exacting standards. Later, he remodeled the master bedroom. He was afraid that fire might trap us upstairs, so he had a metal staircase built in a hidden stairwell that leads to his library and study downstairs. There is a door in the study that leads to the basement where there is a push-up door leading outside at the side of the house. From the outside, the push-up door is concealed by thick bushes."

Kaitlin pointed to an ornate bull's head that served as a candle holder, and which was mounted head-high on the wall. "Pull on the ring in the bull's nose, and the bookcase will open to reveal the hidden stairwell."

Stone pulled the heavy ring in the bull's nose, and the bookcase sprang open about two inches. He tugged on the bookcase, which easily opened ninety degrees, and observed the black metal stairwell descending into the darkness below.

"The colonel found this to be a convenient exit when he wanted to work in his study or to use the facilities outside without waking visiting company. We have no children, so the only occupants were visiting family, friends, and associates from academia and the army. Feel free to use it as you wish."

"This is amazing," said Frank. "Did you know about this stairwell Allan?"

"Not until this very moment," answered an equally amazed Pinkerton. "I've known the colonel for several years and have visited here fairly often, but I am just as amazed as you are," he said as he examined the bookcase. "This is an incredible piece of carpentry," said Pinkerton. "There are no tell-tale marks on the floor because the bookcase does not touch the floor when it is opened or closed," Pinkerton marveled.

Kaitlin lit a candle and started down the hidden stairway. The two men followed. When they reached the bottom landing, Kaitlin pointed to what appeared to be a small window on the right side of the door, and which looked out into the study. There was a certain curiosity about the window as it had etchings lightly scrolled across the surface. This was like no window that Stone had ever before seen. Kaitlin explained by saying, "This window is really a one-way mirror. The colonel had it made in France when the stairwell was built. Please check to be sure no one is in the study before you open the door. Like the master bedroom, the door is a bookcase in the study. Another bull's head candle holder in the study is the key to opening the bookcase." Both men listened in wide-eyed disbelief.

Kaitlin placed the candle in a holder on the wall behind her and pointed to a metal rack mounted on the wall to the left of the secret door. The rack firmly held two shotguns and two Colt Dragoons.

"The weapons are loaded. Also, the weapons are cleaned and reloaded weekly to ensure that they will not fail when needed; a chore that I would gladly turn over to you, Mr. Stone."

"I will gladly accept that chore, Mrs. Jenkins."

Kaitlin rested her hand on a wall-mounted metal box below the gun rack. Slowly opening the lid, she removed a round metal ball saying, "There are six bombletts in this box; what the colonel called grenades. Just light the fuse and smoothly but rapidly toss the grenade at the enemy. It will explode within three to five seconds. The resulting explosion is horrible, and the metal casing fragments into small pieces of metal inflicting injury and even death to anyone in the area. It's a horrible weapon, but the colonel was quite proud of it. He estimated that it had a kill radius of about five yards."

More by habit than by necessity, especially since no one else was in the house, Kaitlin looked through the one- way mirror and then pulled the o-ring that unlocked the secret door. Pushing the door she entered the study, but then returned to the hidden chamber where she blew out the candle nestled in the holder on the wall and closed the secret door behind the men as they entered the downstairs room. Other than the click of the locking mechanism, the bookcase-door made no sound when it was closed. It was truly a work of quality cabinetry.

"I will leave you gentlemen to your needs here in the study. Would you like tea, Mr. Stone?"

"Would you happen to have coffee, Mrs. Jenkins?" "Yes, with blueberry muffins?" asked Kaitlin who showed a warm smile. "Please."

"Mr. Pinkerton?"

"Kaitlin, you know I can't resist your muffins," Pinkerton said, smiling widely.

"Tea or coffee, Mr. Pinkerton?" "Coffee, if you please."

"Certainly," Kaitlin said as she left the room.

The two men sat in a pair of cherub chairs in front of a massive oak desk.

"Allan, I've never seen anything like this. Who was this colonel?"

"He was a very smart man. He was a scientist who worked in the U. S. Army's Bureau of Mines. But he was also a science professor at universities in and around Washington. He rose quickly through the officer ranks because he was so inventive. Also, he was a very likable man who never involved himself in politics. No one outside of academia and the military took note of him, other than his civilian contemporaries in the Bureau of Mines. He foresaw the outbreak of war two years ago and subsequently remodeled his house so that he could continue his very secretive work without prying eyes."

"He must have been an amazing man," Stone reflected.

"He was, and we will miss his genius."

Kaitlin knocked on the door to announce her presence and then entered with coffee and blueberry muffins wrapped in a cloth napkin in a small wicker basket on a serving tray. Placing the tray on the desk, she immediately left the room without further interrupting the two men.

"Allan, I've got to ask, how old was the colonel? Kaitlin doesn't look to be a day over twenty."

Pinkerton smiled broadly and said, "Twenty-five actually. She is a handsome woman, isn't she? The colonel was ten years her senior. They met while she was attending university. He was immediately smitten, as most men are, and after a couple of years of courtship, Kaitlin agreed to marry him."

"How did you meet the colonel?" Stone asked.

"I met Ben several years ago when I was looking for new weapons with which to fight train robbers and gangs of thieves who were robbing banks. I was directed to the Bureau of Mines. Because of our meeting, Ben made some grenades for us. He also improved cannons, taking the Federal Army away from its smooth bore weapons to rifled cannons. His improvements increased both accuracy and the distance that cannon shells travel. Those two inventions alone will help win the war, but there were other inventions as well."

"Well then, how, when, where, and why was he killed?"

"He was killed by a single shot to the back of his head, probably from a forty-four caliber handgun. He was found by a Union cavalry patrol in the early morning hours on one of the back roads to Washington, about two miles from here. We know that he was going to his laboratory at the Bureau of Mines, because he was in uniform. On those days when he was scheduled to teach, he wore civilian clothes. Few of his students or even his academic colleagues knew that he was an army colonel. Because he was a senior officer, a dispatch rider from the patrol informed my office in Washington at about five in the morning. My investigators rode out and examined the area where Ben was killed. It had rained earlier and the hoof prints that weren't obliterated by the patrol indicated that Ben had come up on a wagon and four riders. He was found face down in the mud. That was six months ago."

"Ever find out who did it?"

"Not yet. We're still looking, but my agency has more pressing issues such as protecting the president and developing intelligence for the war. So I will be passing the murder investigation to you."

"Okay Allan, what do you want me to do?"

"You get settled in, and I'll get you the files on Ben's murder. Also, the president wants you to look at some disturbing information we have on a ring of thieves who appear to be selling weapons and ammunition to the South. Every time we get close, our investigators are killed. The killers seem to be able to operate with impunity. It's almost like they have advance information about our investigations. Also, Mr. Lincoln said he had another matter for you to look into—something about girls disappearing from a school for women in Washington. I'll come back with the files and information from the president sometime in the next day or two. You need a hand with that trunk and suitcase?

"No," said Stone, "I can manage."

"Okay. I'll say farewell to Mrs. Jenkins and head back to Washington. I'll see you soon."

Stone went to the carriage, tied the horse to a rail, and retrieved his trunk and suitcase, which he easily carried upstairs in one trip to the master bedroom. After depositing his clothes in the dresser and closet, Stone returned downstairs, noting that Pinkerton and the carriage had already gone.

Stone examined the horse, gently rubbing the animal's neck and talking to him in a soft manner. The horse responded with a soft neigh, his left front hoof pawing at the ground like he wanted to move on. Stone mounted the high horse and barely moved the reins to the left. The horse responded by tuning left. He was obviously well trained and had a soft mouth. Stone turned in circles to the left and right, and with several hints of backward reining, noted that the animal easily backed up, a maneuver that was foreign to many horses. As they got to the main road, Stone leaned forward in the saddle, a signal for the tall horse to move out in a gallop. The horse responded so rapidly that the momentum caught Stone off guard. Recovering, Stone let the horse have his head. When they reached what appeared to be maximum velocity, Stone urged the horse to go even faster. The horse responded with even more speed. After a half mile or so, Stone lifted the reins slightly and the horse slowed to a walk. "What an amazing horse," Stone said aloud. The horse answered with what Stone took as a confirming neigh. Stone laughed aloud. Dismounting, Stone walked the horse, talking with him until they turned into the driveway.

"You are a magnificent animal," Stone said to the horse. Your name shall be Hermes, for the Greek god of speed, for never have I seen a horse move so fast. "Do you like that name?"

Hermes nodded his head up and down as if he had understood the question. Stone laughed a long-light hearted laugh. *Yes, this is a magnificent animal,* he thought.

Stone walked Hermes to the barn where he removed the saddle and bridle and rubbed down the horse while continuously talking to the animal. He found a bucket and poured oats into a trough in a stall, filled the water trough, and later led Hermes into a stall, closing the gate before returning to the house.

Instead of entering, Stone walked around the edifice and noted a couple of repairs that should be made; nothing major, just some sanding and paint in some weathered places. He found a shed at the rear of house that contained tools, a sanding brick, and paint. He spent the afternoon making the needed repairs. When finished, he looked at his handiwork with the experienced eye of a first-class carpenter. His father had taught him well. Happy with the result, he cleaned and returned the tools to the shed, and then walked to the barn where he threw a sheaf of hay into Hermes' trough and talked again with the big horse as Hermes ate his fill.

It was almost dusk when Stone reentered the house.

Kaitlin met Stone in the entryway saying, "Supper will be served in an hour." She turned without further conversation and returned to the kitchen.

Stone went into the study, opened the secret door, and examined the weapons by the light of the candelabra in the study. The weapons were in excellent condition; ready for use at a moment's notice. Stone replaced the weapons in the gun rack, lit the candle in the holder on the inner wall of the hidden chamber, and then closed the secret door. Taking the candle, he climbed the metal steps to the master bedroom. Placing the candle in the holder on the wall next to the four-poster bed, he went to the dresser where Kaitlin had filled a white porcelain pitcher with clean water. An empty ornate porcelain bowl sat next to the pitcher along with a cloth hand towel. Pouring water into the bowl, Stone washed his face, letting the cool water refresh him. He dried hands and face, combed his hair, rubbed his chin, which by then had a full day's stubble, and then walked downstairs using the creaky main stairwell that led to the hallway below.

The smell of cooking permeated the house. "If the smell was any indication, Kaitlin was indeed a good cook," thought Stone. Entering the dining room, Kaitlin had already set the table.

"Have a seat, Mr. Stone. Dinner will be served as soon as the biscuits brown."

"Can I help?" Stone asked.

"Why? Do you think I don't know how to brown biscuits, Mr. Stone?" Kaitlin asked in teasing banter.

"No, I just wondered if there was something I could do to help you?" Stone replied, fearing that he might have offended her.

"Mr. Stone, you spent the afternoon repairing the house. I think that's enough for one day, don't you?" Kaitlin said in a half-mocking voice.

Stone looked up and saw that Kaitlin was smiling. "Yes, quite enough Mrs. Jenkins."

"I do thank you for your work, Mr. Stone. I just never got around to those repairs."

Stone and Kaitlin sat at opposite ends of the eight- foot long table. Each would have to get up and walk to the other end of the table to get various food servings. Stone moved his setting to the other end of the table so that he was seated next to Kaitlin.

"Mrs. Jenkins, we need to talk and I don't feel comfortable talking to you from that end of the table."

Kaitlin kept her eyes on her plate and said nothing. "Mrs. Jenkins, if I am to play the role of the colonel's cousin, I really should know the name of the colonel's brother, don't you think?"

"That would be Edward."

"Where is Edward now?" asked Stone.

"He died in a cholera outbreak two years ago," Kaitlin said, looking defiantly at Stone.

"I'm sorry."

Looking deep into Kaitlin's eyes, Stone asked, "But now Mrs. Jenkins, what is it that I should know about you?"

Kaitlin looked at Stone as if she was surprised by the question. She blushed and immediately returned her gaze to her plate.

"My mother and father were Irish immigrants who arrived in the United States nearly thirty-five years ago. My father was an artist and a sculptor. He landed a job at the Bureau of Engraving and remained there until he died three years ago. My mother is also dead. Because of my father's influence, I was able to get a job at the Library of Congress while I attended university. I met the colonel on campus. We married. Now he's dead, and I have no family in this country."

A long silence followed. Stone carried the dishes into the kitchen and heated water in a kettle on the wood stove in preparation for washing the dishes.

"Mr. Stone, you will kindly remove yourself from my kitchen. I am perfectly able to wash the dishes. Mr. Lincoln has more important things for you to do with your time, to be sure."

Stone jumped as if he had been scalded by the tone of her voice. He looked at her furtively only to find that she was grinning. What a woman, he thought. She moves with the grace of a refined lady, but can hammer me with just the slightest change in the tone of her voice. He hurriedly left the kitchen and returned to the study where he looked over the extensive collection of books and papers. They were mostly scientific, but there were some editions of history and social sciences too.

After a few hours, he returned to the master bedroom where he lay in bed thinking that this would be much harder than he initially thought. How could he sleep under the same roof as the most beautiful woman he had ever met, especially knowing that she was just down the hall? Burned into his memory, her picture played repeatedly in his mind until sleep finally overtook him.

Chapter Five

Mid-August 1861

SHORTLY AFTER MIDNIGHT, four Union soldiers mounted on horseback escorted a wagonload of stolen Union-made rifles and ammunition from a warehouse on the edge of the district to a larger warehouse on a farm in Maryland. The driver, also in a soldier's uniform, wore a white cotton, ankle-length dust coat common to riders who wanted to keep their clothing free of the mud and dust from the road. But the purpose of his wearing a white duster was quite different than merely keeping his uniform free of road grime. Rather, its purpose was to create an illusion that would allow the contraband-laden wagon to pass unquestioned at military checkpoints leading out of the District of Columbia. The ruse was effective.

The uniformed men had common traits. Each had served in the army and had been in battle, and each man had left the army after completing a three month enlistment. They had become disgruntled with the hardships of army life, especially after having determined that there was really no glory in killing on behalf of their government, and there was not much money in it either.

Although they had not previously known each other, each man had mustered out of the army in or near the Washington D.C. area and had turned to a life of crime on which to subsist. They had killed in the army, and each one willingly plied his skills in the capitol city where there was no police force. Between them, over a period of a few months, they had not only killed some thirty or forty hapless victims for their money and valuables, but they also killed for the thrill of murdering a hapless human being. They had one other common trait. They had all survived a small pox outbreak as evidenced by the telltale pox marks on their faces. Those traits brought them together in the Brotherhood.

The small Roman Catholic Church located on the edge of the district had been abandoned after its fiery destruction years earlier. The diocese had since deserted both the edifice and its impoverished parishioners due to the lack of funds to rebuild or even to demolish the burned out shell of a building. The homes and small family-owned farms surrounding the old gothic church had long ago given way to slum houses. That run-down part of town was now used mainly by drunks and heroin addicts as a place to feed their habits outside the view of more urbane Washingtonians. Few people entered the area, especially at night.

Although the old church had been gutted by the fire, most of the rock walls were still upright, as was the stone confessional inside. Heavily charred, the confessional retained a small wooden seat for a long absent cleric and a kneeling bench for those seeking absolution. The rock wall separating priest from confessor contained a small screened window that allowed the absolutionist to see the penitent in the light of a single candle that was mounted in a receptacle in the corner of the parishioner's cramped space. The door to the cleric's side of the confessional had recently been replaced, the outer surface having been burned to look as if it had somehow survived the intense heat of the fire that had destroyed the church. The door had no handle on the outside, and it always remained bolted from the inside. A thick black canvas curtain covered the confessor's entry, allegedly to provide privacy during confession.

The cleric's side of the confessional had an inside door that had survived the fire. It opened into a small dark windowless passageway that led to a stairwell and another passageway that crossed underneath the church to the basement of the rectory next door. It was the secret passageway that had resulted in the post-fire purchase. Harrison had purchased the church and a couple of nearby slum houses under the cover of an umbrella corporation in order to meet in secret those with whom he could not associate in the light of day.

Harrison entered the rectory by way of a back door that faced an alley so that no one would see him on the street that faced the priesthouse or the church. He always arrived hours early so that his eyes could become accustomed to the darkness. In that way, he could see anyone approaching the rectory or the church in both the night and in the still dark early morning hours.

It was in the confessional that Harrison gave instructions to the leader of the gang of thieves and murderers that he called "The Brotherhood," in honor of the priests and brothers who had previously ministered and celebrated mass in the gothic temple. In fact, he dressed in the robes and cowl of the departed monks to further conceal his identity while providing instructions in a whispered voice. The irony was not lost on Harrison. In fact, he relished the role of monk and high priest of treason.

If members of the Brotherhood needed to contact their benefactor, they would put an ad in the newspaper that read, "Brother Magnus, contact us as soon as possible." Conversely, if Harrison wanted to meet with leader of the Brotherhood, he would place an ad in that same newspaper for "Brothers of Magnus – return home as soon as possible." The words "as soon as possible" always meant at 3:00 a.m. the very next morning following the day that the paper was published and disseminated.

The leader of the Brotherhood always knew when Brother Magnus, meaning "the great one," would appear. The candle inside the confessional would be lit. The prior Brotherhood boss had once extinguished the candle while receiving instructions in an effort to see Bother Magnus. He was immediately shot and killed in the confessional, and his body dragged to a nearby empty slum house. After a few days, his rotting corpse smelled so bad that not even the drunks and addicts would enter the building. A new boss was appointed and was told what would happen if he attempted to identify Brother Magnus. No attempt was ever again made.

The only man who had actually met Harrison face-to- face was blind. He knew the sound of Harrison's voice, but he couldn't describe him, even if he were forced to under torture. It was because he was blind that Harrison had chosen him months earlier. The blind man was known to members of the Brotherhood as the messenger. His real name was Roger Burkis, but lately, he was more commonly known simply as "the blind man."

Roger had been blinded early in the war and had made his way to Washington to plead his case for a small pension. But the majors and colonels who ran the day-to- day operations of the War Department, and who themselves had never been in battle, were too busy and too self-righteous to care about the needs of a used-up private who was no longer of value to the army. Harrison, who had regularly seen Roger hanging around official Washington, had gotten to know the bitter young man blinded in service to his country, and who had been thrown on the trash heap of military and civilian bureaucracy.

Harrison gave Roger money from time to time, and provided a place to stay in one of the recently purchased slum houses near the old church. For this, Roger was deeply indebted to Harrison and would do anything he asked. The blind man knew his benefactor only as Magnus. It was the blind man who carried messages from Magnus to the Brotherhood when newspaper ads were too slow or inefficient to meet Harrison's needs. He also met with agents of the South.

The wagon and its escorts moved slowly through the dark Washington streets toward a bridge that separated the district from Maryland. Lanterns hung on hooks fashioned from metal rods attached to each side of the front of the wagon. The lanterns illuminated signs with skull and crossbones and one word—POX.

Four Union soldiers stood watch at the intersection of two main roads leading to Maryland to catch spies and seize contraband. The sentries took their duties very seriously and they would normally thoroughly search any wagon crossing into Maryland. This wagon, however, was well known to them. Recognizing the wagon's escorts, the sentries waved the escorts through, while giving the wagon a wide berth. Initially, soon after the war had begun, the sentries ordered the driver to remove the wagon's white canvas shroud so that they could see the cargo. Three grotesque rotting corpses, obviously dead from the pox, caused the sentries to wretch and retreat, waving the wagon through. After checking the cargo on several trips, they no longer wanted to view the contents of the wagon with the skull and cross-bones. Knowing that, the Brotherhood had stopped putting corpses in the load. Instead, the wagon was loaded with Union guns and ammunition in a compartment hidden underneath the floorboards.

A FEW MILES away in Maryland, Chief of Detectives Franklin Stone studied the files that had been given to him by Allan Pinkerton several weeks earlier. He entered notes in each file. As the midnight hour gave way to the early hours of morning, Stone extinguished the lanterns in the study and made his way up the metal steps of the hidden stairwell to the master bedroom where he fell into the feather-erbed without bothering to undress. He slept soundly.

Waking near midday, Stone bathed as best he could by pouring fresh water from a pitcher into the matching white porcelain bowl on the dresser. He sorely missed the men's club near his apartment in New York City where he could sweat in newly installed saunas, then bathe in the large baths of the clubhouse. He bathed regularly at a men's club in Washington D.C., whenever he traveled there as he found it awkward to use the much too small metal tub that was kept in the pantry for that purpose; especially since Kaitlin might walk in while he was bathing. He wanted to spare her the embarrassment, and he wanted to minimize any loose lips of day workers. He supposed that Kaitlin did use the metal tub, but only when no one else was around the house. He couldn't help but picture her standing naked in the metal tub, a most alluring picture that again caused stirrings. He reluctantly put the thought out of his mind. He dressed casually, used the outhouse to relieve himself, and then returned to his room to wash his hands and to dress more formally for the day.

When he had first arrived, Kaitlin had entered his bedroom in his absence and made the bed, emptied the chamber pot, and drew fresh water for the porcelain pitcher. When he returned, Stone asked Kaitlin to refrain from performing those chores. He assured her that he could—and would—do those things himself. From that day on, Stone, at the very least, ensured that the chamber pot had been emptied and that the pitcher had been filled with fresh water before he left the house. However he was often less inclined toward making the bed. True to her word, however, Kaitlin left the bed unmade except once a week when she changed and washed the sheets.

Stone took the main stairwell to the study, noticing again the creak of the third and seventh steps. As it was the noon hour, he expected no prepared meal because prior arrangements did not include lunch. Shortly after returning to his notes, Kaitlin knocked and entered with a tray containing a full breakfast including eggs, pork, and potatoes. Stone started to protest, but Kaitlin gave him no chance. She exited as quickly as she had unexpectedly entered and said nothing. Stone ate ravenously—suddenly realizing how hungry he really was.

When finished, he returned the tray and dishes to the kitchen and drew a bucket of water from the well on the side of the house. He intended to fill the water jugs in the kitchen so that he could wash the dishes. By the time he got back with the well-water, Kaitlin was in the kitchen wearing an apron and giving Stone that disapproving look that he had come to know so well when he did something that Kaitlin felt was inappropriate.

"Thank you for the water, Mr. Stone. You may go back to work now."

"Thank you for breakfast, Kaitlin."

"You are most welcome, Mr. Stone," she responded.

Stone was returning to the study when he heard the rattle of wagons making their way up the driveway. The delivery men drew their Clydesdales to a stop at the front porch where Stone met them, giving them instructions where cords of wood were to be unloaded: a small cut for the wood stove used for cooking and a larger cut for the fireplace for the coming winter. He had purchased the wood and arranged for delivery several days earlier. Mrs. Jenkins appeared suddenly at his side but said nothing. She disappeared just as quickly wearing that same look of disapproval. She hadn't expected Stone to buy wood for the house, which she viewed as her responsibility because Stone was a renter with no property owner's responsibilities. Inwardly, she was both surprised and thankful as money was tight, and she had held off buying winter wood until she could determine how much she would have left after selling her crops and after paying off the day laborers. But harvesting would not be finished for at least another week.

Stone returned to the study where he reviewed the notes that he had made. Eight weeks earlier, he had been handed three cases: the murder of Colonel Ben Jenkins, dead husband to his hostess, Kaitlin; the continual disappearance of Union weapons and ammunition; and the disappearance of numerous teenage girls from a Washington orphanage. President Lincoln had a personal interest in all three cases.

Because of his own interest in Kaitlin, Stone had started with the Jenkins murder, noting that there were no clues as to why the killing had occurred. The fact that the colonel may or may not have come upon a wagon and four riders on horseback was not real evidence. It was more of a supposition. Therefore, the only course of action was to stake out the area where the murder had taken place with hopes that the wagon and riders would again appear. After several nights of watching the area with no one travelling on the road, Stone was no further ahead than when he had first started the investigation.

While he was in Washington on one of his many trips to the capitol, Stone talked with the director of the orphanage for teenage girls. The orphanage was really more of a boarding school that taught parentless young ladies a trade, including cooking, sewing, homemaking, and nursing. The director admitted that girls did sometimes run off, but noted that they never ran off in the numbers that had come to be missing over the past few years. Then too, runaways usually surfaced in Washington or the surrounding areas after a few days. The girls who were the source of her concern had never been heard of again. She feared the worst had happened to them, and so she had taken her concerns to the president because there had been no police force in the city. Even after the police force was established in August, they had no investigators, only a few uniformed patrolmen. She was glad that Stone was looking into the case of the missing girls. But again, Stone had no evidence—no clues with which to work.

The case of the missing weapons and ammunition was more of a case of weapons having been found on battlefields in the hands of dead Confederate soldiers. No thefts had been reported. No reports of missing weapons or ammunition had been filed as a result of pilfering. After checking hundreds of shipping manifests from Washington, Pennsylvania, and New York, he could find no error in the paperwork, and no evidence that the weapons had gone missing, except that they had unexpectedly turned up on battlefields in the hands of dead or dying Confederate soldiers. He suspected that employees at the manufacturing plants were deliberately siphoning weapons and ammunition to an unknown person or group, but he couldn't prove it. This case, he figured, had a higher likelihood of being solved, so he had moved it to the top of the list. However, after several weeks, he had only caught a few individuals and a couple of small gangs that were stealing and transporting weapons and ammunition to the South. But those apprehensions and seizures did not amount to the numbers of stolen weapons that were being found abandoned on battlegrounds. Somewhere, a larger, more efficient organization was selling large numbers of weapons and ammunition to the enemy. Yet, after nearly three months, answers continued to elude him.

Stone decided that his best chance of solving the big weapons case was to determine how the weapons were being transported to the South. Stone questioned the sentries at each checkpoint from Washington to Maryland. They assured him that they were diligently searching every conveyance. Covertly, Stone alternatively watched each shift of sentries over the following weeks and had to admit that they were properly searching each wagon. But he reasoned that he couldn't watch all checkpoints at the same time. He needed help from Allan Pinkerton.

Allan Pinkerton had his own troubles. With Stone investigating Lincoln's priorities, Pinkerton returned to his primary job; providing military intelligence to President Lincoln and to General McClelland of the Army of the Potomac. And his agency wasn't doing very well.

Before the war, the Pinkerton Agency had hired a number of agents to work bank robberies in the Deep South. When war broke out, the agents were given the choice of resigning to fight for the South or staying with the Pinkerton Agency. Most of them stayed with Pinkerton.

Allan Pinkerton was smart enough to realize that he may have created an avenue for Southern sympathizers and agents to work within the two single-most important areas of the war: protecting President Lincoln and collecting intelligence. Either job would be a windfall for a Southern agent or sympathizer who successfully infiltrated the agency. So Pinkerton vetted his Southern volunteers by placing them in dangerous situations in the South. He waited to read their reports to see if the intelligence they provided had been altered based on known facts that had been previously determined and verified by his most talented and trusted Northern agents. Not once did a Pinkerton agent knowingly falsify the facts in favor of the South. After several months of vetting, Pinkerton felt confident that he could use his Southern agents to conduct assessments for military intelligence. Their assessments did have an impact on the Union Army, but not in the way that was expected.

Pinkerton had placed his agents in strategic Southern towns and cities to gain information on troop strength, weapons, and movements. The agents lived and worked at civilian jobs, and when not working, they hung around bars and saloons where soldiers ventured while on the way to assignments. Based on the conversations with soldiers and town officials, reports were generated and carried north by agents whose only job was to safely take information to the nearest Pinkerton office outside the grasp of the Confederacy. From there, the information was transmitted in ciphered code by telegraph to the central office in Washington.

Once the information was in Washington, Pinkerton analysts would take the patchwork of information from the various towns and cities, along with the independent observations of deployed agents, and develop a coherent intelligence report with which Allan Pinkerton could brief General McClellan and the president.

The fact that the Pinkerton reports almost always overestimated Southern troop strength was due more to soldiers and local officials not really knowing the exact troop strength, and southern bravado or false pride in the number of Southerners who were turning out to fight the Yankee bastards up north. However, the result of those false reports caused General McClellan to wait in Washington until more Union troops, weapons, ammunition, and supplies were available. The wait cost McClellan dearly and worked to the advantage of the Confederacy.

With a mere hundred miles or so separating both capitols, Washington and Richmond, President Lincoln was extremely concerned that Confederate forces might overrun the District of Columbia and disrupt the central Union government and its war-making capabilities. He had reason to worry because during the first year of the war, Confederate forces had made inroads to the D.C. area.

In July 1861, under the leadership of General "Stonewall" Jackson, Confederate troops were literally on the district's door-step, having forced Union troops to flee across the Potomac River and forcing Lincoln to commit large numbers of troops to the protection of Washington.

Lincoln wanted McClellan to take Richmond, and he was irritated at the slow and methodical pace that McClellan had chosen. Lincoln believed that McClellan, if he moved quickly, could defeat Confederate forces around the City of Richmond. But for many months, McClellan waited. He relied on, and wholeheartedly believed, the reports from Allan Pinkerton; reports that said Confederate forces around Richmond outnumbered the Army of the Potomac. They were wrong.

Chapter Six

April 3, 1862

Everett and Andy received the promised letters from Governor Brown directing the two brothers to proceed with all haste to join the army in Richmond, Virginia. Andy, Abigail, and Toby spent that last week with Everett and Barbara in Madison where final arrangements were made to maintain the plantation and the store in the absence of the two brothers. With business concluded, the two men reluctantly packed and prepared to travel northward.

Saying goodbye to their families, they rode out together, parading in full uniform down Madison's main street at mid-morning so that the townspeople would see that the Davis boys were finally doing their duty for the South. Amid smiles and waving, they doubled back and headed out of town for the sixty mile trip to Atlanta. Not pushing the horses too hard, they camped in the woods along the road that night, arriving in Atlanta early the next afternoon. They arranged to take the 4:00 a.m. train on the Western & Atlantic railroad to Chattanooga, Tennessee. Once they arrived in Chattanooga, they would have to catch another train to Danville, Virginia, and yet another to Richmond. The brothers were supposed to arrive in Chattanooga at about 4:00 p.m. Saturday, but they were delayed by nearly three weeks.

Getting tickets to Chattanooga was no problem. The military rate for their passage was reasonable, but getting their horses on the train proved to be costly. Apparently, the government had not negotiated a price with the railroads for shipping a soldier's person-ally-owned horse. So they paid the required exorbitant fees, caught a few hours sleep at a hotel, had breakfast, and made their way to the train station about three in the morning. There they boarded their horses in one of the train's empty boxcars, removing the sad-dles, but leaving the horses bridled and blanketed from the chill of the cold night air.

The train was comprised of three boxcars and three passenger cars, only one of which had any passengers. The conductor, a Mr. Fuller, introduced himself, checked their tickets and the two broth-ers settled in for the first leg of the trip. Promptly at 4:00 a.m. the steam engine, Number 39, which was named the *General*, pulled out of the rail shed starting the one hundred thirty eight mile, twelve hour run to Chattanooga. It would have to stop every thirty-five miles or so to take on water and wood to fuel the voracious appetite of the huge steam engine. The first stop was Marietta.

In Marietta, the train's crew busied themselves, along with sta-tion loaders, loading wood and water for the next leg of the journey. Mr. Fuller was busy getting more passengers settled in. About twenty sleepy-eyed men said they were returning to their Kentucky home to join a Confederate unit there. Considering that the Confederacy had just lost a major battle at Shiloh, a confrontation that had inflicted more casualties than any previous battle in the war, it wasn't unusual for a group of men of that size to be heading home to join a local militia. Shortly thereafter, the train pulled out of Marietta heading for Big Shanty—another wood and water stop—and also a scheduled twenty-minute breakfast stop for the train's crew and passengers.

Dawn was just starting to break as the train arrived at Big Shanty. Station where employees immediately started loading wood and water. Passengers and crewmen moved quickly in pouring rain to Lacy House, a hotel across the muddy street from the train station, where breakfast was waiting.

Andy and Everett decided to use the time to exercise their horses. Once outside the boxcar, the horses whinnied at each other, glad to be free of the dark and dank interior of the boxcar. After about ten minutes of walking, the Davis brothers returned to the platform where the horses reluctantly made the short leap into the dark car after much coaxing.

Thinking that they had enough time to grab a cup of coffee, the brothers closed the heavy freight car door and turned toward Lacy House when Mr. Fuller ran onto the station platform yelling, "They've stolen the train."

Sure enough, Number 39, the tender, and two boxcars were rounding a curve, leaving the other boxcar and the passenger cars sitting at the station platform. The twenty men who had boarded at Marietta were noticeably not among the passengers who by then had returned from Lacy House, and who were stranded on the station platform in the rain. The conductor and three other railroad employees ran after the *General.*

Big Shanty was home to Camp McDonald, a Confederate Army training and staging area that literally surrounded the small town. Everett and Andy talked with the commanding officer, after which a small mounted unit was placed at their disposal for the purpose of chasing the train and apprehending the hijackers. Andy suggested that the commanding officer send a message by telegraph to alert rail stations up the line. But there was no telegraph in Camp McDonald or even in the small town of Big Shanty. The brothers saddled their horses, loaded their saddle-mounted Colt Dragoons and rifles, adjusted their rain slickers, and then joined the chase on horseback, leading a ten-man unit from Camp McDonald. It wasn't much of a chase. The pouring rain had been steadily falling for five days. There was no road near the railroad right-of-way, and much of the right-of-way abutted steeply inclined mountainsides and forests. The more level area next to the tracks was narrow and hoof-deep in slippery mud and sharp rocks. The riders had to walk their horses very carefully, but even at a walk, they made steady progress.

At Moon's Station, a railroad work station, Andy noted that the telegraph wires had been cut and some of the rails were blocked with railroad ties. In the distance, Mr. Fuller and his men were hand cranking a platform car in pursuit of the *General.* The next fourteen miles were all downhill, so it was possible that the pole car could catch up with the slower moving train.

"Captain Davis," the cavalry corporal called out.

Both Davis brothers turned to face the corporal when they heard their name called.

"Sirs, this is as far as we have been authorized to go.

Sorry, but I have my orders."

"Understood, Corporal. Please thank your commanding officer for us," said Everett.

"Will do, Captain."

The corporal saluted, and then led his men back the way they had come. Everett and Andy returned the corporal's salute and pushed on in case Mr. Fuller and his men needed help. In Allatoona, a section of rail had been removed. There were muddy tracks along the right-of- way indicating that the pole car had derailed, likely spilling the occupants into a ditch. But there were no dead or injured railroad men. Muddy footprints suggested that Mr. Fuller and his men had carried the pole car to untouched rails where they continued their pursuit.

Arriving in Etowah, the Davis brothers saw the pole car sitting on a siding. Foundry men at Etowah said that Mr. Fuller and his men had hitched a ride with the foundry's locomotive, and that they were headed toward Kingston.

"Where can we water our horses?" Andy asked.

One of the foundry men pointed to a water trough on the side of the foundry. Andy and Everett dismounted and walked their horses to the trough where the two horses drank their fill of rain water. The rain had let up a little, but it was still misting as the brothers continued their northward trek.

Arriving at Kingston, the stationmaster told Andy that Mr. Fuller had missed the *General* by mere minutes. The *General* had been sidetracked for over an hour while three southbound trains passed through Kingston. The hijackers had seized the keys to the rail switches allowing them to proceed northward even though another southbound train was expected.

"The last of the three southbound trains was still in Kingston when Mr. Fuller and his men arrived. They talked the engineer of the *William R. Smith* into joining the chase," the stationmaster said.

"Is that the *Smith*?" Andy asked pointing to a train that was coming toward them.

"Yes," said the stationmaster. "It doesn't look like they got very far."

The train stopped and the engineer called down saying, "The track was removed about two miles out of town. Mr. Fuller and a few of the railroad men are still following on foot though."

"Any chance of getting a cup of coffee?" Andy asked the Kingston stationmaster.

"You bet. Step inside and I'll draw a couple of cups. It's pretty strong though. I keep the pot on the stove all day, so by this time, its strong enough to float a ten penny nail," the stationmaster said laughingly.

"Just what we need," said Andy. Even with slickers, both riders were wet and cold.

"Thanks for the coffee," said Everett as he placed the two mugs on a desk. "Guess we had better move along if we are going to be of any help to Mr. Fuller."

The two bothers mounted and waved as they continued northward. After thirty minutes of riding, they dismounted and walked their horses for thirty minutes. It was a routine the brothers had learned at an early age.

Arriving at Adairsville, a twelve mile ride from Kinston, the brothers learned that the *General* had again been sidetracked to allow another southbound train, the *Texas*, to pass through the junction. As soon as the *Texas* had cleared Adairsville, the *General* took off northbound over the protests of the Adairsville stationmaster. As the *Texas* continued southbound, the engineer saw Mr. Fuller waving franticly. He stopped the train, and on hearing that the *General* had been hijacked, backed the *Texas* into Adairsville and decoupled the freight cars onto a siding. Since there was no place for the *Texas* to turn around, they had to chase the *General* in reverse. After watering their horses, the brothers gratefully accepted coffee, and then continued the chase.

The rain stopped and the sun peeked out from cloudy skies. The ground was less muddy, and the brothers were able to make better time on the drier earth and the broad path next to the rail right-of-way. Even though they were dog tired from the long day's ride, they pushed on through Ringgold without stopping.

Two miles north of Ringgold, they saw both trains. The *Texas* had caught up with the *General*. Actually, the *General* had run out of wood and water. The hijackers had taken to the woods, heading south into steep mountains. Ringgold was another Confederate Army training and staging area with hundreds of well-armed and mounted Confederate soldiers. The two brothers asked the commanding officer for fresh horses and joined in the search for the raiders. After a couple of days and nights, all of the hijackers were apprehended. A few shots had been fired, but mainly, the raiders gave up when surrounded by superior numbers of Confederate soldiers. The Davis brothers rested in the army camp at Ringgold. As the last of the hijackers were captured, Andy and Everett were asked to stay in camp as witnesses at the trial that was to be held.

Mr. Fuller and his friend returned with the *Texas* to Adairsville, towing the disabled *General*. Andrews, the civilian leader of the raiders, and seven of his soldiers who were wearing civilian clothes were tried and hung as spies. Fourteen others were imprisoned. After the trials, Andy and Everett rode the remaining eighteen miles from Ringgold to Chattanooga on horseback.

The six-day trip to Richmond took several weeks. Rail lines weren't connected, so there were places where they had to ride on horseback from one city or town to another to get on the next train. Other passengers were loaded into horse drawn wagons for the trip to the next rail line. Each railroad was owned and run by different operators, so they had to buy tickets and arrange passage for their horses each time that they caught another train. There was no rail system, just a series of short-line trains. Rail lines also used different types of track. One major railroad used strap iron nailed on wooden ties for about fifty miles, and then switched back to the more traditional iron rail. Most of the trains had a five-foot span between the locomotive's wheels, but others had something just over four feet. One railroad had actually laid a third rail so that trains with a narrower span could use the same railway as trains with a larger span. To Everett, it just seemed to be so disorganized. After weeks on horseback and rails, the brothers arrived by train in Richmond at three in the morning on a weekday in the second week of May.

Expecting the rail depot to be deserted because of the early morning hour, the brothers were surprised to see that the depot was actually quite crowded; so crowded, in fact, that they had difficulty getting their horses out of the freight car due to the throng of people standing on the platform.

A giant of a man wearing stripes of a cavalry sergeant major on his gray shell jacket, and who like Andy and Everett was fetching his horse from the freight car, stepped out on the crowded platform. In a loud penetrating voice he yelled out, "Make way—now!"

It was like the parting of the Red Sea. People scrambled to get out of the way. The brothers followed the sergeant major out to the street where the three men cinched their saddles and checked their horses.

"Know your way around town, do ya?"

"No, this is our first time in Richmond, Sergeant Major."

"Well, you sure look purdy in those nice new officer uniforms. Where you boys from?"

"Georgia," Everett answered. "How about you?" "Virginia boy, born and bred."

"Any recommendations on where we can get a hotel for the night?"

"I don't imagine there will be any rooms in downtown hotels. And if you did find one, you would still have to find some way to watch your horses and equipment, especially your weapons," he said, looking at their saddle mounted Dragoons and Sharps carbines. "Nowadays, people in this town will steal the gold right outta your teeth, if you're not careful."

"So, what do you recommend, Sergeant Major?"

"Well, if you don't mind a ride out of town to the west, I have a friend who owns an inn where you can get a good night's rest, a hearty meal, and a safe place for your horses and belongings."

"Sounds good to me."

Everett introduced himself saying, "Everett Davis, this is my brother Andy."

"Jubal McGraw," said the sergeant major as he offered his hand.

Everett's right hand disappeared in Jubal's, whose loose grip was as tight as a closed steel vice.

The three uniformed soldiers rode west out of the city. After about thirty minutes of easy riding, they arrived at the Boars Head Pub and Inn. The inn was located on an out-of-the-way dirt road next to a small lake made especially attractive by a number of white swans cutting through the water in a most graceful manner. The two- story building was painted white and was of modern construction, but the property was surrounded by a log fence that looked more like a zig-zag redoubt where riflemen could defend the inn, if required.

"Friend of mine owns and runs this place. He lost his leg at Shiloh, so he runs this inn for wayward soldiers like me," said the sergeant major as he grinned. Soldiers only, he won't let any silly-vilians (civilians) stay at the inn, but he will let them eat and drink in the pub. He was a damn good soldier. You didn't have to worry about your back, when he was next to you," he continued.

Andy stayed with the horses while Everett went in to see if they could get a room. Sergeant Major Jubal McGraw grabbed the inn's owner in a powerful bear hug, picking the smaller man off his one good leg saying, "brought you a couple of Georgia boys who need a place to stay tonight."

"Well there is only one room left. We been full every night, what with more and more troops a comin' in to protect Richmond from the Federals. Only one bed though."

"I'll take it," Everett said.

"Two dollars in advance for the room, and two more dollars for your horses, which includes feed and hay," the owner retorted.

"You can put your horses in the barn. My sons stand watch all night, more for thieves than for Federals, so they will be there for ya in the morning."

"Much appreciated," Everett responded.

Everett thanked the sergeant major and got the key to the room, taking most of the gear to the room by way of an outside wooden staircase. Andy took the horses to the barn where he fed, watered, and loosely tied them to a common rail. There were no stalls in the barn. When Andy got to the room, they strapped on belt holsters with their Dragoons and went downstairs to the pub for the promised hearty meal.

The Boars Head Pub was a throwback on the Revolutionary War years with long wooden tables and benches. The main room was candle-lit by two large chandeliers. There was no bar or chairs. Whitewashed walls bore early American flags, and the centerpiece on the wall behind a serving table at the end of the hall bore a large Confederate Flag over the Revolutionary War words, "Give Me Liberty or Give Me Death." It was definitely a soldier's pub.

Andy and Everett took seats at the end of the benches, away from other men who were bunched together in raucous conversation. Sergeant Major McGraw joined them carrying two large steins of brew in each hand saying, "Get em while you can boys. It won't be this good in the field."

The brothers accepted the beer with thanks. A bar girl served pewter plates of greasy pork and home fried potatoes with dark gravy and a large helping of fried okra topped off with a loaf of hot homemade bread. She pointed to the serving table saying, "Rhubarb and raspberry pie is available, if you are so inclined." The men ate heartedly.

"So where do you boys have to report in at?" asked the sergeant major.

Everett answered, "We're supposed to report to a Colonel Myers, the Quartermaster General."

"That's A.C. Myers. His office is located on the corner of tenth and Main Streets, up on the second floor. Well, the Quartermaster won't likely know what to do with you, but I think you'll probably end up going to an outfit that will be fighting the Federals at Seven Pines or Fair Oaks. Union forces are building up breastworks there."

"I know you came in on the train with us, so how is it that you seem to know where everything is, like the office of the Quartermaster General?" Ev asked.

"Been here since day one. Helped set up most of the offices as they moved the capitol from Montgomery, Alabama, last May. I work in an office above the Bank of Virginia on Main Street between Tenth and Eleventh."

Everett continued asking questions saying, "How did you get to be a sergeant major in such a short period of time?"

"Well I was a sergeant major in the Union Army; fighting Indians for the past few years. I was contacted by Colonel James Anderson when I came back to fight for Virginia. He's who I work for now."

"Doing what?"

"I work in the Army Intelligence Office." "What in the heck is that?" Everett asked.

"Well, we try to find out when the Federals are coming, by what routes, troop strength, and the types of weapons that they have."

"How many men you got doing that?" Andy asked intrigued.

"Only a very few of us. Most of the generals think that intelligence is just a waste of time. Of course they want the information that we develop, but they don't want to put any men or money into the office."

"Ever consider listening to their telegraph messages?" Andy questioned.

"Why do you ask?" Jubal responded with a quizzical look on his face.

"I was a telegraph operator while I was going to college. It seems to me that you could learn more by intercepting their messages than you could by sneaking around and risk getting your ass shot off trying to actually see enemy troops."

"Good point," said Jubal without answering the question.

"So what's it like being on the battlefield?" Everett asked.

The sergeant major smiled and said, "Pandemonium—absolute confusion. The more people on the battlefield, the more confused it becomes. Not like fighting Indians. Just imagine sixty or eighty *thousand* men all shooting at each other, cannon and mortars going off on both sides, and officers trying to get soldiers to move from one point to another; themselves not knowing what the hell they are doing."

"That's a pretty grim assessment, sergeant major," Everett said.

"You think that's grim? Wait until you smell the stench of a thousand dead and dying men, and hear the screams of another few *thousand* men who have been wounded, especially when they face the surgeon to have limbs removed with a half dozen men holding them down on a table while the surgeon saws through them like a log with no way to dull the pain. At best, there's only a fifty- fifty chance that they live through the surgery. Many don't make it. That's what's grim."

"That's grim, alright," Everett said, mentally picturing a surgeon sawing through a man's arm or leg.

"Sometimes though, it can get downright comical," the sergeant major continued while grinning.

"A year ago July, I was with General Beauregard at Manassas and Bull Run. I had provided the general with information regarding Yankee General McDowell and his army that was slowly making their way toward our boys at Manassas. General Beauregard prepared a plan to attack McDowell's flank before the Federals could get into position to attack our main force. One Yankee division that was far ahead of the rest of the Federal troops did attack our center. But they were driven back, and they suffered significant losses and casualties. However, owing to the fact that few of our officers actually received or understood their orders to attack the Federal's flank, the whole thing became somewhat of a mess. Add to that, a great many of our troops were wearing blue uniforms, and many of the Federals were wearing gray uniforms, the battlefield became confused early on."

"It was there at Bull Run that General Jackson got the nickname, *Stonewall.* In the heat of battle, confederate lines under Brigadier General Bee started to break and run. General Bee yelled for his men to take heart and look to Virginia's troops, where Jackson was standing like a stone wall. Well, they rallied behind the Virginia boys and finally did beat back the Federal attack. It was only through personal courage and leadership in the face of battle that Jackson was able to hold his men together. Others around him were able to join in and press the attack. As a result, the Federals clearly lost that skirmish."

"Although the Federals were retreating from the battlefield, they had been successful in positioning some cannon and mortars on high ground. The Yankee artillery was causing our boys to fall back instead of continuing to pursue the Federals that we had on the run. A fast thinking infantry officer gathered up as many of our boys as he could find who were wearing blue uniforms. He quickly assembled and marched them in formation, in plain sight, toward the guns of the Union artillery. The Federal artillerymen thought that the blue-uniformed troops were Federals coming to help them. Meanwhile, part of another Confederate brigade made their way through the forest, flanking the Union artillerymen. Boy were the Federals surprised when the troops in blue uniforms started shooting at them. The Federals got away with a few of their cannons, but most of the artillery was left behind, which we recovered for later use."

"But the funny part came later as all the Federals were trying hard to fall back—running as fast as they could. Civilians had come to see the battle for themselves. They brought their carriages with wives and children, and they even had lunch baskets so that they could eat as they watched the ongoing battle from the rolling hillsides. They had been seated on picnic cloths spread out on green grass.

One bridge was central to the escape of the Federals. It was the only road out of the area, and it was jammed with civilians who by then were trying to leave the area after realizing that they too were in the line of fire. A shell from one of our cannons destroyed a large wagon on the bridge, thereby making the bridge impassable.

Everyone, including women and children, were crawling over those in front of them, trying desperately to get away. Because of the women and children, we stopped pressing our attack. Instead, we sat on the recently evacuated hillsides and ate the lunches that had been abandoned by the fleeing sightseers. Like I said, sometimes it can be downright funny," said the grinning sergeant major.

"Funny as it was however, both sides lost a lot of good men at Bull Run."

"Any advice for us?" Everett asked.

The grin on the sergeant major's face disappeared as quickly as it had formed. Suddenly he looked at the two captains in an almost threatening manner as he said, "You're a captain with no battle experience. Find yourself a sergeant who has been in battle and listen carefully to what he tells you. You don't have to do what the sergeant says, but you should carefully consider his words and ask questions. Your job is to be a leader, and being a leader simply means taking care of your men. Officers don't win battles. If your men trust you, they will fight for you. Soldiers—the privates—they're the ones who win battles. Officers lose battles, usually through inept planning or poor execution of battle plans. Look out for your men and they will look out for you. Listen to your battle-tested sergeants, and try not to piss your pants. You can't instill confidence in your men when they see that you've pissed your pants," he said, smiling again.

The two captains remained quiet as they reflected on the sergeant major's wisdom.

"Here's another little piece of advice," the sergeant major said. "Leave your horses here. Don't take them to the battlefield unless they've been gun trained. You don't need a horse that dumps you on your backside the first time a gun goes off next to its ear. Untrained horses will panic at the sounds of battle. You can't lead if you are flat on your back. Get military trained horses from the Quartermaster and leave your personal horses in the safety of someone you can trust while you go to war."

"But we don't know anyone here," Everett remarked. "Talk with Will, the innkeeper. He is as trustworthy as they come. If you can arrange something with him, your horses will be waiting for you when you get back— if you get back."

"Thanks," Everett said thoughtfully.

"Well, if you want to ride back to Richmond with me tomorrow, you boys had better get some sleep. I'll be leaving just after dawn," said Jubal as he got up from the table.

The Davis brothers finished the last of their beer and returned to their room for a good night's sleep, one of only a few they'd had since leaving Madison.

Waking before dawn, the two brothers cleaned up a bit for their meeting with Colonel A. C. Myers. They went downstairs to find the innkeeper to see if they could come to some kind of arrangement for him to keep their horses while they were on the battlefield. They were pleasantly surprised to see that a hot breakfast of ham and eggs, home fried potatoes with hominy and grits, and hot biscuits with bacon drippings were available for an additional dollar. They ate eagerly, not knowing when they would get another hot meal.

After suitable and equitable arrangements had been made with the innkeeper and his sons to take care of their horses, the brothers paid for a month's worth of care in advance. With the most pressing business done, they saddled their horses, checked their weapons, which they placed in saddle holsters and rifle scabbards, tied down blanket rolls and gear, and headed out of the barn thinking that they had likely missed the sergeant major. Jubal was mounted and waiting for them in front of the Boars Head Inn. He wore civilian clothes.

"Good morning Sergeant Major," Everett called out as they approached.

"Please call me Jubal when I'm out of uniform. I have work that requires me to meet people that don't need to know that I'm a soldier."

"Okay, Jubal," Everett responded.

The three men rode in silence, feeling the chill of the early morning, while entering the already bustling city. When they finally arrived downtown, Jubal pointed out the Quartermaster General's office and said goodbye.

Andy and Everett tied their horses to a rail. Remembering Jubal's warning about thieves, they removed their weapons and carried them up the stairway to the second floor where a crowd of officers waited their turn to meet with the Quartermaster General or one of his subordinates. Everett checked in with a corporal and was told to wait until they were called. All morning they waited in the narrow corridor, standing around, sometimes talking with other recently arrived officers who were also waiting for an interview with the Quartermaster General.

The Sharps carbines caused quite a stir among several of the officers. Most had heard of the newer weapons, but none had ever seen one. The carbines were manufactured in Vermont, but only a very few of the newer Sharps rifles and carbines made it south of the Mason–Dixon line. Several of the officers asked to see the carbines, shouldering the weapons to check the weight, which was considerably lighter than the most rifles, and checking the length of the barrel, which was only twenty-one and a half inches. None of the officers had actually seen a slant breech or the pellet magazine in the lock plate that automatically fed a priming disk each time the hammer was fully cocked. Finally, the brothers were called into a small office where they were interviewed by a major.

Just like Jubal had said the day before, Andy was assigned to General D. H. Hill's division southeast of Richmond, while Everett was assigned to General Longstreet's division just north of the city where troops were building breastworks for the anticipated skirmish with the Yankee's Army of the Potomac. Everett asked where they could get military horses, indicating that they had their own tack. The colonel gave them script and directed them to a military corral where they could draw horses for their trip and for use on the battlefields. The interview being concluded, they were dismissed with orders to immediately proceed to their assignments.

The brothers drew two military horses, which they bridled with a lead rope, and then rode back to the Boars Head Inn to quarter their personally owned animals, get some lunch, and then to head out to their separate assignments.

The military horses may not have been gun shy, but they were much more hard-mouthed than either brother expected—probably the result of the fast breaking and harsh military treatment. They also had some bad habits. Andy's mare would rear up when you stepped into the stirrup after having saddled her. Everett's gelding would bolt and run off when another horse unexpectedly came up from behind him on the left side. They realized that they wouldn't have time to work out these flaws, so they just had to deal with them as they occurred. Not knowing what the horses would do under differing circumstances made for an interesting ride back into the city.

The brothers split up. Andy turned southeast and Everett turned north toward General Longstreet's camp. That was the last time that the two brothers would see each other for the remainder of the war.

Chapter Seven

Mid-May 1862

ANDY WAS ASSIGNED to the 24th Virginia, a battalion under Brigadier General Sam Garland's brigade, which was part of General D. H. Hill's division. Within the battalion, only Major Maury, the battalion commander, and Captain Bentley had battlefield experience. Andy and two other captains and two lieutenants rounded out the battalion's officer corps, but none of them had yet been battle-tested.

On May 25th, Garland's brigade marched out of Richmond. They marched up Williamsburg Road, where they set up camp at Bridgewater Field, a large flat field next to a forest that separated them by about two miles from the town of Seven Pines. They spent the next three days reconnoitering the area, standing guard duty, and digging trenches and rifle pits for the day when they would have to defend the area from enemy attack. Even though they were involved in very routine duties, most everyone was nervous because they all knew that the enemy was less than two miles down the road.

On May 29th, Captain Bentley led a small detail of the 24th Virginia, including Andy, into the forest where they were attacked by a reconnaissance detail of Union troops who had been making their way toward the Confederate line. Fighting was brief but fierce. Andy shot several Federal skirmishers with his carbine. Hand-to-hand fighting drove the Federals back to their own lines, but the 24th lost a lieutenant who was killed by a pistol shot to the head.

The next morning, Andy and a squad of soldiers returned to the forest where they spent the entire day observing and making notes about Union redoubts that had been dug near the town of Seven Pines. This time, they didn't stumble onto any Federal troops, and the detail was able to return unmolested to their encampment by late afternoon. By nightfall, pouring rain saturated everyone and everything in the field. Extremely high winds sent lighter objects crashing into tents, people, and wagons. Captain Bentley developed a high fever and became delirious. He was returned to a Richmond hospital, which meant that none of the battalion's junior officers had any combat experience.

On the morning of the 31st, Garland's brigade, including the 24th Virginia, was assembled in battle formation behind the 2nd Mississippi, which was the point formation for the attack on the Federals at Seven Pines. Once again, Andy found himself in the forest under fire from Union forces. But this time, the Union force was much larger than the mere detail that he had faced days earlier. It seemed to Andy that there was a Federal behind every tree. His men were falling at an alarming rate. Still, those who were still standing pushed on. Andy dropped to one knee and rapidly fired. When he ran out of ammunition, the fight continued hand-to-hand using rifle butts, bayonets, knives, and swords.

As ferocious as the fighting was in the forest, the fighting intensified when the 24th Virginia broke out of the woods and faced the enemy in the open. Union and Confederate artillery cut into the infantry of both armies. Minnie balls and grape shot killed or wounded at least a quarter of Andy's regiment in the first charge. Andy's battalion commander, Major Maury, was one of those hit by a Minnie ball. Andy dragged his commander back into the forest, out of the field of fire, where he stopped the bleeding and splinted his commander's broken right arm. Propping Maury against a tree, Andy rushed forward to join his men in the fight. They had advanced only another hundred yards or so. Fighting was still hand-to-hand at that point.

Andy noticed that other Confederate divisions were converging on his left and right. That gave Andy the opportunity to have the 24th fall back and regroup into skirmish lines and reload their weapons. However, the convergence of Confederate units in the center of the massive open field gave the Union divisions a chance to encircle the Southerners. General Garland rode up on his horse, personally taking command of the 24th Virginia, and spreading out the other units to confront the Union soldiers. They were able to stop the Federals in the open field. Though the fighting continued throughout the afternoon, there was no decisive winner. The Yankees fell back. The Southerners took the town of Seven Pines, but spent the night sleeping on the ground in the field that had been so costly in Northern and Southern lives.

The battle resumed at dawn as the Confederate divisions attacked the Federals, driving them back towards the town of Fair Oaks. It was just outside Fair Oaks, during more hand-to-hand combat, that a Union cavalryman nearly slashed Andy with his saber. A sergeant pulled Andy away from the arc of the saber at the last possible second. The tip end of the saber cut through Andy's shell jacket slicing Andy's chest. The Union soldier's horse was shot out from under him, giving Andy the advantage and the time to strike the falling Federal. Andy's anger rose to heights he had never before known. He repeatedly struck the hapless soldier with his saber, hacking at the soldier's neck and head. After repeated angry saber strikes, the soldier's head, hanging only by a thread of neck skin, rolled over onto his back. Momentarily still standing, still holding his saber, the dead Federal had the appearance of a dismounted headless horseman. Blood spattered over Andy, both his own blood from his slashed chest and the blood of the headless dead Federal.

Andy fell back behind the skirmish line where a sergeant began tending to Andy's chest wound. Although the slashing would eventually result in an ugly scar, it was not so deep as to be life threatening, as long as it did not become infected. Andy and the sergeant packed the sliced chest with bandages, which seemed to stop the flow of blood. The sergeant tried to get Andy to make his way back to the rear area where he could get better medical attention, but when Andy rose from the ground, he started making his way forward to rejoin his troops. Just as he was about to reach the skirmish line, a fallen Yankee who was seriously wounded, managed to get off one last shot from his revolver. The bullet hit Andy in the back, knocking him to the ground and rendering him unconscious. The sergeant who had tended to Andy placed a bullet into the Union soldier's head. Other than having been shot in the back, there was nothing particularly distinctive about Andy lying in the field. He was just another soldier lying among the thousands of dead or dying Americans who were wearing blue or gray uniforms. His last thought before passing out was of his wife and son and of his brother Everett, who was fighting less than a mile away.

GENERAL LONGSTREET'S CAMP was about three miles north of Richmond. Just about the time that the smell of the city had cleared his nostrils, Everett began to smell the stench of over twenty thousand men, hundreds of camp followers, and their collective animals camped together in a tent city that was spread out over nearly two miles. Unlike the City of Richmond that had outhouses, the smell of which was usually covered by thick pine oil, soldiers and camp followers alike relieved themselves in shallow open trenches, which remained uncovered as the facilities were used continually every day. The latrines were infested with flies and bugs. It was easy to imagine that you could also smell the excrement of an equally large Union army three miles to the east at Fair Oaks. Add to that the smell of smoke from hundreds of cooking fires, and one could well imagine that army camp life was no countryside picnic. Not only did it smell bad, but there was a dense layer of smoke about ten feet over the valley floor, both over the fields and through the woods.

Everett arrived at Longstreet's camp at about three in the afternoon on May 15th. Even though it was a sunny day, the smoke from the cooking fires made it look more like a gray overcast day. He asked for directions to the Divisional Headquarters Company and promptly reported to the Officer of the Day, where he was assigned to the 3rd Brigade. Finding the 3rd Brigade, he was assigned to the 29th Virginia Infantry Battalion. Checking in with the battalion executive officer, a major, Everett was assigned to D Company as Company Commander. The only indoctrination that Everett received was a short warning not to miss battalion officer's call, which would take place in conjunction with chow call in the officer's tent within the hour. Everett found the mess tent where he met other battalion officers. He learned that the officers lived in a battalion "officer's village" rather than living amongst their troops, a condition that Everett could not abide.

After officer's call and dinner, Everett located D Company, where he met Sergeant McMasters, the company's senior non-commissioned officer. McMasters had been acting as company commander following an injury to the former captain who had been thrown and trampled by his horse two days earlier during a live fire training exercise. Evidently, the horse hadn't been gun- trained. Everett mentally thanked Jubal for his sage advice.

According to McMasters, the company was ill- equipped for battle because it was used as a kind of holding company for the other four Virginia battalions within the brigade. Everett asked McMasters to arrange a company formation before work was to commence in the morning, sometime after breakfast. He wanted the men to form with weapons and ammunition. Normally a company would have about one hundred or more men. D Company had closer to fifty. McMasters indicated that when other companies throughout the brigades had trouble with a soldier, the troublemaker was sent to D Company. It was, according to McMasters, a company of misfits. He sent word by way of two corporals that the company would be formed with weapons, at 6:30 in the morning. Everett asked if there was a spare tent within the company area. McMasters indicated that the tent next to his was not in use, but that officers always stayed in officers' village at battalion headquarters.

"I ain't fighting with a company of officers, Sergeant. I'm going to be fighting with the men of D Company, so I'll sleep with the soldiers of D Company," Everett replied.

Sergeant McMaster's eyebrows rose noticeably, but he said nothing. Everett moved his gear into the spare tent and settled in for the night.

Reveille came a little before dawn. Everett cleaned up, shaving by the light of a lantern and a small metal mirror that had been left in the tent by some prior occupant. He put on a shell jacket to ward off the chill of the morning, knowing full well that a jacket wouldn't be needed later in the heat of the day. He had breakfast with the officers and returned to D Company as the men were forming with their weapons."

Everett approached the formation where Sergeant McMasters saluted saying, "Sir, the company is formed."

Everett began inspecting the men, slowly, looking over every detail of each uniform—looking each man in the eyes, noting the man's reaction, which was usually an indication of how the man felt about himself. Most of the men looked down at the ground when they saw Everett looking directly into their eyes. It was an indication that they were not very proud of themselves. Some looked back with defiance. Others, once they saw the captain looking into their eyes, looked straight ahead, as they were supposed to. Everett sensed that they were all basically good men, but now he would have to find a way to make them into a fighting unit.

As Everett inspected the last row of soldiers, he noticed that one man was not wearing boots. Everett inspected the soldier's rifle and quietly asked, "Where are your boots?"

"Didn't feel like wearing them," the private answered. Then he spit tobacco juice onto the toe of Everett's boot. Everett slammed the butt of the man's rifle onto the private's bare foot. The private was a big man, and he reared back to punch Everett when the private suddenly realized that he was looking at the pointed end of his bayonet.

"You're at attention, private," Everett roared.

Slowly, the private composed himself and stood at attention. His eyes watering from foot pain, he focused his eyes straight ahead, but his face depicted hatred. Everett returned the private's unloaded rifle saying, "Sergeant, bring this man to my tent immediately after inspection."

"Yes sir," McMasters answered.

McMasters brought the barefooted private to Everett's tent.

"Private, why are you not wearing boots?" Everett asked again.

"Sir, I have big feet. Never wore boots before I joined the army. They didn't have the right size, so the boots they gave me hurt something awful."

"Sergeant, where do you draw supplies and equipment?"

"All supplies are kept at brigade headquarters, sir"

"Sergeant, Private, follow me."

The three men walked to the brigade and found a supply sergeant.

"I need to draw some boots for this private," Everett said.

The supply sergeant looked at the private's foot and said, "We don't have any boots."

The supply sergeant was a big man, a big man with big feet.

"Those boots that you're wearing appear to be about the right size, Sergeant. Remove them and give them to the private," said Everett.

"Bullshit," the supply sergeant responded.

Everett drew his Dragoon, cocked the hammer, and pointed it at the supply sergeant's nose.

"Take off those boots now, or I'll remove them from your dead body, Sergeant."

The supply sergeant removed his boots.

"Try these boots on Private," Everett ordered while continuing to point the Dragoon at the supply sergeant.

The private put on the boots and looked up smiling.

"How do they fit?"

"They fit just fine, Captain."

Everett looked at the supply sergeant and said, "Well Sergeant, I'm confident that you will find some new boots somewhere. Thank you for your help."

"You ain't seen the last of this, Captain," the supply sergeant said, sneering.

The sergeant was right. Soon after they returned to the company area, a colonel stopped by demanding that Everett surrender his Dragoon and accompany him back to brigade. Everett did as he ordered. That's when he met General George Edward Pickett, the brigade commander.

"Who the hell do you think you are, threatening to kill my supply sergeant?" the general yelled.

"Sir, I'm a company commander who can't get his men properly outfitted so that they can fight, so I took matters into my own hands. I figured that the supply sergeant would be better motivated to get the right size boots if he had to get them for himself."

The general stifled an involuntary grin, looked Everett in the eye, and said, "Captain, that's not the way we do things around here."

Then he looked at the feet of the aggrieved supply sergeant and noted that the sergeant was already wearing new boots.

"Those boots fit you Sergeant?" he asked. "Yes sir," the supply sergeant answered.

"Then why couldn't you find those boots to give to the private?" the general asked.

Realizing that he had been trapped by his own dereliction of duty, the supply sergeant remained silent.

The general turned his gaze to the colonel while pointing to the supply sergeant saying, "Colonel, this man is now a private. You will immediately reassign him to the 29th Virginia, Company D, and you will personally escort him and his personal property to that area now.

And make sure he has a rifle and remove his sergeant stripes."

Addressing the former supply sergeant, the general continued by saying, "Private, you will learn firsthand what it means to have the right equipment because, as of this moment, you are in the infantry. You are dismissed."

The look on the former supply sergeant's face was one of sheer horror. It turned to pure hatred when he looked at Everett. The colonel handed the Dragoon to the general and left with the former supply sergeant in tow.

General Pickett looked at Everett and said, "Have a seat, Captain."

The only place to sit was on the general's cot. "Captain, while I appreciate your position, I can't have my company commanders threatening to kill supply personnel in order to get what they need or want. From now on, if you can't get what you need, you come see me personally. Is that clear?" he asked,

"Yes sir."

"Captain, I take pride in the fact that I get things done, and not always by the book. So tell me, is there anything else that you might need?"

"Yes sir, there is."

"What exactly is that, Captain?" the general asked with a surprised look on his face.

"Well sir, the first thing I need is to evaluate my men to see if they are fit for battle. That means I need about five thousand rounds of ammunition and four training days, away from digging rifle pits, so that we can do some live firing and unit movements."

"You got your ammunition, Captain. Tell supply what you need and I'll make sure they are more amenable to filling your request. But I can only give you two training days. We may be fighting for real after that. You are dismissed, Captain," said the general as he returned Everett's Dragoon.

As Everett was leaving, the general called out, "Good luck son."

Everett turned, flashed a smile, and saluted saying, "Thank you, General."

Everett returned to the company area where Sergeant McMasters was impatiently waiting.

"I didn't really expect to see you again, Captain."

"I wasn't sure that I would be returning either, Sergeant. But everything worked out fine this time. Where are the men?"

"Digging rifle pits, sir."

"Let the men dig for the rest of the morning, but we will be doing some training this afternoon and tomorrow. Meanwhile, I need to go over to battalion headquarters and let them know what we will be doing. They won't be happy about my going over their heads to General Pickett, so I had better try to mend some fences before we head out for training."

The sergeant got up to leave saying, "Sir, you did a good thing today. The private is showing off his new boots, and telling everyone who will listen how you stuck up for him. Of course, the supply sergeant, now a private, is unhappy, but I have assigned a rather large corporal to personally supervise him for a few days. You did very well today, sir."

"Thank you, Sergeant. I'll see you after dinner."

Everett met with the battalion commander and explained what had happened. The colonel wasn't happy, but there wasn't much that he could do about the unorthodox requisition of supplies. Everett explained that he would be evaluating D Company's ability to shoot and to move as a unit. Again, the colonel acquiesced, even though all the other units would still be digging rifle pits, something which they had been doing for three weeks, and which the men were woefully tired of doing.

Walking around the huge encampment, Everett found a battalion of engineers where he bummed a seven-foot pole that was about two inches in diameter and which was smooth to the touch. He mounted a foot-long sharpened pike to one end. Then he sought out some camp followers, where he found a woman who was willing to fashion a gray pennant with the letter D in bold red letters on each side of the cloth. An hour or so later, he paid the woman and took the pike-mounted pennant to his tent.

That afternoon, D Company fashioned some targets fifty yards from freshly dug rifle pits and ensured that no one was in the line of fire. While they waited for horse- mounted riders to clear the range of personnel, the rest of the company moved in formation. When they weren't parading in formation, Everett had the men aim their rifles from prone, sitting, kneeling and standing positions. It was clear to anyone who was watching that the men had not been drilled as a unit. They were awkward, but in the ensuing hours, they began to get the hang of it.

Finally, the corporals broke out the ammunition and Everett started the live fire sequence of training. He had purposely waited until late afternoon so that he could evaluate his men's shooting abilities, both in bright sunlight and in the subdued light of evening. Everett demonstrated the proper firing of the rifle in each of the four basic firing positions. Once the men saw that Everett could shoot as well, if not better than they could, a quiet competition was started in which each private tried to best the captain. A few of the men were truly expert riflemen. For the most part, those who were good shots were rural men who were used to hunting for their food. Sergeant McMasters spent a lot of time with those who were having difficulty. It was dark when D Company finally cleaned their weapons and returned to camp for dinner. The cooks were angry at having been kept waiting.

The next morning, D Company returned to the firing range. During the night, Everett had pits dug at either end of the target line, and then he had engineers rig a heavy duty pulley system that allowed men on either end of the target line to pull metal targets on ropes across the target line, thereby simulating a moving target. Each man fired at least fifty rounds, and by mid-afternoon, they got progressively better at hitting the moving target. As the word spread about the innovative target system, officers from the battalion, brigade, and even division stopped by. General Pickett stopped by and tried his hand at shooting the moving target.

"Looks like I was right about you, son," he said as he left the range.

When the men of D Company had completed rifle practice, they walked up to the ten-yard line and held pistol practice. The men had never practiced shooting their pistols and they did poorly, all except for one private—the private who had gone to formation with no boots. He was truly an expert with his pistol.

"Where did you learn to shoot a pistol?" Everett asked.

"My father taught me, sir."

"Well you are the best pistol shot in the company. Put away your rifle because I have another weapon for you to carry. Everett went over to where he had stowed the pennant mounted pike, which he handed to the private saying, "You are now a corporal and you are the company's standard bearer. The pike on the end has been sharpened and can be used as a spear. However, your main weapon will be your pistol. I expect that you will always carry this company pennant in formations with pride, and I expect the men of Company D to follow it with pride.

"Will you do that for me, Corporal?" Everett asked. "Yes sir, with pride," the big man answered, grinning widely.

With evening coming on, the men cleaned their weapons and returned to the company area for supper, smartly following the D Company standard by marching in formation. The day had gone by quickly, but Everett was exhausted.

As it worked out, almost two weeks passed before they saw action. Everett used the time to continue training his men, but it was a time of learning for him as well. He went to divisional headquarters and looked up the sergeant major, a grizzled man who had seen action in numerous previous battles. Everett asked if they could talk privately. The sergeant major was accommodating, spending as much time with Captain Davis as he could. The sergeant major asked why the captain had come to him. Everett smiled and related that Jubal McGraw had recommended that he contact the veteran of many battles.

"You know Jubal?" the sergeant major asked. Everett related how the two men had met.

The division sergeant major talked about the difference between tactics and strategies and how they come to play on battlefields. He told Everett what had worked and what had failed in the battles that he had been in. Then he said something unexpected.

"I've heard of you, Captain," he said.

"Heard you sleep in your company area, that you have been seen digging rifle pits with the men, and that you devised a moving target for training. Those are all good things. But it's time to stop digging pits and start being a leader. You will never be one of them; the privates, that is. You are supposed to be an officer and a leader. You got their attention, now it's time for you to lead. And don't try to do the sergeant's job either. You can't become their buddy—you have to be their officer, because that's what you are."

Everett sat there taking in everything the sergeant major said.

"Some men are natural fighters. Others have to learn by doing. Your job is to train them well and lead them well. Or as Jubal says, don't piss your pants. What he means is, on the day of battle, eat sparingly and drink less; one cup of coffee and a few sips of water during the day. Make sure you relieve yourself before going into battle. Encourage your men always. Going into a fight is an unnatural occurrence. Nothing actually prepares you for the sights, sounds, and the smells of the battlefield. It takes some getting used to."

Captain Davis took the sergeant major's advice to heart, but then he had his own way of doing things, so he made it a habit to build a small campfire in front of his tent after supper so that he would be available to those who wanted to talk. Sergeant McMasters usually joined him, as did the corporals. Eventually, the privates started coming around. It was a time where they could talk about home and about the coming battle without rank and position getting in the way. Everett felt that the men of D Company were finally coming together as a unit. But he still didn't know how well they would fight.

Armies are not just men and rifles. A lot of equipment has to move, including ammunition, artillery, medical supplies, and food. Each company started loading equipment in carts and wagons at 3:00 a.m. during one of the worst storms that anyone could remember. Winds whipped around them, sometimes knocking the smaller men off their feet. Within the first quarter hour, everyone was rain soaked, even those who were wearing slickers, and most of the troopers didn't have slickers. Those that did, soon removed them because the slickers did little to protect them from the storm.

The men worked all day and returned that night to tents that were wet inside. Needless to say, the night before they went on the attack, even after having eaten a hot meal, they were thoroughly miserable. Everett visited each man in the company, making sure he had ammunition for the battle. With different types of rifles, getting the right ammunition wasn't easy. Near midnight, Everett returned to his own wet tent where he eventually drifted off for a couple of hours of restless sleep.

The next morning was clear and dry. Everett had a doughy biscuit and one cup of thick black coffee while huddled next to a campfire, both to ward off the morning chill and to dry his still damp uniform. He tied his bedroll to the back housing behind the cantle of his saddle and waited for the order to march. After a hastily-called officer's call at 5:00 a.m., the battalion was formed for the march to Seven Pines.

Everett knew that the Federals had well over a hundred thousand soldiers poised to attack the Confederate capitol. Luckily, three of the five Federal Corps' were stuck north of the Chickahominy River. The storm had destroyed the Union Army's bridges. Ten Confederate divisions were to attack the remaining two federal corps' south of the river near Seven Pines. That meant that the Confederates soldiers were going up against about thirty-three thousand Federals. The Confederates had about fifty-thousand men, so the advantage was with the South.

The key to the attack was to tie up the three federal corps' north of the river. To do that, two Confederate divisions were to attack the three federal corps—not to engage them in all out battle—just enough to distract them. Meanwhile, six Confederate divisions under General Longstreet were to advance to Seven Pines along Nine Mile Road. Major General D. H. Hill, who commanded four divisions, was to advance on Williamsburg Road, which ran parallel to Nine Mile Road, but which was separated by about a mile or so. Hill was to initiate the battle.

Of course, the Federals knew that the attack was imminent. First, they had heard the Confederate rail cars moving men and equipment all night the night before. On the morning of the attack, federal pickets saw the Confederate troops moving in on their positions. But then confusion struck, even before the first shot was fired.

Somehow, Longstreet's divisions (that were supposed to be on Nine Mile Road) ended up on Williamsburg Road in front of Hill's divisions. That meant that they were out of position and that all ten divisions would be bunched up in one place, thereby exposing their flanks to federal fire. The roads were still muddy from the storm, so the going was slow. The battle that was supposed to start at eight in the morning didn't happen while Southern divisions tried to get into position. By 1:00 p.m., General Hill got tired of waiting and attacked federal lines.

Slogging through ankle-deep mud on trails and roads, and tramping through dense forests, Everett and his men knew that the battle had started without them because they heard the federal artillery open up on Hill's men. He knew that Andy was in one of Hill's divisions, so he said a short silent prayer for Andy's safety. Soon, D Company joined the fight and pushed the Federals back to a second line of defense, a Union-made row of rifle pits. Confederate forces took possession of the first row of federally-dug trenches. Suddenly, out of the second row of rifle pits, Union troops surged forward in a bayonet charge.

As the Union troops closed in, Everett slung his carbine on his back, drawing his pistol and saber for close combat. On his left, Sergeant McMaster's pistol jammed just as a Federal was about to gut-stick him with a bayonet. Everett thrust his saber deep into the Federal's chest. The Union soldier fell to his right, dragging Everett down with him. That was fortuitous for Everett because another Federal soldier was about to gut-stick Everett. Instead, the Union soldier bayoneted the right side of Everett's unbuttoned shell jacket. Everett recovered his saber and repeatedly slashed the neck of the Federal in front of him. Blood gushed over Everett's hands, his uniform and his face. The blood had a slightly metallic taste, but there wasn't time to reflect on that because other Yankees were advancing on them in the bayonet charge. Everett's revolver quickly ran out of ammunition, but there was no time to reload. More and more

Union soldiers appeared in front of him, so he continued to slash and thrust with his saber. The fight continued until the Confederate troops were able to overrun the Union line. D Company and the men of the battalion took over the second row of rifle pits and captured six cannons, but the Federals had been successful in removing most of their artillery, which apparently was the main purpose behind the bayonet charge. The Union lost a lot of men protecting those cannons.

The battle raged on with the Federals taking cover in a dense forest. As the Confederate troops approached over open ground, the Federals opened up with murderous rifle fire that caused the Confederate forces to return to the relative safety of the second row of Union-made rifle pits. It was nearing nightfall, and the battle just seemed to stop.

The battalion ate no dinner that night. Sergeant McMasters and Captain Davis checked on their troops and noted that D Company had lost nearly a quarter of its men, far less than other outfits. They replenished ammunition, established sentries, and then hunkered down in the cold night air to catch what sleep they could before morning and the continuation of the battle. Alone in a rifle pit, Everett couldn't stop shaking. Memories of the battle flooded his brain. He got no real sleep.

The battle started again at 5:00 a.m. and continued throughout the morning. One of the federal divisions that had been bottled up north of the Chickahominy River was able to cross the river to bolster Union troops. Confederate forces were driven out of the Union-made rifle pits, falling back to the first row of Union-dug rifle pits. By noon, they\ battalion had fallen back to the field where they had started the day before. The Federals returned to their redoubts, and the battled ended early in the afternoon. General Johnston, the commander of the Confederate Army of Northern Virginia, had been shot and severely wounded. General Smith took temporary command of the Southern army but chose not to advance on the Federals.

The Seven Pines and Fair Oaks battles ended ignominiously. Both the Union and the Confederate forces each lost about five thousand men. Neither side won anything. But the Southern troops counted the two battles as a strategic win because the Federals didn't get to Richmond. Everett counted the battle as a personal win because he didn't piss his pants. Alone in his tent, however, Everett shook uncontrollably because of the cold night air, violent memories and bad dreams.

D Company's casualties were twenty-two men killed or wounded. That included the former supply sergeant, forcefully turned infantry private, who was killed at Fair Oaks. There were no ceremonies. Many of the dead were buried near where they fell, and the wounded that made it to a hospital were treated. Many good men died seeking medical treatment. Even more died when they got to a hospital. General Robert E. Lee took command of the Confederate Army. Longstreet's division, including the Third Brigade and the 29th Virginia Battalion returned to Richmond to defend the Confederate capitol from the Union attack that would surely come in the days ahead.

The first week of June found the 29th Brigade making camp outside Richmond, where the men were again employed digging trenches and rifle pits; hot humid work. Officers' call was held while the men were digging trenches. Because nearly half of the brigade's men of were either killed or wounded, the 29th was consolidated with the 28th Brigade, which had suffered an even more significant number of losses. Everett was reassigned to the staff of General Pickens at Division Headquarters.

That evening before chow, Everett met with the men of D Company. He broke the news of the consolidation. There was a lot of grumbling. Sergeant McMasters called out each man's name and new assignment. It was their last night together as D Company. As was his custom, Everett lit a small campfire in front of his tent. Sergeant McMasters and the corporals sat in silence as the privates came by, both individually and in small groups, to say goodbye. They had become a unit and took pride in that. The big standard bearer corporal came into the firelight with tears in his eyes. Silently, he handed the pike mounted staff with the D Company pennant to Captain Davis. Without saying a word, he saluted, then turned and disappeared into the darkness.

By the time Everett awoke a little after daylight, most of the men had already packed and moved to their new companies. Everett packed his gear and said goodbye to Sergeant McMasters. The two men shook hands.

"You saved my life, Captain. I will never forget you."

"Sergeant, I think we saved each other, several times. I won't forget you either. When this war is over, if you get down to Georgia, I'll be in Madison. You will always have a place to stay in my home."

"Thank you, Captain. I just hope we're both still alive when this war is over."

"Amen to that, Sergeant."

After one final handshake, the two men went their separate ways.

Everett carried his gear to the officer's village at Division Headquarters.

"Don't get too comfortable," a colonel said. "General Pickens wants to see you, now."

"Yes sir," Everett responded as he dropped his gear on an empty cot and headed for the general's tent.

"You wanted to see me, General?" Everett asked. "Have a seat, Captain."

Everett once again sat on the edge of the general's cot.

"You did a good job here, Captain. Your men fought well. I wanted your innovativeness on my staff, but I lost out to General Lee. You have been reassigned to his staff, but I don't think you will be there for very long. He has a special assignment for you."

"What would that be, General?"

"That's for him to say, Captain. He is expecting you at his headquarters early tomorrow morning, so I would imagine that you will want to spend the night in the city." "Yes sir. I'd like to check on my brother who was with General D.H. Hill's division at Seven Pines and Fair Oaks."

"They got banged up pretty bad. I hope your brother is okay. Now get yourself a good meal and a good night's rest, then report to General Lee in the morning."

"Yes sir. Thank you, sir," Everett said as he stood, saluted, and returned to the officer's village to pick up his gear.

Since the encampment was within a thirty-minute ride to the Boars Head Inn, Everett headed there to see if Jubal or anyone at the inn might have news of Andy. Jubal wasn't at the inn, and neither the innkeeper nor his sons had seen Andy since the two brothers had ridden out nearly a month earlier. Everett made arrangements to stay the night. He went to the paddock where he brushed the two horses that had been left behind. They seemed genuinely happy to see a familiar face. He saddled his horse and bridled Andy's horse, and then went for a ride so that the two animals would get some long overdue exercise unfettered by the paddock fence. After an hour or so, with noon approaching, Everett returned the horses to the paddock and entered the inn where he sat down to a large dinner.

"Sergeant Major," Everett said addressing the innkeeper by his former rank, "where is D.H. Hill's division."

"Northeast of the city," said the innkeeper.

Getting directions, Everett saddled his horse and headed to the northeast side of the city in search of Andy. Arriving at divisional headquarters, Everett checked in with a lieutenant who was functioning as the Officer of the Day.

"Excuse me Lieutenant, I'm looking for Captain Andrew Davis."

"Captain Davis was killed at Fair Oaks. At least I think he's dead. He was shot during our first assault on the Union line. I saw him go down, but I haven't seen or heard of him since. I don't know if he made it to a hospital. He was in bad shape."

Everett felt like he had been kicked in the stomach by a mule.

"Has anyone notified his wife?"

"Look Captain, I understand that Captain Davis meant something to you, but we are getting ready to fight for the very existence of the Confederate capitol. If we lose this battle, the war is over and we lose everything. Over five thousand of our men died at Fair Oaks and Seven Pines. We don't even know who most of those men were. I'm not sure we ever will."

"Everett strained to keep a civil tongue. "Captain Davis was—is my brother. I'm sorry about the other deaths, but just now, I'm only concerned about my kin."

"I really do understand. Perhaps he was lucky enough to get to a hospital. I would check with the hospitals in Richmond. But now, I have to get back to my work. Sorry for your loss, sir."

The lieutenant turned and went on about his business. Everett rode into the city. No one at any of the hospitals that Everett visited recalled Captain Andrew Davis. Well after dark, Everett returned to the Boars Head Inn where he took a bottle of whiskey to his room and started a letter to Andy's wife, Abigail. Although he started the letter several times, he never finished. Sometime after the fifth attempt, he passed out sitting at the desk.

Shortly after dawn, Everett awoke with a throbbing headache. His muscles hurt from sleeping bent over at the small desk. He couldn't remember the last time he had felt so bad. He poured water into a bowl and splashed the liquid on his whiskered face, hoping that the cold water would make him feel better. It didn't. If anything, the cold water merely heightened the pain of his headache. Shaving in cold water didn't help either.

Looking at the uniform that he would have to wear that day, he scraped the majority of dried blood and mud from his shell jacket with a knife and brushed the fabric with a horse brush in an effort to bring back some of the luster that had been lost by sleeping in the sludge of wet trenches and rifle pits. He couldn't do anything about the hole in the jacket. It was a permanent reminder of how close he had come to being bayoneted. He brushed his trousers and retrieved his only clean shirt from a canvas bag. He looked at himself in a mirror above the dresser and decided that he could do no better in his effort to make himself presentable for his meeting with General Lee.

Everett went out into the morning chill, stopping momentarily at the outhouse, after which he went to the barn where he fed and watered his horses. Stiffly, he took a circuitous route to the inn, hoping to walk off some of the discomfort of his muscles. His head still throbbed. Entering the inn, the heavy smell of breakfast turned his empty stomach. He drew a cup of coffee and sat at the very end of one of the long benches at a wooden table while holding his throbbing head in both hands. Eventually, his stomach eased, and he took a few sips of the strong black liquid. It helped. Men came and went without conversation. He forced himself to eat and then sought out the innkeeper to make arrangements to leave his personal property in the room until he got back following his meeting in Richmond.

The ride to city-center cleared his head. Muscles began to relax, and the headache finally abated. By the time Everett reached General Lee's headquarters, he felt almost normal. Being in the center of the city, Everett remembered Jubal's advice and unsheathed his carbine, which he took with him into the general's headquarters.

Everett checked in with a skinny corporal and was surprised when the corporal immediately ushered Everett into the general's private office. Several general officers stood around a wall-mounted map arguing back and forth, their voices rising and falling like a tide.

"Captain Everett Davis," the skinny corporal announced.

All conversation stopped as the officers turned to look at the young captain who was intruding on their limited time with General Lee.

"Excuse me, gentlemen," said General Lee. "Please continue with your planning. I will return shortly." The general officers scowled at the young captain.

"Come with me, Captain."

Everett followed General Lee to another office down the narrow hallway.

"Take a seat, Captain," the general said as he turned to tell a private that he was not to be disturbed. The general shut the door and walked across the room where he seated himself behind his desk.

"Thank you for coming so quickly, Captain. Unfortunately, I have very little time to spend with you. I've been told that you are a man of intelligence and wit. I need such a man to carry out an important mission."

The door suddenly opened. The general looked angrily at the source of the disturbance, and then abruptly stood at attention.

"Good morning, Mr. President." Everett jumped to attention.

"Sorry to interrupt you General, but I wanted to meet this young man."

"Our honor, Mr. President," said General Lee, who surrendered his chair to his boss.

Captain Davis remained standing at attention while General Lee moved a wooden chair to sit next to Everett.

"Please sit and relax, Captain," the president said, while inspecting Everett from head to toe.

President Davis turned to Lee and questioned the general about what progress was being made to build defenses around the capitol. General Lee provided a synopsis of what work had been done and described the work that was yet to be accomplished. As the general was answering the president's questions, Everett noted that the Confederate president had many of the same sharp facial features of Mr. Lincoln, the President of the United States. Both presidents wore their hair in a similar manner. Both had high cheekbones that were very pronounced. Both men had deep set eyes with bushy eyebrows. They even dressed a lot alike. That was as far as Everett got comparing the two presidents.

"Captain, what do you think is the most significant reason that we might lose this war," asked the president.

Everett thought for a moment, wondering if he should answer honestly, or answer in a manner that was consistent with the political rhetoric that he had heard around the city. He chose an honest answer.

"Mr. President, I'm new to the role of military officer, so I don't know if anything I say will be of value. However, from what I've seen over the last few months, the most significant reason that the South might lose the war is desertions. Men are returning to their homes instead of remaining at the battle front."

"Governor Brown said you were uncommonly perceptive. Why do you think they are deserting our cause, Captain?"

"Mr. President, there is no one reason. Rather there is an aggregation of reasons including the lack of food, both in the army and at home; and speaking of home, it's approaching harvest season, and there are no men folk to harvest crops; the army lacks weapons and ammunition; and most of all, the horror of dead and dying troops in the thousands on the battlefield."

"And which one of those reasons for desertion can we do something about, Captain."

Everett thought for a moment and then answered, "Providing troops with weapons and ammunition, sir."

"You are exactly right, Captain, which is why you are here. Governor Joe Brown said in a recent meeting that he asked you to coordinate food supply trains from local communities to Atlanta when war first broke out. He said that you were good at getting people to cooperate with you. I need that kind of talent to coordinate the transport of weapons and ammunition from the Caribbean, past the Union blockades and into the hands of our soldiers."

"Sir, I know nothing of ships or running seaborne blockades."

"Neither do I, Captain," the president said with a big grin. "But one of us in this room has to try, and both General Lee and I are otherwise engaged at the moment. You do understand the urgency of this operation, don't you Captain?"

"Yes sir, I do. But I don't know if I'm the right man for the assignment. Surely someone more familiar with the sea and with ships would be a better candidate."

"Captain, I thought so too, at first. Then I began to understand that what we really need is someone who can see the larger picture. I need a coordinator. And according to Governor Brown, you are that man. You have the confidence of the Governor, and now you have my confidence as well. General Lee has your written orders. I just came by to emphasize the urgency and importance of this assignment and to wish you Godspeed because you must leave this very evening to catch a blockade runner to Nassau. Your trip has already been arranged. I am not asking you to go, Captain. I am ordering you to leave immediately, and to carry out the orders that General Lee will provide."

"Yes Mr. President," Everett answered formally. "Good day, General, and good luck, Captain," the president said as he stood to leave.

General Lee and Captain Davis jumped to attention at the departure of their commander in chief.

"Well Captain, you have a long trip in front of you. We've arranged for you to return to Atlanta by train. From there you will have one or two days at home, then you must make your way to Charlestown where you will board a steamship bound for Nassau. You will not wear your uniform. If Federals capture you, and if they find your written orders, you will be hung as a spy. If anyone asks, you are a businessman from Madison, bound for Nassau to buy goods from Europe for sale in your Madison store. Any questions, Captain?"

"Yes sir. I've been looking for my brother, Captain Andrew Davis, who was reportedly killed at Seven Pines. There is a possibility that he was wounded and that he is in one of the many hospitals here in Richmond. I need a couple of days to continue my search for him."

"I'm sorry Captain. Your schedule will not allow you to stay. Your train leaves at three in the morning. And you must be at the station an hour before your train leaves."

"What am I to tell his wife?"

"Tell her that you were assigned to separate divisions and that you have not seen him since the battle of Seven Pines. Meanwhile, I'll have my staff search for him at the hospitals. If we locate him, or if we verify his death, I will send you a telegram in Atlanta. You can check the telegraph office before going on to Madison. That's the best that I can do, son."

"Thank you, sir. That would be a great help."

General Lee took an envelope from the inside pocket of his coat and handed the thick sheaf of papers to Everett saying, "Your orders, Captain. Good luck."

The general walked down the hallway with Everett, shook his hand goodbye, and then entered the office where the officers were still arguing. Everett retrieved his carbine from the corporal in the reception area and left the building. He walked his horse to a nearby café. Seating himself at an outdoor table, Everett ordered coffee and opened the envelope that contained his orders. The envelope contained a draft for one hundred thousand dollars with which to rent an office, living accommodations and to buy unnamed equipment. His orders said only that he was a Captain in the Confederacy who was authorized to coordinate the shipment of equipment as necessary. Never before had Everett felt so unqualified to do a job.

Returning the papers to the envelope, Everett noticed the sign at the Bank of Virginia across the street. He left money to cover his coffee and a tip on the table, and then crossed the street, entering the bank building where he climbed the stairs to the second floor. There was one unmarked door at the end of the hall. Everett knocked, and then opened the door into a single office with a receptionist's desk. The receptionist, a pretty twenty- something year old woman smiled and asked with a heavy Southern drawl how she might help.

"I'm looking for Jubal McGraw." "Your name, Captain?"

"Everett Davis."

"One moment, please."

The woman disappeared behind another door. When the door opened again, the receptionist invited Everett to enter the inner office where Jubal stood with outstretched hand.

"Well, I see you survived Fair Oaks and Seven Pines, Captain," shaking Everett's hand

"Barely," Everett replied.

"So what brings you to my neighborhood, Captain?"

"I need a favor."

"Now how could a mere sergeant major be of service to the Captain?" Jubal asked grinning.

"Jubal, Andy was supposedly killed at Fair Oaks, but there is a chance that he is still alive in one of the many hospitals here in Richmond. I'm ordered to leave early in the morning, so I can't continue to look for him. I need you to use your influence to find him and then to let me know if he's still alive."

"Well, if I did find him, it could be a long time before I could get a letter to you in Nassau," Jubal replied.

"How did you know that? I just learned of it moments ago."

"Knowing things is what I do, Ev. I'll see what I can do."

"I'll check in with the telegraph office in Atlanta in a few days. General Lee said that he would send a telegram if Andy was found, dead or alive, before I leave for Charlestown. Your help would be greatly appreciated, Jubal."

"I'll do what I can, Ev." "Thanks."

The two men shook hands and Everett left the office to pack, return his military-issued horse, and to arrange with the innkeeper to keep Andy's horse for another month. Everett left Richmond on the early morning train on June 4th. He had sold his horse and tack at the public livery for a price far less than their true worth.

June 5, 1862

Andy woke up in a Richmond hospital strapped to a bed lying on his stomach. He struggled to turn over, but was cautioned not to move or he might rip open the stitches in his back.

"What's wrong with me?" he asked.

"You were shot in the back. The bullet must have been partially spent because it didn't go very deep."

Andy knew the voice, but just couldn't quite put a name to it.

"But at least you didn't piss your pants," the voice continued.

"Jubal McGraw! What brings you here?"

"I promised Everett that I would find you, if I could." "Where's Ev?"

"He's been reassigned—out of the country. He's fine. He didn't piss his pants either. He actually made somewhat of a name for himself at Seven Pines and Fair Oaks."

"How bad am I hurt?"

"Nothing that a couple of months of proper care won't heal, according to the doctors. You have some muscle damage, a couple of broken ribs, and you have a collapsed lung."

"Months?" Andy asked incredulously.

"Andy, you're lucky to be alive. You would have bled to death if it weren't for a sergeant. You must have made quite an impression on him because he stopped your bleeding and carried you back through the woods to the rear area and placed you in an ambulance where you were brought to this hospital. The surgeons gave you only a fifty percent chance for survival."

"How long have I been here?" Andy asked. "Just over a week."

"Where's Everett?"

"I'm not supposed to say, but he's in the Caribbean coordinating blockade runners."

Andy drifted off to sleep again. He awoke a minute later saying, "Damn, I'm hungry. Can a guy get something to eat in here?"

"Sure," said Jubal. Today the hospital is serving steak and eggs, potatoes, fried okra, black eyed peas, and homemade cornbread. But you get weak soup."

"Jubal McGraw, you are a cruel, cruel man." Jubal laughed saying, "Yes I am."

"Hey, how come I'm tilted with my head lower than the rest of my body?"

"Your doctor is trying to drain phlegm and mucus from around your collapsed lung. You've been spitting up quite a lot of mucus into that tray beneath you."

"When am I going to be able to sit up again?"

"That will be up to your doctor. He should be checking on you pretty soon. You still want to eat?"

"Weak soup?" "Yes, weak soup."

"Well, I guess that's better than nothing."

Jubal removed the wooden triangular block underneath the bed that kept Andy's body at an angle and summoned a volunteer who brought a bowl of soup and a spoon. Jubal spooned a small amount of soup into Andy's mouth.

"That's horrible. What's in it?" "Garlic mainly, I think."

"What are those little green and brown things floating around in there?" asked Andy who looked suspiciously at the brown liquid.

"Bread mold. If it doesn't kill you, the doctor says it may help fight infection."

"That's horrible," Andy said again. "So you don't want it?"

"No, I don't, but it looks like I don't have a choice," Andy said smiling weakly.

"Here you go, soldier," Jubal said as he spooned more soup into Andy's mouth.

Over the next few days, Andy did get stronger and was eventually allowed to sit up in bed. The stitches, both inside his back and on the surface, held the flesh together as the ingredients of the horrible tasting soup seemed to help the healing process.

His first solid food was a disaster. Not only was it bland, he regurgitated all over his night shirt, which had to be changed with the help of two burley medics. But over the next two days, he got to the point where he could finally hold down some solid foods. He ate hungrily

Jubal stopped by the hospital every couple of days to check on Andy, indicating that he had sent several letters by mail to Everett regarding Andy's improving condition. However, it was unknown when the letters would reach Everett in the Caribbean.

Even though the hospital, one of nineteen in the Richmond area, was overflowing with patients, the surgeon who had worked on Andy would not release him for active duty. It took two weeks before Andy was allowed to walk unassisted, but he tired easily, and initially, he had to be helped back to his bed.

Meanwhile, Confederate forces continued to dig trenches and build defenses around the City of Richmond, preparing for the Union assault. But General Lee was not one to wait. Fighting resumed on June 25th and continued through the first of July in a Confederate offensive. The battlefields were spread out over a vast area in and around cities, towns, and villages, including Mechanicsville, Gaines Mill, Oak Grove, Beaver Dam Creek, Ellerson's Mill, White Oak Swamp, Malvern Hill, ending at Harrison Landing where Union gunboats controlled the waters and provided additional artillery against the Confederate offensive. In all, over thirty-five thousand men were killed or wounded on both sides.

Expecting that Union forces might actually reach the City of Richmond, Andy and other ambulatory officers considered forming an independent corps of walking wounded to protect the hospital from attack. But medical officers refused to let them have access to the weapons that had been collected. The doctors were adamant that weapons would not be allowed in the hospital wards. In the end, however, Union forces withdrew, and the city was not attacked.

Once it was clear that the City of Richmond was no longer under immediate threat, Andy was allowed to assist medical personnel around the hospital, but he still tired easily and had little strength. It took nearly another month before the doctor would allow Andy to return to full duty.

Jubal stopped by the hospital on the night before Andy was to be released. Andy felt fit and couldn't understand why he had been kept in the hospital so long. As usual, Jubal had the answer.

"Andy, you once asked why we didn't spend more time intercepting telegraph messages instead of trying to actually see what the enemy was doing," said Jubal. "Frankly, anybody who could send and receive telegraph was assigned to various army units in the Signal Corps. I talked with my commanding officer. He talked with General Lee, and you have now been reassigned to the Army Intelligence Office. It was necessary that you be completely healed because this new assignment will be both dangerous and physically demanding. Your doctors understood the need for you to be physically able to do the type of work that this new assignment requires."

Jubal, it's been a long time since I did any telegraph work, and I would hardly call telegraph operator a physically demanding job."

"You'll have time to build up your code speed, and while you're doing that, you will be learning the intelligence business. You'll be working behind enemy lines, and that my friend, is very physically demanding, if you live long enough. Do you remember where my office is?"

"Yes, above the bank on Main Street."

"They should release you after breakfast, so come by the office after eight in the morning. I've already arranged for you to stay at the Boars Head Inn where your horse has been well cared for. I'll bring him with me tomorrow morning so that you can ride back to the inn tomorrow afternoon."

"Looks like you've thought of just about everything as usual, Jubal."

"Andy, I'm not doing you any favors. This will be a very dangerous job."

"Well I need to get out of here and get back to doing something useful," Andy replied.

"You'll get the chance to do something very useful. I'll see you in the morning," Jubal said as he waved goodbye.

Andy had a restless night. He was anxious to get out of the hospital. He had written several letters to Abigail, but had not received any mail for quite some time. He was concerned for his family and for his brothers. He had not heard from his wife or either of his two brothers since he woke up in the hospital, and he was extremely concerned about their wellbeing.

Chapter Eight

September 1862

THE BROTHERHOOD HAD grown to nearly fifty men, all killers and thieves. An organization of that size could not long survive without detection on the streets of Washington D.C., especially since a professional police force was now patrolling the district's streets. Harrison subsequently shifted the main part of his treasonous operation—sales, and distribution—to a large farm that was owned by a fervent Southern sympathizer in the State of Maryland. The increased number of men on the farm was easily camouflaged as day laborers who worked in the barns and who drove crops to market. Members of the Brotherhood worked mainly in one of the massive barns, which was actually a warehouse for contraband. They also provided farm and crop security, not only keeping prying eyes away from the farm and its contraband operation, but also protecting crops from foragers.

Of course, day laborers did actually work the expansive fields, but they weren't members of the Brotherhood. Crops were sold to store owners in the many towns throughout Maryland, but the major part of the crop was sold to the Union army. In fact, the farm had become a major contractor, supplying the army with vegetables and salted beef. Farm wagons constantly moved into Washington D.C. and beyond. Drivers no longer had to depend on a ruse to get returning wagonloads of stolen weapons past D.C. guards. They had military passes that allowed them to move freely without inspection between the northern states and the District of Columbia. The false bottom of each wagon was always loaded with contraband when it returned to Maryland.

Since members of the Brotherhood were no longer deriving a living by killing innocent Washingtonians, Harrison began paying them a weekly stipend. Paying the band of killers actually worked to Harrison's advantage because the killers became dependent on him and his Saturday paydays. It was ironic because in one swoop, Harrison had reduced violent crime in Washington D.C., while making a small fortune selling weapons to the South.

Freight hauling became so lucrative that Harrison opened an office in the district. He even opened a security company providing private security at Washington's government offices and eventually, as soldiers could no longer be spared for security duties in and around the district, he provided uniformed guards at the bridges and intersections that led to the South. With this new service, employees were paid to catch spies and gun-runners, which they actually did from time to time. Harrison and the Brotherhood didn't want competition, no matter how small the operation. Everywhere that the government could employ private security, Harrison's unseen hand directed the placement of his killers and thieves under the veil of national security.

Roger Burkis, the blind man, was placed in charge of the security and freight hauling businesses. His status as a blind war veteran provided a cover that was above reproach. His elevated status and increased earnings allowed him to rent a modest home in the heart of the district and to hire a young woman from the orphanage to be his eyes. After a year of close association running the business, as well as simultaneously building financial security that neither she nor the blind man had ever before known, the young woman became his wife.

While Roger Burkis was listed as the company's owner-manager, his covert job was to ensure that members of the Brotherhood manned the most sensitive security positions, especially at border crossings between Washington and Maryland when consignments of contraband were to pass through, which by then was most every day. And he was still the conduit between the Brotherhood and Magnus. His new wife knew nothing about his mysterious boss or of the Brotherhood.

Not only was Harrison stealing from the federal government, the government was actually paying him for his treason. His legitimate security and freight hauling businesses were almost as profitable as selling contraband.

It wasn't long before he got the idea to incorporate a part of the freight business with the security operation, thereby obtaining government contracts to move mail and money to army camps. That gave the Brotherhood the added opportunity to read military dispatches before the letters reached Union Army field command-ers. Telegraph messages were the only war correspondence that the Brotherhood didn't have access to; especially those messages that were restricted to the battlefields by a closed-loop telegraph system.

Harrison's biggest worry was what to do with all of the money he was making. He was careful not to accept Confederate currency. Payments for contraband were made in Union greenbacks or gold. Yet, with all of his ill- gotten wealth, he was a man of few personal luxuries. He had no grand house, no ostentatious carriages, and no fine jewelry except for an ornate pocket watch. He was actually a very frugal man. As his wealth grew, he began to think about life after the war.

He continued to support the orphanage, but did not contribute amounts that might draw unwanted attention. He was a sporadic visi-tor, always encouraging the staff and helping the older girls find jobs in and around the district. It was only after they had left the orphan-age that he would prey on the select few who appealed to him the most.

As chief of staff for Senator Hill, a function that he laughingly thought of as his day job, Harrison continued to attend meetings, craft legislation, and advise the Senator about issues on behalf of special interest groups that supported the Senator with cash and lavish perks. And because the Senator was so well placed, Harrison attended closed-door meetings with his boss regarding military intelligence and the war. Harrison was extremely pleased with himself.

—⤜∞⤛—

CONVERSELY, CHIEF STONE was not at all pleased with himself. He was no closer to solving the murder of Colonel Ben Jenkins. Nor was he any closer to solving the disappearance of the orphanage girls. Most of all, he was discouraged that he hadn't been able to unearth any evidence that would point to those who were stealing Union Army weapons and ammunition in significant quantities, which were subsequently being sold or otherwise provided to the Confederacy. However, at the moment, it wasn't his professional inadequacies that had him edgy. Rather, he was more worried about a domestic issue.

Stone could smell the odor of strong coffee emanating from the kitchen. Unlike most days when he dressed in a suit for his trip to Washington, this morning he was dressed in clothes that were more conducive to manual labor. He had mentally mapped out the day and had decided on a course of work to be accomplished before the evening hours when he was to meet with the president. He had earlier dumped both the chamber pot and the used wash-water from the porcelain bowl on the dresser. He had even made his bed. Realizing that he could no longer put off what would likely turn out to be a confrontation with Kaitlin, Stone exited his bedroom and made his way to the dining room downstairs.

"Good morning, Mr. Stone," greeted Kaitlin as she continued setting the dining room table.

"Good morning, Kaitlin. How are you this morning?" "I'm doing well, thank you. And you?" she asked. "Well, I've been better. Please take a moment to sit. I have a question that has been very much on my mind these past few days," said Stone.

"Well I knew something was bothering you. You've been as nervous as a long-tailed cat in a room full of rocking chairs," Kaitlin remarked, smiling broadly.

"Kaitlin, I have been very reluctant to ask, but the year of mourning your dead husband passed months ago, so I want to ask you to accompany me to dinner with the president this evening. The invitation is partially work- related, but it is a social invitation too."

Kaitlin silently looked down at her hands clasped in her lap. To Stone, the silence was nerve wracking; seconds felt like hours.

"Mr. Stone, I would dearly love to see the president and Mrs. Lincoln again, but I have nothing to wear."

"Is that a yes, then?"

"No, Mr. Stone. I have nothing to wear to visit the President of the United States."

That being said, Kaitlin returned to the kitchen where she finished loading platters with ham and eggs, home fried potatoes and gravy, and hot biscuits, which she placed on the dining room table with a louder than necessary thump.

"Kaitlin, please. The president wants to see you, but in truth, I don't want to be the only unattached male at the dinner."

"It's a large stately affair then?" asked Kaitlin, emphasizing her Irish lilt.

"No, just Allan and Joan Pinkerton, you and me. We won't be going to the Executive Mansion. Rather, the president recently moved to a cottage on the grounds of the Old Soldiers Home about three miles away from the Executive Mansion."

"No, I don't have anything to wear," Kaitlin answered with sternness in her voice.

"Kaitlin, you have worn nothing but black since we first met nearly a year ago. It's time for you to wear something more… colorful," Stone said trying to hide the fact that he was nervous with his boldness.

Kaitlin looked wide-eyed at Stone. She remained silent as she thought, *I have been wrong about you Franklin Stone. You're not as nervous as a long-tailed cat. You're as nervous as a school boy asking a girl for a first date.* Looking in his eyes, Kaitlin felt a stirring that she had not felt for some time.

Kaitlin smiled and said, "Mr. Stone, if you will drive me to town, I will try to find something suitable to wear to your dinner."

Kaitlin and Stone ate breakfast in silence, each contemplating their own thoughts about the other.

After breakfast, Stone washed the horse drawn carriage that had been stored in the barn since the funeral of Ben Jenkins nearly eighteen months earlier. He washed, brushed, and bridled a pair of smallish black Percheron geldings, fast draft horses more commonly used in Europe than the United States. He hitched the animals to the Phaeton carriage and parked at the front door while waiting for his lady landlord.

Kaitlin exited the house wearing a black taffeta dress with embroidered black lace over the bodice and full length sleeves cuffed with lace at her wrists. She wore a large black lace hat to shield her face from the sun. As she entered the carriage, her dainty ankles and the calves of her legs flashed briefly from under a number of black petticoats. *Even dressed in black, she is astoundingly beautiful,* Stone thought.

Town was nearly an hour away. It had been a long time since the draft horses had pulled the carriage, so they had a tendency to want to run. Stone held the horses back until they settled into a more practical stride. Stone was not a man prone to small talk, so he was thankful when Kaitlin asked direct questions.

"Why did the president move to a cottage?"

"Well, even though it's called a cottage, the building has over thirty rooms, I'm told. As you know, Mr. and Mrs. Lincoln are still mourning the death of their son Willie, who died four months ago. I think they just wanted to get away from the city and its oppressive heat, as well as the constant bickering of military and political leaders and the general public who demand so much of the president's time."

"Yes, I was particularly distressed to hear of the death of their son. I can't imagine anything more hurtful than the pain of having a child predecease a parent," Kaitlin answered.

Silence continued until she asked another question. "When will we have to leave, Mr. Stone?"

"We should leave at five-thirty to reach the cottage by seven, I would think."

"Well then, I will be ready at five," Kaitlin said.

With more silence than small talk, they arrived in town where Kaitlin directed Stone to the Emporium.

"I have no idea how long this will take, Mr. Stone. It has been a long time since I have been fitted for a gown; especially one that is to be worn in just a matter of hours," Kaitlin said reproachfully.

"Take as long as you need," Stone said out loud, but inwardly he was thinking, *A man can select a suit, buy it, and wear it out of the store in under thirty minutes. But a lady...* He didn't bother finishing the thought. He was just overjoyed that Kaitlin was going with him. Somehow, he felt like a school boy going on his first date.

"I really am as nervous as a long-tailed cat," he said to himself.

Promptly at five, Kaitlin entered the study where Stone was dressed in a dark suit. She was dressed in an off the shoulder black and ivory gown of velvet, satin, and ribbed taffeta with beaded trim across the bodice. The gown was made even more stunning by an emerald green sash that started at the left shoulder, crossed the bodice, wrapped around the waist, and hung loosely at the bottom of the gown on the right side. The bottom of the sash was weighted with several green stones housed in polished silver ornamentation. Stone was awestruck.

"Never has there been a more beautiful woman. Oh God, did I say that out loud?" he asked.

Kaitlin beamed, saying "Thank you Mr. Stone. Maybe you were right—it is time to wear more colorful clothes.

Then she turned to the right and to the left giving Stone a full view. It had the desired effect. Stone broke out in a cold sweat. Kaitlin smiled a sly grin and left the room to attend to some last minute detail. Stone fell into a chair, trying to recover from the picture of loveliness that had physically taken away his breath. He wiped his brow and tried hard to recover what little dignity he had left. Never before had he been so completely overwhelmed by a woman. He actually felt giddy, an uncommon feeling for the big detective.

As they entered the Phaeton carriage, it crossed Stone's mind that he was glad Kaitlin had not chosen to wear a bustle, commonly worn with Victorian dresses. They just weren't practical on long rides in carriages. Besides, she certainly didn't need one, he thought.

Kaitlin draped a lap robe over the back of the carriage bench for the return trip. Undoubtedly it would be much cooler at night. She noticed that Stone had installed a shotgun and a Dragoon on the front wall of the carriage. It was a reminder that the country was still at war.

Stone decided early on to take the main road to Washington. Although the back road saved a few miles and about twenty minutes, it was the road on which Kaitlin's husband Ben had been shot and killed, and Stone did not want to dredge up painful memories for Kaitlin. They had been riding in silence for about fifteen minutes; the pair of black Percheron geldings easily pulling the Phaeton carriage through the countryside. Air moving around the carriage provided some degree of relief from the mugginess associated with the heat of the early summer day. As evening approached, trees, bushes, and flora competed to saturate the air with heavy perfumes before it turned dark.

There were no other wagons or carriages on the road, so Stone thought the ride was exceptionally pleasant, especially with Kaitlin at his side. Every once in awhile, Stone would cast a sideways glance, just to reassure himself that she was really there. It was while he was stealing such a glance that he ran over a deep rut in the road. Instinctively, Kaitlin reached out and touched Stone's arm to steady herself.

"Well, Mr. Stone, you *almost* missed that rut," she said with a grin.

Defensively, Stone responded by saying, "Kaitlin, honestly, I really didn't mean to hit it."

However, the guilty look on his face betrayed the fact that his derelict driving may have been more of an unconscious desire than an act of poor navigation.

"You have not told me anything of yourself, Mr. Stone. What is it like, living in New York City?"

"New York City is different things to different people. Those of us who live there usually refer to it only as "the city." Everyone in the state seems to understand what you mean. First of all, it's the point of arrival for immigrants. Presently most of the immigrants come from Ireland and Germany. The Irish tend to stay in the city, while many of the Germans seem to locate in rural areas or they go to other states where they join those who came before them to farm the land. The Germans who do stay in the city are generally highly skilled craftsmen. The Irish tend to be less highly skilled, so they take jobs that require muscle. They become stevedores, laborers, and policemen. Of course, that's just my impression. I'm sure others have different views."

Stone continued by saying, "Manhattan, where I live and work, is an island, so it is really quite small when compared with the other four boroughs. And because it is so small, its population, myself included, tend to live in multistoried buildings. In other words, it's crowded. And it smells bad, especially in the summer. Men tend to carry umbrellas. Women walk as close as they can to the buildings, especially in the mornings, so that when someone above empties a chamber pot, the debris won't fall on the pedestrians below. Men use umbrellas to shield themselves and their ladies from the constant morning barrage of spillage. Add to that, horses and draft animals relieve themselves in the street. It really can smell very bad."

"Mr. Stone, you make it sound so foul. Surely there must be something good about the city."

"Well Kaitlin, police officers, even detectives, don't see much good in the city; neither the grand buildings nor the law-abiding people. We usually see the seamier side of life."

"I don't know that I could stand such a life, Mr.Stone."

"The upper east side is a lot different. I don't get there very often, but the townhouses are much nicer, the people more genteel, and the rich certainly live by a standard unto themselves."

"Were you raised in the city, Mr. Stone?"

"Yes, my grandfather came from Ireland and worked as a stevedore on the docks. He met and married an Irish girl, a nurse who worked at a local hospital on the east side of the city. According to the stories my grandmother told, my grandfather was often hurt on the wharves, so he became somewhat of a fixture in the emergency room where she worked. My grandfather says he only got hurt so that he could visit my grandmother. My father also worked as a stevedore, but my mother, who was of British extraction, was a school teacher. She is the one who pushed me through high school and later through college."

"What did you study in college?" "I studied the law."

"Then why aren't you a lawyer, Mr. Stone?"

"I passed the New York Bar and went to work for a rather prestigious law firm. Then I discovered that I didn't like lawyers. Not only are they generally arrogant two-faced liars, most of them who I met were involved in dirty politics. Many of them were involved in graft and corruption. Their only gods were money and power. I came to regard them generally as a shallow and deceitful group, concerned only with themselves and their firms. So I left."

"Did you consider another line of work, I mean besides being a police detective?"

Stone laughed and said, "Yes, for a short while, I considered entering the priesthood."

"The priesthood? So what stopped you?"

"After a period of serious self-examination, I came to realize that I hadn't gotten the call to the priesthood. Then I decided that police work and investigation would be a better use of my education. My mother was terribly upset at my choice."

"Well, I can see why," Kaitlin responded.

Traffic became more congested. The Percheron geldings began to shy—first to the left, and then to the right—as riders guided their horses past the carriage on both sides. Wagons and carriages converged in front and behind the Phaeton carriage causing the Percherons to become even more nervous. Stone pulled over to the right and stopped, then took time to talk soothingly with each of the two horses. Then he led them down the road talking with them, soothing them, and walking with them. After about a quarter mile,

Stone returned to the carriage and continued down the road toward Washington. The two horses remained calmed.

Suddenly, Kaitlin started laughing. "What's so funny?" Stone asked.

"Sorry. I just had this mental image of you as a priest, knocking some freckle-faced altar boy around when he failed to properly learn the Latin." She continued to laugh.

"Well, Mr. Stone, you really are quite a surprise," Kaitlin continued. "First, I would never have considered you for an Irishman. You have no brogue whatsoever. And then a priest? You really are quite a surprise. And do you speak any of the Gaelic, Mr. Stone?" asked Kaitlin with an exaggerated lilt.

"No, I don't speak Gaelic. And being raised in the city, one tends to pick up street language. My mother worked hard to ensure that I spoke the King's English. So, you can imagine how upset she became, even now, when she hears me use street talk. I'm afraid that I am a great disappointment to her."

"She lives in the city then?" Kaitlin asked.

"Yes, but she lives in a relatively nice area, and she is quite happy with her surroundings. She has lived in the same place for several years, since the death of my father."

"How did he die?"

"He died of a heart attack, according to the doctor." "I'm sorry, Franklin."

It was the first time in quite awhile that Kaitlin had called him by his first name. He was thrilled.

"You would have liked him, my father that is. He still had a bit of the brogue and like most Irishmen, he ate too much, drank too much, and worked much too hard. In the end, it killed him. You really would have liked him, though. He laughed a lot and he caused others around him to laugh with him. He was a really great man to be around."

Stone maneuvered past the Executive Mansion and drove the three miles to the Old Soldier's Home on a hill overlooking official Washington. He stopped at Eagle Gate where a guard directed him to the Lincoln Cottage. Dropping Kaitlin off at the front door, Stone continued on to a small paddock where he unharnessed the horses, leading them to a watering trough where the horses drank their fill. He went to a nearby barn and drew some oats and two sheaves of hay, which he took to the paddock. The two Percherons willingly ate and then ran free in and around the paddock. Stone walked to the front door of the cottage and knocked on the door. A staff member answered and escorted Stone to the parlor where the president and Mrs. Lincoln were talking amiably with Kaitlin, Allan, and Joan Pinkerton.

"Sorry for the delay, Mr. President. I was putting the horses in the paddock."

"Chief Stone, how good to see you again," the president answered.

"Let me introduce you to Mrs. Lincoln. Mary, this is Franklin Stone, Chief of Detectives for the New York City Police Department. He and Allan are working together to rid us of spies and killers."

"It is a pleasure to meet you Chief Stone."

"It is my sincere honor, Mrs. Lincoln. Please accept my condolences over the loss of your son, Willie."

"Thank you, it is indeed painful."

The president broke the sudden tension by inviting his guests to make their way to the dining room. He complimented Kaitlin and Joan on their gowns and seated them at the table that was impeccably set by the staff. A salad of fresh lettuce, tomatoes, and apples was first to be served. Mr. Lincoln ravenously ate apples, not only at the dinner table, but also when he was engaged in the business of the presidency. As he was often heard to say, "Apples just seem to agree with me." Mrs. Lincoln confided that the president suffered from intestinal problems.

Wine had been served, but Stone noticed that the president took barely a sip; and then only during Allan's toast to Mr. and Mrs. Lincoln's good health. It was well known that the president didn't drink alcoholic beverages, but he didn't begrudge others from imbibing. Dinner consisted of beef and potatoes, but the president ate sparingly, leaving much of the serving on his plate by dinners end.

Conversation was lively and filled with laughter. Kaitlin and Joan encouraged the president to talk about growing up in the backwoods of Kentucky. Stone noted that Mr. Lincoln was the first president to be born outside of the thirteen original colonies. Mr. Lincoln recalled summers, flat rafting down rivers. He confided that although he lived in the backwoods, he didn't like to hunt or fish, but did so out of necessity to put food on the table. Allan and Joan Pinkerton told stories of their youth in Scotland. They had clandestinely married and had immigrated to the United States following a failed attempt to politically gain voting privileges for the common man.

Following dinner, the group returned to the comfort of the parlor where convivial conversation continued uninterrupted. The president's hand constantly dipped into a silver bowl filled with mixed nuts. Joan, who had been a professional singer in Scotland, entertained the group with a few Celtic songs, accompanying herself by playing a small spinet piano. Allan talked about becoming Chicago's first detective and later starting a private detective agency. Stone talked about early life in New York City. Three hours had slipped by unnoticed until Allan reminded the president that there was business that needed to be conducted. The president excused himself, and the men moved to the formal living room.

Although the chill of the night came through the open windows, the fireplace remained unlit. Rather, the cool night air abated the summer's humid heat. Night bugs flew around the gas lamps in the large room, but the president took no notice.

Allan reported on the activities of his spies in and around Richmond. The battles at Seven Pines and Fair Oaks had been fought to a standstill. Neither side had gained much, but the casualties on both sides had been shocking. Allan lamented that he had failed to accurately estimate the troop strength of the Confederacy around Richmond. There were far fewer Confederate troops than had been estimated by his agency's analysts based on reports from embedded spies. His reports had caused General McClellan to wait until more Union troops and supplies were available, thereby losing any advantage that he might have held when the president had first ordered McClellan to advance on Richmond a month earlier. The president nodded his head, indicating that he understood.

Attention was turned to Stone who had no better news. The fifty some odd cases that had been solved over the past year were of little significance. He was no closer to solving the three major cases that the president had assigned to him.

"Mr. President," Stone said, "I would like to be relieved of my commission so that I can return to New York. I'm doing you no good here. I have failed you."

There was silence in the room as both Lincoln and Pinkerton stared at Stone. Then the president spoke angry words.

"The only failure in this room, Mr. Stone, is mine. I have started a war that we can ill afford to lose. And make no mistake; we are losing this war. Would you have me retreat to the hills of Kentucky to lick my wounds?"

"No, Mr. President—of course not."

"Then I shan't allow you to hide in the boroughs of New York City. We three will just have to find ways to succeed. I'll hear nothing more about running away and hiding. Is that clear, Mr. Stone."

"Yes, Mr. President."

The president's tone became much more conciliatory as he said, "I have a present for each of you that I hope will keep you in good stead. Each time that you look at it, remember that we are going forward, looking for new solutions to solve old problems."

The president left the room but returned almost immediately with a rifle in each hand.

"These are the new Henry repeating rifles that you may have heard about. I give them to you for your added protection. They are only just now available. I believe that they will have an important impact on our ability to win this war. It will take a while to manufacture and ship these weapons to our soldiers in the field, but I do believe that the lever action and the fifteen rounds of rim fire cartridges held within the rifle will significantly add to our ability to win. Please regard these gifts as being symbolic of the same trust that

I place in the two of you. Both of you have my complete confidence that you are indeed contributing significantly to the war effort."

The two men were awestruck by the presents. They thanked the president who also handed each of the men two boxes of cartridges saying, "I do hope you won't have to use them, but if you do, use them well."

That being said, the meeting ended and the men rejoined the women in the parlor. After about an hour of renewed conversation, the president indicated that the one o'clock hour was about as much time as he could afford as he had appointments at the Executive Mansion starting at an early hour. The men shook hands, the women kissed and hugged, and Allan and Joan departed in a commercial horse-drawn taxi. As Stone started to leave to hitch the horses to the Phaeton carriage, the president stopped him and suggested that he and Kaitlin stay the night saying, "I would hate to have anything happen to you and Kaitlin on your night ride back to Maryland. Mrs. Lincoln and I would feel much better if you would stay the night." After a short discussion with Kaitlin, the two accepted the president's generous offer. Staff members escorted Kaitlin and Stone to their separate rooms.

The president had already left for the Executive Mansion by the time Stone and Kaitlin came down to the dining room for a light breakfast. After consuming toast and several cups of coffee, Stone hitched the horses to the carriage, and said farewell to Mrs. Lincoln and the staff. He and Kaitlin started the journey back to Maryland, melding into the thick Washington traffic.

"I enjoyed our visit, Mr. Stone. Thank you for inviting me to accompany you. I hadn't seen the president and Mrs. Lincoln since the inauguration."

"Kaitlin, I can't begin to describe how much I have enjoyed your company," Stone replied. Kaitlin smiled and privately acknowledged the physical stirring that she had not felt in quite awhile.

Perhaps it is time to consider a new life, she contemplated.

Chapter Nine

Early August 1862

ANDY AWOKE EARLY and had several cups of strong coffee and some bread. Food was in short supply at the hospital, and he felt that since he was relatively healed, food at the hospital should be reserved for those who could not get a meal on their own. Besides, hospital food didn't taste very good. At eight in the morning, he boarded a free-to-uniformed-soldiers horse drawn trolley that was headed into city center where Jubal's office was located.

Jubal had already been at work awhile. He was dressed in civilian clothes including gray trousers, and a light blue work shirt with long sleeves that were rolled up. There were noticeable dark sweat stains under his armpits. Although the office was hot and muggy, even with the windows open, Andy was still wearing his blood-stained uniform. He carried his shell jacket because he had nowhere to store it until he settled in to his new job.

Jubal greeted Andy with a wide smile saying, "Welcome to your new home, soldier."

"Thanks, I think."

"No time to sit and chat, Andy. We've got a meeting over at General Lee's headquarters, so we had better get moving. The horses are in the paddock out back, but I think we would be better off walking. The general's headquarters is only a few blocks away, if you think you are strong enough for the walk."

"I'm fine, Jubal."

Since they were going to General Lee's Headquarters, Andy put on his shell jacket to be in proper uniform. He immediately started sweating even more than he had earlier.

"General Lee is seldom in Richmond," said Jubal. "He can usually be found in his field headquarters. However, he maintains office space at the War Department, which is in the old Mechanic's Institute over on Ninth Street across from Bank Street behind the capitol. You can spot the War Department building by the large observatory, over there, said Jubal, pointing to the round observatory building."

Entering the front door to the War Department, Jubal surprised Andy by taking the stairs down to the basement. "The general's offices are upstairs, but the man we need to see is down here."

The windowless hallway was lit by gas lamps, as were the offices. Entering an office with no name on the door, Jubal introduced Andy to Charles Gaston, better known as "C. A." to telegraphers on both sides of the Mason-Dixon Line.

"So, you're the new spy," Gaston said as he shook Andy's hand.

"Sir, I'm no spy," replied Andy, with indignation in his voice.

"You are now," Gaston said.

"We're all spies—all of us who are telegraphers. Some of us just work at it more than others. We copy the enemy's code and they copy ours. That's why you're here. Jubal has convinced General Lee to consolidate the information that each of the various telegraph units receive through a central unit to be called the Confederate Secret Service. So I guess that makes you the first Confederate Secret Service agent," Gaston laughed.

Andy looked at Jubal with a questioning look.

"Don't look so surprised, Andy. You're the one that got me to thinking about a secret service. Look, we are out-gunned, out-manned, and half the time we are out- maneuvered in the field. We need a better intelligence organization if the Confederacy is going to have a fighting chance."

"Well let's see what your new spy can do," Gaston said as he led the way to another office down the half- dark hallway where two men were sending and receiving telegraph code.

"Have a seat and copy along with Charlie here. See what you remember."

Jubal and Gaston watched as Andy took paper and pencil and began copying code. At first, Andy dropped about one out of ten characters. After fifteen minutes or so of copying the silence between the clicks of the telegraph, Andy wasn't missing any characters; even those characters in ciphered messages that made no sense, since they weren't real words.

Gaston slid a telegraph key in front of Andy and said, "Well now let's see how well you can send."

Like most operators, Andy could send characters faster and easier than deciphering them.

"Hey! I know that fist, you used to work the midnight shift out of Williamsburg a few years back," Gaston exclaimed.

"That's amazing, Andy replied. That was more than a few years ago—back when I was attending the university. How is it that you can remember my fist from so long ago?"

"Oh, you'll find that you will remember the fist of most of the operators you worked with while you were a telegrapher. A man's fist is his signature. He can change his name, but he can never change the style and rhythm of the way he sends code. That's going to be very important to you as you copy Union messages. You can determine who the operator is by the operator's unique fist. Ultimately, that will allow you to develop intelligence as to which federal unit is doing what, and where they are doing it. And you must always remember that they will remember your fist as well."

Jubal joined the conversation by saying, "Okay C.A., if you are satisfied, I think we will be on our way. There are a number of other things that we need to get settled before the day is done."

"I see no problem with Andy. If he can work here on and off for the next couple of weeks, he will develop many of the characteristics that he will need to work in your outfit. He will get to know many of the operators on both sides by their fists. Actually, I think Andy is a good choice and will be a great asset for your office."

"Thanks," said Jubal as the two men shook hands. "Nice meeting you Andy," said Gaston. "I'm looking forward to working with you." "Thank you, sir."

"Call me C. A., Andy. Everyone else does, including General Lee."

"C. A. it is then."

As the two men left the building, Jubal added, "Listen carefully to C. A. Gaston. He has more intelligence experience in the field than any of our other telegraph operators. He once spent two weeks behind enemy lines gathering intelligence by intercepting messages. He knows firsthand what he is talking about."

"I'll do that, Jubal."

"Are you getting hungry yet, Andy?"

"I'm hungry enough to eat a bear," Andy replied. "Let's take Thirteenth Street past the capitol over to Broad Street to the Powhatan Hotel across from City Hall. They have a pretty good kitchen staff. We just might meet some interesting people too."

"Jubal, I'm broke. I haven't been paid in months, and someone took what money I had from my uniform pockets while I was in the hospital. I can't afford a meal at a hotel."

"Well, let's get you a meal at the hotel first, and then I'll take you by the paymaster and get you some money to live on. You can pay me back."

"Sounds good to me, Jubal. Thanks."

The two men entered the hotel and went directly to the restaurant, which boasted the best vitals in town, but they weren't cheap. A dinner of beef and potatoes, fried okra, black-eyed peas, cornbread, rhubarb pie and iced tea cost nearly five dollars; more than a week's pay for most privates.

The restaurant was soon filled with Confederate elite from Secretary of State, J. P. Benjamin; Secretary of War, G.W. Randolph; Senate Military Affairs Committee Chairman, Edward Sparrow; a number of judges from the Appeals and District Courts, and a gaggle of deskbound generals and colonels; all of whom were drawn to Andy and Jubal when they saw Andy's blood-spattered uniform.

Andy was uncomfortable with the attention that he was getting, but Jubal was as smooth as a likeminded politician.

Secretary Benjamin asked what unit Andy was attached to. Andy answered, "I've just been released from the hospital and have only recently been reassigned. I work with the Sergeant Major."

"Oh, you're in the Army Intelligence Office," said the laughing Benjamin.

Everyone seemed to know Jubal McGraw and what he did for the Confederacy. As they left the hotel Andy remarked, "Well that was embarrassing."

"Well it's about time they met a real hero." "I'm no hero, Jubal McGraw, and you know it." "They think you are."

"Why would they think that?"

"Well, you are up walking around on two legs, you still have both arms, and you are wearing blood from at least a dozen men on your uniform. What else could you be?"

"Well then we had better get me some money so that I get some new clothes."

The two men entered Suite 67 at Bank and Tenth Streets where the paymaster for officer's pay was located. "I brought you a customer, Captain. This is Captain Andy Davis and he desperately needs to get some back pay," Jubal said.

"What outfit are you with, Captain?"

"I was assigned to the 24th Virginia in General D. H. Hill's Division, but I was in the hospital for the past couple of months."

Jubal joined the conversation saying, "He just joined our operation, so he will be drawing his pay from your office from now on."

"When was the last time you were paid?" asked the paymaster.

"Never been paid. I've only been on active duty for six months, and I was in the hospital for two of those."

"I'm only authorized to give you up to three months pay," the paymaster said as he counted out five hundred dollars.

"That's better than nothing," said Andy.

Andy immediately handed a five dollar bill to Jubal, saying, "Thanks again, Jubal."

"No problem."

"Any chance that we can ride over to D.H. Hill's Division to see if they still have my personal belongings?"

"I don't see why not."

The two men walked over to the paddock behind the Bank of Virginia, above which was located the Army Intelligence Office. Andy's horse shied at the smell of blood on Andy's uniform and ran to the opposite side of the paddock. Andy called out the horse's name and the horse stopped in mid-stride and returned to Andy's side, nuzzling his outstretched hand. Andy talked in a soothing voice as he saddled the mare for the trip to his former unit.

It was an easy ride to D.H. Hill's Division, but once they got out of town, Andy could see all of the rifle pits and trenches that had been dug for the battle to defend Richmond; a battle that started at the end of July while Andy was in the hospital and ended with the Federals returning to Washington unsuccessful in their bid to overrun the Confederate capitol. Andy had a dozen or so questions about the battle, but he remained silent.

Almost as if reading Andy's mind, Jubal remarked, "The war might already have been lost had they taken the capitol."

"Thank God our boys were able to prevent that," Andy replied.

"I don't think that God gets involved in the affairs of men, especially as it concerns their wars," Jubal remarked.

"Yeah, you're probably right."

The two men continued riding in silence. Arriving at D.H. Hill's headquarters, they located the 24th Virginia and reported to the Officer of the Day, a freshly scrubbed lieutenant who looked too young to shave, much less old enough to lead men nearly twice his age into battle. The lieutenant indicated that he had no knowledge as to where Andy's belongings might be. The look on his face said that he didn't care either, but the words went unsaid.

A supply colonel who overheard the conversation said, "Belongings of dead and severely wounded soldiers are normally sent to Richmond where they are held for ninety days to give families time to claim their kin's property. However, owing to the fact that most relatives don't learn of casualties in time, the fallen soldier's property is normally made available to other soldiers. We sell what's left and give the money to the Old Soldiers Home. Records systems rarely provide sufficient information for us to return a soldier's property to families, and frankly, so many thousands of men have been killed or severely wounded, that the government can't afford the cost of shipping property to relatives, even if they knew where they were located."

Andy turned to leave, but the colonel continued by saying, "In your case, however, the sergeant who pulled you off of the field of battle wouldn't let us send your belongings to Richmond. He said that you were alive, and that you would eventually come around looking for your property." The colonel smiled.

"Glad to see that you survived, Captain. Check with the sergeant over at the supply tent. He'll be glad to be rid of your gear. We're packing to move out in a campaign against Washington. The rest of the battalion left a couple of days ago."

"Thank you, colonel," Andy said, as he saluted.

Returning the salute, the colonel again turned his attention to his work.

Andy and Jubal walked their horses to the supply tent where they retrieved the bag that held Andy's belongings. Andy immediately opened the bag because it seemed inordinately heavy. On top of his folded clothing were his two Dragoons and a note from Sergeant Worthington, the sergeant who had saved Andy's life.

The handwritten note read, "Captain, I kept your carbine because I couldn't pack it in your bag, and I didn't want some supply-type stealing it. Stop by if I'm still in camp, and I will return it to you, although I will hate to part with it. Good luck, John Worthington, Sergeant, 24th Virginia."

Andy removed the revolvers, gun belt, holsters, and a box of ammunition and tied the bag behind the cantle of his saddle. Loading the two Dragoons, he passed one revolver and holster to Jubal saying, "For your help and thoughtfulness."

Jubal was genuinely surprised. "You don't have to do that, Andy."

"It's all I have with which to thank you for what you have done for Everett and me. Please take it with my heartfelt thanks."

Jubal took the valuable firearm, removed it from the holster, examined the handcrafted scrollwork on the metal, and carefully checked the action of the loaded weapon. His eyebrows shot up in a silent appreciation for the smoothness of the action and the craftsmanship that went into making the weapon.

"Thank you, Andy. This is truly a fine firearm that I will keep as long as I live."

Andy countered by saying, "Well here's to a long life".

"Amen to that, Andy.

As they were riding back to Richmond, Andy broke the silence by saying, "You know Jubal, I never really got to know the sergeant who saved my life. I didn't even know his name until I read that note." Jubal just nodded saying, "Andy, I don't know why he chose you to save, but I'm sure glad he did".

"Me too," Andy replied as he smiled.

"Andy, you might as well head over to the inn, get situated in your room, and change out of that uniform. I'll meet you there this evening and we can start fresh in the morning."

"That I can do, Jubal. Thanks."

Andy settled into his room at the inn and wrote a short note to his wife Abigail, saying that he was alright, but his job, which he couldn't explain, kept him away from regular mail routes and that she should not be alarmed if she didn't hear from him for long stretches of time. He also cautioned her not to write to him as mail sometimes fell into enemy hands. Finishing the short letter, Andy took what he thought would be a short nap. He was surprised when he awoke late at night. The exercise of the day had taken more out of him than he thought possible.

CAPTAIN EVERETT DAVIS arrived at the deepwater port of Nassau, on New Providence Island in the Bahamas. He settled into the Grand

Victoria Hotel, and then went to the Maritime Agent's office in the port district to introduce himself as the designated coordinator for the government of the Confederate States of America. Everett handed his letter of appointment, which had been signed by President Davis, to Johnny Fernandez, the Maritime Agent who handled most of the shipping affairs for the Confederacy in the Caribbean. After reading the letter of appointment, Fernandez handed a half dozen letters that he had been holding pending Everett's arrival. Everett thanked the agent and went down the street to a curbside café, where he ordered a cup of coffee and read the letters from Jubal. Andy was alive, but it was going to take awhile for him to recuperate. Also, Andy was going to be assigned to Jubal's office, but Jubal said that he could not explain further as to what duties Andy was going to perform. Everett was overjoyed to learn that Andy was still alive and mobile, which resulted in a silent prayer of thanks to God almighty.

Everett walked around the downtown area of the city. He was surprised to find that Nassau was large and well populated. He returned to the office of the Maritime Agent where he asked for assistance.

"Mr. Fernandez, I don't know anything about ships or the sea captains that are running the Union blockades along our Atlantic coast. I don't even know how to contact them. Could I prevail on you to introduce me to the ships' masters?"

"Well, those who are in port usually get together for nightly parties at the Grand Victoria Hotel. But when they want to discuss business away from the watchful eyes of Union spies, they venture to the back room of Blackbeard's Pub in the early evening. They are a suspicious lot, so don't expect them to accept you based solely on that letter of appointment. But I'll do what I can to assist you. Come by at five this evening, and we will go see who is in port."

Thank you, Mr. Fernandez. Your assistance will be gratefully appreciated."

Everett returned to the office at five in the evening where Johnny Fernandez was just finishing his work for the day. The two men walked without conversation to Blackbeard's Pub. The main room of the pub was filled with sailors who were boisterously telling sea stories of ships sailed and ports visited. A chalkboard behind the bar listed many of the regular seagoing customers by name, followed by a record of P's and Q's (Pints and Quarts) of ale consumed but not yet paid for. It was a system used worldwide for sailors who got paid at irregular intervals. And it was from that system that came the old saying, "Watch your P's and Q's." Unscrupulous bartenders had long been known to add a few pints and quarts when a sailor got a little too drunk to pay close attention to what he owed.

Fernandez pushed open a heavy oak door that led into a back room. Inside, the thick oak door was adorned with extra heavy, black strap iron hinges and a black, steel throw bolt to lock the door from forced intrusion. Everett noted that there were about twenty grizzled men sitting in quiet conversations. No boisterous or rowdy conversation, these were serious men who were discussing issues of a dangerous and serious business, that of running the Union blockade along the Atlantic coast of the Confederate States of America. They were in the high-stakes business of making vast sums of money by running guns, ammunition, and war-making materials to the South. And they all knew that one miscalculation could result in the loss of their ships and cargoes, their crews, and their lives.

When the door opened, all conversation ceased. Twenty pair of eyes examined the two men who were entering their personal domain. Initially, there wasn't a friendly face among them. However, upon recognizing Fernandez, most of the captains returned to their prior conversations. Closing and bolting the door, Fernandez greeted the ships' masters cordially and continued by saying, "I would like to introduce you to a man who may be of help getting you through Union blockades. This is Captain Everett Davis of the Confederate Army. He has been sent to coordinate the safe passage of your ships through the blockades."

Conversation immediately stopped as the captains took a closer look at the civilian-clothed Confederate Army soldier. The quiet of the room was suddenly broken as the captains broke out in raucous laughter.

"How the hell are you going to do that, soldier boy?" one sea captain loudly rebuked.

The captains continued laughing and again returned to their private conversations, ignoring Everett and any answer that he might have given. Fernandez directed Everett to an unoccupied table where he poured two glasses of rum from a bottle that was previously situated on the table for other sea captains who might join the nightly ritual gathering. The two men sat in silence sipping the dark rum for over an hour. Finally, one captain joined Fernandez and Everett asking, "Okay soldier, how are you going to get us through the blockades?"

"There is no one answer to getting your ships through the blockade, which over the past year has become increasingly more effective. However, I have developed a number of potential options based upon conditions along the coastal regions. While we build a navy that can fight, I am working with an army colonel who will attack blockade vessels using well disciplined soldiers who have been specifically trained for that mission. In some instances, we will ask you to unload your cargo where the Union doesn't expect you to be. Instead of always using deepwater ports that can be easily blockaded, I want to try using a system of shallow draft vessels to unload your cargo at sea. Your ship will be the mother ship for a score of boats and watercraft that can negotiate shallow waterways in undeveloped areas of the coast. If a Union ship shows up while you are unloading your cargo, you will immediately stop unloading cargo and return to the open sea. The shallow draft vessels will dart off in different directions so that the enemy can't chase all of them at one time. That way we won't lose all of the cargo if the Union does capture a boat. Your ships will be able to get away to make another run at another time in another place. These are options designed to give you a better chance when a Union warship does show up unexpectedly."

"How will you coordinate our arrivals with shallow draft vessels?" the captain asked.

"To date, your large ships have been using deepwater ports, primarily in Charleston and Wilmington. Florida, which has no deepwater ports yet, is ripe for the use of shallow draft vessels. We have put together a large cadre of boat owners who have volunteered to offload cargo from mother ships and to transport the cargo to various small boat ports along the Florida coast for further transfer to army logistics centers in Georgia, Alabama, and Mississippi under army guard. And because the Florida coast is only fifty-five miles away from Nassau, the whole operation can be accomplished in much less time than trying to get in and out of the deeper ports of the Carolinas. Some of the small boat owners have volunteered to serve as message runners from Florida to Nassau and then back to Florida where the Confederacy is installing new telegraph lines throughout the South. Where it has taken weeks to get messages to and from the capitol, it will now take a matter of a few hours or days."

The room grew eerily quiet. Everyone was intently listening to what Everett was saying.

"Will we still use the deepwater ports?" one captain asked.

"Yes, but we will attack the Union gunboats and warships in the deepwater ports, prior to your arrival. That's why close coordination is so important," Everett responded.

"Does the Confederate Navy really have enough gunboats and warships to attack the Union vessels in deepwater ports? They haven't done very well so far."

"No," said Everett. "The Confederate Navy does not have a new fleet of warships to take on the Union. Most of the battles being fought by the Navy are taking place on rivers that connect the various states in the South. I am working with an army colonel who has a dual commission as a commander in the navy and who is familiar with the ways of the sea. He will remain nameless for the time being to protect his men and his mission. But he has convinced the president that he can move from port to port and attack Union ships at will. This is not a theory. Rather, he has already proven his concept of operations by successfully attacking the enemy's vessels in two different ports, hundreds of miles apart. It was only after he was able to demonstrate the capability and effectiveness of his unit that the president accepted this plan. But again, it takes very close coordination to accomplish the goals of this mission."

"Just what are the goals of the mission?" a skeptical captain asked.

"To give you sea captains the best possible chance to effectively run the blockades, offload your cargo, and return to the open sea without being attacked by Union warships in port."

"What about when we leave port," another captain asked.

"Currently, you are on your own. There's no change from the way it is now. However, I'm told that naval engineers have devised a new class of vessel about eighty feet in length, with guns fore and aft and with heavier cannon on each side. They can fire on a vessel that they are chasing, and they can fire on vessels that are chasing them. They are designed to be used in pairs. The engineers call them destroyers. They have steam engines, but they are not paddle wheelers. They will be outfitted with two propellers—what the engineers call screws. It is expected that they will be very fast—faster than a paddle wheeler. But until the new vessels are built, tested, and sent out here to protect your ships, you are on your own."

"Well, I'm willing to try anything that gives us a better chance at keeping our ships and our crews safe," the captain who had joined Everett and Fernandez said." "However, I want to know more about how it's going to work—this coordination thing, that is."

"Mr. Fernandez, our Maritime Agent will continue to coordinate the logistics between the British ships that bring the cargo from Europe into Nassau for transfer to your ships. As your ship is being loaded, I will contact our people in Florida and coordinate whether your ship will use the deepwater ports, or use the mother ship approach off the coast of Florida. If you are destined for the deepwater ports, the colonel will survey the ports for Union warships and plan the attack. If successful, he will let me know through the message system that I talked about earlier, and I will give you your sailing instructions on the day that you are scheduled to depart. If you are to use the mother ship approach, I will coordinate with the shallow draft vessels, and again, I will give you sailing instructions and destinations on the day that you set sail."

Not all the captains were comfortable with that approach, but they indicated that they were willing to give it a try. Everett's work was cut out for him. Not only did he have to coordinate the arrival and unloading of ships running the blockade, he had to win over the captains in a new and daring plan of operations.

MEANWHILE, COLONEL DWAYNE Davis, the eldest of the Davis brothers, sat in his London office disillusioned by the lack of progress with European governments. The "Trent Affair" made it easier for the two envoys, Slidell and Mason, to argue their case before the European public and the official governments of England and France. But public indignation soon waned and the governments of those nations were reluctant to provide the diplomatic recognition of sovereignty that the Confederacy needed and repeatedly requested.

Dwayne spent his time going between France and England assisting James Mason who represented the Confederacy in London, and John Slidell, who represented the Confederacy in Paris. After all of the pretty words had been said in never-ending meetings, and after many inferences were made by Ambassadors and representatives of both European governments, the Confederacy was no closer to gaining European support than when Dwayne had first arrived in England.

As an army colonel and military attaché, Dwayne implored senior officers of both England and France to talk with politicians and senior government officials; to convince them to provide the line of credit and weapons that the Confederacy needed. More importantly, he implored that they convince the admiralty to allow French warships to enter the war on the side of the South. The Union was becoming increasingly more effective in both their naval blockades and in winning naval battles on rivers that connected the Southern states. It became clear to Dwayne that the military officers and the politicians of both England and France were waiting for the South to win a really decisive battle; something that would convince European nations that the South would eventually win the war with the North.

Dwayne was also concerned about the number of dispatches from Europe that seemed to be falling into enemy hands. Dispatches routinely went to Halifax in Nova Scotia, Canada, on a British ship, where they were handed to Southern agents for a covert trip into the United States and then on to Richmond. After receiving a letter indicating that Everett was coordinating blockade runners out of Nassau, Dwayne directed the ship's masters of British ships to deliver Confederate dispatches to his brother in Nassau. The dispatches then went from Nassau to Florida on flat-bottomed blockade runners and then on to Richmond on Southern trains. That shift in tactics significantly reduced the number of dispatches that were falling into Union hands, and it even reduced the time that it took to get the dispatches to Richmond.

Dwayne repeatedly asked to be allowed to return home to fight on the battlefields of the South. His requests were always denied, saying he was of more value in Europe. Dwayne read the latest request that had been denied and shook his head. He wanted to fight for the South and felt that he was wasting time as a military attaché.

Chapter Ten

October 2, 1862

IT WAS A glorious fall Sunday morning. Trees still had most of their leaves, although they had already started to turn colors of red, yellow, and orange. The Maryland air remained abnormally warm, especially for the early morning hour; although it was clear to everyone that winter was just around the corner. Crops had been harvested, bills had been paid, and there was no hint of war in that part of the countryside. Kaitlin looked at the rolling hills outside the kitchen window. The rural setting was idyllic.

She had set the breakfast table, where Stone sat staring into his cup of coffee, thinking about the past week's work. Entering the dining room, Kaitlin asked, "When was the last time you attended mass, Mr. Stone?"

"What?" Stone asked, as he was mentally jerked back into the moment by Kaitlin's voice.

"When was the last time that you attended mass?" Stone thought for a few moments then answered,

"Not since I was considering the priesthood, almost fifteen years ago, I guess."

"And why not, Mr. Stone?" Kaitlin pressed.

"Well, most police officers work weekends, at least they do when they are assigned to the uniformed division. I worked weekends as a new detective too. I guess I just got out of the habit, so I didn't attend after I became Chief of Detectives. Why do you ask?"

"I think that I would like to go to mass this morning.
Would you drive me to church in town?"

"What time is mass?"

"Nine o'clock."

Looking at his pocket watch, Stone noted, "We'll have to get a move on if we want to get to church on time. It's nearly seven-thirty now",

"I'll be ready at eight," Kaitlin said."

"I'll have the carriage ready at eight then," Stone replied.

Stone grumbled all the way to the barn where he went to hurriedly wipe down the carriage and hitch the horses for the trip to town. He parked the carriage in front of the house and rushed upstairs to quickly shave with cold water, nicking himself just under his jaw. Grousing, he pressed a linen handkerchief to stop the bleeding with one hand as he pulled on a collarless white shirt and black trousers. The bleeding had stopped by the time he was ready to attached a stiff cellulite collar to the shirt. He wrapped a thick black tie around the stiff collar, and put on a moderately heavy black frock coat that was lined with brass buttons from the collar to the waist. It was what some would call his Sunday-go-to-meeting coat. As he hurried down the central stairway, he noted that Kaitlin was already in the carriage. He grabbed a small revolver from the desk in his office, checked that it was loaded, and literally ran out the front door.

Mounting the carriage, Stone took the reins, forcefully slapping the backsides of the horses. The Percherons bolted down the driveway knocking Kaitlin askew as Stone made the turn from the driveway onto the road. The rear carriage wheels skidded slightly in the turn.

"A little grumpy this morning, Mr. Stone."

"No, not at all," Stone grumbled.

"And Killarney's not in Ireland either," Kaitlin laughed loudly.

"You, Mr. Stone, may not have an Irish brogue, but you have inherited a full measure of the Irish blarney," she said as she continued to laugh.

Stone quickly veered just enough to cause Kaitlin to fall to her left as he drove over a deep rut in the road. Kaitlin reached out and grabbed Stone's arm to steady herself, but still she kept on laughing.

"Come now, Mr. Stone, it's a glorious morning and we are going to enjoy the day."

Kaitlin collected herself, straightening her clothes and the hat that had been knocked askew by the sudden veering. Had she looked up, she would have seen that Stone had a smile on his face. He was enjoying putting her on the defensive for once.

Being considerate of the fact that Stone wasn't in the best of moods, Kaitlin restrained herself from talking, thereby allowing the wind, the early morning hour, and the steady clip-clop of the horses hooves on the hard-pan road to weave it's magic on the big detective. She could tell the exact moment when Stone's mood had softened. As he returned to a mellower mood, he had allowed the horses to settle into a gentler gait. *Yes*, he thought, *it is a glorious day.*

Kaitlin directed Stone to the Catholic Church; a small wooden building that had aged poorly and was in need of paint and maintenance. It was a far cry from the large stone and marble edifices that Stone had attended in New York City. The priest, who was greeting parishioners at the door, appeared to be frail and nearly as old as the hundred-year-old building. Stone noted there were relatively few people attending mass; thirty at most. The town's residents were predominantly Protestant, and the several Protestant churches around town would likely fill at a later hour, he thought. Parking the carriage under a tree to give the horses a break from the sun, after having allowed them to drink from a trough in front of the building, Stone and Kaitlin walked across the dusty driveway and walked up creaky wooden steps where they greeted and shook hands with the old priest and entered the house of worship. The priest's hand was surprisingly strong.

Stone would have preferred a pew in the back, but Kaitlin made her way toward the front of the church, selecting the second row of pews. Genuflecting and crossing herself with the sign of the cross, she settled into a well-worn wooden pew. Adjusting the faded kneeling pad, she knelt in prayer. Stone genuflected and took a seat in the pew where his thoughts were less about prayer, and more about examining the interior of the church. Where the outside of the old church was in dire need of maintenance, the inside was well painted, maintained, and nearly immaculate. The Stations of the Cross were celebrated in mosaics mounted in the proper order on the walls from front to back on the left side and from back to front on the right side of the church. Fresh cut flowers adorned each side of the small wooden alter. Clearly, the church had known better days. Stone suddenly felt very comfortable in the old church. He glanced at Kaitlin who, having finished praying, had seated herself in the pew. Stone said a silent prayer of thanks for the blessings that he had received, and for the company of Kaitlin, who had forced him to come to this quiet respite from the deadly worries of both crime and war.

The old priest looked to be unexpectedly agile as he went about his long-practiced duties of celebrating mass. Stone felt a little guilty at receiving communion as he had not been to confession for a very long time. The old priest spoke about the need to help others during perilous times such as these. He was careful not to offend the mostly Southern-leaning parishioners in this Maryland town, while simultaneously explaining that war was not an excuse for straying from the path of Christ. His comments were filled with compassion for his fellow man, but they were not condescending. He fully understood man's inhumanity during war but cautioned parishioners to look to Christ for answers regarding questions of conscience.

The old priest blessed his parishioners and walked toward the back of the sanctuary spewing white smoke from an incense pot to the left and to the right as he made his way down the aisle to the vestibule. He again greeted and blessed each person as they made their way out into an uncertain world.

Kaitlin approached the priest saying, "Thank you, Father. It was a wonderful service with great words of wisdom."

"Thank you, my child. Go with God."

Stone stuck his hand out, which the clergyman grasped saying, "I don't believe that I have seen you at mass before now. I'm Father

John, and I am glad that you have accompanied Kaitlin as she is not able to attend very often."

"Father, I assure you that accompanying Kaitlin is more of a blessing for me than it is a chore."

The priest smiled a knowing smile saying, "God bless you, my son."

Kaitlin took Stone's hand and said, "So I'm a blessing, am I?"

"You know what I mean," Stone said, hoping that Kaitlin didn't see that he was blushing.

"No, Mr. Stone, what do you mean?" she teased. Stone didn't bother to respond.

Kaitlin and Stone settled in the carriage for the trip home. Stone held the horses to a slow but steady pace as the sun rose higher in the fall sky. He wanted to experience as much of the moment with Kaitlin as he could. He was in no hurry to get home or to return to work. He felt that being with Kaitlin was as close to heaven as he would likely get today. He didn't want the trip to end.

At about the halfway point in their return trip, Kaitlin pointed to a shady meadow and asked Stone to pull over. Stone did as he was directed. Kaitlin exited and walked to the rear of the carriage where she reached into the rear luggage compartment and withdrew a picnic basket and a large folded blanket.

"Come, Mr. Stone. I have prepared us a lunch." She spread the blanket on the ground under a large oak tree. Stone tied the horses to a low hanging branch over a spot that had long blades of grass for the horses to nibble. Stone paused at the carriage long enough to remove his coat, and to watch Kaitlin as she removed the hat from her head and shook out long curls of hair that had been piled high on her head like a crown. *My God, she is so lovely*, he thought, wondering how he could possibly win her over to be his bride. Joining Kaitlin on the blanket, Stone kept his thoughts to himself.

"How do you see the war going, Mr. Stone?"

"I think that our troops lost the opportunity to win this war quickly when they failed to take Richmond a few months ago. I fear that the war will drag on several more years."

"Have you given any thought as to what you will do when the war ends?" Kaitlin asked.

"No, not really. I guess I will return to New York and resume my duties with the police department."

"Is there no other life that you would prefer?"

"I haven't really considered any other life. I'm comfortable doing police work. Why do you ask?"

"I was just thinking that the dreams and aspirations of men are often dashed on the rocks of life. This war will change the way many people think about their lives. They may want to consider alternatives in peacetime, to reach out for different opportunities that they did not see, or which were not available before the war."

"Like what," Stone asked, perplexed by her line of questioning.

"Like actually living in peace; raising a family; getting to know and respecting your neighbors without being suspicious of their intentions. Like enjoying life, not being afraid of it."

"Have you ever known a life like that?" Stone asked. "Yes, I grew up in a small village in Ireland where people prized peace more than war and trusted their friends and neighbors until they proved themselves to be unreliable."

"Well here in the United States, that may just be a child's dream or a foreign memory. I see a lot of really mean-spirited people— people, who would rather take advantage of you, then beat you to a pulp and leave you to die in anguish and pain."

"Yes, Mr. Stone, you have seen many bad things. That's why I'm asking if you are yet ready to seek another life away from such privations."

"Kaitlin, I don't just experience privations. I even out the process. There are some really bad people out there who take undue advantage of others; those who are unable to protect themselves. I find the evil-doers and put them away so that they cannot continue to prey on the public. I fill a useful function for the public. And I'm proud of what I do."

"Yes, Mr. Stone, you are truly a knight in shining armor. However, at what personal cost?"

"What do you mean, at what cost?" Stone asked in a slightly aggravated tone.

"Please forget that I asked. Anyway, it's time to leave."

Stone felt that somehow he had failed an important test, but for the life of him, he could not identify what test he had just failed. He rose, taking the basket to the carriage as Kaitlin folded the blanket. The two rode in silence the rest of the way home.

As they approached the driveway, Stone noticed a uniformed dispatch rider sitting in the shade of a maple tree, holding the reins of his horse that nibbled at the grass under the spread of the tree branches. As the carriage approached the house, the soldier stood and approached the carriage.

"Colonel Stone?" asked the dispatch rider. "Yes, I'm Stone."

"I have a dispatch from Allan Pinkerton, sir."

"Thank you," Stone replied, taking the sealed parchment from the soldier.

"Would you like a glass of lemonade?" Kaitlin asked the dispatch rider.

"Yes, ma'am, I would be very grateful," the soldier answered.

Kaitlin disappeared into the house only to reappear several minutes later with a glass of lemonade for each of the two men, after which, she again disappeared into the house.

The soldier finished the lemonade in three quick gulps and placed the glass on the railing of the porch. He saluted, saying, "Please thank your lady for the thirst- quencher, but now I must be on my way, Colonel."

"I understand, soldier, thanks for bringing the dispatch," Stone replied without indicating that Kaitlin was not his lady, although he certainly wished otherwise.

Stone tucked the dispatch into his inner coat pocket and walked the horses to the barn where he unhitched them from the carriage, and set them free to run around the paddock. He grabbed both glasses from the porch rail as he entered the house. After placing the glasses on the kitchen counter, Stone entered his office where he opened the dispatch from Allan Pinkerton.

"What is so urgent that Allan sent a uniformed dispatch rider?" Kaitlin asked from the doorway.

"Apparently, one of Allan's operatives near Richmond has developed a reliable source of information, a Southerner who has information about stolen weapons and ammunition that have been making their way into Confederate hands."

"What does that have to do with you, Mr. Stone?"

"Since the very beginning of the war, a large number of weapons and ammunition that were made in the north have been found in the hands of dead Confederate soldiers at nearly every major battle in the south. It was one of three major cases that Mr. Lincoln asked me to solve. And to date, I've gotten nowhere. That informant just might have the information that I need to break this case wide open. I'll have to go down there to interrogate him."

"Let's see if I understand this, Mr. Stone. You, a colonel in the Union Army, will travel through the front lines of battle to a southern town to interview a Southerner in the heart of Dixie. Is that about right, Mr. Stone?"

"Yes, that's about it, Kaitlin."

"And what will you use for identification, Mr. Stone?"

"Well, I have my commission from President Lincoln to get through Union lines. I guess that I will just have to be careful not to be stopped by the Confederate Army as I get close to Richmond," Stone said smiling weakly.

"How will you do that, Mr. Stone?"

"Mainly by travelling at night and staying off main roads, I guess."

"If I may say so, that's not much of a plan, Franklin".

"And do you have a better plan, Mrs. Jenkins?" Stone asked somewhat sarcastically.

"I think so, Mr. Stone."

"Pray tell."

"You are aware that my father was an engraver in the Bureau of Engraving at the Treasury Department. You also know that I worked for several years at the Library of Congress."

"Yes, I was aware of that."

"Are you also aware that I worked in the Documents Division authenticating documents, and that my father taught me the art and craft of engraving?"

"No, I wasn't aware of that. But what does that have to do with me?"

"If you will take me to Washington tomorrow, I should, within a few hours, be able to produce a commission from President Jefferson Davis that would be unquestioned by most Confederate troops," said Kaitlin.

"You can do that?" Stone asked in awe.

"I can, I will, and I must if we are ever to see that handsome face of yours safely at home," said Kaitlin, greatly emphasizing her Irish lilt.

"Handsome face?"

Kaitlin blushed and looked away.

"In a roguish sort of way," she answered, laughingly.

"That would certainly be a great help, I'm sure. What time would you like to leave, tomorrow?"

"Seven, I think. It might take longer than expected to do the research needed to duplicate the hand-script of Mr. Davis. Also, we will need to find some recent letters, preferably letters signed by Mr. Davis that have the current Confederate capitol letterhead."

"Seven it is," said Stone who was growing excited at the prospect of another ride to Washington and back with Kaitlin.

The morning was gray and cloudy. Rain was expected, but Stone and Kaitlin made it into the district without getting wet. Kaitlin got out of the carriage on Fifteenth Street where she entered a side door to the Treasury Department. Most employees used the side entrance rather than the front entrance at 1500 Pennsylvania Avenue. Inside the employee's entrance, she asked for the director, David Johnson.

Johnson greeted Kaitlin as a long lost friend. Without telling Mr. Johnson what she intended to do, Kaitlin indicated that she had been asked to do some research for the Executive Office and needed access to the Department's files. Mr. Johnson readily agreed, escorting Kaitlin past the guard to the staircase where they went upstairs to meet with the Documents supervisor. Johnson explained that Kaitlin was a former Library of Congress employee who was working for the Executive Office and was to be given access to any and all documents that would help her meet her mission requirements. The Documents supervisor wasn't happy about an outsider looking through Treasury's documents, but he acquiesced in the presence of the director.

After Kaitlin entered the Treasury Department, Stone drove over to Allan Pinkerton's office where the two detectives talked about the informant that the Pinkerton spy had developed. The informant wanted money for information, and Pinkerton was willing to pay. Allan handed Stone an envelope containing one thousand dollars to be delivered to the informant when and if Stone believed that the information was of subsequent value.

"Frank, how are you going to travel?" Pinkerton asked.

"Well, the Union still controls most of the rails between here and Fair Oaks. It would take five days to get there by horse, so I'll take the train. If I'm lucky, I'll be back in Washington in three or four days," Stone replied.

"What cover story will you use for being in Fair Oaks?"

"Kaitlin is working on that over at Treasury."

Pinkerton laughed. "War is a funny thing. Kaitlin worked hard to authenticate documents at the Library of Congress while she took classes at the university. Now she is forging them at the Treasury Department. Well, if there is anyone who can do the job, it's Kaitlin."

"I hope so. My life may depend on those documents," Stone replied.

"Are you going to take your Henry rifle with you?" Pinkerton asked.

"I hadn't thought about it. Why?"

"To the best of our knowledge, the Henry repeating rifle has not yet fallen into Southern hands. Mere possession could be your death sentence; not to mention the fact that any number of Southerners would kill you just to get their hands on that rifle."

"Good point. Any trouble that I might get into would be close up and personal, so I'll take my ten-gauge and a couple of Dragoons."

"Good choice, I would think," Pinkerton responded.

"How will I know your man when I get to Fair Oaks," Stone asked.

"Check into the Fair Oaks Hotel. Our man works there, and he will contact you. He will ask if you were at Shiloh. Your answer is, No, I was in Missouri at the time. Ross Hanrahan is short but stout and walks with a slight limp. He's about forty but looks more like fifty. He's had a rough life, but he is a good man—tough as nails—and his information has been accurate so far."

"Anything else that I need to know?"

"Not that I can think of at the moment, except that we don't know if the informant's information is valid. You will have to find a way to determine that. Also, he could be a double agent. He may be trying to find out who we have there in Fair Oaks. So be extra careful!"

"That I will do," Stone replied as he rose to leave.

The two men shook hands with Stone saying, "I'll report in as soon as I get back."

"God speed," Pinkerton replied.

Stone looked at the Regulator wall clock, noting that he still had a few hours before he was to pick up Kaitlin. He drove the carriage to the Men's Club where he had lunch and soaked his body in the hot baths until his skin began to shrivel. Refreshed and relaxed, Stone dressed and took time to read the Washington newspapers in the lobby until it was time to fetch Kaitlin.

Stone arrived at the Treasury Department promptly at 4:00 p.m., the agreed upon time, where Kaitlin was already waiting at the side door.

"Have you been waiting long?" Stone asked.

"Just a few minutes," Kaitlin responded as she adjusted herself into the seat of the carriage.

"Any luck?" Stone asked.

"Yes, I think I have just what you will need, Mr. Stone."

"Isn't it about time that you start calling me by my first name?"

Kaitlin smiled slyly and answered, "Perhaps, Mr. Stone, perhaps."

Stone shook his head from side to side with a dejected look on his face.

"Oh, Franklin, quit pouting."

Stone smiled a wide grin as he guided the Percheron geldings into the Washington traffic, heading back toward Maryland.

"I have two documents that I think will serve you well on your trip to Fair Oaks and beyond. One is a commissioning letter from Jefferson Davis. You are now commissioned as a Colonel in the Confederate Army. The second is a personal travel permit from General Robert E. Lee that says you are on special duty, assigned to the staff of Jefferson Davis, and that your travel is not to be questioned or impeded."

Kaitlin continued without interruption by saying, "Jefferson Davis was a U.S. Senator, so the Documents Division had several documents on file with his handwriting. General Lee had written several letters to the War Department when he was the superintendent at West Point, so they had his script on file too. The hardest part was to age the parchment that the letter from Davis was written on so that it looks to be about a year old. I dated the letter a year ago. The travel permit is dated one month ago so that no one would question whether the travel permit has expired. So, what do you think?"

"Well, if I have the commissioning letter from Lincoln in my right coat pocket, and the commissioning letter from Jefferson Davis in my left coat pocket, I just hope I don't get mixed up as to which one is which when I have to present one of them," Stone joked.

"You can make jokes now, Mr. Stone, but just watch out that your joke doesn't become a sick prophecy."

"Right, no sick prophecies," Stone grinned. "Oh, hush, Franklin."

Both Stone and Kaitlin grinned, thinking private thoughts for the next mile or so.

Arriving at home, Stone busied himself feeding and watering the horses after a brisk rub-down. Then he entered his room and packed for his trip to Virginia. Once satisfied with his packing, he took the canvas bag to his office and went over a report that he was going to drop off at the Pinkerton office before leaving on the morning train.

Just before sunrise the next morning, Stone saddled Hermes, tied the canvas bag with clothes and a box of ammunition for his revolver and another for his ten-gauge shotgun behind the cantle of the saddle, and headed down the driveway for the back road to Washington. Stone couldn't see Kaitlin's pained expression as she looked out of the window from her still dark bedroom—watching Stone as he rode away.

Hermes was used to this daily road trip and needed no real guidance as to the direction or pace. He took his cue from Stone's manner as transmitted to the big horse by leg pressure and the way Stone sat in the saddle. The more relaxed Stone became, the slower Hermes paced himself. As Stone leaned forward in the saddle, and as Stone's leg muscles clutched at Hermes sides, the big horse increased speed until he was at full gallop. Man and animal had long ago become a team that needed little in the way of verbal or reining communications. Stone rode for thirty minutes and walked for thirty minutes. Neither man nor horse became overly tired, yet they traversed the miles effectively and efficiently. After an hour or so, Stone took a brief pause in their journey to let the horse nibble grass before they entered the city. The detective continued to talk in quiet conversation. Hermes was prone to neighing on occasion, as if in answer to some question being posed by the big detective. Man and beast could talk together that way for hours on end.

When Hermes wanted his master's attention, he would head-butt him on the shoulder or in Stone's back. A lesser man might have been knocked down by the force, but Stone accepted the head-butting amiably. This morning, Hermes wanted the carrot that Stone usually buried in his coat pocket before leaving the Maryland farm. Hermes head-butted Stone until he finally handed over the desired delicacy. When Hermes had finished with the edible, Stone remounted and the two continued down the uninhabited dirt road as the sun rose a few degrees above the eastern horizon.

Passing the Pinkerton office, Stone guided Hermes down Cherry Lane, a nearby street where Allan and Joan Pinkerton had a modest home. Pulling up to the Pinkerton house, Stone dropped the reins on the ground, confident that if Hermes walked off, he wouldn't be very far away. And God help the stranger who might try to take Hermes or ride off on him. Just as Stone was about to knock, Allan opened the door.

"Have a nice ride?" Pinkerton asked.

"Yes, as a matter of fact we did."

"I thought you would be on a train headed for Fair Oaks."

"I didn't want to leave Hermes at a public stable while I was gone, so I thought that I would leave him here with you until I get back."

"Of course. Put him in the corral, and I'll take care of him as I do my own horses."

"Thanks. I'll see you in a few days. By the way, I was going to drop this report off at the office, but if you will get it to Mr. Lincoln after you have read it, I would appreciate the assistance," Stone said handing the multi- page report to Pinkerton.

"No problem, Frank. Have a good and safe trip."

The two men shook hands, and then Stone took Hermes to the corral where he rubbed down the big horse. After feeding and watering Hermes, Stone retrieved his bag and shotgun and headed into the city on foot.

Stone's timing was near perfect. Arriving at the train station, he was able to buy his ticket and board the train within minutes. After another fifteen-minute wait, the train pulled out of Washington, headed for Fair Oaks on the outskirts of Richmond and the Confederacy. The ride was slow as stops had to be made for water and wood. Each stop held the potential for an attack by Confederate troops. It was a nerve-wracking ride for most passengers, but Stone used the few hours to catch some sleep. Passengers were somewhat relaxed as long as the train was moving. However, as the train pulled into wood and water stops, the passengers held their rifles at the ready and watched out of the windows for signs of enemy troops.

Arriving at the Fair Oaks station, Stone exited the railcar with the other passengers. Confederate soldiers were checking the papers of each person. Although the Union controlled the rails, the Confederacy had regained control of Fair Oaks and the surrounding area following the Seven Days Battles. A young captain asked to see Stone's travel permit. Stone produced both his Confederate commission and the travel permit allegedly signed by General Lee.

"We don't see many permits like this one," the captain said.

"No, I don't expect that you do," Stone answered. "I'm going to hold on to these papers while I check them out."

"*Colonel.*"

"What?"

"My rank, Captain, is Colonel. You will address me as such. And you will not hold on to my papers. What you may do is have your commanding officer call on me at the Fair Oaks Hotel later this afternoon. But you are not holding those papers. Am I clear about that, Captain?"

"Yes sir, very clear," the captain said as he handed the papers to Stone.

"You may pass, Colonel."

Stone took one step then turned and asked, "Do junior officers no longer salute senior officers, Captain?"

"Sorry, Colonel," the captain said while he rendered a snappy salute.

Stone returned the captain's salute and continued on out of the station to Main Street, and then on to the Fair Oaks Hotel.

He was able to get a room without difficulty. Stone walked up creaky wooden steps and inserted the hotel's key into the room's lock. Turning the key with a loud click, Stone turned the doorknob and pushed open the door to find a gray-haired man standing in the center of the small room. At first, Stone thought that he had entered the wrong room and started to apologize for the intrusion. Before Stone could say anything, the unidentified man said, "You look familiar, were you at Shiloh?"

"No, I was in Missouri at the time."

"I'm Hanrahan, the man said. I saw you in the lobby and came up while you were signing the guest book."

"How did you get in the room?" Stone asked.

"I work here at the hotel, so I have a skeleton key. It helps when I'm trying to check out someone. I wait until they leave their room and go through their belongings."

"Ever get caught going through someone's gear?"

"Not yet."

"I'm Frank Stone."

"You're bigger than I thought you would be."

"Yeah, I tend to stick out a bit."

"That you do, Frank."

"Allan said to say hello.

"Yeah, it's been nearly a year since I was at the main office."

"Well, Ross, how do we handle this meeting?"

"I have a room on the ground floor on the right side of the hallway, next to the back entrance. The informant will stop by my room at eight tonight. If you come by a few minutes beforehand, I'll introduce you when he arrives."

"Fair enough, I'll see you just before eight."

Hanrahan opened the door, checked the hallway, and departed. Stone changed into work clothes and walked through the small town noting the location of the livery in case he needed to rent or buy a horse. He entered a nearby restaurant where he ate lunch—dinner to Southerners. And because Stone was a stranger, he was the recipient of more than a few unfriendly glances.

Following lunch, Stone made his way to the hotel where the over-stuffed bed enticed him into an afternoon nap. Rising refreshed at six in the evening, Stone went to the hotel's restaurant where he ate a meal of pork roast, fried potatoes, and homemade bread, a meal which he topped off with rhubarb pie and iced tea. He decided that he really didn't care for rhubarb all that much. The rhubarb had an overly tart taste, owing to the fact that sugar had become somewhat of a luxury. He left the small hotel restaurant and stopped to lounge in the overstuffed chairs of the lobby where he watched people come and go, while he read the *Daily Richmond Enquirer* and the semi-weekly *Richmond Dispatch*. Both papers extolled the virtues of the Southern soldiers who had repulsed the Yankee incursion into Richmond in an attempt to take the Southern capitol. Both papers talked about the Southern push to Washington and suggested that the war would soon end after General Robert E. Lee took Washington.

Just before eight o'clock, Stone walked toward the hotel's rear entry. Knocking lightly, Hanrahan immediately opened the door and ushered Stone into his room. They waited in silence for the few minutes that it took for the informant's arrival, which was announced by the opening of the rear door to the hotel, and the creak of the wooden floor just outside Hanrahan's room. Stone stood in the shadows, pointing his revolver toward the doorway. Hanrahan cracked opened the door and admitted the nervous informant.

"Were you followed?" Hanrahan asked.

"No, I was careful to keep to the back streets," the informant answered.

"Have a seat," said Hanrahan gesturing toward a small table with a whiskey bottle and shot glasses.

The informant sat and immediately poured a glass of whiskey, which he downed in one short gulp while he looked around the familiar room. His eyes widened noticeably and his face changed to a look of fear when Stone stepped out of the shadows with a gun in his hand.

"Are you armed?" Stone asked. "No," the informant answered. "Stand up," Stone ordered.

The man stood and was searched by a heavy handed Stone, which only added to the fear that the informant was experiencing. Finding no weapons, Stone ordered the man to sit.

"I told you I was unarmed," the scared man said. "And now I believe you," Stone replied.

"This is Henry Slater. He says he has information about arms sales that you might find interesting," said Hanrahan.

"Well, what about it?" Stone asked. "I don't know you," Slater responded.

"I'm the guy with the money. I'll determine how much you get based on what I think your information is worth."

Slater looked at Stone with penetrating eyes and then determined that he would go through with his end of the bargain.

"Until recently, I worked on a farm in Southern Maryland. The man I worked for has Southern ties. I worked in the fields mostly, but during harvest time, I was put to work in the barns; all except one barn that no one was allowed to enter except for some very unpleasant guys who provided security for both the farm and for the crops. They also transported the crops and meat that was slaughtered and cured on the farm for local markets. After working in the barns for a few weeks, I noticed that the wagons used for taking crops to market always came back empty but heavier than when they left with the crops. The horses seemed to work harder at pulling the supposedly empty wagons, and the tracks left by the wagon wheels were always deeper when they came back."

"Go on," Stone said.

"Well, I got curious, and one night when I finished my work, I saw that the side door to the barn that we weren't allowed to enter was open. I entered the barn and hid behind some crates in the corner. Some of the men who worked security, and who I had seen taking crops to market, were sitting on boxes in the middle of the barn drinking hard liquor and talking—bragging really."

"What were they bragging about?" Stone asked.

"One big guy with yellow hair was bragging about how he killed a Union colonel on the back road to Washington near the farm. He said the wagon in which they were returning to the farm had broken a wheel, and the colonel, who was on horseback, stopped to see if he could help. Two other men had gone to the farm to get another wheel. The colonel offered to help them lift the wagon while they changed the broken wheel. As they were tightening the new wheel, the colonel walked around the wagon asking why an empty wagon was so heavy. That's when the yellow-haired man said he shot and killed the colonel, leaving his body on the road but taking his revolver; a fancy Dragoon with the colonel's name on the frame."

"Did the braggart say the name of the colonel?" Stone asked.

Yeah, he said that the colonel had a farm a couple of miles south. His name was Jenson or Jenkins— something like that."

Stone's face did not give away his feelings as he asked, "And you think we would pay you for information about a dead Union colonel?"

"No, I think you would pay to know what was in those boxes that the men were sitting on and what was in the boxes that were stacked throughout the barn."

"And what would that be," Stone asked. "Guns—rifles, revolvers, and ammunition." "How do you know what was in the boxes?"

"First of all, the boxes were marked 'U.S. Army.' Some of the boxes were marked Rifles, Revolvers, or Ammunition. There was one open box where the men were sitting. They were passing a rifle around. I had never seen a rifle like that. They called it a Henry repeating rifle. But they only had a few of those."

"You can read?" Stone asked. "Read and write," Slater answered.

"What happened then?" Stone asked.

"Well I continued hiding in the shadows behind some of the boxes while they kept drinking. Finally, I was able to sneak out of the side door without being seen. I was scared. The next morning, I went to the boss and told him that I needed to get paid because I needed to get home before winter set in so that I could take care of my family. Several of the other farm workers had already returned to their homes, so he didn't question me further. He paid me what I was due, and I left."

"Where's home?" Stone questioned.

"Missouri," said Slater.

"So how come you are here in Fair Oaks?"

"I took a job at the livery until I could afford to buy a pack horse, food, and supplies for the rest of the trip to Missouri. I got trapped here by the war, but now that the Yankees have been beat back, I want to go home."

"What's the name of the farm where you worked?" Stone continued.

"It's the Smith farm on the back road to Washington from southern Maryland. It's the biggest farm in the area, so it's easy to spot. But those security guys won't let you on the farm."

"Which one of the barns has the weapons and ammunition?" Stone pressed.

"The barn that is furthest away from the main entryway."

"How much will you pay me?" Slater asked.

"I'm going to take the morning train back to Washington. I'll check your story. If you are telling the truth, I will send a telegram, and Mr. Hanrahan will pay you five hundred dollars. If you lied, I will come back and kill you myself."

"I'm not lying."

"Other than for the money, why are you telling us?" "Sir, I am a Southerner. I believe the South has a right to break away from the Union if it wants. But those killers are selling guns. I don't believe in war- profiteering, especially when it's a group of thugs and killers. They deserve to get caught."

"Okay Mr. Slater, I'll check out your story and you should get your money within a few days, given that you haven't lied to us. You can leave now, but lay low. Don't do anything that will call attention to yourself."

"Don't worry about that. I just want to get home with money enough to take care of my family."

Hanrahan and Stone listened as Slater left the building by the back door. Hanrahan checked the hallway and then reentered the room.

"Well that's quite a story. Any truth to what he said?" Hanrahan asked.

"I'll let you know within the next few days. If you are to pay Slater, I will send you a telegram saying that your cousin Gertrude died of the pox. If he lied, I'll send a telegram saying that a trip to Missouri is not feasible at this time."

"Got it. Let's hope he didn't lie," Hanrahan answered. Stone stood and opened the envelope with the money that Pinkerton had given to him. He counted out five hundred dollars, which he handed to Hanrahan.

"This is for Slater, if he's been truthful. I'll leave in the morning."

"A pleasure to know you, Mr. Stone," said Hanrahan as he shook Stone's hand.

"Ross, if this proves to be true, your work here will have been very worthwhile. Thanks for putting this together for us."

"Please tell Allan hello for me," Hanrahan answered as he opened the door.

Stone was as excited as he could ever remember being. He couldn't sleep. He just kept thinking about the information that he had received. The next morning, he had breakfast at the hotel and checked out, thanking the desk clerk for a good night's rest. But in truth, he felt like he had been on an all night stakeout.

Stone walked to the train station and bought a ticket for the ride back to Washington. The train left at ten in the morning, arriving in Washington on time at two in the afternoon. Unknown to Stone, a telegram arrived an hour later at Army Headquarters in Fair Oaks saying that Colonel Stone was unknown to the staff of General Lee, but that they might want to check with the staff of the president before taking action. The Commanding Officer, a major, didn't want that kind of presidential attention, so he burned the telegram and withheld the information from his over-exuberant captain.

Stone stopped by the Pinkerton office, but Allan wasn't there. He left word that he needed to see Allan as soon as possible. Then he walked to the Cherry Lane residence, said hello to Joan, and then saddled Hermes for the ride back to Kaitlin's farm. He toyed with the idea of stopping by the Executive Mansion to tell the president what he had learned but decided against that until he had a chance to talk with Allan Pinkerton.

Stone arrived at Kaitlin's farm just before sunset. He brushed, watered, and fed Hermes, and then he entered the house soon after darkness had fully enveloped the farm. Kaitlin flew across the room and wrapped her arms around Stone's waist.

"Well, that's a pleasant surprise," Stone remarked.

Realizing that she was holding Stone in her arms, she jumped back, holding her hands in the air in front of her saying, "I'm sorry, Mr. Stone. I was just so very worried about you."

"Well it's nice to have someone worry about me, Kaitlin. I missed you too."

I didn't say anything about missing you, Mr. Stone. I was just worried about your safety," she said with a sly smile.

"And with good reason. However, your papers worked well."

"I'm so relieved, now that you are back safe and sound."

It was near nine when Pinkerton rode up. The two men quietly discussed the information that was gleaned from the informant Slater. It was decided that both men should meet with President Lincoln the following morning. Kaitlin was told nothing. Pinkerton left for his home near midnight.

Chapter Eleven

November 6, 1862

STONE FORCED HIMSELF to get out of bed before dawn. He would have rather gone back to sleep, because sleep had not come easy during the night. Every hour or so, he had awakened wondering how the president would view the information that he had received in Fair Oaks. He lit a kerosene lantern and shaved in cold water, dressed in the flicker of the dancing flame, and then extinguished the lantern making his way downstairs by way of the hidden steel staircase so that he would not wake Kaitlin by going down creaky wooden stairs. He thought briefly of putting on a pot of coffee, but decided not to so that the aroma of freshly brewed coffee would not wake his sleeping beauty. He smiled at the image of Kaitlin that he projected in his mind's eye.

The house was cold, so he fired up the kitchen woodstove, knowing that Kaitlin would come down soon after sunrise, the coldest part of the day. He paid a visit to the outhouse, and then walked to the barn, thinking that maybe he should have worn a heavier coat. Fall was finally giving way to winter.

Hermes heard Stone's footsteps and softly whinnied a greeting as the barn door opened. Stone talked in soft tones as he produced the anticipated carrot, gently nuzzled the softness of the nose of the big horse, and then adjusted the bridle, blanket and saddle. As they walked side by side out of the barn, Stone noticed vapor coming from the stallion's nostrils as if confirming the coldness of the morning.

Hermes was alert to the fact that his rider, once mounted, sat more erect than usual. There was stiffness in his rider's body, which caused Hermes to move just a little faster than normal through the early morning air. No verbal conversation took place between man and horse this morning. Stone had issues of great importance on his mind.

Arriving at the Pinkerton house an hour after daybreak, Stone was surprised to see Allan's horse saddled and ready for the trip to the Executive Mansion. The two men greeted each other in quiet tones, neither one feeling particularly rested. They rode without conversation. Allan entered the Executive Mansion while Stone waited outside with the horses. Allan returned within minutes with a cup of coffee in each hand.

"Courtesy of the staff," he said lifting a cup up to Stone who was still mounted.

The two men drank hot coffee while Allan Pinkerton explained that the president had left hours earlier for the War Department where he waited for telegraph messages from his generals regarding the status of the war. Returning the empty cups to the house staff, Stone and Pinkerton rode the few blocks to the War Department, where they made their way to the telegraph room. Stone noted that the president looked years older than when they had first met just a little over nineteen months earlier. President Lincoln led the way to a room where the three men could talk privately. The briefing that Stone thought would take about fifteen minutes turned into a five hour operational planning meeting attended by generals, colonels, and their respective planning staffs.

The best scouts in the Union Army, those that were still in the district, were deployed in civilian clothes to covertly watch the Smith farm and to make regular reports by courier every four hours starting at noon. A company of cavalry and a company of light infantry were put on alert for an early morning raid. The soldiers were sequestered in a remote wooded area north of Washington so that word would not leak out regarding the impending raid. None of the soldiers knew where they were going. They only knew that they would be in harm's way that night. A supply company was similarly deployed south of Washington with twenty wagons and teams of four horses for each wagon. Several ambulances and medical doctors and their aides were staged with the supply company. The president wanted to strike immediately but wisely decided to take the advice of his generals to conduct the main part of the raid at dawn.

Pinkerton would go with the cavalry while Stone would take part with the infantry on foot. Both men warned the president and the generals of the need to take prisoners so that they could interrogate them for information concerning the clandestine arms operation. But like almost all battles, that plan was shattered when the first bullet was fired.

At four in the morning, Stone led the mounted infantry to the woods a mile east of the Smith farm. They would cross the fields of the Smith farm on foot. When necessary, the soldiers would have to crawl on their bellies to avoid being seen. They left anything that would rattle or make noise with their horses and the soldiers who were assigned to remain behind to guard their mounts. An hour before dawn they started their concealed approach onto the Smith farm.

Pinkerton and the cavalry staged one mile north of the Smith farm. They would make their approach one half hour before dawn. They were not worried about the noise their mounted unit would make. Union mounted units were fairly common in Maryland, even in southern Maryland. Few people who resided in the area would be alarmed by mounted soldiers riding by their farms. The supply company staged their wagons and horses about a mile away from the Smith farm. They would remain encamped there until they were given new orders by courier.

Stone and his men had made it across the fields in the darkness. At dawn, they rose from their prone positions in close proximity to the barns. Shots unexpectedly rang out at the farm's entryway. Three members of the Brotherhood who were secreted in blinds set up for concealment, opened fire on the mounted soldiers as they turned into the farm's driveway. A squad of cavalrymen dismounted, fell prone on the ground, and engaged the unseen shooters while the rest of the company charged up the driveway at full gallop. Those who had continued riding up the driveway suddenly found themselves in a murderous crossfire from the farm house and the bunk house. Pinkerton and the cavalrymen took what cover they could, but they were easy targets, especially for the shooters on the second story of the farmhouse.

Stone and the infantrymen began charging the rear of the farmhouse and the bunkhouse when they were engaged by shooters from the loft of a barn in which the arms and ammunition were stored. The Brotherhood had the advantage of concealment and elevated positions. The Union soldiers had the advantage of a larger force. But many of the soldiers paid the ultimate price that morning. Toward the end of the skirmish, members of the Brotherhood deserted the bunkhouse and ran for the barn where they would have access to more weapons and ammunition. They were cut down in mid-stride. But one man, a yellow-haired man, made it to the barn without being hit.

Stone made his way cautiously to the barn where the weapons were stored. He and several of his soldiers entered and were immediately fired upon by the Brotherhood. The soldiers took cover as best they could. Members of the Brotherhood were using the shadows of the barn to conceal themselves as they fired on the soldiers. Pinkerton and a group of soldiers entered the barn by way of a door on the opposite side of the barn. Stone gave the members of the Brotherhood the opportunity to surrender. They chose to shoot it out instead. As the Brotherhood ran out of ammunition, they turned to using knives, pitchforks and axes—any implement they could reach out and grab that could be used maim or kill. The soldiers used bayonets. By then, it was a one-sided battle with the soldiers winning. Pinkerton walked toward the center of the barn, thinking that the battle was over. The yellow-haired man came out from behind a stack of crates and grabbed Pinkerton around the neck, placing a Dragoon in Pinkerton's right ear.

From the shadows behind a stack of crates, Stone yelled "Charge." Instinctively, the yellow-haired man pointed his revolver toward the perceived new threat. As the barrel of the Dragoon moved away from Pinkerton's head, Stone fired his Henry repeating rifle, placing a forty-four caliber bullet in the blonde man's forehead. Stone came out of the shadows and knelt by Allan Pinkerton who had been dragged down by the yellow- haired man who still had his left arm wrapped around Pinkerton's throat.

"Are you hurt?" Stone shouted.

"Just my pride, Frank—just my pride. Thanks. I thought sure I was a goner."

Stone pulled the ornate Dragoon from the hand of the yellow-haired man. He read aloud the name on the frame: *Ben Jenkins, Colonel, United States Army.*

"I'm keeping this for the colonel's widow," he said hefting the heavy weapon. No one challenged the decision of the big detective.

The supply company moved in with their wagons and began loading the crates from the barn for transport back to Washington. It would take several trips before the contents of the barn were returned to Union warehouses because half of the wagons had to be used to transport dead and wounded soldiers back to Washington. Most of the wounded would die before they got to a hospital. Medical personnel treated the walking wounded.

Ambulances transported those who had the best chance for survival.

Pinkerton examined the bodies of the dead Brotherhood members in the barn's loft.

"No wonder the shooting had been so murderous," he said to Stone.

"Look, these three were using Henry repeating rifles." "A lot of young soldiers lost their lives today because of those rifles," Stone said.

Pinkerton and Stone collected the repeating rifles to show the president. Then they went about identifying those Brotherhood members who were still alive so that they could interrogate them. None of the surviving killers knew who was actually running the operation. They found Smith in his house. He and his wife and two sons were dead. They had all been firing on the troops and died as a direct result of the battle. Pinkerton and Stone were no closer to identifying the head of the contraband operation, but they had collected a valuable storehouse of weapons and ammunition. They also seized what crops were stored in the barns. When the last of the troops and shackled Brotherhood members returned to Washington, a cavalry officer gave the order to torch the buildings and fields.

Stone and Pinkerton rode two miles south where Kaitlin sat worried on the front steps of her home. She, like other neighbors, had heard the shooting at the Smith farm. She could see the plumes of smoke too. Riding to the front steps, Stone said, "We need to talk."

"Shall I make coffee?" Kaitlin asked.

"No time," said Pinkerton. "We must get back to Washington and report to the president."

The trio went into the parlor where Pinkerton escorted Kaitlin to the couch.

"Please be seated, Kaitlin. Our news will not be easy to hear."

Stone recited the story that the informant in Fair Oaks had told him as to how and why Ben Jenkins had been killed nearly two years earlier. When he finished, he handed the unloaded Dragoon to Kaitlin. Tears immediately filled her eyes as she recognized the ornate weapon with her dead husband's name engraved into the frame.

Pinkerton told her that the man who had shot her husband was killed in the fight at the Smith farm. The two detectives sat with Kaitlin as she openly wept. After a half hour, Pinkerton stood and indicated that he and Stone had to return to the president. Kaitlin thanked them for the information and watched as they rode off. She returned to her grieving. After a couple of hours, she said aloud, "Rest in peace my gentle husband. Rest in peace." With those words, Kaitlin mentally closed the door on her married life.

Stone and Pinkerton rode past the burning Smith farm and headed to Washington at a quick pace. Arriving at the Executive Mansion, Pinkerton briefed the president on the raid, including the number of dead and wounded.

"We had more casualties than I thought we would, Mr. President. They were well armed and well prepared for a fight."

Lincoln shook his head as he listened to the Pinkerton report. Stone remained silent. Pinkerton finished by saying, "Frank saved me from certain death."

The president looked over his notes saying, "Well at least I have something worth telling the Congressional leadership at our meeting this evening."

"You have both done well," he continued. "After all of the defeats that we have suffered at the hands of the South, I think that we may be on the verge of turning a corner on the war. This raid of yours proves that we are starting to get a handle on some of the clandestine activities that have been serving Southern interests to our detriment. Well done!"

Standing, the president said, "I'm sorry that I can't continue to discuss this and other issues, but I must prepare for my meeting with the Congressional Committee on Intelligence."

Stone and Pinkerton shook hands with the president and left the Executive Mansion. They rode their horses to the Willard Hotel where they downed two glasses of authentic imported Scotch whiskey in the elaborate "Men Only" bar. Allan raised his glass saying, "My homeland still makes the very best whiskey in the world."

The two men clinked their glasses and downed the burnt umber liquid.

"Yes," said Stone, I can't argue with that. But I want to finish interrogating those men we apprehended today. What did they call themselves? The Brotherhood?"

"Yes, they seemed to be quite proud of the organization. Okay, let's go," Pinkerton responded after he had drained the last of the whiskey from his glass.

The two men mounted their horses and rode to Fort Massachusetts, located on the outskirts of northwest Washington D.C. near Maryland. The Brotherhood prisoners had been taken there for medical treatment and for incarceration pending trials for treason.

Following hours of questioning, both Stone and Pinkerton were convinced that the prisoners did not know who actually ran the Brotherhood, although one prisoner did refer to a shadowy figure named Magnus. None of the captured men knew anything about Magnus. According to the survivors, only the dead yellow-haired man, identified as Jeffrey Parsons, had ever met him. The prisoners were to be tried by military tribunals, and soon thereafter, military executioners would hang them. Their murdering and war-profiteering days were over.

While Stone and Pinkerton questioned the prisoners, President Lincoln briefed the Congressional Intelligence Committee Chairmen from both houses about the Smith Farm activities and the capture of the rogue members of the Brotherhood. Winston Harrison, as Chief of Staff to Senator Aaron Hill, had accompanied the Senate Intelligence Committee Chairman to the evening meeting as he had for the past two years. The intelligence briefings were always a source of information that he could use to great advantage. He sat spellbound as the president related the information that had earlier been provided by Allan Pinkerton. As the president continued to tell about the raid and the interrogation of prisoners, Harrison barely breathed.

My God, he thought. *How close they've come.*

Out of natural curiosity, Senator Hill asked, "I know Allan Pinkerton, Mr. President, but who is this man Stone you keep referring to?"

"He is the Chief of Detectives for the New York City Police Department. I asked for his help at the outbreak of the war. He has been working with Mr. Pinkerton to identify those responsible for transporting and selling Union weapons and ammunition to the South, as well as other cases of murder and treason."

"His name doesn't appear in any Pinkerton Agency reports or budget requests," the Senator remarked.

"No, he resides and works out of the home of Colonel Ben Jenkins in Maryland, which ironically, is only two miles from the Smith Farm. As you may remember, Colonel Jenkins was murdered nearly two years ago. And now we know why and by whom. But Stone does work closely with Mr. Pinkerton and uses the resources of the Pinkerton Agency when he needs them."

"So he's an employee of the Pinkerton Agency."

"No, he is actually a colonel in the army assigned to the Executive Department," the president responded with some irritation in his voice.

Senator Hill, who couldn't care less, kept no notes, but Winston Harrison wrote furiously. No one took notice, since the chief of staff characteristically took notes for his patron. The meeting broke up at nine in the evening. Harrison, as usual, accepted a carriage ride with Senator Hill who groused about the late night meeting with the president.

"I don't like the idea of having an agent working in secret for the president. He could be investigating Members of Congress, and we wouldn't even know it. I don't like it one bit."

Harrison agreed. "This president seems to think that he can do whatever he wants without first getting Congressional approval. We need to find a way to limit presidential power. He needs to understand that it is the Congress who represents the people, therefore it is the Congress who controls this country."

Senator Hill responded by saying, "Maybe if we reduce the budget of the president and the Secret Service, he'll get the message. See if there are any laws that will allow us to curtail who and what the Pinkerton people can investigate."

"Yes sir. I'll get on it first thing in the morning." Senator Hill was still grousing about the president, Muttering to himself as he entered the front door of his riverside mansion. The taxi driver turned the coach around and headed for Harrison's hilltop residence on Adams Mill Road. Harrison's mind was racing over the events of the day, events that had diminished the Brotherhood by half, and had eliminated entirely his distribution system for shipping Union weapons to the South. After tipping the driver, Harrison entered his home, started a fire in the woodstove, and then he paced the living room floor.

"Maybe it's time to get out of the weapons business," he said out loud.

The more he thought about it, the more he became afraid. Now that he knew for sure that Stone and the Pinkertons were actively investigating his illegal enterprise, the more he was ready to give it up and concentrate instead on the legal and profitable business of providing security and freight hauling for the army. However, it would be necessary to make some immediate adjustments.

At midnight, Harrison saddled his horse and made his way down the hill to an even seamier side of town where the burned out shell of the old Catholic Church still stood in silent testament to its fiery desecration and the abandonment of the formerly thriving farm community. Leaving his horse with other animals in front of an all night pub, Harrison walked the back streets of the derelict community to the rectory next to the church. There he went upstairs in the darkness to watch the alley in back and the road in front for anyone approaching the area. This biweekly meeting with the Brotherhood leader would take on greater urgency.

Twenty minutes before the three o'clock hour, Harrison put on the monk's cloak and cowl, taking on the embodiment of Magnus, the monk of high treason. He made his way through the underground tunnel to the confessional in the old church. There, he lit the candle in the small parishioners side of the confessional and sat in the dark on the priest's bench holding a sawed off double- barrel shotgun. A revolver was held to his waist by a doubled up white braided cord. Almost exactly on the hour, the canvas curtain was pulled back, and the new senior member of the Brotherhood kneeled in the confessional saying, "Bless me Father, for I have sinned."

Magnus whispered the important elements of the raid on Smith's farm and told the Brotherhood leader that the prisoners at Fort Massachusetts were a threat to the remaining members. Magnus directed the killer to open an envelope that had been placed in the confessional. The two men discussed the contents of the envelope for several minutes. Business being concluded, the Brotherhood leader was dismissed. He hurried out because there was much to be done before daylight. Magnus returned to the rectory where he removed the monk's clothing and returned to his normal persona. He retraced his steps to his hilltop home where he unsaddled, fed, and watered his horse. He put the animal in the barn for the night. Then he entered the house where he fell into bed, physically and emotionally drained.

At dawn, six mounted uniformed Union soldiers rode two by two in a column followed by a canvas covered wagon distinguished by the words, "U.S. Army." They stopped at the gate and displayed a written order, which gained them entry to the military installation. The soldiers remained mounted while the sergeant of the guard summoned the commanding officer who read the order and gave instructions for the prisoners to be escorted to the wagon for transport to a more secure military installation that was closer to the War Department, where the murderers would be tried for treason. The commanding officer was glad to be rid of the killers. Based on the expressions on the faces of the prisoners as they were being chained inside the wagon, they were equally glad to be leaving Fort Massachusetts. As the wagon rolled out of the stockade, the fort's guard noticed that the prisoners were actually smiling.

About two miles away from the fort, the column pulled into a wooded area where two soldiers dismounted and made their way to the inside of the wagon. The prisoners greeted the two soldiers as friends and held their wrists in the air so that the soldiers could release them from their shackles. Instead, the two soldiers unsheathed large hunting knives and systematically slit the throats of the six former Brotherhood members among screams of terror, all of which ended in gurgles as blood escaped from their butchered throats. The two soldiers didn't immediately leave the inside of the wagon. Rather, the soldiers waited patiently until they could confirm that each victim had bled to death, a procedure that took several minutes. When the six men were confirmed dead, the two soldiers unharnessed the two draft horses from the wagon, and rode off with the column. The deaths of the six killers were meant to convey two messages to other Brotherhood members: first, you don't fail the

Brotherhood and live, and secondly, not the federal government or even the U.S. Army can protect you.

It was dark when the two teams of assassins forcefully entered the district homes of two different purchasing agents, men who had long ago made arrangements with Harrison to divert a portion of each shipment of government weapons and ammunition to the Smith farm. The killings were particularly brutal. No one in the two homes was spared—men, women, or children. In all, nine people were deprived of their lives—their throats having been butchered in a manner similar to those Brotherhood members in the wagon. The assassins left unnoticed by residents of either neighborhood.

Five men quietly entered the front and back doors of the two story farm house. The doors had not been locked. Three of the men splashed kerosene over the interior of the house, dousing curtains, furniture, and the floors until the cans were empty. Two men simultaneously made their way up the stairs with revolvers in hand.

Stone, having risen at his usual hour, just before dawn, heard footsteps downstairs and supposed that Kaitlin had risen early to make breakfast. He was fully dressed and about to exit the bedroom when he heard the familiar creak of the third stair. But this time it was immediately followed by a second creaking. That meant two people, and at this early hour of the morning, that could only mean trouble.

Stone pushed a loaded revolver into the waistband of his trousers and grabbed his ten-gauge shotgun that was leaning on the wall next to the doorway. The shotgun was always loaded and ready for use. The seventh stair creaked as he cracked open the door observing two men with guns in the dim light of the low-burning lantern that illuminated the hallway. The two men were nearly at the top of the stairs. The lead man turned and took one step toward Kaitlin's room. The back of his head disappeared in an array of bone and blood, splaying in the air from the discharge of the ten-gauge shotgun. Almost immediately Stone fired his second shot, striking the second man in the chest, the force of which knocked the would-be assassin back down the stairway. Dropping the shotgun, Stone grabbed his

Henry rifle and ran toward Kaitlin's room as he repeatedly yelled her name.

Kaitlin had heard the shotgun blast and had hurriedly put on slippers and a housecoat. She took her dead husband's Dragoon that she had loaded and placed on the table beside her bed the night before and made her way to the bedroom door where she could hear Stone yelling her name over and over. She swung open the door and stood menacingly with the large revolver. Stone grabbed her arm and said, "This way, quickly."

As they ran toward Stone's room, she could see that the lower part of the house was almost fully engulfed in flames. Pulling on the bull's nose ring, the bolt unlatched, but the door did not spring open. They were trapped.

Stone took a hunting knife from his trunk at the foot of his bed and pried open the secret door. Taking a lighted candle, Stone and Kaitlin ran down the spiral steel steps just as large billows of smoke and flame entered the bedroom. Stopping momentarily at the bottom of the stairs, Stone filled his coat pockets with grenades. He glanced through the one way mirror. The office was not yet fully engulfed. He pulled the nose ring on the bull's head and the secret door to the office sprang open. Since the hallways to the front and rear kitchen door were fully engulfed in flame, Stone entered the office closet that contained a ladder that led to the cellar. They exited the house by way of the push-up door that was concealed behind a row of twisted juniper trees and bushes. He motioned for Kaitlin to remain concealed behind the trees and bushes as he made his way along the burning building to the rear of the house.

It was twilight and two mounted assassins were in full view as Stone lit the fuses on two grenades and lobbed the round bombs in their direction. When the grenades exploded, shrapnel flew through the air hitting men and horses. Stone charged the two men, repeatedly shooting at them as they fell from their mounts. The horses whinnied in pain, writhing on the ground. Stone side-stepped the horses and placed a bullet in the head of each of the fallen assassins. Two more riders came from the front of the house at full gallop.

Stone ducked down behind one of the fallen horses and opened fire on the oncoming riders. The lead man went down with Stone's first shot. Stone rapidly fired at the remaining rider, but the distance between them had swiftly closed and the rider was nearly on top of him when Stone realized that his rifle was empty. Stone reached too late for his Dragoon. The now dismounted rider pointed his revolver at Stone's head and was about to pull the trigger when a shot rang out from behind him. The assassin felt the bullet penetrate his body and turned to defend himself when he was shot a second time, and a third time and a fourth. He didn't feel the fifth bullet. He was already dead when it pierced his body. He fell to the ground with a surprised look on his face. His glazed eyes didn't see Kaitlin or her dead husband's Dragoon. The irony of his being shot with the very pistol that had belonged to the colonel that the Brotherhood had killed nearly two years earlier was lost on the dead Brotherhood member.

"May your soul forever burn in hell!" yelled Kaitlin.

Then she fainted, falling ungracefully—like a sack of potatoes.

Stone stood and reloaded his rifle with bullets from his pocket. He placed a bullet in the head of the two horses that has been hit by shrapnel, putting them out of their misery. Then he placed another round in the heads of the four assassins, confident that the two men inside the house were dead and cremated. Stone was glad that Kaitlin had fainted so that she wouldn't have to see him shoot both men and horses, but his trouser legs bore the gory evidence of the violent encounter.

Kaitlin returned to consciousness in the arms of Stone.

"It's over," said Stone.

"No, it's not over. The war is still raging—for years, you yourself said."

Kaitlin looked at the still burning farmhouse. "I've lost every-thing," she cried.

"I'll hitch the horses to the carriage and take you to Pinkerton's house. I'm sure they will care for you until we can rebuild."

"I don't want to rebuild. I just want to get away," Kaitlin cried.

The trip to Washington was eerily quiet. Kaitlin physically shook most of the time, and there was nothing that Stone could say that would reassure her. He covered her in the lap blanket to shield her from the cold and drove silently to Washington.

Arriving at the Pinkerton house, Joan took Kaitlin inside and dismissed Stone, saying that Allan had already left for the office. Stone untied the saddled Hermes from the back of the carriage and unhitched the Percheron geldings, putting them in the paddock. He pushed the carriage inside the small barn to get it out of the weather, and then mounted Hermes for the short ride to the Pinkerton Agency.

Entering the office, Allan started to greet Stone when he noticed the blood and gore on Stones trousers. "My God, what happened?"

Stone gave a full verbal report and asked Allan if he would make the necessary arrangements to bring the bodies of the assassins back to Washington for identification and for burial in a common grave. Allan quickly agreed and made the necessary arrangements while Stone sat and drank a cup of hot black coffee.

"I guess we had better brief the president," Allan said. "Yes, as if he needs more bad news," Stone remarked. The two men rode to the Executive Mansion where they waited for well over an hour to see the president. After briefing the president about the fiery attack, the president ordered, "Bring Kaitlin to the Executive Mansion."

Both Stone and Allan started to object, however, the president cut them off saying, "Kaitlin lost her husband and all of her worldly possessions as a result of this war and my request that Mr. Stone stay at her house. Mrs. Lincoln and the staff here at the Executive Mansion will see to it that she gets the medical attention and the rest that she needs to see her way through this. Gentlemen, this is not a request."

Early that afternoon, Joan and Allan Pinkerton drove Kaitlin to the Executive Mansion. Mrs. Lincoln was courteous, but she also made it known that this was not a social call. Joan and Allan Pinkerton were dismissed. They returned crestfallen to their home on Cherry Lane. Stone was uncharacteristically nowhere to be found.

Once it was clear that there was nothing that Stone could do to help Kaitlin, he left Washington, returning to the burned out Maryland farm to examine the crime scene. As he and Hermes approached the driveway, Hermes suddenly veered left into the woods. Surprised, Stone was about to rein Hermes back onto the road when he noticed two horses hitched to a small wagon hidden by a stand of trees. Stone dismounted and whispered sarcastically in Hermes ear, "I thought I was supposed to be the detective." The big horse grunted and stamped his left forefoot on the ground. Hermes gently head-butted Stone's back, propelling Stone toward the wagon. "Smart-assed horse," Stone said aloud. Hermes snorted again. Stone grinned.

Examining the ground around the wagon, Stone could see that five men had walked from the wagon across the road and up the driveway. Knowing that there had been six men who attacked the house, he surmised that one man must have held the horses for the attackers as they carried cans of kerosene to the house. Stone unhitched the two horses from the wagon and walked them up the driveway to a watering trough where the two horses drank thirstily. Going to the barn, Stone retrieved a couple of sheaves of hay and turned the two horses loose in the paddock. Hermes drank his fill, then walked with Stone to what had been the front of the burned out house. Footprints in the fine dust of the driveway indicated that three men had walked to the front door and two other men had gone around the side toward the rear of the house. That explained why Stone had not heard horses coming up the driveway.

Entering the burned-out shell of the house, Stone saw two charred cans the size of milk jugs, one in the living room, and one in the office. Walking to the rear of the house, Stone spotted two more cans—one in the kitchen and one in the dining room. Each could hold about five gallons.

"Obviously they were serious about burning the house down," he said aloud.

The staircase and the second story had collapsed in the fire. The barrels of two Sharps rifles stuck up out of the ashes. The wooden stocks had burned. The bones of two men were partially buried by ash and debris. Their clothes had burned away along with the fatty tissue of their bodies. Any personal property that they had was also burned beyond recognition. Stone collected the two rifles and looked through the rest of the debris to see if there was anything that could be salvaged. All that he could find that was useable was some jewelry and a slightly burned Bible. He collected those for Kaitlin and returned to the front of the house where Hermes waited patiently.

Stone and Hermes rode through the fields and located two saddled horses in a hollow munching on grass and the stubble of hay that had been left in the field after the harvest. Stone dismounted and gathered up the loose reins of the horses and walked them to the paddock where he fed and watered them. Hermes followed behind unattended. Going to the barn, Stone fashioned four lead ropes, which he installed on necks and muzzles of the attacker's horses. It was difficult and very slow riding with four horses in tow, but Hermes needed no special reining as the group made its way back to the Pinkerton office in Washington. Allan Pinkerton met them in front of the building.

"Have you decided to become a horse wrangler?" Pinkerton asked with a broad smile.

"Just what I need—another smart-ass. First Hermes, now you," Stone answered grinning.

"Of the two of us, you probably ought to listen to Hermes. He's pretty smart, you know."

Ignoring Pinkerton's remark, Stone continued by saying, "These are the attacker's horses. I also have their rifles that I retrieved from the house. We should be able to get the serial numbers from the rifles. Maybe they will tell us something of the assassins."

"Would be assassins. You're still alive." "Thankfully."

Allan took the rifles from Stone and examined them saying, "Yes, I'm sure we will be able to get the serial numbers. What are you going to do with the horses and tack?"

"I thought that some of your men might take them to the various public liveries to see if anyone can identify the owners."

"Yes, we can do that for you. What do you want me to do with the horses and tack when we've finished with them?"

"Well, I guess we should sell them and give the money to Kaitlin."

"Okay, we can do that too," Allan responded.

The two men entered the agency office where Pinkerton offered Stone a cup of coffee.

"Actually, I could use something a little stronger," Stone said.

Pinkerton pulled a bottle of scotch whiskey out of his desk drawer and poured a water glass full, which Stone swallowed in three quick gulps.

"Okay Frank, what now?"

"I think that the would-be killers were likely part of the Brotherhood, which means that the Brotherhood is much larger than just a group selling illegal weapons from a Southern Maryland farm. Have you telegraphed your agent in Fair Oaks authorizing him to pay the informant yet?"

"No, with all the excitement, I was going to do that this afternoon."

"Well, I would like to go back down there and talk with Slater one more time. Maybe he can shed some light on this group. I'll tell Ross Hanrahan to pay Slater when I'm through talking with him, if that's okay with you."

"That's taking a very big risk, Frank."

"Someone tried to kill Kaitlin and me. It's worth the risk if I can find out who is behind this."

"Well, I don't think Slater knows anything more than he's already told you."

"He may not realize what he knows. I'll have to work it out of him gently."

"Okay, when will you leave?"

"There's a train to Fair Oaks that leaves this evening. It pulls in late tonight. With luck, I can return on the morning train, arriving here about noon tomorrow."

"I'll telegraph Ross to set up a meeting with Slater for this evening. I won't give him the payment code, but I will indicate that you will meet with them when payment is to be made."

"Thanks, Allan."

"By the way, if you want to leave Hermes at my house, just put him in the barn, and I'll take care of him."

"I think that I will take him with me on this trip. Things are heating up again down there, and I may not be able to ride the train back to Washington. I would like to stable him at your house while I get some shopping done in city center. All my gear was destroyed too."

"No problem, of course. Oh, and I almost forgot, the president authorized me to reimburse you for your loss."

Pinkerton handed Stone an envelope with five hundred dollars in cash.

"Thanks, I haven't had a chance to stop by the bank yet, so this will come in handy."

The two men silently looked at each other for a few seconds, shook hands, and Stone turned to leave.

"Good luck, Frank." Stone just nodded.

Stone stopped by the railway station; bought tickets to Fair Oaks, including cargo space for Hermes, and then he went to the shopping district to buy another canvas bag and some clothes.

The train ride was uneventful. He still had the forged identification papers and travel permit in his inner coat pocket, so he was confident that all would go according to plan. He left Hermes in the hotel's public stable and then went to the hotel's restaurant where he ate a fine supper. He was famished. He suddenly realized that he hadn't eaten since the night before the attack.

Stone went to the desk, where the clerk remembered him from his last visit and welcomed him back. Stone paid for a room, collected the key, and took his canvas bag to his room. He half expected Ross Hanrahan to be in the room, but he wasn't. It was another hour before Hanrahan and Slater showed up. Slater was noticeably scared.

"What are you doing here?" Slater asked. "Are you trying to get me killed?"

"No, I just have a couple of questions. Then you will be paid, and you can be on your way."

"I'm not leaving. I'm going to stay here until it's safe to travel."

"Your choice," said Stone.

Stone questioned Slater for the better part of an hour. When it became apparent that Slater really didn't know anything more about the Brotherhood or Magnus, Stone said his goodbyes and walked to the train station while Slater counted the money that Hanrahan had given to him; five hundred dollars in twenty-dollar greenbacks. Meanwhile, the stationmaster indicated he had received word by telegraph that Union troops near Fredericksburg had removed rails thereby disrupting service.

Stone returned to the hotel, where he stayed the night. He awoke early, had breakfast, and started back to Washington on horseback. Stone didn't want to push Hermes, so he would ride for thirty minutes and then walk for thirty or so minutes as the two held a somewhat animated conversation. On the evening of the fifth day of travel, they arrived at the Willard Hotel in Washington where Stone paid room rent for a week. Putting Hermes in the stable, taking time to feed, water, and briskly rub down the stallion before going to his room. He slept until ten in the morning, highly unusual for Stone no matter how tired he may have been the night before.

Stone had a light breakfast in the restaurant and then walked to the exclusive Metropolitan Men's Club where he languished in a hot bath for over an hour. He stopped by the barber and got a haircut and shave. By noon, he almost felt normal.

Stone walked to the Pinkerton office. He accepted a cup of coffee and admitted sheepishly that Slater had no useful information. It had been a wasted trip. Pinkerton seemed nervous, like he was reluctant to talk with Stone.

"What's the matter, Allan? You don't seem to be yourself today."

"That's highly perceptive of you, Frank. I have news that I don't want to give to you."

Stone's eyes narrowed; his face noticeably hardened. His voice deepened as he asked, "What's wrong Allan?"

"Kaitlin's gone," Allan said quietly.

"*Gone!* Gone where?" Stone asked.

"Ireland."

"Ireland? When did she leave?

"Yesterday. She asked me to give you this letter," Pinkerton said as he handed Stone an envelope embossed with the presidential seal. Stone read and reread the letter, then left the office without gesturing and without saying another word.

Chapter Twelve

December 9, 1862

Everett Davis sailed on a packet boat to Florida on calm seas, even though it was still hurricane season. Thanks to Everett's coordination, there were over twenty volunteer boat-owners who sailed between their various Florida homeports to Nassau and back with messages for the Confederacy. New telegraph lines had been installed down both Florida coasts. Messages between Richmond and Nassau took mere hours, where earlier it had taken weeks to get messages through by courier.

Arriving in the Florida Keys, Everett transferred to a commercial fishing vessel that took him to Sullivan's Island at the north entrance to Charleston, South Carolina, a port that was blockaded by the Union. The fishing boat was stopped and inspected outside the harbor, but owing to the fact that the boat contained no contraband and that both the boat and crew smelled heavily of sweat and fish, they were allowed to quickly enter the harbor. Everett, who was wearing work-clothes and who had worked with the crew as they fished their way up the coast, gave no indication that he was anything more than what he appeared to be; a commercial fisherman.

Making his way to a Confederate safe house, Everett bathed, shaved, changed clothes, ate supper and rested before heading out on his true mission—a meeting with the colonel who would lead an attack on the Union's paddle-wheel steamer that was currently blockading the port. The two men met on the sand dunes of Goat Island.

The City of Charleston and the surrounding areas were still in the hands of the Confederacy, but the Union had successfully blockaded the port for nearly a year.

This particular time was chosen for an attack because two other Union warships that had been blockading the port were recently redeployed to blockade other deepwater ports along the coast where Southern ships had successfully unloaded war-making materials. For the first time in over a year, only one warship prevented delivery of weapons and ammunition to Charleston.

Everett and the colonel needed no passwords for recognition. They had met on prior occasions and knew each other by sight.

"Good evening Colonel."

"Good evening Ev. I didn't expect to see you here." "Three of our largest ships are waiting over the horizon to enter the port. The ships' masters are a suspicious lot, and they trust nobody except their crews. I have been trying to convince them for some time now that we can disrupt the Union's blockade long enough for them to unload their cargo and return safely to sea. Since this is the first time that we will actually attack a warship on the coast so that our ships can gain access to the port, I wanted to join you on the mission."

"How will they know if we are successful?"

"I have three packet boats watching the Union ship from a distance. If they see the explosion, they will sail to the various locations and let the runners know that the port is open."

"Okay, but we won't start the attack until about three in the morning."

"The packet boat owners are dedicated Southerners.

They will wait, either way."

At about two in the morning, two row boats made their way out of Breach Inlet under cover of a thick fogbank. The Union warship was anchored about a half mile off of Sullivan's Island. Six men strained at the oars of each boat, silently propelling the small boats toward the Union ship. They arrived fifty yards off the stern of the ship, with one boat going to the paddlewheel on the right and the other boat going to the paddlewheel on the left. The boats were loaded with explosives and fuses that would withstand the sea while wreaking havoc on the shafts and the ship's paddlewheels once they were detonated. Four men from each rowboat slipped into the cold waters to pack the explosives with black sticky goo from the marshes of Goat Island to the steel shafts and thick wooden paddles of the Union blockader. The swimmers lit long fuses and returned to the row boats where they pulled away from the Union ship and waited for the results of their night's work. They didn't have long to wait.

The explosives on the left side of the ship were first to detonate. A yellow and orange plume lighted the dense fog. Splintered wood debris from the paddles flew through the air like spears, seriously injuring one of the Confederate soldiers. A water column caused a wave to hit the bow, nearly upending the boat and its crew. The charges on the right side of the ship detonated seconds later with nearly the same results. As the two row boats departed, they could hear the ship's bell clanging repeatedly to alert the crew to the emergency. Buckled steel plates around the paddlewheel shafts allowed seawater to spill into the damaged hull. Both paddlewheels were tilted at odd angles because of the damage to the shafts.

Unnoticed by Union sailors, three packet boats quickly got under way from their nest nearly a half mile away. They headed out to sea in different directions to alert the merchant ships that the way had been cleared for their arrival in port. The ship's masters waited until dawn, when the fog had cleared, before entering the Port of Charleston. They stayed well away from the Union ship and its still-dangerous deck cannons. However, with its propulsion system severely damaged, Union sailors could only watch as the three merchant ships entered port, unloaded their cargos, and departed before the end of the workday.

In a way, it was somewhat ironic because the hulls of several Confederate blockade runners that had previously attempted to enter the port were lying on the seabed around Sullivan's Island, almost directly underneath the incapacitated Union ship.

Everett returned triumphantly to Nassau with the first of the three merchant ships. The nightly party at the Grand Victoria Hotel lasted well into the morning hours with many of the attendees asking Everett to relate again and again the story of the attack on the Union ship that blocked Charleston Harbor. He retold the story to the sailors' delight.

———— ∞ ————

ANDY DAVIS HAD been working at the telegraph office at the War Department in Richmond each morning to build up his code speed. After noon, and sometimes well into the evenings, Andy read dispatches from the various telegraphers who were assigned to different commands both for the Union and for the Confederacy. He began to formulate a strategy as to how he should work to gain information from Union telegraph wires, but he would need the approval of senior officers assigned to the Confederate Secret Service—something that they would be reluctant to give because his strategy was far different than theirs. While the goals and objectives were the same (gaining intelligence from the enemy by listening to his telegraph transmissions), he felt strongly that the methods that he should use needed to be different than those of other Confederate telegraphers. He needed to be invisible to everyone, Northerners and Southerners alike.

Outlining his strategy to Jubal, Andy explained that since telegraphers were able to distinguish the fist of one operator from another, he would obtain the information from Union telegraph wires, then ride to the nearest Confederate telegraph train or office and have other telegraphers transmit the information back to headquarters. In that manner, Andy would not disclose his fist. He would essentially remain invisible. If a situation became so dire that it became necessary to immediately provide battlefield information, he would transmit the information in numbers only. No words would be used. The enemy would not be able to decipher the meaning of the numbers, which would be agreed upon before Andy left on a specific mission. Using numbers only, Andy would disguise his fist by sending the transmissions very slowly, as if he were just learning how to use the telegraph.

To show Jubal what he envisioned, Andy took a map of the battle at Fair Oaks. Dividing the battlefield into grid squares, and giving each grid a number, Andy could send information by telegraph as to the number of enemy troops that were moving in a particular direction. The formula 3.21–3–4 would indicate the three thousand two hundred troops were moving from grid square three to grid square four on the map of the battlefield. The number one meant that the first number was to be read in thousands. If the number of enemy troops were in the hundreds, a zero would follow the number 3.2. Also, by adding a different number to the equation each day, say the number six for today, the equation would read 9.81– 9–10, which would further complicate efforts to decipher the message. Grid square numbers could be mixed up so that there was no discernable pattern.

Senior officers were slow to warm to Andy's suggestions. The South did use a code. They called it the Diplomatic Code and felt that it was the only code necessary to prevent Union telegraphers from deciphering their messages. However, based on actions taken by Union commanders in prior battles, Andy was convinced that Union telegraphers had indeed broken the Diplomatic Code. Some Southern generals were reluctant to use telegraph because telegraphers needed to be supported by a telegraph train. Not a train made of railcars necessarily, but a train of five or six wagons and about twenty linemen to spool out the heavy telegraph cable from one field headquarters to another. It was a cumbersome chore that required more food and supplies to feed and house the telegraphers and linemen. Most Southern generals preferred to use semaphore flags in the day and lanterns at night. They had learned that system early in their careers, and they were comfortable with its use.

Andy believed that codes used by the Confederate Secret Service should be different than the codes used by the military in order to protect the men who were gathering intelligence. He also believed that the only way to test his theories was to try them out in the field. Jubal agreed.

Jubal volunteered to stay with General Lee's telegraph train to decipher Andy's messages so that General Lee could send new orders to the various Divisional Headquarters during the battle. While a few of the Southern generals quickly accepted the use of the telegraph for tactical use in a battle, General Lee was convinced that the telegraph could influence strategic objectives too.

General Lee approved Andy's plan and asked when Andy would be ready to move out. As Andy was about to answer, Jubal interrupted saying that he and Andy needed to pay one last visit to C. A. Gaston at the War Department telegraph office before heading out to the battlefield. They would be ready to leave for the battlefield in two days.

Early the next morning, Andy and Jubal met with Gaston at the telegraph office. Gaston understood the dangers of conducting battlefield intelligence wiretaps. He had performed numerous such wiretaps himself. He had been shot at and chased by the enemy, avoiding capture more by luck than by skill. In his opinion, it was the cable that he had used to tap into the enemy's telegraph system that gave away his position. It was thick and relatively inflexible. By following the wire, soldiers had nearly discovered his hiding places, causing him to flee for his life on more than one occasion. He needed a better device, a device that didn't require heavy cable. He found such a device being manufactured in the North. But of course he couldn't just order one.

It had taken months to find the device. However, one was finally seized from a telegrapher who had been taken prisoner along with a squad of Yankee soldiers who were protecting a railroad station, and subsequently a telegraph station, well behind Union lines. Another half dozen keys and sounders had been manufactured by Confederate machine shops based on the specifications of the seized device. C. A. handed a small wooden box to Andy saying, "This is a copy of the Caton lineman's test set and pocket relay. It looks a lot like a snuff box, but it contains a key and sounder for tapping into telegraph lines."

Andy opened the wooden box and examined the brass key and the two thick coils of tiny wire that provided the electromagnet that allowed the sounder to work. He noted too that the brass parts were mounted on hard rubber, which had been fitted into the small oval-shaped box.

"This is certainly a lot smaller than a standard key and sounder. Does it really work?" Andy asked.

"Yes, it works very well. But the best part is yet to come."

Gaston reached into his desk drawer and retrieved a small roll of tiny wire of the same diameter as the wire used in the magnetic coils—just a little larger than the diameter of a human hair. The wire was covered with a brown colored silk shroud.

"We have discovered that you don't need a thick wire to tap into a telegraph line. This wire is very thin and it is flexible, meaning that you can bury it or hide it in bushes without fear that it will give away your position. The clip on the end allows the user to connect to a bare telegraph wire quickly."

"I wouldn't have believed that you could use such a tiny wire," said Andy.

"Remember, the wire is very delicate; however, the silk shroud gives it added strength when using it in the field. It's very expensive, and we have to get the wire from England because we have no easy access to silk or to the machines used to cover the wire. Since both the roll of wire and the key set are so small, you can carry them in your pocket. If you do have to abandon your wiretap, you can still take the key and the tap wire with you. If you yank on the wire, the clip will disengage from the telegraph cable and you can quickly wind the wire on the small wooden spool for use again later. Use it well, Andy, and good luck."

"I will, C. A., thanks."

Jubal and Andy returned to the Boars Head Inn to pack, to have dinner at the pub, and to have one final good night's sleep before returning to the battlefield. It took two days of hard riding to catch up with General Lee's Army of Northern Virginia in the hills above Fredericksburg.

Uncharacteristically, the Union was conducting a winter campaign in a renewed effort to take the Confederate capitol. But first, General Burnside, Commander of the Union Army of the Potomac, wanted to take Fredericksburg, a Confederate city on the Rappahannock River that was halfway between Washington D.C. and Richmond. Fredericksburg would be of great importance to the Union supply line, should they successfully take the Confederate capitol. In his view, taking the capitol was one thing. Holding the capitol would require an unobstructed road, rail, and river for the movement of men and supplies.

Burnside and well over a hundred thousand Federal soldiers had arrived at the edge of the Rappahannock River in mid-November. Only a few thousand Confederate soldiers stood in their way. The Confederate soldiers destroyed the three bridges that crossed the river from the east and waited for the enemy to find other ways to cross the river. The Federals had to wait for three weeks before a sufficient number of pontoons arrived to ford the river.

Andy and Jubal arrived at Lee's headquarters while the Union troops were staging across the river. General Lee's telegraphers had already laid telegraph cable between the headquarters of General Lee and his subordinate commands. Miles of cable formed a closed-loop telegraph system that allowed General Lee to stay in contact with the various divisions under his command. When Burnside had become entrenched on the eastern side of the Rappahannock waiting for pontoons, he too had miles of cable laid so that he could communicate with his subordinate generals. The question on Andy's mind was where he should infiltrate the Northern line to intercept messages from Burnside to his generals. Looking over the city, Andy discussed the situation with Jubal.

"Jubal, I just don't see any way to get behind enemy lines at this point."

"I don't either, Andy. I think that this is one of those times when we will have to be content with finding a place where you can watch what's going on, so that you can transmit information back to me at General Lee's telegraph wagon train."

"Any suggestion as to where I should go to see the action as it occurs?"

"I've been looking at the dispatches from the troops in the forward elements. I think the main Union attack will occur on the south side of the city. We're kind of thin there, and I think that the Federals know it."

"Why don't we ride down there and take a closer look," Andy suggested.

"Okay."

Residents who were fleeing in anticipation of the attack made Andy and Jubal's ride into the city somewhat more difficult. Stopping at Richmond Road, Jubal and Andy noticed that there was a lone Confederate cannon mounted on a high point overlooking the city and the river.

"Jubal, I need to stay away from artillery or I won't be able to hear the sounder."

"Well Andy, I don't think there will be much to listen to. I think you will be sending messages, not receiving them. Look at the river. The Federals already have a pontoon bridge nearly half way across. The other pontoon bridges farther north aren't nearly as complete as this one. This is where the attack will begin."

"The telegraph line between General Lee and Jackson's division is just about a half mile up the road. If you can get the linemen to extend the line, I'll take cover and report what I see from here," said Andy.

That night, the linemen extended the telegraph line as requested. Meanwhile, Confederate soldiers took to the highest rooftops along the city's riverfront. Early the next morning, as Union troops began crossing the river south of the city. Confederate sharpshooters began a torrent of deadly rifle fire to slow the Federal advance. When a superior number of Union troops successfully crossed the river, Confederate sharpshooters fell back to the hills, joining General Lee's Army of Northern Virginia. Federal troops spent the next two days preoccupied with looting the City of Fredericksburg.

From his hiding place above the city, Andy could see a substantial Union force making its way into the south side of the city. The single Confederate cannon mounted in the heights on Richmond Road stopped the attack cold. The Federals would have to find another way, and they did. They found an unprotected area just a little north of the Confederate cannon, out of the cannon's range, but still on the south side of the City of Fredericksburg.

Andy could see Union troops pouring through a gap in the Confederate line and quickly telegraphed 5.21–4–3. Jubal deciphered the report to General Lee who directed General Jackson to fill the gap immediately. Jackson's troops moved forward and took a stand on a road protected by a rock wall overlooking the city. The Union artillery fired volley after volley from across the river while the infantry surged forward. Confederate counter- attacks pushed the Union troops back. As the Union troops fell back, the previously unprotected area was reinforced with Confederate infantry from other divisions taking positions on the road behind the rock wall.

Once the Confederate line had been reinforced, Andy took advantage of the night to move forward where he had observed Union linemen laying a telegraph cable across the pontoon bridge into the city, thereby installing communications between Burnside and his forward commands. Taking refuge in a depression a few yards behind the outhouse of a deserted home, Andy covered himself with weeds and dead bushes next to a marsh. Union soldiers came and went, using the outhouse, oblivious to the faint clicking sounds of the Caton keyset that was mixed with the sounds of katydids, frogs, and other night creatures. Hiding in the darkness, Andy clipped onto the Union telegraph cable and copied the messages between the various Union generals.

Just before dawn, Andy made his way through both the Union and Confederate lines, where he connected his telegraph key to the Confederate telegraph line. Reading his notes, Andy transmitted the messages that he had intercepted in plain text. There was no numerical equivalent for the actual messages that he had intercepted, so he had no choice but to relay what he had heard verbatim. As long as there were no Union telegraphers intercepting his messages, his fist would continue to remain hidden from those Federal telegraphers who might recognize it. It took two hours to relay the messages that he had intercepted. He was interrupted repeatedly while orders were transmitted to various commands that were fighting along the walled road.

All day, the Union surged troops—whole brigades— in an effort to overcome the inferior Confederate force. By nightfall, it was clear that they had failed to penetrate the Confederate line. General Burnside recalled his troops to the east side of the river, having lost over thirteen thousand soldiers. General Lee lost about five thousand soldiers, but his troops had retaken the city of Fredericksburg. General Lee congratulated his troops for having fought and won a glorious battle. In the privacy of his headquarters, General Lee took the time to congratulate both Andy and Jubal for keeping him informed regarding enemy intentions. He credited them with much of the day's success.

Dismissed, the two intelligence specialists silently huddled beside a campfire sipping strong coffee, allowing the tension of the day to drain away and fade into the cold starry night of mid-December. Andy's thoughts turned to his wife and son in Georgia.

Andy said aloud, "Damn, I'm not going to be with my family for Christmas. Do you have family, Jubal?"

"I have a brother in Fork Union, here in Virginia. It's about seventy five miles southeast of Richmond. That's where we were born and raised. I never did marry, so I ended up out west fighting Indians until war broke out here."

"Will you go back to Fork Union after the war?" "Probably; for awhile at least. Nothing much there for me though."

Jubal paused before saying, "Well, Andy, I guess I had better turn in. I've got to go back to Richmond tomorrow."

"Okay Jubal. Have a safe trip back. I'll stay by the fire awhile longer."

The two men parted. Jubal was up and on the road to Richmond before dawn. Andy was still asleep when Jubal left.

Chapter Thirteen

December 15, 1862

FOR THE FIRST time in many years, Winston Harrison was afraid. As a lawyer and Chief of Staff for Senator Aaron Hill, Harrison believed that he had wielded power as few men could. For years, he had crafted legislation, coercing Congressional staffers to have their patrons vote for the special interests that Senator Hill wanted to support. On occasion, he even convinced U.S. Supreme Court Justices concerning actions that they should take on behalf of big money interests. He had been content with his position, answering only to the Senator and to certain special interests. He was extremely confident in his ability, having helped advance the Senator to chair the most important committees and subcommittees. Even his secret life as Magnus, the high priest of treason and head of the Brotherhood, had gone well. He had netted several hundreds of thousands of dollars in personal wealth. And his liaisons with young women from the orphanage, although ending in their undetected deaths, had given him great physical and emotional satisfaction. But now, things were changing, and he felt afraid.

The fear started a month earlier when he learned from the president that half of his Brotherhood organization had been killed when the U.S. Army, Franklin Stone, and Allan Pinkerton had raided the Maryland farm where he warehoused Union weapons to be sold to the South. The fear grew when many of his remaining men were killed while attacking the Jenkins farm. And it grew exponentially when he learned that Stone and Kaitlin Jenkins had survived. He realized that the president had told only a select few men about the raid on the farm and he feared that becoming a suspect would eventually cause him to be executed for treason.

Harrison walked out of the nation's capitol and headed toward the taxi stand in front of the north wing. The ride home went relatively quickly. However, during the ride, he decided that it was time to take his money and leave Washington. But first, he would have to remove the only two people who might be able to identify him.

Arriving at his run down home on Adams Mill Road, Harrison put on a rain slicker and placed the deadly removal tool in his pocket. And just to be sure, he loaded and pocketed a small revolver in case his primary plan went awry. Saddling his horse, Harrison returned to the district where he found a suitable pub at which to leave the animal while he continued to his destination on foot.

Softly knocking on the front door, Harrison took the straight razor from the pocket of his slicker and readied it for use. Mrs. Burkis, the blind man's wife, answered the door as Harrison expected she would. Recognizing him immediately from her days in the orphanage, Mrs. Burkis invited Harrison to step inside.

"Mr. Harrison, Merry Christmas. What a pleasant surprise. Won't you come in?"

"Thank you, Mrs. Burkis, and Merry Christmas to you. I'm sorry to intrude on your evening, but I need to talk with your husband, Roger."

Mrs. Burkis closed the door and turned to get her husband when Harrison grabbed a fist full of thick black hair on the back of her head and sharply pulled downward, raising her chin upward and exposing her neck, which he slashed with the straight razor. He quickly slashed her throat twice more to be sure that she would die as quickly as possible. Initially, she had started to call her husband's name, but that changed when she felt the pain of having her hair violently pulled. She was only able to let out a short cry of surprise when all verbal communications ceased. The sound that came out of her throat was mixed with burbling blood. Her body writhed in spasms, blood squirting all over Harrisons hands, face and rain slicker. Harrison eased Mrs. Burkis to the floor with his fist full of her thick black hair.

Roger Burkis heard his wife answer the door and started for the living room door when he heard unfamiliar and threatening sounds. Feeling for his desk, Burkis removed a small revolver and walked toward the living room. Harrison moved across the living room and was waiting for Roger beside the doorway leading to the rest of the house. He was surprised to see a gun in Roger's right hand, but he quickly adapted to the changing situation. Harrison dropped the straight razor and grabbed Roger from behind, forcing his gun-hand toward the side of his head. Placing his finger over Roger's, Harrison pulled the trigger. The report of the gun was deafening.

Harrison's ears were ringing as he let Roger's body fall to the floor. He picked up the straight razor, wiped the blade on Roger's shirt, and placed the open razor in Roger's left hand. Checking to make sure that Roger Burkis was dead, Harrison wiped the blood and gore from his face and hands, locked the front door, removed his slicker, which he folded inside out. He turned down the gas lamps, and walked out of the back door of the Burkis home. If anyone heard the shot, they took no action. Harrison returned to the pub, retrieved his horse, and rode home.

Now that the major impediment had been removed, he cleaned his rain slicker and turned his thoughts to where he would go and where he would transfer his money. Harrison was still excited by the evening's kill and wished that he had ensnared another female victim on which to shed his physical and emotional arousal. He had a stiff drink of whiskey instead. And then he went to his cold bed where he suffered through a restless night, thinking about how his life was about to change.

Sunlight was streaming into the bedroom window when Harrison finally got out of bed, shaved, washed his hair and face to ensure no blood or gore remained, and started the long downhill walk to the Senate Office Building. The exercise seemed to relieve him of his anxieties, and he felt almost normal as he entered his office. Senator

Hill was gone to New York to spend time with constituents and special interests that were important to funding his next election campaign. He would be gone for at least a week, so Harrison was free to do as he wished.

Harrison found it difficult to concentrate on the work of crafting new legislation. Knowing that this was his last day, he took a break from his deskbound duties and walked around the offices. Subordinates scurried to look busy in his presence. He walked to the capitol grounds and visited the rotunda. His visit to the rotunda had always been empowering. This time, it was merely a symbol of all that he would lose by choosing a new life.

I will miss the trappings and power of government, he thought to himself.

At noon, he walked over to the bank and requested a draft for something over three hundred thousand dollars, the entire amount in his account. The bank clerk went to check the records and to make out the bank draft. He seemed to be gone an inordinate amount of time. When he returned, he was accompanied by the bank manger that held a sheaf of transaction records in his hands.

"Good afternoon, Mr. Harrison," the manger said. "I understand you want to withdraw your entire amount."

"Yes, I will be leaving for New York, and I will transfer my money to a bank there."

"I don't understand, sir. Our records show that you withdrew your money last week."

"Impossible," said a suddenly irate Harrison.

The manager pushed the sheaf of papers toward Harrison and said, "See right here, you received a bank draft for the entire amount from your account a week ago."

"There must be a mistake, I did no such thing. I want to see the bank president."

"I'm sorry, Mr. Harrison, the bank president is at a conference in New York and won't be back until Monday."

Mumbling to himself, Harrison left the bank and hurried across the street to another bank where he had another three hundred thousand dollar account. There too, he was told that he had withdrawn his entire amount a week earlier. The president of that bank was also at the New York financial conference and would not be available until Monday. Harrison left shaking with rage and fear.

"Who took my money?" he demanded to no one in particular.

Waiting until Monday to confront the bank presidents didn't fit into his plans. He wanted to leave immediately, tonight if possible, tomorrow at the latest. But he wasn't going to leave without his money.

Harrison had lunch and returned to the office where he tried unsuccessfully to pay attention to the work that needed be done. He couldn't concentrate on anything except his missing money. He refused to meet with his subordinates or with other Congressional staffers, citing pressing legislation that needed his full and immediate attention. He told them that he would meet with them on Monday afternoon.

As night fell on the capitol, Harrison waited, as was his habit, until the employees had gone for the day. He walked to the north wing of the capitol building to catch a ride home. Even though the hour was late, there was one carriage parked in the taxi zone. He gave his address to the driver and entered the carriage. After getting situated for the ride home, Harrison closed his eyes momentarily when both doors opened and two men entered the carriage from opposite sides. A burlap bag was forcefully placed over Harrison's head and tied to his neck. His hands were tied behind his back. The carriage started moving away from the capitol building. Harrison yelled for the driver to stop, but the carriage continued moving out of the district. Harrison tried to kick his abductors, all to no avail. The two burley men tied his ankles and beat him about the head until he stopped yelling. If he was afraid before, now he was terrified.

The carriage moved west out of the district. After what seemed like an hour to Harrison, the carriage stopped, and he was dragged into some kind of a building. He knew that because he felt the threshold plate of the doorway as he was dragged over it. Hearing the door close, Harrison yelled for his abductors to remove the bag on his head so that he could talk with them. They responded by beating and kicking him. Another door was closed and a throw bolt was locked into place. He could hear the fading footsteps of his two abductors as they walked away.

Harrison called out to see if someone else might be in the room, but no one answered. There were no sounds except his. He struggled for awhile, but getting nowhere by struggling, chose to analyze his situation and to approach the circumstances of his capture rationally.

After thinking about it for awhile, Harrison was able to slide his arms over his butt, and later with pain, he was able to slide his arms over his bound feet. With his hands now in front, he located the knot on the rope that held the burlap bag to his head. After several minutes of manipulation, Harrison removed the bag and realized that he was in a dark windowless room. Using his teeth, Harrison was able to untie the knot on the rope that bound his hands. After a minute of flexing painful arm muscles, Harrison untied his legs. Agonizingly he moved to a kneeling position. His back and his sides hurt where he had been beaten and kicked. Reaching out and using a nearby wall for leverage, Harrison slowly stood. With both hands touching the wall, Harrison shuffled his feet as he moved around the perimeter of the room. He neither tripped on anything on the floor, nor felt anything except the rough hewn panel of wood on the walls.

Finding the door, Harrison realized there was no doorknob. Pounding on the door, he could tell only that like the walls, the door was thick and strong. Harrison repeatedly tried to force the door open to no avail. All that did was to hurt his shoulders. He checked the left and right side of the door, but the hinges had been mounted on the outside. He had hoped that he would somehow be able to remove the hinge pins that held the door in the frame, but even that option had been denied to him. He checked the bottom of the door and found that it just barely cleared the cement floor.

Rationally, that left only the ceiling as a possible avenue for his escape. But he couldn't reach the ceiling, and there was nothing to stand on. He repeatedly jumped as high as he could, but he couldn't jump high enough. Although he had freed himself from the bindings that had held him, he was still a prisoner. "So," he thought, "I will have to overcome my abductors." Kneeling on his hands and knees, Harrison felt all over the cement floor for something that he might be able to use as a weapon. He found nothing.

Placing his back against the wall opposite the door, Harrison prepared himself to propel past his guards when they came for him. Even though he knew not what their purpose was, they would surely come for him. He waited.

If I can overcome them for even a few moments, I might have a chance to escape.

First, he heard footsteps, and then he heard the throw bolt sliding. He braced against the wall so that he could spring past his abductors as soon as the door opened. When the door did open, Harrison was frozen in his tracks. A look of astonishment crossed his face. There centered in the frame of the door was the one man he never expected to see under these circumstances.

"Senator Hill?" Harrison said completely baffled.

"Yes Winston, it is I."

Two very large men, one holding a lantern, stood behind the senator.

"I see you have relieved yourself of your bindings." Talking to the men behind him, Senator Hill continued by saying, "See, I told you he was smart."

Then to Harrison the senator said, "Come along Winston, we have a great deal to do before this night is finished."

Something in the way the senator said those words sent a chill down Harrison's spine. Never before had he heard Senator Hill's voice sound so cold or detached. Harrison didn't move. The lantern was handed to the senator as the two abductors pushed past Senator Hill. Harrison scurried to a corner where he scrunched down and whimpered.

"No," he cried out.

The two men placed metal manacles on Harrison's wrists and dragged him out of the wood paneled cell.

"Come now, Winston. This is so unlike you", the senator crooned.

"What are you going to do?" Harrison whined.

"Your fate has already been determined, Winston.

Tonight, you will die."

"Why?" Harrison asked sobbingly.

"That's what I'm about to explain, my boy. I believe that you have a right to know why you must die tonight." The three men climbed wooden stairs leading to the main part of the building. Harrison was dragged up the stairs, his legs hitting the leading edge of each stair.

"Come sit down," said the senator. "Would you like some water?"

Harrison answered by nodding his head up and down. For once in his life, words failed him.

Harrison accepted a metal cup of water, grasping it in both hands. He downed the cold liquid in two gulps. His body shook, but not because of the room temperature or the cold water. He was genuinely terrified. Tears ran down his face. His hands and the cup therein trembled.

"Winston, my boy, you are a hypocrite. You have been the instrument of death for many. I expected better of you. Aren't you even a little curious as to why you must die tonight?"

Harrison didn't answer.

"For years now, you have looked on me as a lazy gentleman farmer and legislator. I am both a farmer and a senator, but I am not lazy. I think that before this night has ended, you will discover that I am really quite industrious.

Several things may surprise you, however. For instance, you may be surprised to learn that we have been watching you closely for nearly a year, ever since your bank deposits substantially exceeded your salary. We know that you have been siphoning off nearly ten percent of most arms shipments from northern manufacturers. We weren't overly concerned about that because the government had already paid for the weapons and ammunition that you stole. We know that you were storing and distributing those arms from the Smith farm in Maryland. You made a few measly thousands of dollars

while we made millions lending money to the government and manufacturing the weapons that they needed to buy."

"We know that you are a pedophile. You sexually abuse young
women, and when you are finished with them, you kill them and
bury them in a makeshift graveyard in the woods on the hill behind
that shack you call a home. And since I am a family man with three
daughters of my own, I would like to spend the night torturing you
by extracting your genital organs before you die. But you may rest at
ease because torture does not meet our needs.

We know that you have formed a group of killers and thieves that
you call the Brotherhood. And that has become a problem for us."

"By now you must be wondering who *We* are. We are the men
who exercise real power in this country. We are a select number of
bankers, industrialists, railroad executives, Members of Congress,
and yes even the largest of farmers. We control virtually every facet of
life in this country. You and your Brotherhood have called unwanted
attention to how those weapons were stolen. You foolishly used secret
intelligence information that was provided to only a select few people. You were incredibly easy to identify as the traitor. However, there
are those in Congress, those who are not within our legion of power
brokers, who are questioning those of us who are profiting from the
war. And since the members of our circle of power have become
enormously wealthy at the expense of the American taxpayer and
the government, we can't afford for anyone outside our circle of
friends to push such an agenda, not even in the Congress. So tonight
you must die after confessing your sins in writing."

"I will never write such a confession," Harrison objected with a
bit of bravado.

"You don't have to. We have prepared and signed your confession for you. I have it right here, my boy," Aaron Hill said as he
displayed a signed handwritten letter.

"We have people who are experienced at duplicating handwriting. Yours was pathetically easy, I'm told."

"By now you realize that you are not the great and powerful
man that you thought Actually, you are vermin. And tonight, you

will be squashed like the irrelevant rodent that you are. For years, you strutted around our nation's capitol; you were pompous, conceited, and arrogant. You treated your subordinates poorly. You even thought you were better, smarter, and more important than those who really do wield national power. You thought we didn't know you, but we do. And now we are going to eliminate you and the need for a Congressional inquiry into war profiteering.

It is my wish that you burn in hell forever—and that those who you have tortured and killed will greet you at the door to perdition to testify against you. Goodbye, my boy. I won't miss you. You are already a distant and unpleasant faded memory. Oh, by the way, we removed the money from your bank accounts. Your ill-gotten money will pay for your death tonight. I just thought you might want to know."

Senator Hill stood and handed the signed letter to one of the three men who would become Harrison's executioners. "You know what to do," Hill said coldly as he walked out the front door.

One of the men stuffed a rag in Harrison's mouth and tied a long rectangular rag around his head and over his mouth to ensure that Harrison did not spit out the gag. Another man placed a chain around Harrison's waist and coupled the manacles to the chain with an iron padlock to keep the waist-chain and manacles in place. The first man then tied Harrison's ankles together, tying the rope extraordinarily tight. Harrison, again in pain, was dragged to the waiting carriage for the trip to the house on Adams Mill Road.

Harrison whimpered on and off during the hour-long trip back to the district. The two men ignored him. There was no conversation. There was only the sounds of horses' hooves on the hard pan dirt road and Harrison's whimpering.

Arriving at the house on Adams Mill Road, the driver dismounted and untied an empty barrel from the luggage compartment in the rear of the carriage. The two men remained in the carriage with Harrison. Rolling the barrel to the barn, the driver returned to the carriage where he retrieved a coiled rope, which he also took to the barn. Lighting a lantern in the barn, the driver led Harrison's unbridled horse outside, where he slapped the horse on the rump, causing the startled animal to run down the driveway and then down Adams Mill Road. The driver returned to the small barn where he stood on the top of the righted barrel, measured the rope, and lashed the rope several times around the exposed overhead beam. He tied the loose end with two half hitches, and then tucked the bitter end neatly under one of the lashings. He pulled on the rope above the noose, stretching the hemp strands with his weight.

The two abductors dragged Harrison into the barn where the driver was still standing on the barrel. The burley men lifted Harrison as high as they could. The driver placed Harrison's squirming head into the noose. Pulling the noose tight, the driver jumped down off the barrel and kicked the barrel out from under Harrison's feet.

The short drop off the barrelhead did not sever the spinal cord as would normally be the case on a professional gallows. Harrison remained conscious for several minutes. He thrashed about, his eyes bulged, and after a minute or so, his face began to show the tiny tell-tale red spots where blood from burst capillaries made its way under the surface of his skin. His bulging eyes similarly developed red spider lines from ruptured capillaries. Harrison passed out after nearly ten minutes of thrashing around. His face turned blue from the lack of oxygen, but his heart continued beating for another twenty minutes. The limp body spasmodically rippled as muscular reflexes reacted to the sudden loss of life-sustaining blood and air. Toward the end, the three men moved closer to the partially open barn door to breathe fresh air as Harrison's bladders voided.

"A fitting end to a cowardly pedophile," said the driver to no one in particular.

Shortly after death was confirmed, one of the abductors took the signed confession and enclosed the document in Harrison's right hand. He held Harrison's hand in place for several minutes until the hand's muscles retained the letter without external support. He up-righted the barrel and removed the gag, waist chain, and shackles, and untied the ankle restraints from Harrison's limp body. Then he again knocked over the barrel as if the barrel had been knocked over by Harrison's thrashing body. The driver extinguished the kerosene lantern and returned it to its original position on a wooden shelf. The door was left wide open so that anyone passing the building in the light of day would see Harrison's remains. The three men walked without conversation to the carriage, where the driver took the reins and leisurely drove into the district. Their gruesome night's work done, the killers returned to their homes and families.

Chapter Fourteen

January 2, 1863

"HA, HA, HA!" laughed Pinkerton. "This is the one place I never ever expected to find you, Franklin."

"Oh, shut up, Pinkerton".

"Sorry, Franklin, but the president wants to see us." "Well, tell the president that I can't go to the executive mansion because I'm in jail."

"The president knows where you are. He told me to come get you."

"How did he find out where I am?"

"The police sergeant sends him a report each morning. The report had you listed as having been arrested for drunk and disorderly and for breaking up a bar and about ten soldiers. Five of them are in the hospital. That surely must have been some brawl, Frank."

"Yeah, a real donnybrook," Stone answered sarcastically.

"Well, let's get you out of here and get you cleaned up a bit before we go see the president."

"Tell him I like it here. I'm not leaving."

"He said you would say something like that, so there are twenty cavalry soldiers outside who would dearly love to escort you to the Executive Mansion. But I don't think you would get there in one piece, Frank. They heard about the donnybrook too."

"Okay, okay."

The jailer unlocked the door and returned Stone's property to him without comment.

"Man, I've got one hell of a headache," said Stone.

"You must have been drinking American whiskey," Pinkerton laughed. "Scotch whiskey won't give you a headache," Pinkerton said, widely grinning.

"Well you are a Scotsman, Allan, and you're giving me a headache right now."

"Just doing my job, Frank. Come along now."

"You don't have to talk so loud. I can hear you," said Stone while holding his head in both hands.

The two men stopped by the Willard Hotel where employees took one look at Stone and gave him a wide berth. Stone cleaned himself up in the restroom and had a cup of coffee in the lobby before he and Pinkerton headed across the street to the see the president.

"Good morning Allan, I see you found Franklin okay."

"Yes sir, but it was the twenty soldiers that convinced him to come."

"Good morning, Frank."

"Good morning, Mr. President. At least I'm guessing that it's a good morning, sir."

"What happened, Frank?"

"Nothing much really, sir. I guess I was celebrating the New Year a little too much last night. I had been drinking pretty much all day at different places. I was in the corner of the bar having a quiet drink before heading back to the hotel when some soldiers got a little rambunctious. I had to straighten them out."

"Five soldiers are in the hospital, Frank."

"I'm really sorry about that sir, but they didn't take to just talking."

"Well I'm sorry I missed the fracas, Frank. I haven't seen a brawl like that since I left Kentucky," Lincoln laughed.

"I could have used your help, sir."

"It sure doesn't sound like you needed my help, Frank. Plus, I'm sure there's some law about the President of the United States brawling in public. I'll have to wait until I go back to private life. But thanks for the offer," the president said, grinning.

"How about some coffee, Frank?"

"Anything that will stop my head from hurting will be appreciated, sir.

"We better have the doctor look at you before you leave. You just may have a concussion, Frank."

"Sir, I'm an Irishman. Haven't you heard that you can't hurt an Irishman by hitting him in the head?"

"Well, let's have him look at you anyway, Mr. Stone."

"Yes, Mr. President. Thank you."

Once coffee had been served, the president got down to business.

"Frank, how about briefing me on your activities since Winston Harrison was found hanged in his barn last month."

"Well sir, it's been one hell of a grisly investigation. Even though the police have deemed the hanging a suicide, it is my opinion that he was murdered. There were bruises on his neck and on the trunk of his body; bruises that indicate he had been beaten and kicked. There were bruises on his wrists. Either his hands were tied, or more likely, his wrists were manacled. There were bruises across his lower back, indicating that he might have been wearing a waist chain on which the manacles were attached. There were bruises on his lower legs as if his ankles had been tied with rope prior to his being hanged. I feel quite sure Harrison was murdered."

"So Harrison was a victim?"

"He was a victim of being murdered, but he was also guilty of many other murders and of selling arms to the South. He was a very bad man, Mr. President."

"What other murders?"

"We think that he was probably responsible for murdering Mr. and Mrs. Burkis, the blind man who was providing freight and security services for the army.

Investigation reveals that Mr. Burkis was blinded in the war and came to Washington seeking a pension, which he never received. Several months after he arrived in Washington, he suddenly started a business, questionably winning several service contracts with the army. We think he was somehow tied to Harrison and was, at least initially, moving the stolen weapons past checkpoints that were manned by his employees. He may, or may not, have known about the weapons. Based on the number of employees who have since disappeared as a result of the death of Mr. and Mrs. Burkis and the failure of their company, we think that those employees were members of the Brotherhood."

"We think that Harrison was also responsible for the deaths of two families. The men were buyer agents for Union arms manufacturers. I had interviewed both of the agents about a year ago, and I felt then that they were somehow involved in the disappearance of the weapons and ammunition. However, the paperwork reflected that the arms were stolen during or maybe even after delivery to the army."

"More grizzly than that, however, is the graveyard that we found as a result of the written confession. The graveyard is behind the Harrison house in a remote part of the district. It contains the bodies of over thirty young girls who went missing from the orphanage. It took two weeks for a whole company of soldiers to uncover their graves on a steep forested hillside. You remember that you directed me to look into how the girls came to be missing. I did, but nothing led me to finding them until we read the written confession that was taken from Harrison's body. We doubt that he wrote the confession, but the information appears to be accurate. Harrison was a very bad man and certainly deserved what he got."

"I believe that it was Harrison who organized the Brotherhood, just as the confession says. He may not have ordered the killing of Colonel Jenkins, but he was ultimately responsible for Ben's death," Pinkerton added.

"And that, Mr. President, concludes the three investigations that you assigned to me. I'm ready to return to New York, if you please."

"Well Franklin, it seems to me that you won't be finished until you find out who is responsible for killing Harrison. There may be a larger organization at play here. If they knew that much about Harrison before they killed him, enough to fabricate a written confession that appears to have been true in all respects, then they may be more insidious than was Harrison."

"I've thought about that, Mr. President. I have no ideas as to who they may be, but certainly it was someone who had contact with Harrison and knew more about him than any one person would normally know. Frankly, I think they did the nation and the district a great service. Do you want me to continue to look into the Harrison killing, sir?"

"Yes, definitely. I want to know if there is a larger threat at stake. Did Harrison intrude on a larger operation? I definitely want to know, and I do appreciate the fact that you are willing to stay and to serve and to work with Allan on this matter."

Turning to Pinkerton, the president continued by asking, "How about you, Allan? Do you have anything to add?"

"No, Mr. President. Frank detailed everything that I am aware of."

"Okay Allan, thank you for briefing me this morning. If you don't mind, I would like to talk with Frank privately. If you have nothing further, then I'll say good day."

"Thank you Mr. President," Pinkerton said as he stood to leave. "I'll see you later, Frank."

"Okay, thanks for bailing me out of jail, Allan."

"Don't thank me. Thank the president, said Allen grinning."

Allan Pinkerton closed the president's door and returned to his office in the district.

"Franklin, I am concerned about you. You don't usually drink to excess. What's going on with you?"

"It's personal, sir."

"Well, I figured that, Frank. Talk to me, man to man."

"Well Mr. President, I just can't get Kaitlin out of my head. More importantly, I can't get her out of my heart."

"I see. I figured as much. Frank, I want you to stay here in the executive mansion for a couple of days. I really do want to have the physician look you over, but more importantly, I want you to relax. You are as tight as a snare drum."

"Mr. President, I would be more comfortable in a hotel."

"It's just for a couple of days, Frank. I'm not asking you to live here, God forbid. I really must insist. You see I feel personally responsible for Kaitlin's leaving."

Stone's head snapped up. His face hardened as he asked, "How are you responsible?"

"Well Frank, Kaitlin was extremely distraught. She kept saying that she wanted to get away from the war. She wanted to return to what family she has left in Ireland. I had the staff arrange for her to return to Ireland. So if there's anyone to blame, blame me."

After a long silence, Stone's face softened as he said, "No, Mr. President. You were just trying to help Kaitlin. I likely would have done the same under the circumstances. I guess the really hard part is that I don't even know where she is. I can't write to her, and I don't know how she is. She just dropped out of my world, and there's a really big hole where she was."

"Frank, we will talk about this later. Now I want you to go upstairs and go to bed. I'll have your meals brought to you, and I want the doctor to look after you. Will you do that?"

Stone looked blankly at the president and nodded his head in the affirmative. A staff member escorted Stone to an upstairs bedroom, the same bedroom that Kaitlin had occupied before returning to Ireland. But there was no trace of Kaitlin in the room. Stone undressed and went to bed. Later that evening, the president's physician checked Stone and decided that he was likely going to live. There was no sign of concussion, but he recommended that Stone lay off brawling for awhile. Even the physician had heard about Stone's New Year donnybrook.

Stone awoke early on the second day. After stretching, he had to admit he felt much better. He dressed and went downstairs to the kitchen where he poured a cup of black coffee. A breathless staff member entered the kitchen saying, "Mr. Stone, I was afraid that I had missed you. The president asked me to notify you that he wants to meet with you here in the Executive Mansion promptly at one o'clock this afternoon."

"One o'clock. Okay, please advise the president that I will be here at one."

Stone returned to his room at the Willard Hotel where he changed clothes and went to the Metropolitan Men's Club for an extended bath, a haircut, and a much needed shave. Feeling more alive than he had in weeks, Stone walked to a café, ate lunch, and returned to the Executive Mansion for his meeting with the president.

Promptly at one, a staff member escorted Stone to the president's personal office upstairs. He was surprised to see that Pinkerton was in the office too.

"Hi Frank," said Pinkerton grinning. "You look a whole lot better than the last time I saw you."

"Yeah, I guess I was a sight to behold."

"Good afternoon gentlemen," the president said as he entered his office.

"I don't have much time. I have a meeting at the War Department in a few minutes, but I wanted to meet with you first. Have a seat gentleman. Frank, you seem greatly rested."

"I am, sir."

"Good, because I need you here—all of you—no holes. I need all of your expertise and talent. I have another trip for you."

"Yes sir, I'm ready."

"Good. The staff has arranged for you to board a ship this evening. It will sail early in the morning, so you will have to catch the afternoon train to New York. I do have to go to the War Department now, but Allan will explain the details of this mission. I expect that you may be gone for as long as three months, so please pack accordingly. You have my best wishes and may God bless you."

"Is this a particularly difficult mission, sir?"

"It could turn out to be, but I'm hopeful that you can successfully pull it off without becoming a danger to yourself or others, Franklin. Now I really do have to go. Good luck."

Stone and Pinkerton stood as the president hurried out of the door, leaving the two men to finish their business in the privacy of his office.

"What's this all about, Allan?"

"Well, as the president said, you're going on another trip."

Pinkerton withdrew an envelope from his coat pocket saying, "You will find a train ticket for the three o'clock train to New York City. You will arrive in New York about ten this evening. There is a first class ticket for the sailing of the *Britannia Rose*, which leaves at seven in the morning. You will arrive in London in about three weeks, depending on the weather. Once you get to London, you will have to arrange for transportation to Ireland. My friends in Scotland contacted Her Majesty's Secret Service and located Kaitlin. You will find her address and some particulars about the village in this envelope."

Handing the envelope to Stone, Pinkerton smiled and said, "The president cares a great deal about you, Frank. And he really does hope that you will be able to convince Kaitlin to return to Washington with you. I'm not supposed to tell you this, but he is having Kaitlin's house rebuilt as it once was. He and Senator Hill convinced the arms manufacturers to fund the rebuilding of the house, since they were inadvertently responsible for the fire. His staff located the original architect and construction company. They started working on the house a week ago."

"I don't know what to say."

"You don't have time to say anything. Just get packed and meet that train. And of course, get Kaitlin back here. By the way, Kaitlin has been using her maiden name. That's why we couldn't find her on the manifest of the steamship that took her to London. However, there was only one Kaitlin on the manifest, so we tracked her down using her maiden name, which by the way is O'Riley. And don't worry about Hermes. I'll take him home with me until you get back. Now get going, you're almost out of time to pack, check out of the Willard and get to the train station."

"Thanks Allan, and please thank the president."

"Get a move on, Frank. There will be time enough for thanks when you and Kaitlin get back to Washington."

Both men left the president's office. The staff wondered why both men were grinning. Pinkerton took Hermes from the hotel's stable and placed him in the paddock behind his home before returning to his office. Stone packed, checked out of the hotel, and caught a taxi to the train station. He made his connection to the train with only minutes to spare. The train ride took longer than anticipated; it was close to midnight before they entered the New York train station. Because of the late hour, he decided not to visit his mother. Stone went directly to the pier and settled in for the night on the British ship.

His first class quarters were surprisingly comfortable. It was his first Atlantic crossing and he just couldn't stop grinning. He went over the papers that Pinkerton had given him, reading, then re-reading and then re-reading them again. He was headed to Ireland to get Kaitlin, but it was also the land of his Irish ancestors; a land that he had only heard stories about from his father. His British mother usually pooh-poohed the stories as "just so much Irish blarney." But his Grandmother and Grandfather assured him, with twinkling eyes, that the stories, even those of leprechauns and magical fairies, were absolutely true. It had been many years since Stone had been this excited.

***

IT TOOK SEVERAL weeks before the linemen and telegraphers of the wagon train accepted Andy as one of their own. When they weren't laying or retrieving cable on battlefields, and when they weren't ducking bullets and artillery, or when they weren't standing watch sending and receiving traffic, they sat around the campfire at night and swapped stories of boyhood life in small town Virginia.

Andy was an outsider, having been raised on a plantation in Georgia. Even though they were raised in the south, they knew nothing about plantations. Most of the men were raised closer to Washington D.C. than they were to the large plantations of the Deep South. They listened to Andy's stories about farming and the genteel life of ladies and gentlemen with awe. To them, life in the Deep South seemed somehow idyllic, especially since they had mainly been the sons of merchants, teachers, and blacksmiths. Oh, they all had small gardens that they tended. Every family grew gardens for vegetables, but the really large farms outside of the towns were nonetheless called farms, not plantations. But the men of the wagon train had things in common with Andy, too.

They all recalled cooling themselves from hot humid southern summers in cold water streams, of fishing and hunting, getting their first horse, and teasing girls at school until they came of an age where female companionship was pleasing.

As young boys, they had each been rubbed raw by mothers who ensured each Saturday night that the children were scrubbed clean for church the next day. They recalled coming home from church and changing into work clothes, wringing the neck of one or more plump chickens, gutting and bleeding them dry, putting pots of water on a wood stove, and pouring boiling hot water into a metal tub where they hung the chicken from a rope on a tree branch after soaking the chicken in the hot water to soften the feathers. They recalled having spent over an hour pulling feathers, then taking the bird indoors for their mothers to cook.

Sunday supper was usually attended by friends and neighbors, or the local minister sitting at tables under a spreading oak tree. Of course, the kids had to change back to Sunday go-to-meeting clothes if the minister showed up for supper. And then as the telegraphers got to know each other better, they talked of wives and girlfriends left behind and the lack of adequate mail service with which to stay in touch.

When Andy returned from the battlefields with information gleaned by surveillance and tapping Union telegraph lines, he would check his notes and prepare a written report to be transmitted by wagon train telegraphers. It was then that they learned how much more dangerous Andy's job was when compared with theirs in the relative safety behind the lines of battle. And when Andy wasn't tapping Union telegraph lines, he took turns standing watch with wagon train telegraphers for the purpose of receiving administrative traffic—messages from Richmond and from the various divisional headquarters that had telegraph operators assigned to their commands. Even while standing night watches in the telegraph wagon train, he protected his fist by asking others do the transmitting. Nonetheless, the wagon train telegraphers appreciated the extra respite they received while Andy stood watch in the message center, a chore that was not part of his job description. Andy came to be close friends with the linemen and the operators of the telegraph wagon train. Like other men in combat, he came to regard them as his extended family.

<hr />

THE NEWS MEDIA had been running the story of the Brotherhood and the murders around the district for nearly a month. They repeatedly questioned Senator Hill, who stated for the record, that neither he nor his staff knew anything about the secret life of his former chief of staff. He stated that he was just as surprised to learn of Harrison's misdeeds as was the general public, but that his work at the capitol had been adequate.

The Congress, both the House and Senate, took no official interest in the violent death and confession of Winston Harrison; however in private, individual Members of Congress were just as interested in the case as were the gawkers outside the capitol building. After a month of sensationalism, some contrived by overzealous reporters, Winston Harrison became old news. The stories about Harrison were seemingly buried along with Harrison the man.

Chapter Fifteen

February 1863

AFTER THREE WEEKS at sea, Stone was more than anxious to get ashore. The seas had been calm, and overall, the trip had been a pleasurable experience. Meals had been bland but plentiful, and the ship's master went out of his way to ensure that Stone's first Atlantic crossing was an enjoyable experience. Stone sat at the captain's table during evening meals, and the two men became fast friends when Stone asked to see the boilers below decks, and asked many questions about life at sea for both the ship's master and the crew. After three weeks without real physical exertion, Stone was anxious to walk the streets of London.

The *Britannia Rose* sat at anchor all night before entering port the next morning. It took nearly an hour for the ship to tie up at the London pier and for Customs inspectors to process the paperwork that would allow passengers to disembark. Stone had packed the night before and waited patiently for permission to leave the ship. He was surprised when the purser knocked on the cabin door and introduced him to an official visitor.

"Good morning, Colonel Stone. I'm Colonel Edward Jones, military attaché at the U.S. Embassy here in London. I've been asked to see you to the train station for your trip to Dublin."

"Good Morning, Colonel. I'm curious, how did you know that I would be arriving in London this morning?"

"Official dispatches are offloaded onto a pilot boat while the ship is at anchor outside the harbor awaiting permission to enter the port on the morning tide. There are a lot of twists and turns up the Thames River, so ships don't enter at night. The pilot boat takes the dispatches to Customs House, where they are sorted for Her Majesty's Government and the various embassies. I was alerted to your arrival earlier this morning."

"Well Colonel Jones, I'm sorry for intruding on your schedule."

"Please call me Ed. The letter from the president made it clear that the Ambassador was to provide all possible embassy assistance and courtesies; so you get me," Ed grinned.

"Okay Ed, please call me Frank. I am definitely in need of your service, as I have never before been to England or to Ireland."

"It can be a little confusing, Frank. It took me over a year to learn my way around. You will be going by train from London to Chester. Normally it takes about two or three days, but depending on conditions, it could take longer. The rails from Chester to Holyhead, where you catch a ferry to Dublin, won't be completed until later this year, so I have arranged for a private carriage. The ferry company does provide a wagon for passengers and their luggage, but it's very crowded and slow. The wagon takes a good three days. Even with a private carriage, you will have to stay at a hotel overnight. You will arrive in Holyhead about noon the next day. So your trip could take between five and seven days."

"I didn't realize that it was so complicated going from England to Ireland."

"The most direct way is to take a ship from London, around the coast, and into Dublin, but after your Atlantic crossing, I expect that you have seen enough of the sea for awhile."

"Yes, I need to get out and walk around. Three weeks of just sitting and laying around saps the energy out of a man who is used to being active."

"Your train leaves in an hour, so we had better get going."

A stevedore loaded Stone's two suitcases onto a waiting carriage. Stone tipped the stevedore, after which the carriage driver headed to the train station only a few blocks away. Stone purchased tickets to Chester, watched as his luggage was loaded into a first class car, and said goodbye to Colonel Jones. He suddenly felt very alone. Even the English language, as spoken by the British, sounded foreign to his ear.

Stopping every thirty or forty miles for fuel and water, the trip to Chester took three days. He was glad that he had taken the advice of Colonel Jones to purchase first class accommodations. He would not have wanted to travel for three days in a crowded coach. The seat in the first class car made into a bed, and he had enough privacy when he pulled the curtain over the window in the door to exercise. Arriving in Chester, the driver of a private carriage held a small sign with Stone's name. Once loaded, the driver headed without conversation through the city toward Holyhead.

Even though Stone was anxious to get to Dublin, he was glad when they finally stopped for the night at an inn. After getting situated in his room, Stone took a long walk through the countryside. He returned to the inn after several hours of walking, had dinner and went to bed., but he didn't rest. He was too concerned about how Kaitlin would react to his arrival on her front door step unannounced. Also, the bed was not particularly comfortable—it sagged in the middle—and he just couldn't fall asleep. He tossed and turned and by morning felt absolutely miserable.

Just before noon, the carriage pulled into the ferry station. Stone paid the driver and tipped him well. The words "thanks, mate," were the closest thing to a conversation that the two men had during the day and half trip. Taking his bags into the station, Stone bought a ticket and waited for the one o'clock ferry to Dublin. By four in the afternoon, he was situated in a Dublin hotel on the west side of the city, near what had once been the village of Se Fheirm.

According to the notes that Allan Pinkerton had provided, Se Fheirm (meaning six farms) started as a collective as farm owners banded together in the mid- 1500's to sell their crops to Dublin buyers. Where previously the farmers had competed with each other, they realized increased earnings through the collective. In the years that followed, enterprising local residents began opening shops to sell hardware and other goods to the farmers, and a small community was formed. However, as Dublin expanded into a large metropolitan city, Se Fheirm had been devoured sometime after Kaitlin O'Riley and her parents had immigrated to the United States. Her childhood home was now just part of the larger city.

Kaitlin's uncle, Duncan O'Riley, was a retired iron worker and shipbuilder who had worked throughout his life in Dublin. He had never married, but he had a modest house (Number 64 College Road) near Phoenix Park, about two miles west of downtown Dublin.

Stone sat reading his notes in a hotel just two blocks away from that address. But he would wait until the morning before walking over to try to convince Kaitlin to become his bride. First, he had a number of things that he wanted to accomplish.

He found a public bathhouse and enjoyed a hot bath, haircut, and shave. He brought a new suit. The tailor worked all day to have it ready that afternoon. He went to a jeweler where he bought an engagement ring with the largest diamond that he could afford and two gold wedding bands, one for Kaitlin and one for himself. He returned to the hotel, had an early dinner, and then walked for several miles in an effort to wear off the uneasiness that he felt. It was well after dark when he finally returned to the hotel for the night.

The next morning he carefully shaved, dressed himself in his new suit, and had a very small breakfast, as his stomach wasn't up to his usual large morning meal. He dawdled for a couple of hours, waiting for a more appropriate time of day to visit his beloved. Stuffing the rings in his left jacket pocket, Stone stiffly walked the two blocks to 64 College Road. He was so nervous, he was afraid that he was going to throw up.

Stone walked up the short walkway, stepped up on the cement step in front of the row house, and knocked on the door. He waited, but there was no answer. He knocked all the harder, and again no one answered the door. He turned, stepped back down onto the walkway, and was about to leave when the door finally opened. As he turned, he could see Kaitlin standing in the doorway. He immediately forgot everything that he had rehearsed for the past month.

"Kaitlin, I…"

That's as much as he was able to say. Kaitlin kissed him hard on the lips. Stone lightly returned the kiss. Then Kaitlin kissed him long and passionately. Duncan O'Riley, who by then was standing in the doorway asked, "Is this someone who you want to introduce me to? Or is he just a passing fancy?" Kaitlin blushed.

"Oh, uncle, this is Franklin Stone from New York City in America."

"You're smaller than I thought you would be. Based on what Kaitlin told me, I thought that you would be at least ten feet tall," Duncan O'Riley said, grinning widely. Come in, Mr. Stone. Come in, please."

"Thank you Mr. O'Riley," said Stone as he took Duncan's hand in a firm handshake and entered the house.

"Please, call me Duncan."

"Only if you will call me Frank."

"Done and done," O'Riley said, still grinning. "May I serve tea?" asked Kaitlin.

"Only if you don't have anything a bit more stout," said Stone.

"Aye, a man after my own heart; a bit of the Irish, if you please girl," Duncan beamed.

Kaitlin gave both men a disapproving look and served two short glasses of Irish whiskey saying, "Here is your devil's brew, and it being just so early in the morning."

Both men ignored Kaitlin's scolding, clinked their glasses together, and downed the amber liquid, finishing with an audible "ahhh."

"Welcome to Dublin, Franklin Stone." "Thank you for that, Mr. O'Riley."

Feeling left out of the conversation, Kaitlin asked, "And what exactly has brought you all the way to Ireland from America, Mr. Stone."

"You have, Kaitlin O'Riley."

Smiling, Kaitlin teased, "And I'm supposing you thought that you could just waltz in here and sweep me off me feet and carry me off to Washington, Mr. Stone?" as she turned toward the kitchen to return the bottle of whiskey to the shelf, sporting a sly smile.

"No, not at all. I had no such intention."

"No?" said Kaitlin as she instantly spun around to face Stone with her hands on her hips and the look of extreme hurt on her face.

"No, I came to ask your uncle for your hand in marriage. I came to marry you here in Ireland and to visit the land of my ancestors with my new wife."

Kaitlin's mouth opened, but no words came out.

"Hush girl, this is talk only for men," said Duncan.

Kaitlin was suddenly flush with anger, except she didn't know who she was angry with more, Franklin or her uncle. She continued to stand with her mouth open but the flash in her eyes let both men know that they were suddenly on very dangerous ground.

Duncan continued by saying, "Mr. Stone, as you know, Kaitlin is no mere girl anymore. Aye, she has no dowry to speak of, and she is a bit worn. And as the widow Jenkins, she needs no such permission from me to marry. But have you thought this through, man? Do you really want to marry a woman of such foul temper?"

Both men were enjoying the moment—standing there smiling at each other, knowing that Kaitlin was just itching to smack them both.

"A bit worn, is it? I'll show you a bit worn," as she uncorked the bottle and took a full mouthful of Irish whiskey, which she downed in one gulp. Coughing and sputtering, she grabbed up the broom from the corner, slammed the whiskey bottle on a table, and attacked the two men with the broom.

Both men feigned extreme fear and ran out of the front door while laughing. Once outside, Duncan smiled and said, "I think I need another drink."

The two men walked to a nearby pub. Meanwhile, Kaitlin, who had expected both men to reenter, was at a complete loss over where the two men had suddenly gone. The more she waited, the more she fumed. The more she fumed, the angrier she got until suddenly her anger thawed, her heart warmed, and she thought, *He came to marry me.* She smiled and ran upstairs to the bedroom where she changed into a dress that was more flattering of her youthful figure.

"I want to be his wife," Kaitlin said out loud. "I do so want to be his wife. Where are they?"

Suddenly, she was fuming again with her fists doubled up on her hips. She wanted to hold Franklin and he was probably at some pub, drinking Irish whiskey with her bachelor uncle.

The two men returned after a little more than an hour. As they entered the parlor, Franklin got down on one knee in front of Kaitlin, produced the rings, and said, "Kaitlin, will you be my wife? Will you marry me?"

Kaitlin hesitated out of pure orneriness for having been left alone.

Stone continued, "Kaitlin I don't want to live without you anymore. And both the President of the United States and Chief of the United States Secret Service join with me in begging you for your hand."

Kaitlin immediately envisioned the mental picture of Mr. Lincoln and Mr. Pinkerton standing patiently behind Stone who was still on bended knee. She giggled and then said, "Oh Franklin, stand up and kiss me. I want to be your wife more than anything in the whole world." He stood and kissed her, long and passionately. Duncan politely coughed and left the room. Stone placed the engagement ring on Kaitlin's finger. "We will have a good life, I promise you, Kaitlin." She kissed Stone again.

The rest of the week was taken up by arranging with the local Catholic priest for a wedding mass and for notifying relatives, friends, and neighbors. The wedding was held at the church on Friday, just before noon. The wedding reception was held in the O'Riley home, as was the custom in Dublin. The reception lasted well into the nighttime, and few people were particularly concerned when the bride and the groom left for a downtown Dublin hotel after having said their farewells to Duncan.

For two weeks they traveled all over Ireland, visiting the ancestral homes of their forbearers—and making love. For the first time in several years, both Kaitlin and Franklin felt at ease in the world. Then suddenly, it was time to return to Washington. They stopped in Dublin, spending the night at Duncan's house while Stone arranged to take a ship directly to London. The one-day trip to London found them in a downtown hotel while Franklin arranged passage to New York. They were fortunate in that they were able to book passage for the return trip on the *Britannia Rose*. The ship's master greeted them warmly, and in fact, the return trip felt more like an extended honeymoon.

Mr. and Mrs. Stone arrived in New York City where they stayed at the Grand Hotel pending travel to Washington. Stone penned a short letter to his mother saying that he and Kaitlin had married, but that they were unable to stop by as they had to leave for Washington very early the next morning.

They arrived in Washington the next day, stopping by to see the Pinkertons. Joan and Kaitlin cried tears of joy upon seeing each other and for the marriage of Kaitlin and Frank Stone. Frank went out to the barn and saddled Hermes, then hitched the two Percheron geldings to the carriage. Allan refused to take any pay for the feeding and caring of the horses. He helped load the luggage into the carriage and rode with Kaitlin to the Willard Hotel, while Frank rode Hermes. While Kaitlin settled into the hotel suite, Franklin and Allan talked about the war.

Chapter Sixteen

March 1863

Captain Andrew Davis was ordered to return to Richmond for a meeting at the office of the Confederate Secret Service. He said his goodbyes to the linemen and telegraphers and headed back to Richmond on the afternoon train, arriving just after three in the afternoon. Walking from the train station to the office, he saw little change in the city. He stopped by the paymaster's office collecting another three months pay and arrived at the office a little before four in the afternoon. There was a great deal of activity. Officers from General Lee's planning staff were heatedly and animatedly talking about potential strategies for the next big battle in the Union's effort to take the Confederate capitol. Jubal left them to their arguments and followed Andy into a private office that the two men shared when they were in town.

"It's good to see you Andy."

"You too, Jubal. What's going on?"

"We have received information that General Hooker and his Army of the Potomac may be considering another attempt on Richmond."

"My God, Jubal, not again."

"I'm afraid so, Andy."

"How many times have they tried so far, Jubal?"

"Well, there was the Battle of Bull Run in '61, the Seven Days Battles in '62, the Second Battle of Bull Run in December of '62, and the Battle of Fredericksburg, all fought for the purpose of taking the capitol."

"And here we go again, Jubal."

Jubal shook his head in the affirmative.

"Andy, we're not getting the information we need from listening to Union telegraph lines. They have developed a number of codes that have effectively blocked us from reading their messages. Yet, they seem to be able to read ours, even some of our encrypted messages. We want you to look over the situation and see what you can come up with in a relatively short time for collecting information on their operations for a new campaign."

"Okay, I'll see what I can do, Jubal."

"On the good side, at least you can sleep in your bed at the inn for awhile. My one-legged friend has been keeping your room for your return. Of course, he gripes a lot about not being paid for an empty room, but he's a trooper. He just likes to gripe," Jubal grinned.

"So do you, as I remember, Jubal."

Jubal gave Andy a look of complete innocence. Both men laughed.

Andy hired a taxi and went to the Boars Head Inn where he was greeted by the owner, Will, as a long lost friend. They talked about the Battle of Fredericksburg over a warm beer, and then Will returned to his work. Andy went out to the paddock where he brushed, fed, and watered his horse.

After nearly three months of absence, the animal was ambivalent toward Andy, who tried to overcome the horse's feeling of uncertainty by talking soothingly to the animal. When Andy tried to bridle him however, the horse ran to the other side of the paddock. It took more than a few minutes to get the horse to accept the bridle. Tying the reins to a paddock rail, Andy fetched his saddle and blanket from the barn. But when he tried to saddle the animal, the horse shied and bucked halfheartedly. Finally saddled, Andy led his horse out of the paddock gate and mounted the animal for a short ride. Again, the horse bucked halfheartedly, but quickly came under control when Andy kicked its underside with the heel of his boot.

After leaving the driveway and riding away from the inn, the horse suddenly turned and made a dash for the paddock. Andy reined the horse into a tight right-hand circle until the horse realized that he wasn't going to get to go back to the barn. So instead, he tried to bite Andy's right knee. Andy started back down the road when he heard a familiar voice.

"Looks like your horse has turned barn sour, Andy."

"Hi, Jubal. Yes, it's been awhile since he's been ridden. I'll take him down the road a couple of miles and come back. He'll get the idea of what he's supposed to do over the next few days."

"See you for supper?"

"Yeah, Jubal. In about an hour okay?" "Perfect. See you then."

Andy studied Union dispatches for two days and came to the conclusion that the Confederacy would not be able to break the Union codes in time to garner pertinent intelligence information about the next attack on the capitol. In late March, he met with Jubal and suggested that the only way to get verifiable information was to send an agent behind enemy lines to gather intelligence by what he saw and heard and also to tap into Union lines closer to Washington. Andy received independent duty orders to accomplish that task.

Early the next morning, Andy left the Boars Head Inn and headed toward Washington. He arrived in Southern Maryland, which was still sympathetic to the South, where he decided that he was close enough to tap various Union telegraph lines, especially those that were along railroads. He found a place in the woods where he could camp unseen by prying eyes in towns and along established roads. By and large, he ate cold meals from supplies that he purchased in small towns. He wore civilian clothes and was never questioned about his status in the area.

<hr />

ONE GLORIOUS SPRING Sunday in mid-April, Stone escorted Kaitlin to the lobby where Allan and Joan Pinkerton were waiting. Together they boarded a carriage and took the long way to the Jenkins farm without telling Kaitlin where they were going. As they got close to the property, Kaitlin, who had been talking non-stop with Joan, realized where she was and drew quiet. As they turned into the driveway, Kaitlin saw the newly constructed house and let out a cry of surprise. Allan explained how the house came to be rebuilt, crediting the president for the quick reconstruction.

Together, the foursome entered the house. The burnt smell had been replaced by the smell of new lumber and paint. The house was exactly as it had been with the exception of the secret passageway and steel spiral steps leading from the master bedroom to the office below. Then too, the furnishings were different. But all in all, the house was the same as it had been before the fire. Kaitlin was deliriously happy with the outcome.

"Oh Franklin, when can we move in?" she asked.

"We just did. A wagon will follow with our luggage from the hotel. You are home, Kaitlin."

Kaitlin cried tears of joy as she went into the kitchen. "Oh look, the kitchen is stocked with food," Kaitlin said with surprise.

"Joan stocked the kitchen yesterday," said Allan. "Oh, Joan, how can I ever thank you?"

"Go check out the rest of the house while I start dinner."

"I'll cook," said Kaitlin with a surprised look on her face.

"Not necessary, Kaitlin; I have two big strapping men to help me. You just relax."

The foursome gathered around the new dining room table and celebrated by eating a sumptuous meal and enjoying the company that only good friends can provide. The wagon arrived with luggage from the Willard Hotel. Kaitlin filled closets and drawers after the Pinkertons left, and with everything done, she inspected each room. She was truly happy with the new house. It would be up to Frank and Kaitlin to make the rebuilt house into a home.

ANDY HAD BEEN in the woods for over a week. His camp was located a half mile from the nearest road where telegraph lines were located. He left his horse in camp and walked to the road where he tapped into the telegraph line and buried his cable from the road to a well concealed area just under one hundred feet into the woods. He would have gone further into the woods, but he only had a hundred feet of cable. He carefully cut poison ivy and placed the plants just inside the forest near the road. He had chosen an area with dense foliage and trees that were close together. No one would have reason to enter the area where Andy copied code day and night. As a rule, he would go back to camp to sleep from noon to six, have a cold meal, and then return to his hideaway to copy code most of the night. He had discovered that the most promising intercepts were transmitted for four hours shortly after first light and then again throughout the night. He adjusted his hours of operation accordingly.

Most of the intercepts that he could read were administrative in nature. But even administrative traffic gave him clues as to the movement of the Union Army. Messages regarding the movement of food, weapons, and supplies were generally transmitted as administrative traffic. Therefore, even though he was unable to make sense of tactical traffic, he still copied the unreadable ciphers in case Confederate code breakers had broken the Union codes while he was deployed behind Union lines. This part of Maryland might be sympathetic to the South, but it was still controlled by the Union Army.

His supplies just about used up, Andy decided it was time to go back to Richmond to provide planners with the information that he had gathered. Based on where Union supplies were being sent, Andy believed that the next attack on Richmond would start around the Chancellorsville area.

Andy packed his gear and walked back to his hiding place near the road to retrieve his cable. As he approached the area, he could make out a mounted rifleman watching the road from just inside the forest. It was almost dusk, and slight darkness was just starting to turn the foliage from bright green to black shadows. Andy hunkered down on his haunches to watch the rider who held his rifle in his left arm as he puffed on a cigarette with his right hand. Suddenly, the rifleman flicked the cigarette away and took aim at the road. A single rider was coming up the road oblivious to the rifleman hiding in the trees.

Frank Stone was tired, having ridden to Washington just before dawn. He was looking forward to getting home. He was looking at the Smith farm on his left side, recalling the ferocious battle that had taken place there, when Hermes suddenly bolted to the left just as a rifle shot exploded from the trees on the right. Stone felt the bullet enter his right side, but he instinctively threw himself onto the ground on the left side of the road. Unfortunately, his head hit a large sharp-faced rock that was unseen in the oncoming darkness. Stone was incapable of moving; he was unconscious.

The rifleman continued to train his weapon at the spot where he had seen Stone fall. He didn't pay attention to Stone's horse, which had run off as startled horses are prone to do. Instead of passing the mounted rifleman, however, the big stallion veered to the right, snorting as he slammed into the rifleman's smaller horse, knocking the animal to the ground and pinning the rifleman's right leg to the ground.

Sudden pain hit the rifleman, and he struggled to free his leg. The rifleman's horse panicked. Struggling to get his legs underneath him, the horse's movements kept grinding the rifleman's broken leg into the ground sending shockwaves of pain up the leg, through his cortex, and into the rifleman's brain. The big stallion reared up on his hind legs and came down striking the head and chest of the stricken rifleman. The smaller horse was finally able to get up and run away. However, Hermes continued to press his attack on the rifleman again, and again, and again, until there was no noise or movement except those of Hermes. Snorting and whinnying, Hermes returned to Stone's side; however, Stone remained unconscious. Hermes pushed at Stone with his nose, but Stone still did not respond.

Andy went to his camp and got his horse and equipment. He was careful to enter the road a considerable distance from the hurt man and the big stallion that had just killed the rifleman. He didn't want the stallion to attack him. He slowly rode up toward the stallion, making quiet talk to calm the big horse. Andy tied the reins of his horse to a tree branch about twenty- five feet away. He kept talking softly as he approached. The big stallion reared up and Andy stopped where he was. He continued talking to the stallion for a couple of minutes, and then slowly stepped toward the fallen rider. Hermes was nervous, but he finally allowed Andy to approach.

Andy examined the fallen rider. There was a bloody gash on his head where he had landed on the rock, and his right side was bleeding where the bullet had entered and exited. Andy could see a rib and knew that the fallen rider would need a medical doctor. Taking water from his canteen, Andy washed the gashed head. Andy shed his jacket and took off his shirt, which he cut into strips for use as bandages. Just about the time that he was finishing wrapping the injured man's head, the big man regained semi-consciousness and started to struggle.

"Easy, big fella. I'm trying to help you, not hurt you." Stone relaxed and let Andy finish bandaging his head. Then Andy propped Stone up and tied a bandage around Stone's chest with compresses over the entry and exit wounds. He pressed on the compresses in an effort to stop the bleeding. Stone yelled out in pain and Hermes snorted a warning to Andy.

"Who shot me?" Stone asked.

"I don't know who he was, but he's dead now. That horse of yours pummeled him into the ground. His head is nothing but sticky goo. His chest is caved in too.. I've never seen anything like that before—haven't even heard of such a thing happening before. That's some horse you've got there."

"Yeah, he's pretty special alright."

"You live around here?"

"About two miles down the road on the right side." "Well, you're going to need a doctor."

"Just get me home, and I'll worry about seeing a doctor later."

"Okay, but getting you on your horse is going to hurt."

"If you give me a hand, I'll make it okay."

Andy helped Stone mount Hermes. The horse stood perfectly still as Stone finally made it into the saddle.

"You just hold onto the saddle horn, I'll hold your horse's reins so that he doesn't run off," Andy counseled. "No need, Hermes knows the way home. Just make sure I don't fall off again."

"Okay, I'll get you home, Colonel." "What did you call me?" Stone asked.

"I called you Colonel. I went through your pockets while you were unconscious to see if I could tell where you lived. Don't worry, I didn't take anything."

"Who are you?"

"Andy Davis. I'm just passing through. I saw the shooter point his rifle and fire, but I didn't see what he was shooting at."

"That would put you in the forest behind him."

"Yes, I was camped there for the past couple of days, resting up before continuing on down the road."

Conversation stopped as Stone was in great pain.

The horses were held to a slow walk, so it took nearly an hour to get to Stone's home. When they arrived, Andy helped Stone down off the big stallion and up the stairs to the front door. Hearing noise on the porch and expecting her husband an hour earlier, Kaitlin opened the door and saw Andy holding her husband. She grabbed Stones free arm and helped Andy half drag Franklin to the couch in the parlor.

"He's been shot, ma'am, and he hit his head on a rock. He needs a doctor."

"The nearest doctor is an hour away. It will take at least a couple of hours to get him here.

"Well I don't think we should move him anymore than I already have. Ma'am, I'm a telegraph operator, and there's a telegraph line that follows the road out front. I can try to contact the telegrapher in the nearest town and ask him to contact the doctor, if you want."

"Yes, please. That would save at least an hour." "What's the name of the nearest town with a doctor?" "Ellsworth and the doctor's name is Forrester—Doc Forrester. Tell him to come to the Jenkins farm."

Andy went outside and got his equipment, then rode to the nearest telegraph pole where he tapped into the wire. Andy realized that he was likely exposing his fist, but he felt that this was a matter of life or death. He called the telegrapher at Ellsworth to see if there was anyone actually on duty at that hour. There was. "Please contact Doc Forrester and tell him that we have a man who is badly hurt at the Jenkins farm. Ask the doctor to come as quickly as he can. I will await your return signals." He signed the message A. J., his first two initials.

The operator in Ellsworth acknowledged the emergency traffic and indicated to his supervisor down the line that he was shutting down momentarily to get the doctor. About twenty minutes later, the operator in Ellsworth sent code to A. J., saying that the doctor was on his way to the Jenkins farm. Andy thanked the telegraph operator for his help and signed off. Just as he was about to pull the tap away from the main cable, the Ellsworth operator asked A. J. to identify himself. Andy explained that he was an army telegrapher who was on his way to another assignment when he witnessed the incident.

"Which army?" the reply asked.

"Does it really matter at this point?" Andy asked. "Not to me," the Ellsworth operator said. However, you might consider clearing out of the area as soon as possible. There's been a lot of Yankee activity in your area over the past few days."

"Thanks, I hope I can repay the favor someday.

Andy closed his transmission with the common telegraphers code, A.J./SK.

Andy disconnected his key and sounder and headed back to the house. Knocking on the door, he indicated that Doc Forrester was on the way and should arrive within the hour.

"Thank you Mr...?"

"Davis, but just call me Andy."

"Thank you, for contacting the doctor, Mr. Davis, but could I prevail on you further to help me get Mr. Stone to the bedroom up the stairs?"

"Of course."

Andy struggled to get Stone to the bedroom where he removed Stone's boots and left it to Mrs. Stone to get him ready for the doctor. As he was leaving he said, "I'll take care of your horse."

"Hermes—his name is Hermes. Two scoops of oats and a sheaf of hay from the barn, if you will please."

"Oats and hay. Will do."

Andy could make out the form of the big stallion under a tree nibbling on the new sprouts of grass. He went over and took the reins and led Hermes to the barn where he fed and watered the big horse. While Hermes was eating, Andy washed his legs and hooves, all the time talking to the horse and calling him by name. Then he brushed him until he heard the clip-clop of a draft horse and carriage coming up the driveway. Closing the barn door, Andy met the doctor at the steps leading to the front door of the house. Andy described the injuries and led the doctor to the upstairs bedroom.

The doctor asked Stone to urinate in the chamber pot and then he examined the injuries.

"Well, it doesn't look like there are any internal injuries—no blood in your urine anyway. I'll have to stitch up your side and that gash in your head. I don't have anything to dull the pain, so it's going to hurt."

"Do what needs to be done, doctor. I'll manage," Stone responded.

Stone bit down on a thick leather strap while the doctor began stitching Stone's side. Under other conditions, Stone would have yelled out, but with Kaitlin standing there, watching the procedure, Stone bit down even harder on the leather strap thinking that the doctor would never finish. When the stitches were in place on Stone's side, the doctor stitched up his gashed head. The whole procedure took about an hour. The doctor bandaged the two injuries, after which he examined Stone's eyes and determined that he likely had a mild concussion and cautioned Kaitlin that Mr. Stone would have to stay in bed for at least three days, if not longer.

Escorting the doctor downstairs, Kaitlin paid the doctor his fee and saw him to the front door.

"I'll be back tomorrow afternoon. Don't let him get out of bed."

"I won't," Kaitlin promised.

"As the doctor was leaving, Andy asked, "Can I talk to your patient for a few minutes?"

"Keep it under five minutes." "Yes sir, less than five minutes."

Andy entered the house and asked Kaitlin if he could talk with Mr. Stone for a couple of minutes.

"Of course, Mr. Davis, I'll go with you."

Andy and Kaitlin entered the bedroom where Andy asked, "Feel like talking for a couple of minutes?"

"I think I can stay awake that long. What's on your mind?"

"I was wondering why that guy shot you. Do you know?"

"I don't even know who it was that shot me, and I certainly don't know why."

"Well, in that case, I'll stand watch outside on the front porch until daylight, if that's okay with you and Mrs. Stone."

Stone thought about it for a minute or so then said, "I would certainly appreciate that. We were burned out of here a few months back, so having a guard would set my mind at ease. Are you sure you don't mind?"

"No, I think it's a prudent decision. It's what I would want if it happened to me."

"Okay, Andy, thanks. I'll see you in the morning."

Andy took his horse to the barn where he helped himself to some oats and hay and put the horse up for the night. He took a shirt from his canvas bag and put it on, then removed his rifle from the scabbard and took a seat in the chair by the front door on the porch. He caught himself nodding off, so he got up and walked up and down the driveway in an effort to stay awake. The only movement he saw was a fox crossing the road near daybreak.

Kaitlin exited the house and handed a cup of coffee to Andy saying, "Do you take milk or sugar?"

"No thank you, ma'am. Black's fine."

The coffee helped drive away some of the grogginess that Andy felt from a night of forcing himself to stay awake.

"How's your husband doing?" Andy asked.

"Well, he had a good night's sleep. He's hurting, but I think he'll be okay in a week or so."

"I'm glad to hear that, ma'am. But it's time for me to get along. I have a lot of miles to travel before sundown."

"Where are you headed, Mr. Davis?" "Richmond."

"Please wait a few minutes while I make up a food wrap for your trip."

"Thank you, ma'am."

Andy used the time to get his horse and to visit the outhouse. By the time he returned to the front of the house, Kaitlin was waiting on the porch.

"I wish there was something more that I could do, Mr. Davis."

"You've been very kind, ma'am. Thank you."

Heading down the driveway, Andy checked the road in both directions looking for Union soldiers. Seeing none, he turned left and headed past the road to Washington on his way west to Richmond.

When Stone didn't show up for an eight o'clock meeting at the Pinkerton office, Allan rode to the farm. When he saw Stone laid up, he rode back to the office and set up a four man watch around the clock until Stone was able to resume his duties. He also sent a wagon and a team of men to recover the shooter's body, which remained in the forest near the edge of the road. Then he notified the president of Stone's condition.

THERE WERE TIMES when Andy would have to wait in the forests while Union troops passed. He traveled mostly at night, sleeping on and off in the saddle. It took five days to get to Richmond.

Entering the office, Jubal greeted him saying, "Hi Andy, you sure look like hell."

"I feel like it too. Jubal, I'm going to give you my notes, and then I'm going to the inn where I'm going to sleep for a week."

"Okay," said Jubal as Andy handed him a leather binder filled with notes, messages that he had intercepted and maps of the areas that he had visited. Andy rode to the inn, put up his horse, and fell into bed. He was exhausted. He slept for two days and woke on the morning of the third day ravenously hungry. Entering the pub, Andy ate the first hot meal that he had eaten in nearly a month while working behind enemy lines. Feeling better, Andy decided to go to the office.

"Good morning sleepyhead, I thought you said that you would sleep for a week," Jubal greeted Andy.

"What day is it?" "Tuesday, the 28th."

"It feels like I slept for a week."

"You will be happy to learn that your information was right on target. The Union Army crossed the Rappahannock River yesterday. It looks like the battle will center on Chancellorsville."

"I thought as much, but watch out for another attack around Fredericksburg. The Union was sending supplies in that direction too."

"We saw that in your reports. General Lee has General Early's troops at Fredericksburg while General Lee is personally leading part of Stonewall Jackson's division to face the main force at Chancellorsville."

"Sounds like our lines are pretty thin."

"They are, Andy. The Federals have twice as many soldiers. But Lee has a few surprises that might even up the odds somewhat."

Fighting started at Chancellorsville on the first day of May and continued through May 6th. Front lines extended from Chancellorsville to Fredericksburg, just as Andy had predicted. Stonewall Jackson led a force of about twenty eight thousand Confederate soldiers undetected around the front lines and attacked Hooker's right flank. On the sixth of May, General Hooker withdrew. The Union had suffered over *seventeen thousand* casualties. The Confederacy had suffered over *thirteen thousand* casualties, but they had rebuffed the Federals, and the Confederate capitol remained untaken.

The most foreboding news came when it was learned that Stonewall Jackson had been shot by his own men while he and his staff members were conducting reconnaissance. Returning to camp in the darkness, pickets on watch mistook the small reconnaissance party as Union troops and opened fire. Jackson's arm had to be amputated, and he died days later of pneumonia. The loss of General Stonewall Jackson was demoralizing to the Confederacy. But more importantly, his death would surely affect the outcome of battles yet to be fought; such was the boldness of Jackson's character and his expertise in battle.

Chapter Seventeen

Mid-May 1863

Doc Forrester rode out from Ellsworth every other afternoon of the first week following the shooting to check on Stone, ensuring that infection was not setting in, and changing his patient's bandages. Even with stitches, Stone would have a nasty-looking scar on the left side of his head. Doc Forrester said the scar would add character to his otherwise youthful face. The wound on Stone's right chest was showing signs of healing, but it would take another month before he could stretch or bend without pain. The doctor recommended another week of bed-rest, but Stone was anxious to get up and get back to work. The doctor extended his visits to once every four days as Stone showed improvement. Kaitlin sat with her husband day and night for the first week, mainly to ensure that he didn't get out of bed.

There were times when Kaitlin would have to talk with the day laborers who tended the farm. It was then that Stone got up and walked around, staying away from windows that faced the fields. But even having taken that precaution, Kaitlin once unexpectedly entered the house through the front instead of the kitchen door that she usually used, and saw him standing on the balcony overlooking the entryway. Stone looked down, saw that Kaitlin had seen him, and prepared himself for a verbal assault. Instead, she did something he did not expect. She stuck out her tongue and made a face, the likes of which he had never before seen on his wife. He started laughing and grabbed his side saying, "Don't make me laugh. It hurts."

"Good," Kaitlin responded with enthusiasm. "Maybe next time you get the urge, you'll stay in bed like you're supposed to."

That evening, as Stone lay in bed and Kaitlin sat in a chair beside him, Stone said, "You took my getting shot better that I expected."

"Franklin, I've come to terms with life. When I ran off to Ireland, I just couldn't deal with the fact that I had taken a man's life."

"Thank God you did, Kaitlin. Had you not shot that killer when you did, I would be dead. You would likely be dead as well."

"I am aware of that, and I now understand the need to take a life, when it is necessary."

"I ran off to Ireland expecting to find a land without violence. But what I learned was that the Ireland of my early youth never existed. I was overly protected. I attended private schools, and my parents made sure that I didn't experience any of the political and religious differences that Irishmen seem to hang onto. Ireland's history is one of being conquered. And now that no one is trying to conquer the Irish, I fear they will fight each other just as we are here in the America; except theirs will most likely be more of a religious war. I just don't understand why supposedly Christian people can't live together in Christian harmony."

"Nor can I, Kaitlin. Nor can I," Stone responded.

———— ∞∞∞ ————

June 1864

Following the Confederate-won Battle of Chancellorsville in May 1863, the war started turning in favor of the North. Battles at Vicksburg, Gettysburg, Chickamauga and Chattanooga all favored the North at great human cost to both sides. Andy provided General Lee with telegraph intercepts as he tapped Union telegraph lines and hid from Federal troops that moved across the battlefields to attack or counterattack Confederate soldiers. He was nearly caught at Vicksburg and again at Gettysburg, but he was able to blend in with the bodies of the dead and dying and was overlooked by Union soldiers until he could make his escape in the dark of night.

Several thousand Confederate troops rushed the ten miles from Richmond to Cold Harbor after the Union cavalry had seized control of vital crossroads there on May 31, 1864. Andy arrived in Cold Harbor that night to tap into telegraph lines from General Sherman's Headquarters. Most of the messages were sent in plain text rather than in cyphers. The Federal troops just didn't think that the Confederacy could get telegraph personnel into the area that quickly. Andy was glad that he could finally read messages and forward useful tactical information to General Lee. It was that information that allowed General Lee to repulse a Federal attack by surrounding Union forces on three sides, forcing them to withdraw.

Meanwhile, Southern engineers built up barricades of a type not before seen by the Federal troops. Confederate artillery covered nearly every approach. Federal troops advanced on the defenses and were cut to pieces. In the two weeks that both sides fought at Cold Harbor, and in the seven miles of fields adjacent to Cold Harbor, Federal forces lost over *fifty-two thousand* men. The South lost an estimated thirty-three thousand soldiers. The Union took hundreds of prisoners, mostly made up of units from Georgia including one Georgia telegrapher, Andy. Luckily, Andy had worn his uniform because Cold Harbor was so close to Richmond. Otherwise, he would have been shot as a spy. Instead, he and the other prisoners of war were loaded into boxcars on a Union held railway and shipped off to Maxwell House, an unfinished hotel that was being used as a prisoner of war camp in Nashville, Tennessee.

The prison, comprised of old buildings that had been converted to hold Confederate soldiers, was dangerously overcrowded. Designed to hold no more than twenty-five hundred men, it housed a war-time population of nearly seventy-five hundred soldiers. Sickness permeated the prison population. Union soldiers maintained order through random beatings, torture, and starvation that resulted in over three hundred fifty deaths in the two years that the penitentiary was used as a war prison. Only thirty six men ever managed to escape from Maxwell House.

Andy tried twice to escape but was caught each time as a result of information provided by starved and tortured Confederate soldiers who were in utter despair. They no longer held allegiance to any single individual; it had been beaten out of them.

Captain Andrew Jefferson Davis was personally targeted for torture because of his name. Union tormentors mistakenly believed that he was named for Jefferson Davis, the President of the Confederate States. Actually, the name Jefferson was conferred on him by his father in honor of Thomas Jefferson, the third President of the United States. His father, like Thomas Jefferson, strongly believed in states' rights over federalism. Hence the middle name Jefferson. Andy was tortured often.

Union guards took his leather boots and tied his hands behind his back as they beat on the soles of his feet with oak truncheons. He never got his boots back. Often, he would have to crawl to the chow line, which usually served watery potato soup or thick tasteless porridge. Occasionally, the first in line would get stale bread, but they didn't share it with others. Rather, they fought over the few scraps that were handed out.

At times, guards had tied his hands behind his back and hung him by his ankles from rafters in the interrogation room. They lowered him into a large barrel of fetid water until he nearly drowned. Johannsen, a hulking sergeant known among Union troops as the Swede—but who was actually of Danish extraction— particularly delighted in administering torture. It was the Swede's heavy military boots that Andy hated most. As he lay on the ground, unable to stand following a beating on the soles of his feet, Johannsen would stomp on Andy's fingers or kick his head. And when Andy could stand, Johannsen delighted in grinding his booted heel on Andy's unprotected toes.

After a few months, Federal soldiers turned most of their attention to the new arrivals, leaving alone those who were sick and weak from months of torture and near starvation. For the most part, that included Andy too. However, on one gray day in September, Andy was sought out and escorted to the headquarters building where the Swede administered another round of beatings. When Andy was no longer able to stand, the Swede smiled broadly.

"I'm told your wife, Abigail, and your young son Toby, squealed like pigs while they were being raped. A fat corporal took out his lust with your son. But your wife and son are okay now. They are what we call good Southerners. They're dead. Your plantation was burned to the ground during General Sherman's march through Georgia."

Andy could hear the Swede's laughter as he was being dragged back to his barracks by two Union privates. What the Swede missed was the look in Andy's eyes. Where months of torture and malnourishment had taken its toll on Andy physically, his inner strength was now renewed with extreme hatred.

Somehow, somewhere, I will kill you, Swede.

New prisoners were normally the only real source of somewhat reliable communications. Information from federal soldier-guards was always suspected of being just another form of torture. Andy sought out new prisoners who had been captured in Georgia, asking what they knew about Madison. No one had specific information about Madison, but they told of plantations, towns, and cities being burned to the ground throughout Georgia. Nothing was spared, he was told. Still, the desire for revenge grew as a raging inferno within. Andy was resolute that he would survive.

Christmas, 1864 was particularly bad for Andy. He hadn't seen his family for over two years, and now he was convinced that they were dead. Had the Swede not known their names, there might have been hope. But he felt no hope now. The mental picture of his wife and son at Christmas-time played in his mind repeatedly, until he thought he would go mad.

Four months later, on a pale blue-skied spring day, prisoners could see their guards jumping and whooping with joy. The guards gleefully shared their information: Richmond, the Confederate capitol, had finally fallen. Eleven days later, Union guards again were jumping for joy. Lee had surrendered at Appomattox. The South was lost. Five days later, it was the prisoners turn to jump with joy. President Lincoln had been assassinated.

———∞∞∞———

PINKERTON RODE TO Kaitlin's farm on the afternoon of April, 15th, the day that the president actually died. He was angry, frustrated, and felt guilty for not having been with the president, even though it was not his job to be there. When in the district, the president was protected by the army. But still, he thought, "If only I could have been there, I might have been able to prevent the assassination."

The news hit Frank and Kaitlin particularly hard. Lincoln had been more than their president. He had been their friend.

———∞∞∞———

IN THE MONTH that followed, it was clear that the war had ended. Treaties that allowed Confederate enlisted troops to keep a horse and officers to keep their sidearm went unrealized by those who had been taken prisoner. Rather, when authorized, Union soldiers at Maxwell House merely opened the gates at midnight, and then disappeared from view. Nothing was ever said to the prisoners. A few men ventured through the open gates, fully expecting to be shot. They no longer cared whether they lived or died. When nothing happened, others followed until the prison eventually emptied late in the day. Those who were too sick to walk were left behind. Broken in spirit, the prisoners sullenly walked out of Maxwell House and headed toward the only homes they had ever known. With no food, water, or transportation, save for their feet, many died looking for the freedom, families, and homes that they had left behind years earlier.

Although Andy's body would bear the marks of Union torment and the long walk home without shoes, those wounds would eventually heal. However, the memories of war, the hardships of prison, and the torture and murder of his family would always lurk in the shadows of his mind. Now that he had walked out of prison, he thought all that was behind him. He was headed home. He hadn't realized that arriving home would be just another form of even more torture.

Home was a little over three hundred miles away. If he was lucky, Andy could walk about fifteen miles each day. Before the war, he would have been able to walk the three hundred miles within two weeks or so, but now it would take at least a month, maybe longer. The first thing that struck him about his release was the long line of prisoners who were, like him, trying to get somewhere. Southerners, who had near nothing, shared what little they had. Andy began looking for those things that would help him survive: rags to be tied to his feet to cushion the blow of each step, and a bottle to hold spring water, when he could find a freshwater spring near the road. When he was too tired to continue walking, he would find a place in the woods and look for edibles before napping for a few hours. When he awoke, he would check his sometimes bleeding feet, readjust the rags that served as bandages, and then continue on his way—each step a painful reminder that he had lost everything. Occasionally, he would get a ride in a wagon loaded with possessions as people moved from place to place throughout the South. He arrived at his plantation of the night of July 6th.

Andy sat alone in the dark by a small campfire in what had once been his Georgia plantation's expansive front yard—sobbing uncontrollably. It had taken thirty minutes of vigorously rubbing two dried twigs together to generate enough heat to produce the first flicker of flame in the small mound of dried grass and that thirty minutes had used up just about all of the energy that Andy had. He sat on his haunches looking into the fire and remembering the good days before the war. He prayed for strength throughout the night, strength to somehow find those who were responsible for the death of his family so that he could extract revenge. He was not content to leave revenge to God.

Dawn broke to find Andy totally and completely spent from disgorging his emotions all night. He had nothing left to expel. Rail thin, he was a mere shadow of his former pre-war self. He would now have to deal with his own survival.

Andy left the cold campfire and hobbled several hundred yards along the property behind the burned out plantation-house. Nearly four years of weeds concealed the narrow entryway to a natural cave that had served as a winter block-house during those years when ice had formed over still waters in an inlet near the cave. It was there that the family had routinely stowed cane fishing gear. The cave, located near their favorite fishing site, was a convenient repository for equipment. He hoped that no one had found their way into the cave or that the cool cave had not become home to any of the variety of poisonous snakes that inhabited the area, because he had no torch to light his way.

Being careful not to trample the weeds any more than necessary, Andy peered into the dark cave. It was cool and dry, just as he remembered. He heard no movement, and there was no evidence that the cave had been found by marauding Union troops or passers-by. After his eyes adjusted to the dim entryway, he made his way inside, stopping after a few steps to adjust his eyes to the depths of the darker cavern. The main grotto, where blocks of ice had at one time been stacked one upon another, was empty, yet it still had a musty smell. Andy turned left into a smaller alcove where the fishing gear had been kept. He exhaled a sigh of relief. The fishing gear was still intact. Taking a filleting knife and a long cane-pole with line and hook attached, he exited the cave making sure that the weeds continued to conceal the entrance.

Making his way toward the nearby stream, he tested the line to ensure it had not rotted. He knelt by the still water of the inlet and, using the knife from the cave, dug up earthworms in the moist sandy loam for use as bait. Dropping the line in the water, a large catfish hungrily struck at the wriggling worm. Shaking with anticipation and hunger, Andy built a stream-side fire with flint and steel from the cave, cleaned the catfish, and stuck a fillet on a forked willow branch to cook. He retched after the first few mouthfuls, his stomach at first rejecting solid food. After several attempts, his stomach muscles finally relaxed, and Andy was able to eat some, but not much. Still weak from his ordeal, he stretched out and slept in the warmth of the rising sun.

It was about noon when he awoke, the sun being directly overhead. It was peacefully quiet save for the sound of a mocking bird. Andy dug up more earthworms and went back to fishing as he contemplated survival. He cleaned and filleted another half dozen fish, which he took downstream to where the water ran wild and free. Using rocks that had been smoothed by the running water, he built a rock container in the shallow water to keep the fillets cool and secure. They would make for his next few meals until he was well enough to leave. Moving under the shade of a knurled oak tree, he again slept for a few hours, waking as the sun was descending toward the western horizon. After eating again, Andy reentered the cave where he slept through the night.

The next morning, having paid his last respects to his dead wife and son, Andy wrapped his feet with what rags he could find, ate another meal of fish, and headed on foot for the town of Madison to see if his brothers had survived. Unbeknownst to Andy, Dwayne and Everett had returned to Georgia nearly two months earlier. It was almost three years since he had seen them.

After having walked about a mile, Andy, still wearing his threadbare Southern Army uniform, heard the sound of hooves on the dirt road behind him—not more than two horses, he guessed by the sounds. The horses had a walking gait, so he paid little attention to them other than to move closer to the edge of the road. The first horse and rider, a Union cavalry sergeant, passed Andy in the center of the road. The second horse and rider was much closer. As Andy started to look over his left shoulder, the rider's boot forcefully hit Andy in the head sending him crashing to the ground in pain.

"Get off the road, you Dixie trash," yelled the private, who then laughed as he kept riding, picking up the pace a bit to catch up with the sergeant.

Andy shook his head, trying to clear the ringing from his ears. Rage overtook him. He made it to one knee when he suddenly realized that both horsemen had wheeled about, and were riding toward him at a gallop. One of the troopers was yelling "Yeehaw, get Johnny Reb!" The private again outstretched his leg, getting set to kick Andy, but this time Andy was ready. He crouched, slightly, and as the cavalryman's leg made contact with his chest, Andy grabbed the leg with both arms, and using the momentum of the horse, swung up behind the surprised rider.

Andy drew the filleting knife and deeply cut the cavalryman's throat. Blood gushed out and dribbled down the front of the Union soldier's uniform. More pulsating blood flew through the air, spattering the dying soldier and the face of the rider behind him. The dying private tried to yell, but blood had entered his throat and the only sound that came out was a loud gurgling.

Sensing that something was wrong, the sergeant wheeled about again and saw the Confederate soldier mounted behind the Union private. The sergeant drew his side arm and tried to aim, but the body of the Union private was in the way. The two horses closed rapidly. Andy drew the sidearm from the dead private's holster, and as the sergeant came within a few feet of passing, Andy placed two well-aimed shots into the sergeant's chest. The force of the forty-four caliber projectiles from the Colt Dragoon knocked the sergeant from his horse, which soon returned to his rider's side as the horse was trained to do.

Andy quickly checked the road for other travelers. Seeing none, he draped the body of the sergeant across the saddle of his horse and led both horses well into the forest. He dumped the two bodies into a shallow depression, covering them with small branches and leaves so that passersby wouldn't easily see them, even if the riders were on the road's edge. He striped the horses of the U.S. Army saddles and horse blankets, which he threw to the ground, covering them with leaves. He then washed the blood off his face in a nearby stream and returned to the road with a leaf-covered tree branch to obliterate telltale hoof prints and blood.

What a waste, he thought, looking at the two dead soldiers. He pulled his shirt out of his trousers and jammed their Dragoons into his waistband. Calmly, he mounted the sergeant's horse and rode bareback, leading the second horse through the woods to the spot where the Union soldiers had first made contact with Andy. There were no longer any tell-tale hoof prints in the dirt road to indicate what had happened. To the casual rider, it looked like two horses had been ridden without stopping. He carried the dead men's rifles across the withers of the horse he was riding, while simultaneously leading the second horse by its reins.

Andy muttered to himself, "It sure is good to be on a horse again."

His feet still hurt. About a mile out of Madison, Andy again turned deep into the woods where he removed the bridles and let loose the two horses, allowing them to forage as he continued his journey on foot. He would have kept the two horses, but the "U.S." burned into their left front flanks would be a death sentence; especially if the bodies of the two dead soldiers were soon to be uncovered.

Andy entered Madison, keeping to the back streets and alleyways so as not to call attention to his Southern Army uniform. Madison, like most southern towns of any size, would be filled with carpetbaggers and administered by Union officials, he correctly surmised. He was stunned to see that the town still existed. None of the buildings, at least none that Andy could see, had been burned as a result of Sherman's march through Georgia.

Andy tried to enter the back door of Everett's store, but the door was bolted on the inside, something that would never have occurred during business hours before the war. He softly knocked on the door and waited. No one answered. He knocked with a heavier hand. After a few seconds, the door was opened just a crack so that whoever was inside could get a look at the stranger at the back door. After just a moment, the door was flung fully open and there stood Chiggers.

"Andy!" Chiggers yelled in complete surprise. "Come in. Come in."

"Massa Ev—Massa Ev, come see who's here at the back door," Chiggers yelled.

Chiggers wrapped his powerful arms around Andy, almost knocking him off his feet.

"Andy," said Chiggers, "We was all afraid you was dead."

"I almost was, several times."

"Oh my God," said Everett, as he barely recognized his younger brother. "We had given you up for dead."

"So Chiggers said."

Just about the time that Chiggers released Andy, he was enveloped in the arms of his older brother.

Praise God, praise be to God," Everett said repeatedly.

"Aiieee!," screamed a black woman as she entered the room.

It took Andy a moment to recognize Lila.

Tears flowing, Lila all but smothered Andy in an embrace.

"You home, you home," she kept saying.

"Sit yourself down over here," said Chiggers, pointing to an overstuffed chair.

"My wife, Barbara, turned the storeroom into an apartment for Chiggers and Lila after the plantation was burned," said Everett. "They help us run the store now."

Andy turned to Chiggers smiling as he said, "So are you and Lila a couple now?"

Chiggers looked lovingly at Lila. "Yessa, we truly are." Lila had a big toothy grin on her face.

"Well, it's about time," said Andy.

"Chiggers," said Everett, "go fetch Dwayne from his office down the street."

"Yessa," said Chiggers, as he hurried out through the store.

"Andy, you want something to eat or drink?" asked Lila.

"Well I haven't had a cup of coffee in over a year. A good cup of hot coffee would be a blessing from heaven."

Lila stoked the fire and put a big black kettle of water on the small wood stove. When the water began to boil, she grabbed a canister and threw three handfuls of coffee grounds, a pinch of salt and some egg shells into the steaming kettle. The aroma of fresh-brewed coffee permeated the small apartment.

"My God, there isn't a sweeter smell in all the world than your coffee, Lila," said Andy.

"Oowee, from the looks of you, I'm gonna be doin a whole bunch of cookin. You looks like a scarecrow, Andy," Lila said in return.

Before he could answer, Dwayne hurriedly entered the small apartment. Andy tried to rise out of the overstuffed chair, but Dwayne quickly crossed the room and placed a heavy hand on Andy's shoulder saying, "Rest easy, Andy. You look like hell."

"It's good to see you too, Dwayne, Andy smiled." "We had just about given you up for dead," said Dwayne.

"So everybody keeps saying," said Andy.

"Well, it's been almost three months since the war effectively ended," said Dwayne.

"It took me awhile to get back from Nashville on foot."

"You were in Maxwell House?" Everett asked. "For almost a year."

"My God," Everett paled. He had heard so many horrifying stories about the Maxwell House prison.

Dwayne, as the head of the family, immediately took command of the situation.

"Chiggers, you take Andy to my house and get him situated in the downstairs guest bedroom. Lila, you go to Everett's house and help Barbara arrange a family dinner for tonight. Everett, you get some clothes and boots for Andy. Have Chiggers deliver them to Andy at my house." The back-store apartment suddenly became a flurry of movement as everyone jumped to fulfill their assigned chores.

Chiggers escorted Andy to Dwayne's house where he drew a tub of well water, built a fire, and put a large pot of water on the stove. After the water had just begun to boil, Chiggers poured the hot water into the tub of cold well water so that the bathwater was comfortable to the touch. It had been a very long time since Andy had bathed with bar soap in clean hot water. Andy's muscles began to relax in the heated water. Chigger's eyes widened measurably as he saw the roadmap of torture and deprivation that marked Andy's body. Unhealed discoloration from beatings, both with boots and blunt instruments, jagged scars from beatings with whips, a few scars that might have been made by sword or knife, and one roundish scar that had healed so that it looked more like a crater. Chiggers involuntarily shuddered but kept his silence.

When the water cooled, Andy stood and dried himself with a large soft towel, which he wrapped around his middle as he padded to the large four-poster featherbed in the downstairs guest bedroom. Sliding under the sheets, Andy surrendered to the luxury of the bed, and for the first time in well over a year, fell soundly asleep.

Night fell on Madison and the Davis family gathered at Everett's house for dinner. Gas lamps brightly illuminated the interior of the house. Andy had walked the two blocks to Everett's house with great difficulty. He wasn't used to wearing boots. They hurt his feet even more than walking barefoot. Everyone could see that Andy was having a hard time walking, even when walking around the house, but they looked the other way and said nothing. After dinner, a hearty meal of beef, potatoes, green beans and fried okra, followed by cherry pie, the men moved to the parlor, while Barbara, Lila and Chiggers cleared the table, washed the dinnerware, and cleaned the kitchen.

As the men moved to the parlor, gas lamps were lit while Andy removed his boots and wiggled his toes inside cotton socks. With a smile on his face Andy said, "That feels a little better. It's going to take awhile to get used to wearing boots again."

"Well, Andy," said Dwayne, "we have a lot of questions."

"I have a few questions myself," said Andy.

"How is it that Madison is still standing?" he asked. "Why didn't Sherman and his troops put the town to the torch like he did so many other towns and cities?"

Everett answered, "Old man Joshua Hill went to Atlanta to pick up the body of his son, Legare, who was killed at Cassville. While Hill was in Atlanta, he went to see Sherman. They had supposedly known each other in Washington D. C. when Hill was a U.S. Senator. I don't think they were friends exactly, but I'm told that they did work together while Sherman was assigned to the Headquarters Brigade in Washington."

Andy listened carefully as Everett continued by saying, "Senator Hill was an anti-secessionist who tried to convince the Georgia Legislature not to secede."

"I remember," said Dwayne, who had been a state senator when the question of secession had first surfaced. He too had argued against secession, believing that they should remain part of the Union until all legal avenues had been exhausted. "Supposedly," Dwayne continued, "old man Hill was a friend of Sherman's older brother. They had attended West Point together."

"When Georgia did secede," Everett said, "Old man Hill resigned from the U.S. Senate and returned to his home here in Madison to retire. I don't know if he was elected or not, but at the time that he went to see Sherman, old man Hill said he was acting as the town mayor. Hill convinced Sherman not to burn Madison, but Hill and the townspeople remained skeptical, and rightly so, because Sherman and his main force took another route. Sherman never came to Madison. Rather it was the left wing of Sherman's force under General Slocum, who came to Madison. Old man Hill and two other townspeople met with General Slocum, but the general made no promises about whether or not Madison would be burned. In the end, Slocum honored the agreement between Hill and Sherman and only burned the courthouse, train depot, a cotton gin, a few hundred bales of cotton, and the old factory on the south side of town. A few houses were burned, but they were torched by drunken soldiers rather than by Slocum's orders."

Everett continued by saying, "My wife said that they were doing okay when General Slocum and his troops left Madison, but it was the bummers, scavengers, who followed Slocum's troops that looted the town, including our store. But Barbara, Lila, and Chiggers had earlier removed most of our stock to the house, leaving just enough hardware to make it appear that the store was still doing business. When the bummers moved on, she waited for a week or so and then slowly started returning food stuffs, clothes, and hardware back to the store. She said the bummers even stole a communion service from the Presbyterian Church over on Main Street, but Slocum made them return them to the church. All-in-all, Madison came out okay. I'm told there were only seven cities and towns that Sherman decided not to burn."

"Old man Hill is the town's hero," Everett said. "And rightly so," Dwayne added.

"So who killed my Abigail and Toby?" asked Andy with a strained look on his face.

After a few seconds of silence, Dwayne answered, "We don't rightly know, Andy. I've been looking into the matter for over a month. I contacted both of the Corp Commanders who were under Slocum, and I talked with the Regimental Commander in Atlanta. They all disavowed any knowledge of the killings. They all told me that they suspect the bummers who followed the main force did the killings."

"Who are these bummers you keep talking about?" Andy asked.

"Sherman had no supply line. He forced his men to live off the land. Bummers were commissioned from every regiment to scour the land and take anything that could be used to feed the 60,000-plus men under Sherman's command. Every time they came to a farm, they took every horse, every farm animal, and anything of value, including silverware, jewelry, paintings, furniture—anything they wanted, really. They even took food off the table and out of the pantry, leaving the farmer and his family with nothing. "Then they put the farms and plantations to the torch," Dwayne continued.

"They did the same to the slaves," said Chiggers from the dining room.

"It was even worse in the cities," said Everett. "But it wasn't just the bummers. The main forces, when they were allowed, also took everything of value, and then they burned the towns to the ground, leaving the townspeople with nothing. Hundreds of villages, towns, and cities were burned to the ground throughout Georgia and the Carolinas, which just proves how fortunate Madison really was that old man Hill did what he did."

"Killing Abigail and Toby was not an act of war. It was murder. It was so horrible that I actually heard about it at Maxwell House. I didn't want to believe it, but I couldn't deny it after I saw the plantation-house for myself," said Andy. The room remained silent for several minutes.

"So, what about you?" Dwayne asked.

"Before we talk about the war," Andy replied, "I have to advise you that I bring great risk to you and your household," Andy said grimly. "This morning, I killed two Federal cavalrymen about a mile from the plantation."

Dwayne and Everett looked at Andy with shock and dismay.

"What happened?" asked Dwayne.

"One cavalryman tried to run me down, and the other tried to shoot me."

"That's self-defense," Dwayne retorted.

"Yes, but with the carpetbagger court system, I wouldn't get a fair trial, so I will have to leave. If their bodies are discovered, I may have to leave sooner rather than later."

"Nobody knows you killed them, so why leave?" asked Everett.

"The killing took place close to the plantation, and I just got back to town. I think suspicion would be cast on me just for that. But also I kept the soldier's rifles and Dragoons, which I intend to keep. If those bodies were to be found, the possession of those weapons would be all that would be needed for a carpetbagger judge to hang me."

"Why not just get rid of the weapons?" asked Dwayne.

"If it was just the revolvers, I would. But did you get a look at the rifles?"

"No," answered Dwayne and Everett in unison.

"The rifles are Henry repeaters. They hold fifteen rounds. It was with that rifle that Union forces were able to repulse four separate Confederate Army attacks at Allatoona Pass in the fall of 1864. They killed over two thousand of our soldiers, while only thirty-eight federal troops were felled. If I have to a fight, I want a Henry repeater."

Both Dwayne and Everett nodded their heads in agreement.

"Brothers, in all honesty, the real reason I must leave is that I just can't live here anymore—not with the memories of my Abigail and Toby surrounding me everywhere I look."

"Where will you go?" asked Everett.

"I thought that I would go to the cabin on Blood Mountain," Andy responded. "The Federals won't look for me there."

"No one would look for you there," said Everett, smiling. "But how will you live?"

"The same way we did when we were kids—when we went there with Dad. I'll hunt, fish, and gather whatever edibles I can off the land."

Dwayne looked at his younger brother with concern and said, "You're not well enough to make such a trip by yourself, much less hunting and foraging all winter. But I do agree, you will have to leave Madison as soon as possible; hopefully before the bodies are discovered."

"Ev, can we borrow a couple of your horses?" Dwayne asked.

"I'll ride to Blood Mountain with Andy and get him situated for the winter. If anybody asks, you can tell them we went hunting for fresh meat in the mountains."

"I have one good riding horse and two draft horses that I use to pull the supply wagon," Everett said.

"I will take my horse, Andy can ride yours, and we'll take the two draft horses to carry supplies. Can you get by without your horses for a month?" Dwayne asked.

"Yes," said Everett. "I can get a couple of horses from the livery when I need to make a delivery."

"I'll bring your horses back with me in about four weeks," Dwayne said.

"When will you leave?" asked Everett.

"Andy, do you feel up to leaving tomorrow night?"

"Yes, as long as I don't have to walk," said Andy, smiling weakly.

"Think anyone found Dad's cache?" asked Everett

"Not unless they ripped up the floorboards," answered Dwayne. "He was pretty crafty, the way he hid the cache. He always said we needed to be ready for any eventuality. He wrapped the rifles and ammunition in oil cloth before he buried them underneath the cabin."

"What about the money?" Everett asked.

"Dwayne can bring back your share. It's only a hundred dollars for each of us in double eagles," said Andy, "but it was supposed to be enough to keep us going if everything went to hell in a hand basket."

"Well, the war sure did that, Andy, but you can keep my share. Barbara and I will make out okay. The store is still profitable, and we have some Federal money put away that will get us through the winter," said Everett.

"Where will you go in the spring, Andy?" Dwayne asked.

"West, I think. I sure can't stay here."

"What do you want us to do with the plantation?" Dwayne asked.

"I would like to put a thousand acres aside for our darkies—those who return, that is. I promised them ten acres each if they worked for ten years. The war interrupted that, but I want to make good on my promise. I'd like to give one hundred acres to Chiggers and Lila. They might be able to lease it out to someone who wants to farm. As for the rest of the land, I think it will be a long time before agricultural profitably returns to the plains. I want to sign a deed over to you two tomorrow. Maybe you can find someone who wants to farm the land, or you can sell it off in parcels. I want nothing more to do with the plantation."

"That's understandable, Andy, but the land is worth a lot of money," said Dwayne.

"The double eagles from dad's cache will be enough to get me away from here. I'll make out okay. You two decide what to do with the land and split any money that you can get. I'll be fine."

"Well, now that that's settled," said Everett, "what happened to you? How did you end up in Maxwell House?"

"That's not a topic for mixed company." Andy replied.

Dwayne nodded his head in agreement. It also ended the Davis family reunion. Dwayne and Andy said goodnight and returned to Dwayne's house for the evening. Andy had a hard night. He kept having dreams of his tortured family.

Chapter Eighteen

July 8, 1865

ANDY WOKE UP slightly after ten in the morning with a splitting head-ache. Dwayne was already gone, but he had left a pot of coffee on the wood stove, which by that hour of the day was barely lukewarm. Andy hastily poured and drank a cup of the tepid dark liquid to wash out his mouth, which felt like it was filled with cotton. He stirred up the fire in the wood stove, adding fresh fuel until flames were once again heating the coffee pot, and then he sat at the kitchen table holding his head, wishing he had not had so much brandy the night before. After two more cups of coffee, his headache somewhat abated.

Andy dragged out the metal bath tub and placed a large pot of water on the stove. After several trips at filling the tub with well water, he poured the boiling water in the tub until it was almost hot to the touch. He gingerly entered the tub and let the hot water work its magic on his sore muscles. His next bath would likely be in the icy streams of Blood Mountain.

Shortly after noon, Dwayne returned to the house where the two men ate a light supper and discussed the coming journey. Dwayne had drawn up the legal documents necessary to transfer the planta-tion back to Dwayne and Everett, which Andy signed, believing that he was somehow admitting a final defeat at the hands of the North. Chiggers had dropped off more new clothes, some medical supplies and a couple of large canvas bags that were more practical than were suitcases for use on pack horses. Dwayne returned to his office while

Andy packed, checked the Henry repeaters and Dragoons, napped for a couple of hours. At six in the evening, the family met at Everett's home for what would likely be their last meal as a family.

Following dinner, Everett went to the barn and retrieved his two draft horses, which would be used to haul the supplies that Andy would need for the next few months. Lila and Barbara filled a large canvas bag with food that they had canned, along with packages of dried beef. After dark, Andy and Dwayne led the two pack horses and Everett's Tennessee Walker to Dwayne's house to finish packing the clothes, weapons and supplies that they would take to the mountains. Dwayne retrieved his horse, a high spirited Arabian, and packed a few clothes and a bedroll for the trip. By ten o'clock that night, they headed out of town.

Andy felt that he could not leave town without stopping by the Bennett home to tell the banker and his wife how sorry he was that the banker's only daughter, Abigail, and their grandson Toby, had not survived the war. Although getting ready for bed, the Bennetts took time to talk with Andy. They were understandably bitter about the murder of their daughter and grandson, but they made it a point to tell Andy that they did not hold him responsible. Andy reiterated that he could not stay in Madison because of the murder of his family. It was just too painful. When Bennett asked where he was going, Andy lied, saying that he was headed for Montana or Idaho. Although he trusted Bennett, he didn't want to take a chance that he would reveal Andy's destination due to economic pressures placed on their bank by carpetbaggers. After saying good bye, Andy and Dwayne left town by way of back streets, none of which had lights by which the two men could be identified.

The trip of a hundred and fifteen miles due north would take the better part of four or five days. They had decided to resupply in Watkinsville and Jefferson, going around Athens, which would be more likely to have a contingent of Yankee soldiers, being one of the larger cities in the central region of the state. They rode during the night for the first three days to reduce the possibility of running into patrols and law enforcement officials. They stayed off main roads whenever they could, taking roads headed north that were sometimes little more than trails. They resupplied in Gainesville and again in Cleveland, the last town of any size to speak of before heading into the mountains of North Georgia. The last store-bought meal was eaten at Turner's Corner in the foothills leading to higher mountains and the Chattahoochee Forest. There was no restaurant in Turner's Corner; rather, the wife of the local general store owner cooked for travelers out of her home next door to the store. Travelers ate whatever was available, but fresh eggs, hot biscuits, and gravy was a staple that was always offered, along with beans and occasionally some beef or pork.

At midday, Dwayne purchased a bottle of Tennessee sipping whiskey in the general store and then they headed north into steeper mountains. Turner's Corner, with an elevation of about fifteen hundred feet, was still quite warm; however, the temperature dropped rapidly as they reached the forty-five hundred foot level of Blood Mountain.

The cabin on the Davis property was still standing and appeared to be in good condition. Few people actually owned property on the mountain, but Augustus Davis had bought ten acres when it was offered for sale by the State so that he could build his cabin within hiking distance of his preferred hunting area. Most cabins were built just above Turner's Corner, so there were no other actual human residents on the higher elevations of the mountain. Most of the undeveloped mountain was still owned by the State of Georgia. Other mountain hunting areas in the state were closer to main roads and civilization. Only the more serious hunters ever came to Blood Mountain.

Dwayne and Andy unloaded the supplies from the horses. Dwayne took the horses to the barn that was attached to the cabin, where he fed them oats from the supplies that the animals had carried up the mountain. Andy took two of the canvas bags that had been used as luggage and filled them with water from a nearby stream. After the horses had been fed and watered, Andy returned to the stream to get water for use in the cabin both for cooking and cleaning. Five years of dust coated the floors and the handmade furniture that their father had built many years earlier.

The two room cabin contained a main room with a fireplace that was used both for warmth and for cooking. It also contained chairs and a couch Augustus had made on the mountain, and which was adorned with cushions Beth had made at the plantation. The second room was a windowless bedroom that had two bunk beds, one on each side of the dark room. Instinctively, Andy threw the clothes that he had packed on the top bunk on the right, the bunk that he had used as a kid when the Davis family men-folk came to the mountain for their annual hunting trip. The lower bunk had been his father's bed. Dwayne and Everett had always used the bunk beds on the left side of the room.

Since darkness had yet to descend, Dwayne decided on reconnoitering the property to see what, if anything, had changed. Andy took the time to clean the cabin and to stow supplies. After a couple hours, Dwayne returned, reporting that there were no signs that anyone had been on the property and that there was abundant game for hunting.

Dwayne went to the barn where he got a small pry bar from a wooden toolbox. Returning to the main room of the cabin, he lit a kerosene lantern, which he hung on a hook in the center of a rafter in the dark bedroom while he examined the floorboards. The two men moved the bunk bed on the right side to the center of the room. One floorboard appeared to be a quarter inch shorter than the other floorboards. It would be easy to regard that lesser length, if noticed, as being the result of rough carpentry in a remote area. But Augustus Davis was not the type of man who would allow such a miscalculation to occur. Rather, that quarter inch was the key as to which board should be pried to unearth the weapons, ammunition, and money secreted below. The weapons and ammunition were still in the oilskins where Augustus Davis had placed them, years earlier. So were the three small deerskin medicine bags that each contained one hundred dollars worth of double eagles. The brothers just looked at the money and weapons, remembering when they had been placed there, reminiscing over better days—fun days with their father and with Everett. After retelling stories of memories past, the two men replaced the board and the bunk bed and took the weapons, ammunition, and the three deerskin bags to the front room for further examination. Andy extinguished the lantern to conserve fuel for use during the weeks or months that he would live in the cabin.

The weapons were still free of rust. The action on the Sharps rifles worked smoothly, and although old, the ammunition appeared to be fit for use. Dwayne prepared a light meal, which the two men ate while sitting outside under the covered porch. They watched birds and small animals curiously examine the two men who had invaded their peaceful world.

Sunset came quickly on the mountain, and the sounds of larger game could be heard, including the occasional growl of a cougar and the far off howl of a wolf. The sounds were music to the ears of the two men who had fond memories of both the area and the animals that lived in the forest.

Dwayne woke up and put on a pot of coffee, used the outhouse, and was waiting for the coffee to boil when Andy wandered out onto the porch where Dwayne was sitting admiring the beauty of the early morning forest.

"Morning, Dwayne."

"Good morning, sleepyhead. How're you feeling this morning?"

"Better, I think. At least the bunk was more comfortable than sleeping on the ground."

"You going to be alright up here by yourself? Is there anything you need?"

"No, I think this will be just fine, brother. You don't need to worry about me."

"Well, you always were the best hunter in the group." The two men sipped the boiling hot coffee and quietly watched squirrels scurry around looking for food. Finishing his cup of coffee, Dwayne saddled Everett's Tennessee Walker and said, "I'm leaving my Arabian here for you, Andy. I'll find another horse when I get home."

"Thanks, Dwayne. I know how much you love that horse, so I will always treasure the gift with great fondness."

"Family first, as dad used to say," Dwayne responded. "Family first," Andy repeated.

Andy packed the two Sharps rifles and ammunition on the draft horses. Dwayne swung up into the saddle. Andy handed him the lead rope for the two pack animals.

"Let us know where you end up, Andy."

"Count on it, Dwayne. My best to the rest of the family. I will miss you all."

"We will miss you too, Andy. Be careful."

"Don't see how I can get into trouble up here, Dwayne."

"You'll find a way. You always do," Dwayne grinned as he started down the mountain.

Andy watched until the horses were out of sight.

For the rest of July and throughout August, Andy hunted, fished, and gathered edibles. Day by day he got stronger and eventually got to the point where his boots no longer hurt. When he didn't need to hunt or gather food for the day, he gathered dead dry wood for warmth and for cooking. And when there was no work to be done, Andy began riding the Arabian around the mountain. By the first week in September, mountain coolness had turned cold. Andy decided to ride down to Turner's Corner to buy more supplies before winter snow set in on the mountain. He longed to hear human voices and to hear what news there was since his arrival at the cabin.

Filling two canteens, Andy placed his ten-gauge shotgun in the scabbard on the right front side of the saddle, and the Henry repeating rifle with the butt sticking out to the rear on the left side of the saddle. He placed extra ammunition for the shotgun and the rifle in his vest pockets and a box of each type of ammunition in his saddlebags. *I might do some hunting on the way back*, he thought. He strapped on a holstered revolver and took a coat for the ride back in the cold night air. The ride to Turner's Corner took nearly six hours. He arrived in an area above the store at mid-afternoon.

Andy dismounted and continued on foot while he was still a few hundred yards above the store, a habit he had gotten into while tapping Union telegraph lines. Stopping just inside the tree line, he watched the front of the store for a few minutes before venturing toward the dirt road on which the store was located. Just as he was about to exit the cover of the trees, batwing doors flew open and a pile of fighting men fell out of the store punching, gouging, and yelling profanities. Five of the men wore Union uniforms. The sixth man was in civilian clothes.

Andy tied the Arabian's reins to a tree branch and removed both the shotgun and the rifle in case the soldiers decided to fire on him. He edged closer to the road and propped the rifle against a tree, cocked the two hammers on the shotgun, and watched from the edge of the forest.

"Get a rope!" the sergeant ordered. "You got no right," the civilian yelled.

Two cavalry soldiers mounted their horses. One private uncoiled a rope from which he made a noose. The two remaining soldiers, who were kneeling on the back of the struggling face-in-the-dirt civilian, tied his hands behind his back and helped him to his feet. The civilian continued to struggle to no avail.

Two soldiers lifted the civilian onto his horse and placed the noose over his head and around his neck.

"Throw that rope around the tree branch over there," the sergeant ordered, pointing to a large oak tree.

It was then that the sergeant saw Andy standing by the tree.

"Move along Mister. This ain't no concern of yours," the sergeant said.

"What did he do?" Andy asked.

"Like I said, it's not your concern. Now move along."

"Well, if you're going to hang him, seems like he ought to know what he did," said Andy.

"He's a damn Texas Confederate," a private blurted out.

"The war's over," Andy responded.

"It will be for him in a few minutes," the private laughed.

"Then he will be a good Southerner," the sergeant said grimly.

The words "good Southerner" hit Andy like a fist. His mind replayed the Swede saying those very same words when he described the death of Andy's wife and son. Andy drew cold inside, but he didn't betray his feelings.

"So, you're going to hang him because he's from Texas?"

"No, we're hanging him because he is a Southerner." "I wouldn't do that, if I were you," Andy cautioned. "Why not?" the sergeant laughed again.

"The war's over and he's done nothing wrong."

"He's a Southerner, that's all we need to know to hang him."

"Too bad," said Andy as he pulled the trigger.

The sergeant was thrown back a few feet as the blast from the shotgun tore out his chest and the vital organs therein. He was dead before he hit the ground. The second shot took out the private with the rope, knocking him off of his horse. The other mounted soldier went for his revolver. Andy dropped the shotgun and picked up his rifle, which already had a bullet in the chamber. He fired a bullet into the private's head then turned toward the two soldiers who had been holding the civilian. They were clawing at their flapped holsters, trying to draw their Dragoons, as Andy fired again, hitting one soldier in the chest.

"Why did you shoot us?" the wounded private whined.

"If you were willing to kill him because he was a Southerner, then I guess you'd have killed me too. I'm a Georgia Southerner," Andy said.

The wounded private didn't hear the answer. He died standing on his feet clutching his wound. He fell to the ground.

Andy pointed the Henry at the soldier who was not shot. "Remove your holster and throw it into the street." The soldier did as he was told.

"Don't shoot me," he pleaded.

"Do as you are told, and I won't shoot."

Two men watched from the batwing doors. One was the owner.

"Got a pick and a shovel?" Andy asked.

"Sure do," the store owner responded.

"Give them to the private here," said Andy as he pointed to the private with his rifle.

"Private," Andy continued, "Dig a common grave for your dead comrades, and dig it deep."

The private took the pick and shovel, crossed the road toward the woods, and started digging a common grave. The man dressed in civilian clothes just stood there silently, not knowing what his fate would be. Andy stepped out into the street and cut the ropes that bound the civilian.

"Thanks," he said. "I'd be dead by now if you hadn't stepped in," he said, looking with distain at the store owner.

"Jeb Smith, from Amarillo, Texas."

"What brought you to Georgia?"

"Trying to get back to Texas," said Jeb. "Where from?" Andy asked.

"Moline, Illinois."

"So why are you in Georgia?" Andy asked again. "There are more direct routes to Texas from Illinois."

"I thought there would be less chance of getting killed by Union soldiers if I traveled in the South."

"So what do you think now?"

"I think I had better get back to Texas as fast as I can."

It took three hours before a sufficiently deep grave was dug and the bodies interred. Andy said a prayer over the dead soldiers then turned his attention to the remaining soldier. Andy reloaded his shotgun, untied his horse, putting the rifle back in the scabbard, and brought his horse to a water trough to drink.

"Take off your boots," Andy said pointing his shotgun at the exhausted soldier.

"No," said the defiant soldier.

"Take them off, or die," said Andy menacingly. The soldier took off his boots.

"Take off your socks too," Andy ordered.

The soldier reluctantly did as he was told. Andy handed the soldier a half full canteen and said, "Now walk."

"Where to?"

"Wherever you came from."

The soldier started walking down the mountain road toward Fort Smith, which was only ten miles away from Turner's Corner. He thought that since it was a fort, there might be a Union presence. However, he would be wandering around for a long time. Fort Smith, Georgia, was a deserted outpost in the mountain wilderness.

Andy went into the store and bought oats for his horse and some canned goods that the owner's wife had put up. After paying with one of the double eagles, a coin that the owner had not seen since before the war, Andy collected his change and started to leave when Jeb Smith said "Let me at least buy you a drink."

"Not necessary. What's done is done."

"You're not an easy man to get to know."

"Perhaps I would be more amenable if you start telling me the truth and stop avoiding my questions," Andy said in a harsh voice.

"Look, I'm not the bad guy here. Ask the store owner. I was minding my own business having a drink before continuing on with my travels down the mountain. Those soldiers came in and asked me where I was from. I told them, Texas. They made a few caustic comments about Texans, and the fight was on. Then they decided that I should be hanged."

The store owner nodded his head affirmatively, but said nothing.

"Where were you coming from," Andy asked again. "I told you. Moline, Illinois."

"What was a Confederate trooper doing in Illinois?"

Jeb was silent for about thirty seconds. Then he got a look of resignation and said, "I was in Rock Island Prison for six months until the end of the war."

"That's nothing to be ashamed of," said Andy. "No, but it's nothing to be proud of either."

"I'll ask you again, what brings you to Georgia?"

"Fewer Union troops and warmer weather."

"I don't understand. Why warmer weather?"

"Have you ever been to Moline, Illinois?"

"No."

"Well, I'm tired of being cold. The prison was bitterly cold, especially in the winter. And with winter coming on, I wanted to travel in warm weather."

"I guess that makes sense. But you are wearing some pretty expensive clothes. How does a Confederate prisoner of war get such expensive clothing?"

"A friend gave me these."

"That horse and tack outside are very expensive. How can you afford those?"

"I stole them from my friend's husband."

"Horse theft is a hanging offense. You want to explain?"

"No, not really, but I will. While I was a prisoner, I was put to work as a carpenter. I did a lot of work on the warden's house. While I worked, I got to know his wife, who was a very lonely woman. The warden, a colonel in the Union Army, believed that he was far superior to anyone else. After the war, I stayed in Moline and worked at odd jobs trying to make enough money to return to Texas. I continued working at the colonel's house because his wife kept finding things for me to do. The colonel was seldom at home during the day. Recently, he came home unexpectedly and caught me talking with his wife. He was going to shoot me, but his wife stopped him on the stairwell as I escaped out of the window. I stole his horse and have been on the run ever since."

"He was going to shoot you for talking to his wife?" Andy asked incredulously.

"Well, we were talking in the language of love in the upstairs bedroom."

"Oh," said Andy.

The store owner laughed and said, "That's the most ridiculous story I have ever heard. It's so ridiculous; I'm guessing it's true."

Andy continued with his questioning by asking, "So did the colonel send those troops after you?"

"No, I don't know where they came from or where they were going. The colonel would never publically admit that a former Confederate prisoner of war, who was intimate with his wife, was walking around wearing the colonel's clothes, and had stolen his prize horse and saddle. The colonel's reputation would be permanently tarnished. He would be the butt of many jokes for years to come."

"I see what you mean. It is pretty funny. Okay, let's have that drink now."

"What about you?" Jeb asked. "You live around here?"

"No more. After today, I'm going to have to move on. I was going to stay on the mountain for the winter and then head west. But after today's events, I guess I had better move on now."

"Why not join me, and we'll head to Texas together?" Jeb asked.

"I don't know, Jeb. Being with you seems to put me in dangerous situations."

"I can't guarantee you won't be placed in dangerous situations, but I think we would be good company for each other. We could watch each other's back along the road."

"Well, I can't argue that. There are some things I need to get, so I'll be back by noon tomorrow. If you still want to partner up, I'll see you then. If you decide differently, then good luck and goodbye."

Andy started to leave when the store owner asked, "What do you want me to do with the soldier's horses and tack." Andy examined the horses and found one without the "US" brand.

"I'm going to use this one as a pack horse. I guess that means the rest of them are yours to do with as you please."

Jeb, who had no weapons before the attempted hanging, examined the army rifles and revolvers and said, "I'm going to take a Henry rifle, two dragoons, and ammunition."

He also took a scabbard from one of the army saddles. He strapped one Dragoon and holster on his hip and saddle mounted the second Dragoon on his horse.

"Thanks again for saving my life," Jeb said as he offered his hand.

The two men shook hands, and Andy rode back to the cabin, arriving near midnight. He fed and watered the two horses and then went inside and packed everything that he thought he would need for the trip west.

The next morning, Andy securely tied the gear to the pack horse and headed back down the mountain. When he got to within a mile of Turner's Corner, he hobbled the two horses with soft cloth hobbles and continued on foot. He watched the buildings for most of the morning. Seeing no signs of Union troops or anyone that looked like they might become a threat to him, he returned to the horses and rode to the store, arriving close to the noon hour. Jeb was ready to go. He had few possessions to pack and to carry on the trip. Andy bought more food for the journey, packed the food with the rest of his gear, and suggested that he and Jeb eat a meal prepared by the store-owner's wife before they headed off. Jeb agreed. After a meal of eggs, bacon, and homemade bread, the two men headed northwest. As they were riding over the mountain, Andy thought about what Dwayne had said about finding ways to get into trouble. It looked like Dwayne had been right.

Chapter Nineteen

September 1865

ANDY FIGURED THAT he was at least ten years older than Jeb, but then Jeb wasn't the talkative type, so he didn't know for sure. The two got along well on the trail. At night, sitting around a campfire, both men at times loosed their tongues and talked about life before the war. Andy had noted that Jeb treated his horse well, tending to indicate that Jeb was not an arrogant man. Arrogant people tend to take their conceit out on others, especially their animals. Andy couldn't stomach people who felt they were superior to others, so he and Jeb had started on a good footing.

The two men decided to ride north over the mountains toward Chattanooga, Tennessee, and then diagonally across Alabama through Birmingham. It would have been an easier and shorter trip had they taken the route south through Atlanta, but having killed four Union soldiers at Turner's Corner, it would have been more dangerous. Few people would expect them to travel north in the winter, especially with snow expected any day.

Andy had little need for the compass mounted in a wooden brass-hinged case that he had taken from the cabin on Blood Mountain. He had walked these same mountains following his release from prison. He remembered all too well each painful step. On his way home from prison, he had made the decision not to stop at the cabin because he didn't want to walk the extra miles to the cabin and back to the one-lane road, especially since it was another hundred miles or more to Madison. He never imagined that he would be retracing his steps to Chattanooga, at least not so soon.

Travelling the northern route, the trip to Texas would cover over a thousand miles. In the snow, the pair barely made ten miles a day, but they only had a few days like that. The cold made travel unpleasant, but the two men stopped at night, rubbed down the horses by the campfire, and warmed icy drinking water before allowing the horses to drink. The horses were covered with blankets to keep them warm at night. Only when the horses had been cared for properly, including a careful inspection of hooves and horseshoes, did the two men pay attention to their own needs.

Depending on when they decided to call it a day, usually an hour or so before sundown, they would start looking for game. If no game was available, they ate what food they had in their dwindling supplies. Although it was only eighty miles from Blood Mountain, it took two weeks to get to Chattanooga, Tennessee. Jeb and Andy were glad to get out of the high country. Their food supplies were exhausted. The City of Chattanooga, which lies at seven hundred feet above sea level, was much more comfortable and considerably warmer than riding around at the nearly six thousand-foot level in the surrounding mountains in winter.

The city had been a center for many terrible battles during the war. President Lincoln had made its occupation a main objective because it was a major railway hub for men and war-making materials. Part of the city had been subjected to artillery bombardment merely as a diversion for an attack on Confederate troops located elsewhere. But after two years of occupation by Union troops, and with the war finally finished, the people of Chattanooga were busy trying to find ways to get on with their lives.

Hotels, those that had empty rooms, were relatively inexpensive. The average Southerner had little or no money, so Northern carpetbaggers and minor officials tended to be the only hotel residents. Jeb and Andy checked into a downtown hotel, taking a single room with two beds to save money. Their horses were quartered at the livery stable. Following a noontime dinner, Jeb returned to the room for a nap, while Andy made his way to the Methodist Church, not to pray, but to repay the kindness that had been shown to him on his walk to Madison.

Andy knocked on the door to the parsonage. The aging pastor answered the door but after a few minutes of talking, had to admit that he did not remember Andy. There had been so many Southern soldiers walking or riding to homes all over the South. Andy had been just another forlorn face in a sea of hundreds of people that the church had tried to comfort.

Members had pooled what food they could gather from merchants and parishioners each day, and fed travelers a meal each evening. They had opened the church's sanctuary to weary men, women, and children so that they could get a night's sleep out of the elements. The pastor had managed to secure cots and blankets from departing Union supply officers who didn't want to bother shipping the material back to warehouses in Washington.

They still fed needy people once a week, but the main groups of traveling Southerners had peaked a couple of weeks earlier. Andy handed the pastor a twenty dollar double eagle and thanked him for the courtesy that he had received on his way to Madison. The pastor looked at the gold coin. Tears sprang to his eyes. It had been awhile since he had money in his pocket. Andy returned to the hotel and slept through the late afternoon and all night until five in the morning.

The two men talked about how they would approach the rest of the trip. They decided to take the train from Chattanooga to Birmingham, Alabama and then they would take another train across Mississippi and Louisiana where they would ride their horses into northern Texas.

Jeb was a little short of money, but Andy said he would make up the difference so that the two men could continue to travel together. Jeb had other ideas.

Jeb went to the parlor that evening and watched as hotel residents played poker—poorly he thought. When a chair emptied, he asked the players for permission to join them. They readily agreed and Jeb took what money he had and filled the empty seat.

The other players were northern carpetbaggers who had come to Chattanooga to make their fortunes at the expense of Southerners. One man in particular, Addison, lost several hands, but then Jeb noticed that each time Addison was the dealer, he won. He watched Addison closely, but could not detect any chicanery. As the night wore on, the players who had lost money left the table. Only Addison and Jeb played on.

Sometime after midnight, the pot grew to a point that it became clear this would be the last hand. Most of the money that had been piled in front of each man was now in the pot. Addison dealt the first five cards for a hand of draw poker. Jeb had three queens, a duce, and a six. He bet most of the money that was in front of him, saving the rest for the last bet. Jeb asked for two cards, discarding the six and the deuce. Addison saw the bet and threw one card into the discard pile. He drew one card—from the bottom of the deck. Jeb grabbed Addison's right hand before he could complete the card pull exclaiming loudly that Addison was cheating by dealing off of the bottom of the deck. Only the bartender heard Jeb, but everyone on the ground floor heard the shot that followed. Addison pulled a Derringer from his vest pocket and shot Jeb in the head. Then he shoved the money into his coat pockets and spit in Jeb's dead face saying, "You damned Southerners will just have to learn your place. This is the new South." He tipped the bartender and walked to his room, packed, and took the three a.m. train to Birmingham; leaving Jeb slumped across the table with the deck of cards still in his hands.

The hotel clerk ran to the city police department, and shortly thereafter, the hotel parlor was filled with uniformed police. A detective questioned the bartender who told the investigator what he had seen and heard, including the fact that the dead man had accused the killer of cheating just before the killer shot the unarmed dead player. After the police gathered the information they needed for their reports and for the local newspaper reporter, they returned to their normal duties. They didn't try to find the killer. After all, the dead man was just passing through. It wasn't as if he was an upstanding local citizen with demanding relatives.

Andy did not hear the shot that killed his travelling companion. When he awoke and realized that Jeb had not been to bed. He walked downstairs to see if his friend was still playing poker. The hotel clerk told him that Jeb had been killed. Andy questioned the clerk, but he received no satisfactory answers. He went to the police station and asked more questions. They asked if he was a family member.

Andy answered, "No, but we were travelling together."

"Well," the police sergeant said, "I guess you will be travelling alone now." The sergeant turned away to pay attention to some other function.

Andy realized he was not going to get any straight answers, so we went back to the hotel where he talked with the manager.

"Who shot my friend, Jeb?"

"Addison Crowley," said the manager. "Crowley was a guest at the hotel, but he packed and left after the shooting."

"Where did he go?"

"Personally, I don't know. I wasn't here at the time of the shooting. But the rumor is that he took the early train to Birmingham. It left at three in the morning."

"What does Crowley look like?"

The hotel manager described the card playing killer as best he could remember. Andy asked the manager for the location of the city's undertaker. The funeral home was just five blocks away. Andy thanked the manager and walked over to the undertaker's office. Andy explained the situation and asked the undertaker if he would be willing to take Jeb's horse, saddle, and weapons as payment for a decent burial and headstone. The funeral director agreed. Andy went to the livery, paid the fee for the release of the horse and tack and took them back to the funeral director. Andy retraced his steps to the hotel where he took Jeb's Henry rifle and two Dragoons to the funeral parlor. The funeral director assured Andy that Jeb would get a decent burial—not a burial in a pauper's unmarked grave. Andy thanked the man for his kindness.

Stopping at the train station on his way back to the hotel, Andy purchased a ticket to Birmingham and made arrangements for his two horses to ride in a freight car designed for livestock. The train would leave at four in the afternoon. After packing, checking out of the hotel, and eating a light supper, Andy made it to the train station by two.

Because of his incarceration at Maxwell House in Nashville and the killing of his friend in Chattanooga, coupled with the fact that carpetbagger city officials couldn't care less about finding Jeb's killer, Andy vowed never again to come to Tennessee. The train pulled out on time. Six hours later, he was in Birmingham.

Putting his horses in a livery, Andy checked into a hotel, ate dinner at the hotel's restaurant and after dark, went on the hunt. He checked the parlors of various hotels first. No one was playing poker. He checked bars, pubs, and saloons, watching players that looked similar to the description that he been given. Around midnight, he found his quarry. He was sitting in a gaming parlor in a saloon playing poker with a number of local men. When a vacancy occurred at the table, Andy asked if he could join them. The players answered in the affirmative. Andy sat and introduced himself, shaking the hand of each player. The players introduced themselves and shook Andy's hand. His quarry, Addison, gave his name, confirming what Andy already believed, and shook hands smiling. Andy played a few hands, intentionally losing, and then said that the game was too rich for him and excused himself.

Andy sat nursing a beer in the bar until the game broke up slightly after one in the morning. He went outside as the players paid their debts and waited. Addison left the saloon and walked up the street. Andy followed at a discrete distance. He watched as Addison entered a hotel. He was about to enter the hotel when he noticed a gas lamp being lighted in a second story room. Andy could clearly see Addison as he opened the window and closed the curtains. Andy waited, studying the construction of the hotel. Just after three o'clock, Andy climbed up the back steps of the hotel, and then made his way along the slightly canted roof that covered the sidewalk below. Entering the open window, Andy drew his Dragoon, crossed the room, and sat on the bed next to the sleeping Addison. Shaking the killer from a deep sleep, Addison awoke with a start. The barrel of the Dragoon immediately got his attention.

"What do you want?" Addison asked, recognizing Andy from the card game.

"Heard you killed a man in Chattanooga yesterday evening in a card game."

"You the law?" "Nope."

"Are you family?" "Nope."

"Then what do you want?"

"Justice."

"Are you going to take me to the police?"

"Nope. Not here anyway. Why don't we go back to Chattanooga?"

Andy caught Addison's hand as it came out from under the pillow with the Derringer. He forced Addison's hand and subsequently the Derringer to Addison's temple. Then he covered Addison's trigger finger and pulled. The gun went off, instantly killing Addison.

Andy walked over to the dresser where he washed his hands in the bowl provided for that purpose, then poured the bloody water into the chamber pot. It was unlikely that anyone would check the chamber pot for evidence of a shooting. By the time he finished washing his hands, someone was pounding on the door to Addison's room. He quietly moved to the wall next to the back of the door.

Within minutes, the hotel clerk entered, as did several residents of nearby rooms. While they were looking at Addison's dead body, Andy slipped out of the room, walked down the hallway, down the stairs, and out of the hotel.

The lobby was empty. He walked the few blocks to his hotel and entered through the back door. No one saw him enter his room. He left Birmingham the next morning on a train bound for Jackson, Mississippi, where he caught another train to Shreveport, Louisiana, arriving in Shreveport just three days after leaving Birmingham. Andy once again checked into a hotel and quartered his horses in a public livery. He was less than a day's ride from Texas.

THE MEETING WAS by invitation only. It was organized, but the attendees were not part of a formal organization. Rather they were Chief Executive Officers, owners, media moguls, and Captains of Industry of the nation's most profitable and influential businesses. They were meeting at the Grand Metropolitan Hotel, the most luxurious hotel at the time in Manhattan. The meeting in the hotel was well within public view, yet outside of the public's prying eyes and ears. A whole floor had been reserved for the weeklong meeting. The meetings were private but allegedly not secret. However, since media moguls controlled what the public read, the meetings actually did provide a veil of secrecy. Minutes of the meetings were never ever made public.

Although Senator Hill had set up the meeting, there were no politicians in attendance. Politicians were important to the courses of action that would be set in motion, but they weren't necessary to the planning process. After all, any politicians, including judges, who might have been invited, were already in the pockets of those who were attending the meeting. Politicians were generally considered to be minor inconveniences that had to be paid at least annually, some more than once a year, to keep them in line with the wishes and desires of the elite heads of big money special interests. Senator Hill was the one exception to the rule. For years, he had been the go-between for big money interests and the Congress and subsequently to state and local governments.

Publically, the meeting was held to allow the nation's most influential businessmen the opportunity to plan for rebuilding the country: "To help the nation's people rebuild their lives in the post-war period of reconstruction," they said. Privately, they were there to see how they could extend their wealth and influence, and to find ways to dominate governments and the public. Keeping wages low and prices at wartime highs were just two ways to accomplish their goals and objectives. Other ways would be determined throughout the week. Each of the nation's infrastructure was discussed—discussions that could influence the nation for well over the next hundred years.

The fifty-some-odd attendees were broken down into committees based upon their areas of expertise and influence. The committees included Agriculture, Public Health, Military-Industrial Development, Government, Public Media and Communications, Transportation, Banking and Finance, and Shipping.

Each member contributed one million dollars for investment into the common vision under a financial development organization that was generally shielded from public and government view by layers of legalese. With a budget of over fifty million dollars, they could financially influence the direction that smaller businesses would take, and because of political affiliations, they could shape the actions of governments. By the end of the week, each committee was to make recommendations for further development, which would then be voted on by the entire membership. Their common vision was simply to expand their personal wealth and influence, under the protection of government, with little or no regard for how their plans might affect others.

The Agriculture Committee reported that, due to the freeing of slaves in the South, the national food supply was significantly lagging below need. Lands in the Deep South would be near worthless without slave labor. They recommended that members, through the development company, invest in the invention and production of farm machinery so that farms could be productive without much in the way of human labor. Their rationale was that older slaves who could no longer perform heavy labor could be shuttled off to the service industry, or if they couldn't find work, they would eventually die off, in time. Others, those who were fit for heavy labor, would be available for work for low wages in other infrastructure areas such as building railroads. They opined as how individual members could buy Deep South land at a fraction of the actual value to be held for future development as more efficient farm machinery became available. Until then, the cost of taxes for unfarmed land would be relatively low. They also recommended that individual members consider developing chain stores to provide food to people throughout the urbanized nation, thereby driving small family-owned stores out of business. Profit projections over the next twenty-five years were staggering; well beyond what the average family could even imagine. Members smiled at the projections.

The Public Health Committee indicated that the war had killed over one million American citizens and had injured many more times that. They projected that many of hospitals that had been hurriedly built to meet the needs of the war would be torn down or closed. Small towns, especially those in the Midwest and the West continued to be serviced by individual doctors with no hospital accommodations. The need for doctors during the war had created new opportunities for aspiring medical practitioners; however, a glut in big eastern cities would now cause many doctors to move to small town America.

They also reported that the continuous flow of immigrants, especially now that the war had ended, could result in the emergence of diseases that could affect large populations, but they saw no immediate financial advantages by investing in pharmaceuticals at this time.

The committee also noted that because the war had killed or wounded so many men, the available workforce was greatly reduced. Therefore they recommended that child labor be institutionalized, especially in mines and in the mills of the northeast, and that the development corporation set aside funds to grease the hands of Congress and state legislators to ensure that child labor laws would be forestalled until future generations could fill workforce needs. The members voted to establish a fund of two hundred thousand dollars for that purpose.

The Military and Industrial Committee reported that there was a glut of weapons available and that individual members could make a substantial return on investments by buying up older weapons for sale to Indians in the west and to militants south of the border and throughout South America. The sale of weapons to Indians especially was viewed as a good investment as a continuing war between indigenous peoples and the federal government would create the need for increased numbers of newer weapons. Those individual members who were involved in the manufacture and sale of weapons smiled and accepted the recommendation.

Industry representatives reported that starting with the Industrial Revolution and now with the end of the war, industry would play an increasingly larger role. They anticipated that over the next fifty years, members would see a dramatic change in the way the people of this country lived and worked. As machinery replaces human labor, they said, there will be much unrest. Therefore, it will be necessary to protect mills and foundries and other places of manufacture. The committee anticipated that workers would attempt to form unions for collective bargaining. Therefore, laws must be passed to outlaw such labor force organizations. In the event of a failure to outlaw unions, we must be prepared to protect our investments with strike breakers. This was not welcome news, but the murmuring members accepted the forecast as necessary to their collective goals and objectives. They voted a one million dollar budget for strike busting.

The Governments Committee reported that they had a number of issues that they were studying that would require passage of laws at the state and federal levels and that they would work within the already established network to accomplish those goals. They recommended a three million dollar budget be made available for influencing government officials. The measure passed unanimously.

The Public Media and Communications Committee reported that although they controlled mainstream media, smaller publishers were still able to print and distribute papers that were critical of the goals and business practices of member companies. It was recommended that large media organizations purchase small competing print media in or near large cities in order to reduce the voice of dissent and to create a base for the election of member- preferred public officials.

Furthermore, the committee recommended that individual members might want to further invest in telegraphy, to buy out small investors and to establish nationwide telegraph lines so as to control which communications would get through in what timeframe. The recommendation did not require a voice vote since no collective development money was to be spent.

The Transportation Committee reported that it wouldn't matter how much food was produced or weapons manufactured if you couldn't transport the end product to buyers. They recommended that the membership lend ten million dollars to members within the rail industry at no interest, to establish a rail line that stretched across the country. They recommended that the money be used to buy state and local rail lines that already existed within the projected new rail system and to pay for a coordinator who would fend off problems from governments and private individuals. Specifically, they wanted the Committee on Governments to quickly have Congress enact laws that would give the railway coordinator the power of eminent domain so that they could force landowners off lands where a right of way was required. The recommendations passed.

The Banking and Finance Committee recommended that several new laws be enacted by Congress allowing individual citizens to have access to the newly created New York Stock Market. By extending investment opportunities to the general public, Chief Executive Officers and Board Chairmen could direct investments without investing their own money. Meanwhile, the corporations that they owned would make sizeable profits in the stock market. All the members smiled at that recommendation. The motion passed unanimously and enthusiastically.

The Shipping Committee reported that steamships were now the heart and soul of international freight hauling. Although ships of sail still navigated international waterways, steamships cut travel time and therefore, reduced overhead. It was recommended that the members look into consolidating shipping companies that used steam power so as to take control of that market. No further action was recommended.

One last piece of business had to be resolved before the members could adjourn and go celebrate. Who would be the coordinator for their undertakings, and under what format? It was decided that one member of each committee would be elected to fill a position as board member of a new company, the National Development and Research Organization. After the board members were elected, one member of the board was selected as Chairman. But who would be the coordinator? The members decided that the new board members should select the new coordinator.

The board met and selected the one man they thought was so unethical as to do the job without qualms. They met in private with that man, and after an hour of forceful haranguing, the man reluctantly accepted the new position. One week later, Aaron Hill resigned from the Senate, "...to pursue new opportunities in the private sector," a news release said.

KAITLIN SOLD THE crops, paid the day workers who had worked in the fields during the summer, and arranged for an extended trip to New York City. She was anxious and a little frightened at the prospects of finally meeting Frank's mother. With the war's end and with improved mail service, the two women had corresponded for the past three months. However, Kaitlin wondered whether she would ever really be accepted as part of the family. This trip was more than a mere visit. Stone had to meet with the police commissioner to see if he still had a job.

Since the assassination of President Lincoln, Stone and Kaitlin had long discussions about his return to New York to resume his duties as Chief of Detectives. Kaitlin didn't want to live in the city, but Stone didn't see any other option if he was to continue with his career. They decided to wait until Stone talked with the commissioner before they made any final decisions about life after the war.

Stone was surprised to see his aging mother at the train depot.

"Mom! I didn't expect you to come to the depot." "Hello, Franklin," she responded, walking past her son and embracing Kaitlin.

"Oh Kaitlin, I am so excited. I couldn't wait for you to get here. I have a taxi waiting out front. I have so much to show you in the city."

The two women continued talking while they walked out of the depot's front door, leaving Stone to grapple with the luggage. They continued talking during the taxi ride to the eastside Third Avenue apartment, and continued talking nonstop up the stairs to the second floor, where Mrs. Stone handed a key to Kaitlin saying, "This key is for you so that you can come and go as you wish. I don't know if Franklin still has his key, but we will find out in a minute."

As the two women entered the spacious apartment, Mrs. Stone closed and locked the door, winking as she ushered Kaitlin into the parlor. Frank Stone made two trips up the stairs with luggage and turned the door handle only to find that the door was locked. He knocked on the door.

"Well I guess that means he doesn't have his key," Mrs. Stone said with a smile as she walked back to the door.

"Yes, who is it?" she innocently asked through the closed door.

"You know damn well who this is, mother. Now open the door."

Mrs. Stone unlocked the door and walked back into the parlor where both women giggled.

"I see now where Franklin gets his devilishness," Kaitlin whispered as she grinned.

"My dear, I have no idea what you mean," Mother Stone replied with a sparkle in her eyes.

The two women laughed out loud. Stone, who had entered the parlor by then, gave them his coldest police stare. They laughed even harder. Stone groaned, suddenly realizing that he was outnumbered and would likely remain so for the entire time that he and Kaitlin would be staying at his mother's apartment.

Stone went downtown to police headquarters early the next morning, leaving the women to fend for themselves. Because he had been gone for four years, he waited in line to ask the desk sergeant to announce him to the Chief of Police. He wanted to talk with the chief before meeting with the commissioner. A young uniformed officer accidently bumped into Stone saying, "Get out of the way, you big oaf."

Before Stone could respond, the desk sergeant, who recognized Stone said, "Right this way, Chief." He emphasized the word "chief" to ensure that the young patrolman heard what he had said. The young patrolman paled and scurried off down a hallway in the opposite direction, hoping that the big man would not recognize him if they ever again met.

"You'll have to excuse the rookie, Chief. He means well, but he still has a lot to learn, especially if he is going to continue working here at the headquarters precinct."

"I'll look forward to talking with him another time, Sergeant."

"Yes sir. I'll be sure and let him know," the sergeant said with a big smile.

The sergeant knocked on the chief's door saying, "Chief Stone is here to see you sir."

"Send him in."

Stone entered the spacious office and walked to the chief's desk. The chief stood and offered his hand saying, "Hi Frank. You don't look any worse for wear. Heard you got shot in the war."

"Just once, you big Irish galoot."

The two men laughed and hugged each other. "We sure missed you around here," the chief said.

"I hope that's true Chief. I'm about to see the commissioner to see if I still have a job."

"Oh, you still have a job, alright. Crime's up, population's up because of the war, and there's a stack of cases that you won't believe. I think your detectives have been stacking them up, waiting until you got back to give them your special guidance," the chief laughed.

"Oh, great," Stone said, rolling his eyes.

"How bad was it, Frank?" the chief asked with a somber look on his face as he sat down behind his desk?

"Over a million men killed; many by disease. Five million or more wounded; many were severely wounded, and the President was assassinated. The only way that it could have been worse was for us to lose the war."

The unformed chief remained silent and shook his head in understanding.

"Well it was no picnic here either, Frank. We had riots after the president announced the implementation of a draft. And the number of Copperheads, Northerners who had southern leanings was unbelievable. They were always causing some kind of mischief."

"I saw the reports, Chief. I knew that it was affecting the department. I just hope we can soon get back to some degree of normalcy."

"Yeah boyo, me too. By the way, Frank, I heard that some high-faluting Washington woman set her hooks into you, and that you ran off and got married."

"No Washington lady, chief. She's an Irish lass so beautiful that she makes you forget what day of the week it is."

"Ahh, an Irish lass, you say. Frank, I always knew you had good judgment. When will I meet this young lady of yours?"

"Soon, Chief. Soon."

"I'll look forward to that. It's good to have you back, boyo."

That being said, the chief stood, the two men shook hands again, and Stone took his leave.

Stone walked to City Hall and climbed the stairs to the commissioner's office.

"This is where it all started," Stone said to himself, remembering the conversation that he had with the senior commissioner. Unlike his last visit to the third floor, which had been empty, this time the hallway was packed with people waiting to see one official or another. Stone gave his name to the clerk, a young girl he had never seen before.

"Please have a seat, Mr. Stone." "Chief."

"What?"

"That's Chief Stone as in Chief of Detectives, New York City Police Department," Stone said.

"Sorry Chief. I'm new here."

"No problem, I've been away for a while."

The young clerk disappeared inside the suite of offices and returned almost immediately saying, "Chief Stone, Commissioner Kennedy will see you now."

"Thank you," Stone replied as he moved passed the throng of people lining the hallway.

Commissioner Kennedy met Stone in the inner lobby of the five offices with his hand extended to shake hands.

"Welcome home Franklin. Welcome home."

"Thank you, Commissioner. After four years, it feels a little strange to be back in the city."

"I'm sure it does Chief, but now it's time to get back to work."

"Well, that's what I came to see you about, Commissioner. I wanted to make sure that I had a job to come back to."

"Yes Chief, your job awaits, and there's plenty to do." "So I hear, Commissioner."

"Franklin, I won't hold you. I have meetings scheduled with the mayor and other city officials, so I will look forward to talking with you later about the war. Good to have you back home though."

"Thank you, Commissioner. I'll look forward to talking with you at another time," Stone said as the commissioner ushered him through a private door leading to a stairwell behind the offices.

"That was sure short and sweet," Stone thought, as he walked down the stairs and back to the headquarters building.

"Good to have you back, Chief," the desk sergeant said as he passed through the wooden barricade that separated the lobby from the police offices.

"Thanks Sergeant. It's good to be back," but Stone wasn't really sure that it was so good.

Stone walked to the Detective Bureau and entered the office with his name still painted in black block letters on the door. The office was dark but it looked the same as when he had left, except that case files that had been on the desk had long since been removed. Stone opened the back door to his office, which emptied out into the Bull Pen, a common area where detectives worked and met with those members of the public who got past the desk sergeant.

Two young detectives who Stone didn't recognize looked up. They knew that the chief was supposed to come back to work today, but they were expecting a fat old cop. This very large man was not fat, nor was he old.

"I sure as hell don't want to piss him off," one detective whispered to the other rookie detective.

"Yeah, I sure wouldn't want to meet him in a dark alley either," the other rookie whispered.

The other detectives—those who had been on the force for several years—gathered around Stone saying, "Welcome back, boss."

Stone was about to respond when the Assistant Chief of Detectives entered the Bull Pen from his private office saying, "So you finally decided to come back from vacation, did you?" He grabbed Stone in a bear hug saying, "Welcome home, Frank." The other detectives clapped their approval at having their boss back. They had all heard hair raising stories of his exploits during the war. To them, he was a hero.

"What's the matter? You guys solved all the cases and you have nothing better to do than stand around gawking?" Stone said as he broadly smiled at their welcome, trying to hide the tears that were welling up in his eyes.

Frank walked over to the cupboard and grabbed his cup as if he had never been gone and poured a cup of hot steaming coffee while he surreptitiously wiped his eyes.

"So, how about giving me a short brief about the cases you guys are working."

One by one, each detective explained his caseload. When they had finished, the assistant chief introduced the two rookies. Stone took more than several seconds to examine each man's appearance and then he individually looked each man in the eyes until they became noticeably uncomfortable.

"You've both worked hard to become detectives. Your gold shield tells everyone, cop and citizen, that you are the best of the best. But being the best carries with it certain responsibilities that I will hold you to every day. You may never fail your city, its citizens, your precinct, your squad, or your partner. Do we understand each other?"

"Yes, sir," both detectives quickly responded.

The more experienced detectives all smiled. They had received that same cautionary word when they had become detectives. It was like a rite of passage, the chief telling you what he expected.

Frank reached out and shook the hands of the two rookies.

"Welcome to the bureau. I look forward to working with each of you."

"Thank you, Chief," they said in unison.

"Okay, break's over. Let's get back to work," Stone said with a big smile.

Smiling or not, everyone knew he meant it. They scurried back to their desks and tried to look busy, even if they weren't.

Stone and the Assistant Chief walked into Frank's office for a more thorough briefing about city crime and cases to be investigated by the detective bureau. By the end of the day, Stone was worn out. He was anxious to get back to his mother's apartment and to Kaitlin.

"Oh, hello, Franklin. Did you have fun playing with the boys down at the stationhouse?" Mother Stone asked, knowing that her choice of words would bedevil her son.

Stone, who knew how to push his mother's buttons, responded by saying, "Yes, mum, we had a good time playing."

"Franklin, you know full well that I don't approve of the use of Irish slang in this house. I'm your mother, not your mum," she said with a disapproving look.

"To others, you are my mother, but to me, you are and will always be, mum," Frank responded playfully.

"Be respectful of your mother's wishes, Franklin," Kaitlin joined in.

Franklin rolled his eyes but said nothing. Both women loudly laughed.

At dinner that evening, a dinner served at one of New York's restaurants generally known only to those who lived within the city, but which served some of the best food in a city that had the reputation of being the gourmet capitol of the eastern seaboard, Mother Stone announced over dessert, "Franklin, we have decided that you will remain in the city through the holidays."

"And where will I work after the holidays, mother?" Stone asked." Oh, Franklin, you know that I have always told you that you can be anything you want. You're not getting any younger; it's time to do something important, to fulfill your destiny," his mother responded.

"And as long as we are on the subject of getting older, when are you going to give me a grandchild?" she continued.

"Yes Franklin, when are you going to give your mother a grandson?" asked Kaitlin smiling broadly.

Stone's face reddened as he excused himself and retreated to the "Men Only" bar for a drink in privacy.

Women, he said to himself as he downed a shot glass of Scotch whiskey.

"Women, indeed," he said out loud, smiling.

Chapter Twenty

ANDY STOPPED BY the telegraph office and sent a wire to Dwayne in Madison, indicating that he would spend some time in Shreveport, Louisiana. He reported that he was staying at the Crossroads Hotel and that he expected to head into Texas within the next week or so.

It was nice being in a Confederate-friendly city again. Shreveport had been the state capitol during the last two years of the war. Confederate troops had continued fighting for several weeks after General Lee had surrendered at Appomattox. Even Jefferson Davis, the President of the Confederate States of America, had been attempting to make his way to the Confederate stronghold of Shreveport when he was captured in Georgia, following the fall of Richmond. Yes, there were carpetbaggers in the city, but unlike Atlanta and Chattanooga, they tended to keep a very low profile. The people of Shreveport were very independent and Confederacy-minded. And they were individually very well armed.

The situation reminded Andy of something that his father had once attributed to Thomas Jefferson; something to the effect of, "*When the government is afraid of the people, you have freedom. When the people are afraid of the government, you have tyranny.*"

Andy walked around the city, especially around the docks and warehouses along the Red River. He was a little surprised by the sight of bales of cotton ready for shipment. The sight tugged at his heart, causing him to long for the days before the war. He bought a paper and returned to his room for a leisurely afternoon when he was startled by someone knocking on his door. Since he knew no one in the city, he was more than a little surprised. Grabbing his revolver, Andy cautiously opened the door where he saw the telegrapher holding a message. "You got a return on the message that you sent out this morning," the telegrapher said.

Andy tipped the telegrapher and thanked him for taking the time to deliver the message to the hotel. Reading the message, Andy couldn't help but wonder what Dwayne was up to. The message read, "Remain in Shreveport until you receive my letter." Fearing the worst, although he couldn't imagine what, Andy remained in Shreveport until Dwayne's letter arrived nearly two weeks later.

Dwayne indicated that he had sold half of the plantation. Included in the letter was a bank draft from the Bank of Madison for ten thousand dollars, which Dwayne said was Andy's share of the sale. Although unexpected, the bank draft would allow for the purchase of land should Andy want to start a new life in the West. Andy sent a telegram back to Dwayne saying that he had received the letter and thanked Dwayne and Everett for their generosity. He also said that he was headed into Texas the next morning and would contact them again when he could.

Andy still had a little over one hundred dollars in double eagles, so he didn't have to cash the bank draft, which would have likely taken weeks to clear a Shreveport bank. He spent the afternoon buying supplies for his trip into Texas, had dinner, and then went to bed early in order to rise early for his trip the next morning.

Andy was sick and tired of cities and trains. He was anxious to get back on the trail and into the forested mountains of northern Texas. Now that he was no longer traveling with Jeb, he had no particular destination in mind. Rather, he planned to take Texas Road, a road that led from northeastern Texas to Mexico, until he found a town of interest or an opportunity for a new life. He spent two days fishing at Caddo Lake, which had been named for the Caddoan Indians who had occupied the land long before European-Americans had settled there. He built a smoke oven out of rock and smoked a half dozen fish, thereby extending his supplies by several meals. Camping along the swampy lake, Andy felt alive again. He left Caddo Lake and turned north toward northeast Texas.

There was no line in the dirt or "Welcome to Texas" signpost. He guessed that he was in Texas after having walked and ridden for about ten hours. The mountain air was cool and clean, and he was at home in the pine forest; however, he noticed that there were plenty of hardwood trees in the forest too. Small animals and birds were abundant. His horses fed and watered, Andy set up camp for the night deep inside the forest.

Andy had been traveling at a leisurely pace for nearly five days. He stopped when he wanted, fished in mountain streams, and hunted for game for an early evening meal. He was enjoying his time in the forest, even when it rained, which it seemed to do once or twice almost every day. He had the feeling that this was more of a vacation than it was a planned trip, especially since he had no planned destination. He had been riding downhill for most of the day, so he was expecting to come out of the mountains by late afternoon. He exited the woods at a road that was headed in a westerly direction and decided to ride to the next town where he could resupply. However, as he approached a rock outcropping that narrowed the road, he was surprised to see a stage coach stopped with passengers aimlessly walking around.

"Did you break down?" he asked.

"No, we were held up. They took the horses, so we're stuck here," a passenger said.

The driver came around from the front of the coach and said, "We sure could use some help."

"How can I help?" Andy asked.

"Golden Eagle Hot Springs is just about ten miles down the road. You could ride to the stage stop and tell them where we are so that they can bring us some more horses."

"Tell me what exactly happened here," Andy said.

"We were going down the road when I spotted that there tree lying across the road," said the stage driver pointing to a tree on the side of the road.

"I pulled up, and they shot my security guard. Killed him right off. Then they had the passengers get out of the coach. They took our weapons and valuables, and then they unhitched the horses, shot up the water keg on top of the coach, and took off."

"How many of them," Andy asked.

"Three of them. Oh, and they took one of my passengers too, a high-born Mexican woman," the driver said.

"Which way did they go?" Andy asked.

"Back up in the mountains to the south. They went up through that draw there," one of the passengers said pointing into the forest.

"Well, I don't think they would take draft horses very far. Draft horses would just slow them down. How long ago did they leave?"

"Fifteen, maybe twenty minutes ago."

"It would take at least two hours for me to get to town, and another couple of hours for your stage stop people to get back, so I'll see if I can find the draft horses that the hold-up men took from you."

"I would sure appreciate that," the driver said.

Andy handed his spare canteen of water to the driver and said, "I'll be back as soon as I can."

He started up the draw looking for signs of the seven horses. He soon found the trail. He removed his rifle from the scabbard, cranked a round into the chamber, and picked up the pace in pursuit of the bandits.

Andy found three draft horses nibbling on grass about a half mile into the forest. He hobbled his two horses, then took a rope and fashioned a three-loop lead line and slowly approached the three horses. They continued nibbling at the grass while Andy tied a lead line around each of their necks and noses. Andy looked for the fourth horse but soon found signs that four horses had continued into the forest. Andy notched a tree to identify where the trail continued and returned to the road where the driver and passengers were still waiting. No one else had come by to offer help.

"I think they kept the fourth horse, probably for the woman they took."

"These three can pull the coach. We'll be slow, but we will get in by nightfall, thanks to you. By the way, what's your name?"

"Andy, Andy Davis."

"Well, Andy Davis, we sure thank you."

"No thanks necessary," said Andy as he swung his horse around and headed back into the forest.

"Where you headed?" the driver asked.

"I'll see if I can find that passenger of yours."

"I'll tell the marshal in town, maybe he can get up a posse to help you."

"I'll mark the trail by notching trees along the way, just in case he does get a posse together."

"I wouldn't count on it though. He and the county sheriff don't get along very well, and that's outside the town's jurisdiction."

"Well, I'll do what I can."

Andy rode off into the forest. He found the marker that he had left and dismounted with his rifle, carefully watching the forest floor for signs of the four horses and their riders. This part of the forest had not been disturbed for some time, so the hoof prints of the four horses were easy to see, even in dense pine needles. He followed the four horses on foot, leading his two animals until he caught up to the bandits some three hours later.

He smelled the smoke from the campfire. Andy secured his two horses to different tree limbs so that if they spooked, together they could not pull down the limb of the tree and run off. He placed a supply of bullets for his rifle in his coat pocket, and checked himself for anything that might make noise and removed his hat before advancing. He approached the campsite, taking cover as much as possible in case the bandits had left a lookout on the trail. Also, he couldn't be sure that there were still just three men. They might have joined a larger group after successfully raiding the stage coach. And then he heard her voice screaming "No! Stop that!" Even with her shouts, he advanced very slowly.

Evidently, the three bandits weren't concerned with being followed, Andy thought as he watched them from the bank above. They had made camp beside a streambed. The bank above them on both sides was six feet higher than the streambed and about ten feet away from their campsite. Their horses had been hobbled.

The woman was staked out in the dirt. Her ankles were tied to stakes with her legs spread. Her wrists were staked above her head. One man was sitting on his haunches with his hand disappearing under the woman's riding skirt from time to time, then reappearing to pinch the woman's breasts. That man was facing Andy and might have seen him had he not been so engrossed with fondling the woman. The two other men were sitting by a small campfire talking, smoking cigarettes, and laughing at the woman's screams.

Andy cocked his rifle and fired a shot into the chest of the man who was molesting the woman. The force of the bullet knocked him backwards into the men sitting fireside. Andy rolled to conceal himself behind thick brush on his left. The two bandits drew their revolvers and opened fire in the direction where Andy had been just moments ago. Andy chambered another round and fired on a second man, hitting him squarely in the chest. The third man stood, looked for cover, and then pointed his revolver at the staked out woman saying, "I'll shoot her if…"

Andy's third round hit the gunman high on the right side of the chest, spinning the gunman away from the woman on the ground. When the bandit's revolver fired, the bullet traveled harmlessly into the bank of the streambed. Andy's next shot finished him off. The bandit would never get to finish his sentence. Andy waited a full two or three minutes before going to the campsite to release the woman. He wanted to be sure that there was no one else watching from the forest. There wasn't.

Andy fully expected the woman to be hysterical when he got to her side. She wasn't. She was composed and remained silent until Andy had cut away the bindings that held her ankles and wrists. She stood and rubbed her wrists as she went to the dead body of the man who had been tormenting her and spit on him.

"Bastard," she exclaimed.

"I'm sorry if that offends you," the woman said as she turned to face her rescuer. "The man had no morals whatsoever."

"I'm not offended. You didn't spit on me," Andy replied grinning.

"Thank you for rescuing me. I fear that I was to be their after-dinner entertainment."

"Sure looked that way to me," Andy replied.

Andy checked to ensure that the three men were dead. He then loaded their carcasses across their horses—all except for one saddled horse. He loaded last man onto the unsaddled draft horse. He tied each corpse tightly so that they wouldn't roll under the animal's belly while they made the trip to Golden Eagle Hot Springs.

"Can you ride in a saddle, Miss?" "Yes, thank you."

The woman mounted the remaining saddled horse, her riding skirt hiking up, slightly exposing her leg. Andy couldn't help but look because the woman was truly beautiful.

"You can look, but don't touch," she said sarcastically.

Andy was embarrassed at being caught in his uncharacteristic voyeurism.

"Sorry," he said. "But you are very beautiful. I guess I just couldn't help myself."

The woman said nothing in reply, but she did smile a coy smile.

Andy drowned the campfire and led the woman and the horses up the stream bank to collect his animals. Once mounted on his horse, he headed out of the forest to ensure that the stage had gotten safely underway. They had followed the road to Golden Eagle Hot Springs for over an hour when three riders appeared riding at a full gallop with rifles in their hands.

With no cover in the area, Andy and the woman dismounted, placing the horses and the dead men between them and the oncoming riders.

"Can you use a shotgun?" Andy asked. "Yes, of course. I'm a Texas woman."

Andy removed the ten gauge shotgun from its scabbard and handed it to her. Then he removed his rifle and chambered a round taking aim at the lead rider. The riders slowed as they approached, realizing that they were the ones at a disadvantage.

"Hola, vaqueros," the woman shouted out her greeting. "It's okay, I know these men. They work for my father."

Andy relaxed a little but maintained a certain readiness.

The woman and the riders talked in rapid-fire Spanish, way beyond the few words that Andy understood. The woman explained, "These men were sent to meet the stage and to escort me to my father's ranch. When they heard what happened, they came after me. They would not want to return to my father without me."

Andy placed his rifle in the scabbard and reclaimed the shotgun from the woman.

"I will ride to my father's ranch with the vaqueros.

Again, I thank you for rescuing me."

As she turned to leave, Andy asked, "Can I at least know your name?"

"No," she replied. "Not today, but soon—very soon." She smiled broadly and waved as she rode off.

Placing the shotgun in its scabbard, Andy mounted his horse and rode the rest of the trip without further incident. All he could think about during the ride was the woman; probably about twenty five years old, he thought. He tried to remember her details, long black hair, startling white teeth, and a figure that any woman would be jealous of...

He arrived in Golden Eagle Hot Springs well after dark. He was surprised to see the town lit up with gas lamps along the main street. The town was much better developed than he had imagined any small town in Texas would be. Madison had not installed gas lamps until after the war, he remembered. Tree-lined streets complemented fairly large homes leading to the downtown area. By the time he located the marshal's office, a small crowd had gathered around him; all of them looking at the dead bodies draped across the horses that Andy had in tow.

"That's him, that's the guy that helped us," the stage driver said loudly.

"Did you find the woman?" he asked.

"Yes, she's okay. She rode to her father's ranch with some of his vaqueros."

The Marshal stepped forward and asked, "Did you have to kill them?"

"Yes," said Andy. "I was concerned that they would shoot the woman. In fact one of them threatened to do just that."

The marshal examined the faces of the three men. "Not from around here," he said out loud.

The undertaker appeared out of the crowd and said, "I'll take care of them for you, Marshal." Then he led the horses to his place of business to prepare the bodies for a common-grave burial.

The stage driver said, "I'll pick up the draft horse when you offload the body." Then he turned to Andy and said, "I want to buy you a drink, Andy."

"I'd like to get my canteen back." "Yep, I'll get that for you too."

The crowd moved in unison to the saloon to hear the story of how Andy had rescued the daughter of the largest rancher in the area. He explained only the most basic facts, leaving out the part that she had been groped and fondled but including the fact that her life had been threatened.

After a couple of drinks—one that the stage driver bought, and one that Andy paid for, Andy left the saloon and went to the livery where he rubbed down his horses and made sure they were fed and watered before registering at the local hotel for the evening. The shootings brought back bad memories of the war and of prison. He got little in the way of sleep that night.

The next morning, Andy shaved and bathed as best he could using only a pitcher of cold water, a bowl, and a hotel-provided bar of body soap. He dressed in clean clothes and made his way to the restaurant on the bottom floor adjacent to the lobby. He ordered a cup of coffee and noted that there were very few people in the restaurant. Taking his coffee cup to the veranda, Andy got his first daytime glimpse of the town. He was impressed.

Most of the buildings were painted white to reflect the sun. The buildings were trimmed with different colors. Nearby houses all had white picket fences and emerald green lawns of varying sizes. The most impressive and surprising thing that he noticed was that the town's sidewalks were made of cement, not wood. Every frontier town picture he had ever seen depicted a shabby and drab town with buildings made of dark stained wood. Golden Eagle Hot Springs was vibrant and colorful, so unlike anything he had ever seen in pictures.

Looking closer, he noticed that with the exception of a wagon passing through the main street every once in a while, there was little in the way of traffic. He could hear the sounds of work being performed, especially at the blacksmith shop down the street, but no one was just standing around. Men weren't wearing firearms either. That in itself was abnormal.

Andy returned the cup to the restaurant and then walked down Main Street toward the marshal's office. Entering the office, the marshal looked up and scowled.

"Just wanted to make sure that you didn't need or want anything more from me," said Andy.

"Nope. I think I got what I needed last night." After a couple of moments of uncomfortable silence the marshal asked, "Will you be leaving soon?"

"Are you in a hurry to get rid of me, Marshal?"

"I don't need killers in this town. When people start glorifying killing, they're more apt to solve their differences with violence," the marshal responded.

Andy looked at the marshal with penetrating eyes for several moments and then said, "In the war, I killed men—men who were trying to kill me and my troops. Yesterday, I killed three men who threatened to kill a defenseless woman—men who were shooting at me. I have killed men, Marshal, but I'm no murderer."

"Well Mr. Davis, that's reassuring to hear, but since I don't know you, I can't tell if you are being truthful or not."

"Well, Marshal, I have no way of convincing you otherwise, so I guess we will just have to let it be." Andy continued by saying, "I noticed that no one seems to wear firearms, Marshal. Is there a law against wearing firearms in town?"

"No, Mr. Davis, wearing a weapon is not against the law in this town. Using them may be. But then you never answered my question. Will you be leaving soon?"

"In a couple of days, maybe. I have no agenda. But I thought I would look around a bit."

"Well, Mr. Davis, let me show you around our town."

The two men exited the marshal's office and started walking down the street. The marshal began talking about the town of Golden Eagle Hot Springs.

"This town is truly blessed. We have the Red River to the north, a cement plant in the hills to the south, and a lumber mill to the east. There is mining in the mountains. We have some of the best ranches in Texas. Now that the Red River is navigable, and with steamboats able to come and go in either direction, we can ship our products to Louisiana, Arkansas, Oklahoma, and the panhandle of Texas by riverboat or by wagon down Texas Road to Dallas and beyond. We have a thriving economy, plenty of fresh water, the public bath in back of the hotel is part of the hot springs that the town is named for, and we have decent, hard working people who take pride in their town."

"Sure sounds like you have it all, Marshal."

"We do, Mr. Davis. And because we're located so far north, most people never get up here. They usually go to Dallas and to areas along the coast. Unlike the desert, we get plenty of rain and our weather is generally very comfortable."

"So what's the down side, Marshal?"

"If there is a downside, it's that there isn't much for young people to do, so they sometimes get into a little trouble. Nothing major though. We have a school for the younger children, but the older kids are expected to work, so they don't get the opportunity of a high school education. That means they don't get into a college, so they can't take advantage of opportunities elsewhere in the world."

"You sound like you've had some education, Marshal."

"Yes, I went to college in Iowa. I came out here and set up the lumber mill before the war, and I've been here ever since. The former marshal died a few years ago, and I was appointed to take his place."

The two men walked by a storefront with a "closed" sign on the door.

"This looks like a telegraph office," Andy remarked. "It is," said the marshal. "We lost our telegrapher to the war. Never could find another telegraph operator who wanted to live here, so it's closed until they can find someone to relocate up here."

Andy turned the door handle and was surprised to find the door was unlocked.

"It's not locked," said Andy.

"Not much need; there's nothing much to steal."

"Mind if I go in and check out the gear, Marshal?"

"You know how to operate a telegraph?"

"Yes, I was a telegrapher during the war."

"Well check it out, and call the station in Dallas, if you can. See if they have any messages for Golden Eagle Hot Springs. It has been several years since we've had a telegraph operator up here."

Andy checked the batteries and added some acid to the battery beakers. He connected the wires and sent off a message. Almost immediately, the stationmaster in Dallas replied. Andy explained the situation and asked if there was any traffic for the townspeople. The stationmaster advised Andy to contact Shreveport and Texarkana, Arkansas.

Shreveport had a couple of messages for the banker, and Texarkana had a message for the marshal. Andy asked the operator at Texarkana to send his traffic. The message explained that the marshal should be on the lookout for three men who were wanted for murder and robbery in Texarkana. The description was that of the three men that Andy had shot it out with in the hills above the town. He showed the message to the marshal who penciled a reply indicating that the three men held up the stage coach that ran between Texarkana and Dallas, and that they were dead; shot during apprehension, the Marshal said in his message.

"Well I guess that explains that," the Marshal said.

"I've got a couple more messages for the bank, so I will be awhile longer," Andy replied.

"Take your time, Andy. I'll see you later." For the first time since they had met, the marshal smiled.

Andy received the two messages and was about to close the station when the supervisor in Dallas asked if Andy was willing to work at the telegraph office on a permanent basis. Andy responded by saying he didn't know how long he would be in town, but with permission, he would check for incoming traffic on a daily basis until he decided what he was going to do. The supervisor agreed.

Andy closed the station and took the two messages to the bank.

"Are you the new telegraph operator?" the banker asked.

"No, I was just checking out the equipment and so I collected the incoming messages. If you have any outbound messages, I will be happy to send them for you."

"You sure that you don't want to take over the office?" the banker asked.

"I haven't decided on what I will be doing in the near future," Andy replied.

Returning to the hotel, Andy had a light dinner, what they called "lunch" in Texas and went to his room for a short nap. He had no sooner drifted off to sleep when he was awakened by someone knocking on his door. Grabbing his Dragoon, Andy answered the door where two vaqueros stood smiling.

"Señor Davis?"

"Yes, I'm Andrew Davis."

"Don Diego Alejandro Flores requests the pleasure of your company for dinner at six this evening at his ranch. What is your reply, Señor?"

"Where is his ranch?"

"Ten miles south on the main road, Rancho de los Angeles, Señor."

"Please tell Mr. Flores that I would be honored to join him at his ranch for dinner."

"Muchas gracias, Señor. Buenas tardes."

"Good afternoon, and thank you too."

Andy shook out the suit that had been rolled up for months in his canvas bag and asked at the hotel desk where he could get the suit cleaned and pressed. He was told of a laundry down the street that catered to townspeople, lumberjacks, and miners. He arranged with the laundry to brush and press his suit. They didn't have dry cleaning chemicals. He bought a new shirt, stiff collar, and tie at the general store. He also bought a gift bottle of wine for the occasion. By late afternoon, he was on the road to the Flores ranch. All he could think about was the woman whose name he didn't know.

He felt guilty that he had feelings for the woman that he had rescued. After all, his dead wife and son were never all that deep in the recesses of his memory. But still, he was a relatively young man, and he felt strong urges and desires for a normal life, a life between a man and a woman. It was close to six in the evening when he arrived at the ranch in near darkness.

As he rode up the driveway, he noticed a number of vaqueros lounging in front of a bunk house, having an early evening cigarette after dinner. Others were just leaving the ranch kitchen. Some of the vaqueros had stringed musical instruments and were playing maria- chi music near the open front door to the main house. Andy tied his horse to the rail in front of the house, nodded to the musicians, and, carrying the bottle of wine, knocked on the door frame.

A woman with graying hair, and who was dressed in colorful Mexican attire, met Andy at the door. She escorted Andy to the parlor where he was introduced to the ranch owner, Don Diego Alejandro Flores. Andy expressed his honor at meeting the rancher and handed the bottle of wine to his host saying, "For your good health and for the enjoyment of your family." Mr. Flores in turn introduced his wife, the Señora Maria Guadalupe Flores de Ruiz. However, the woman he most wanted to meet was nowhere to be seen.

"My daughter told me what you did to save her from the ravages of those animals that took her from the stage coach. You have my undying gratitude."

"I'm glad I was able to help. I was just a guy who was in the right place at the right time. I'm sure anyone would have done the same, Señor."

"I'm not so sure. Taking on three armed men was no small feat. It took great courage."

"Not so much, I was concealed on a bank above their campsite."

"Nonetheless, Mr. Davis, you have my thanks." "Please call me Andy."

"Thank you, Andy."

"You're most welcome, Señor."

After a few more minutes of polite conversation, the room was suddenly filled with the aura of their daughter who had stopped in the entryway so as not to intrude on the discussion.

"Of course you have already met our daughter," Mr. Flores said.

"We met, but we have not been introduced."

Mr. Flores went to his daughter's side where he took her hand saying, "Mr. Davis, this is our daughter and only child, Veronica Marguerita Flores de Ruiz."

"Señorita Flores, it is indeed a pleasure to meet you," said Andy bowing slightly."

"Thank you for coming, Andy."

Mr. Flores gave his daughter a disapproving look for her use of such an informal response.

"As you can see," Mr. Flores said, "Our daughter does not necessarily follow our traditions."

Andy didn't know how to respond, so he remained silent, an uncomfortable silence that was gracefully broken by Mrs. Flores saying, "Let us go in to dinner."

Dinner was less of a meal and more of a feast, which was begun with a prayer in the Catholic tradition, spoken in English by Mr. Flores out of respect for his guest. Strains of mariachi music could be heard from outside, but not so loud as to cover up the conversations that took place around the large rectangular wooden table which was ornately decorated with the leaves of fall made into centerpieces. An ornate tablecloth covered all but the corners of the oak table. Folded silk napkins highlighted a set of heavy, handcrafted silverware. Following dinner, Mr. Flores invited Andy to return to the parlor where there was a full snifter of brandy. Mr. Flores filled a small glass with brandy, which he sniffed and downed with a single gulp. He poured himself another glassful of the liquid laughingly saying, "They tell me that I should sip brandy; however, I find it more satisfying to drink the first glass and sip those that follow."

Andy raised his glass and said, "To your good health."

The two men completed the toast with a sip of the fine fruit of the grape.

"Please, sit down Andy and tell me something of yourself."

Veronica and Mrs. Flores entered the parlor, taking seats across from the two men.

"Yes, Andy, tell us," said a smiling Veronica.

Before Andy could say anything, Mr. Flores interrupted saying, "As you can see, both my wife and my daughter don't believe in leaving men to their own conversations, as women are supposed to do after a fine meal."

"Would you cause us to be uninformed, father?" Veronica teased.

"I will tell you what you need to know."

"Oh father, that attitude is so antiquated. I am old enough to determine for myself what I want to hear and from whom I want to hear it."

"Are you familiar with the name Veronica, Andy?" Mr. Flores asked.

"No, not really. Certainly I've heard the name before, but I cannot say that I am familiar with its derivation."

"It's my understanding that the name Veronica means a person who brings victory. Frankly Andy, I have not had a moment of victory in conversation with either my wife or my daughter since she became a grown woman. They do and say pretty much as they please, so I must ask you to please excuse their lack of tradition."

"Mr. Flores, I must say that I am enchanted by their company."

"I can see that you are not going to be of any help. You're encouraging them." Everyone smiled.

Andy took up the requested conversation by saying, "There's not much to know about me. I am a lawyer by training, but I am a farmer by choice. I grew up on a plantation in Georgia, was formally educated in Virginia, and traveled some in Europe before my parents died, which required that I return to run the plantation. I fought in the war on the side of the South and now I am trying to determine where I shall start a new life."

"Well there's not much need for a lawyer or a farmer in these parts," Mr. Flores responded. "Ranching is king, but we do have some mining and the start of a lumber industry as well."

"The Red River seems to offer opportunities for shipping cotton, meat and vegetables to other markets. I would think this would be an ideal place to farm."

"Farming has always been at odds with ranching," Mr. Flores answered just a little more animatedly. "This ranch was originally part of a Spanish land grant. It has been in our family for generations. When Texas became a state, I went to register our land claim of a little over ten thousand acres. However, the state would only recognize the original land grant, which was one-tenth that size. So we are reduced to a title of one thousand acres. We ranchers need open graze-land so that cattle can have enough to eat, especially through the winter months."

"I pride myself on being a student of agriculture, and I have studied the subject for more than just a few years," Andy responded. "It has been my observation that where there is opportunity, people will rush to participate in those opportunities. Many people in the eastern cities are tired of overcrowding. People in the South, like me, are looking for new opportunities in a land where they can raise families in peace yet make a living commensurate with the amount of work that they are willing to invest. I believe that trains will bring more and more people looking for opportunities in the West. And I strongly believe that farming can complement, not compete with ranching. As the west becomes more populated, I believe that fences will dot the land as they do in Europe. Farming allows the rancher to feed his animals on smaller parcels of land."

"Neither the Indians nor the ranchers will stand idle for that, Andy."

"The army will deal with the Indians; dishonorably, I fear. Ranchers and farmers will have to find ways to coexist."

"Either way, I fear there will be bloodshed," the rancher responded.

"I hope not, but I expect that you are right," Andy concluded.

Noting the late hour and thinking about the hour and a half or two hour ride back to town, Andy suggested that it was time for him to leave. The women got up and left the room, saying goodbye. Andy turned to say goodbye to Mr. Flores but instead blurted out, "Mr. Flores, I would like permission to call on Veronica."

Mr. Flores face flushed with anger, but he restrained himself and answered saying, "I'm sorry Mr. Davis but that is not possible."

Andy responded by saying, "I don't understand why it's not possible, but I will respect your wishes."

The two men shook hands, whereupon Andy mounted his horse and departed feeling utterly dejected.

Veronica, who had been standing in the hall outside the parlor, flew to her father's side loudly berating him in machinegun-rapid Spanish for declining Andy's request to allow him to call on her.

"I will see who I want, father!" she exclaimed. "I am not a young girl who needs to be protected from inappropriate suitors. I am a woman."

"You are my daughter," her father answered loudly, his temper rising. "We have a bloodline that stretches back to the Spanish in this country. You have a duty to retain your Spanish culture and heritage."

Mrs. Flores entered the room saying, "Hush you two, do you want the townsfolk to hear you yelling at each other?"

"No mother, you are right. I will never talk to this man again," answered Veronica who stomped out of the room."

"Hear me woman, you will not see that gringo again," Mr. Flores yelled.

"Veronica is right, there is no talking with you when you are like this," Mrs. Flores said. "I will not talk with you either." She too stomped out of the room in a huff.

And so it was for nearly two weeks. Neither woman would answer or talk to the man they called husband and father. At first, Mr. Flores delighted in the womanly quietness of the house. But after a few days, the silent treatment began getting on his nerves. He tried to bait them into talking, all to no avail. Then he demanded that they talk. The two women ignored him and walked off out of his presence. Finally, the silence became maddening and he decided to take the opportunity to go to Dallas on business. *At least there, I am held in great regard,* he thought to himself. He and his two closet vaqueros rode off early the next morning. The air was wintery cold, but not near as cold as the hearts of the women whom he loved the most.

Andy had made the decision to stay in Golden Eagle Hot Springs until the passing of winter. He knew that he would have to dip into the money from the draft in his shirt pocket, so on a weekday morning, he deposited the draft at the Hot Springs Bank and waited three weeks for it to clear. Word quickly got around town that Andy was not a drifter; and that he had a substantial amount of money in the bank.

Going into the telegraph office each morning, Andy would check in with the supervisor in Dallas to see if there was any message traffic for Golden Eagle Hot Springs. Now that there was an operator working in the out-of-the-way town, the telegraph business picked up.

Because he was not an employee of the telegraph service, Andy would only charge the line fee. He claimed no salary or per-message fee and he personally made no money for the service that he was providing. He kept accurate books and each month sent a bank draft by stage coach with the collected fees to Dallas. Everyone was happy. The townspeople got a cheaper rate, and the company got a telegrapher at no cost.

After sending and receiving morning messages, Andy would close shop and ride into the countryside, looking at land. He returned in the late afternoon to handle any message service that might have accumulated before closing the office for the night. His code speed picked up significantly, and as telegraph lines were installed across much of the nation, his fist was easily recognized, and he made friends with many of the nation's telegraph operators.

One abnormally warm fall day, just as he was considering closing the office to have an early lunch and to ride the countryside, the tiny doorbell tinkled, indicating that someone had entered the office. Turning toward the front door, Andy found himself looking at the smiling face of Veronica. His heart seemed to skip a beat, and he smiled saying, "You are the last person I expected to see."

"Well Mr. Davis, I have brought a one horse buggy. I intend to take you for a ride in the countryside, to feed you a picnic-basket lunch, and to talk with you of a more serious nature."

"What about?" Andy asked.

"Us," Veronica answered with a serious demeanor. "Veronica, there is nothing more that I would like to do. However, I promised your father that I would not call on you."

"Andrew Davis, perhaps you haven't noticed, but you are not calling on me. I'm calling on you."

"I don't think that your father would appreciate the distinction."

"Probably not. But he's in Dallas and you have to make up your mind here and now as to what is more important: Your honor, or the possibility that we might be attracted to one another?"

"I don't need a conversation for that. I'm already attracted to you."

"Then Mr. Davis, we are having lunch together. Now close up shop, and I will meet you in the buggy."

"Are you always so pushy?" Andy smilingly asked. "Yes, and you may as well get used to that right now, too."

Andy rolled his eyes and did as he was told.

Everyone downtown noticed Veronica and Andy as they made their way out of town. Veronica drove the buggy to an area that Andy had not yet visited, about five miles south of town on the west side of the valley. The area was distinctive because out of the ground, a mountain protruded straight up for several hundred feet.

"The townspeople call this the Spires because the tops of the mountain look like church steeples. There is no pass through or over the mountain because the mountain rises straight up. Some people say the ghosts of Indians who lived here several hundred years ago still haunt this place. Personally, I think it is very beautiful. What do you think?" Veronica asked.

"I have never seen anything quite like it," Andy replied as he went over to the mountain and dug out a small sample with his pocket knife. "It looks a lot like sandstone, but there is limestone and decomposed granite too. But you are right, Veronica. It is beautiful." *But not near as beautiful as you are,* he thought.

Veronica drove over to some scrub oak trees on the opposite side of the road. Andy hobbled the horse in a patch of grass so that the horse could nibble while Veronica grabbed the picnic basket and a cloth, which she spread out in the shade of the trees.

After lunch and pleasant but light conversation, Veronica spoke of the more serious side of her mind.

"Andy, I'm a woman, not a girl. I say that to you because I want you to know that I am not enamored with you just because you rescued me. Rather, I see in you compassion that I don't generally see in other men. You are concerned about the feelings of others. And you try to help others when they are hurting or in need. Being a caring person is probably the single most important trait that I look for, and so seldom find in a man."

Andy started to reply when Veronica put her finger to his lips and continued by saying, "Andy, I want you to know who I am; not the girl that my father sees, but the woman I have become, and why."

"I'm listening," he said fully attentive.

"My father shipped me off to finishing school in New York when I was sixteen. I found that I preferred reading books instead of walking with them on my head in order to develop poise. I enrolled in a nearby college, took a flat, had my mother send my allowance there, and when I graduated three years later, entered medical school. My mother made the necessary excuses to my father for my staying in New York. By the time I graduated from medical school, the war was starting and I took my residency at a military hospital so that I could practice medicine where it was needed most. As you can imagine, most of the wounded soldiers didn't want a woman doctor working on them, not even in surgery. So I worked the worst cases, those who were so severely wounded that they couldn't object. I also provided medical care to women and children who were injured; many more than one would think were wounded in the war. Frankly, I'm a damn good physician. But in the process, I have seen things that a woman doesn't normally see. In short, I'm no shrinking violet. But I do have womanly physical needs."

With that, Veronica moved closer to Andy and kissed him, lightly at first, and then more passionately as Andy responded to her kisses. Andy blushed and changed his position to ensure that Veronica could not see his rising passion.

"Veronica, you have to know that I was once married and that we had a son. They were killed during the war. My plantation was burned to the ground along with my family in our house. I returned after the war, but I couldn't remain there. I just couldn't face the shame I felt for surviving while they had been killed."

"I won't ask you to stop loving your dead wife and your son. But I would make you a good and willing wife."

"Are you asking me to marry you?" Andy asked incredulously.

"Yes, because I don't think you would ask me without my father's permission."

"So how do we get your father's permission?"

"We leave that to my mother. I will talk with her tonight if you want to marry me."

"Veronica, I do so want to marry you, but I won't until your father permits it."

"You leave that to me. However, you will have to ask him, and he will not be easy with you. He will try to break you down, to force you to reconsider. And then he will ask for concessions."

"What kind of concessions?"

"He will want us to marry in the Catholic Church, and he will want our children to be raised as Catholics. Can you accept that, Andrew?"

"Yes."

"Then ask me."

"Ask you what?" Andy asked.

"Ask me to marry you, because we are not going through life with you telling people that I proposed to you, even if I did."

Andy took her hand and asked, "Veronica, will you marry me?"

"Yes, if we can get my father's permission. Until then, we can say nothing to anyone about our pledge."

Andy reached over and kissed Veronica passionately.

"I think we had better go, Andy." Her face significantly reddened, she continued by saying, "The ghosts of Indians from hundreds of years may be watching us," she laughed.

"If so, then they are watching with great jealousy," he responded with a smile.

Chapter Twenty-One

January 2, 1866

IT WAS THE Tuesday after the Christmas and New Year holidays, and Frank Stone was getting ready to leave for work when there was an unexpected knock on the door. Kaitlin was sitting in the small apartment-sized kitchen with coffee, and Mother Stone was still sleeping in her bedroom. Stone moved toward the door, puzzled as to who could possibly be calling at such an early hour. Opening the door, Stone was astonished to see Commissioner Kennedy.

"Happy New Year, Franklin."

"Commissioner Kennedy, what an unexpected surprise, especially at this hour of the morning."

"Yes, yes, I know this is unusual, however, I very much need to talk privately with you and Kaitlin, and there's very little time."

"Come in Commissioner, please."

"Good morning Kaitlin, please pardon the intrusion on your morning. I am, however, pressed for time, and what I have to say is for both you and Franklin together."

"You certainly have my interest," said Kaitlin as she moved into the parlor.

After being seated, Commissioner Kennedy got right to the point.

Franklin, Kaitlin, the President of the United States, Andrew Johnson, asked me to meet with you this morning. He wants you both to go to Washington this morning and meet with him on a matter that he believes is quite urgent."

"Why both of us, Commissioner?" Kaitlin asked.

"Honestly, I don't know. I received a telegram asking that you both meet with him at five this evening. You can just make it if you catch the nine o'clock train. I expect that you will return on the morning train tomorrow and let me know how this meeting with the president is going to affect the department."

"You expect it will affect the department?" Stone asked.

"Yes, definitely. So will you go?"

Stone and Kaitlin looked at each other and nodded their heads saying, "Yes."

"Well, if we are going to Washington, I had better get dressed and pack an overnight bag."

"I have a taxi waiting in front, and I will take you to the station," Kennedy said.

Within twenty minutes, Frank and Kaitlin said goodbye to Mother Stone and the group left for the train station. Commissioner Kennedy already had first class train tickets, so there was no need to stand in line at the ticket window. Instead, the group went directly to the gate where Kennedy said goodbye and gave Frank last second instructions to see him first thing Thursday morning.

The train ride went without incident, yet both man and wife questioned why they would be summoned to the Executive Mansion. The trip seemed to take twice as long as it really did. When they got to Washington, Stone had the taxi driver stop by the Willard Hotel where they were surprised to learn that the staff at the Executive Mansion had already made reservations for them. After checking into the hotel, they continued on to the Executive Mansion where the doorman remembered them from their prior visits with President Lincoln.

"Good evening Mr. and Mrs. Stone, the President is upstairs in his private office," the doorman said.

A staff member escorted Frank and Kaitlin to the private office. As they were walking up the stairs, Stone couldn't help but feel that the Executive Mansion had a pall hanging over it; a gloominess that seemed to hang on since the death of its previous resident. Entering the president's office, Andrew Johnson walked to the door and shook hands with both Frank and Kaitlin.

"Thank you for coming on such short notice, especially so soon after the holidays," the president said.

"I admit to a certain curiosity, Mr. President" Stone responded.

"Please sit. Would you like coffee or tea?"

"Not for me, Mr. President," Stone answered.

"Nor for me, Mr. President," said Kaitlin. "So, direct and to the point, eh?"

"At your pleasure, sir," Stone responded, although his curiosity was badgering him.

"Frank, I need to ask you what your position is on handling Reconstruction."

Stone thought for a moment, then answered saying, "I guess I believe that we should do everything in our power to bring the people of the North and the South together to heal the nation as quickly as possible".

"And Kaitlin, my dear, do you agree with your husband?"

"Yes, I certainly do, Mr. President." "Really?" he asked.

"Yes, really," responded Kaitlin, a little irked at having her answer questioned, even by the President of the United States.

"Well I happen to agree with you both. So did Mr. Lincoln. However there are those who want revenge. They would have us enslave all Southerners with unfair taxes to pay for the war and to burden them with regulations that would be harmful both to them and to the nation. It has taken me some time to get through Mr. Lincoln's papers while simultaneously having to deal with a Congress that is split on the issues surrounding Reconstruction. For the most part, the Republicans want revenge. I'm not sure what the Democrats want. But I do know what Mr. Lincoln wanted for the nation, and that's why I have asked you to come to Washington."

"Franklin, it was President Lincoln's intent to ask you to take on the position of District U.S. Marshal: to enforce the laws of the land, to protect those who cannot protect themselves, and to carry out the functions prescribed by the President, Congress, and the Federal Courts. He was assassinated before he had the opportunity to talk with you about accepting the marshal's job."

"Now as to why I asked you both to come, I want you to take over the district office in northeastern Texas. You would be assigned to the Dallas office, but your district covers many hundreds of miles."

"Texas?" Kaitlin blurted out.

"Yes, Texas. It is a state that was aligned with the South, and it is being filled with carpetbaggers and Union officials who are hell bent on persecuting Southerners in violation of the law."

"Texas?" Stone echoed.

"I'll leave you two alone for awhile to discuss the matter. Let me know what you decide, I must know today because I need someone to take over the office by the end of the month."

When the president left the office, Kaitlin said, "I want to get out of the city, but Texas?"

"I'll leave it up to you, Kaitlin. If we move back to Maryland, I won't have a job. In Texas, I will still have my work, and we will be out of New York City."

"Do you want to do this?" Kaitlin asked.

"I wouldn't turn down the president. If that's where he thinks I can help, then that's where I should go."

"I'll have to find a tenet to take over the farm in Maryland."

"Can you do that?"

"Yes, I know of a man and his family who I trust."

"So, what are you saying, Kaitlin?"

"I'm saying that it looks like we are going to Texas, Franklin."

Stone stepped out into the hallway where a staff member was waiting.

"Please tell the president that we have come to a decision," Stone said.

The president walked into the office. Both Frank and Kaitlin stood.

"So I understand that you have an answer. What might that answer be," he asked.

Stone pointed to Kaitlin, who said, "We will go to Texas, if that's what you want, Mr. President."

"I was hoping that would be your answer. Thank you both. You will please take the morning train to New York. Franklin, you have a nine o'clock meeting with Commissioner Kennedy on Thursday. Your meeting should be short, so I will make arrangements by telegraph for a judge at the Federal Court to administer the oath of office at ten, after you have resigned from the police department."

Handing a parchment to Stone, the president went on by saying, "This is your appointment as U.S. District Marshal of northeastern Texas. You will have five deputies to help you. Any questions?"

"Not at the moment, Mr. President."

"Then you should have this too," he said handing a thick envelope to Stone.

"What's this," Stone asked."

"That's the pay you never collected from the army. General Grant was helpful in getting it for me. I believe it will help you get started. The government will pay your salary and expenses, so any money you spend on the move will be reimbursed."

"Thank you, Mr. President. That is very thoughtful." The two men shook hands, whereupon Kaitlin and Frank Stone departed, walking back to the Willard Hotel.

Mr. and Mrs. Stone caught the morning train arriving in New York at four-thirty in the afternoon. They caught a taxi to the apartment where they dreaded telling Stone's mother about the move west.

"Texas!" she shrilled. "They still have Indians in Texas."

"Yes, mother, but New York still has Indians too." "Not in the city."

They had a strained but quiet dinner. Mother Stone was not happy with their decision to go to Texas, and she let Frank and Kaitlin know of her displeasure.

"Mother Stone," Kaitlin said, "Franklin was asked to go by the President of the United States. It is his duty."

"He could have asked someone else, you know."

Yes, but he didn't. He asked Franklin. Now let us have a nice dinner as we will have to return to Maryland this weekend."

"Humph."

It was an eerily quiet dinner in the apartment on Third Avenue, east.

Stone was in Kennedy's office at nine in the morning on Thursday as requested.

"What did the president want with you this time, Franklin?"

"He has appointed me as a District U.S. Marshal. I have to go over to the Federal Courthouse at ten this morning to be sworn in. You're invited if you want to join us. Kaitlin will meet me there."

"I see. President Lincoln did indicate to me that he wanted you to take such a position. I didn't know if President Johnson would follow up on that or not. But I think it's a good decision. You know, Chief Stone, you have served this department well for the past twenty or so years; therefore the other Commissioners and I have decided that you are entitled to retirement pay. The Commission has awarded you a retirement of five hundred dollars a month. You know, Franklin, your Marshal's appointment runs out when a new president takes over, so this pension just may come in handy," Kennedy said smiling. He handed an envelope to Stone saying, "This is your retirement certificate and the contract that the city has to pay you retirement pay. And yes, I will definitely accompany you to the courthouse."

Kaitlin was already at the courthouse when Kennedy and Stone arrived. The ceremony took less than five minutes. Commissioner Kennedy shook Stone's hand saying, "Good luck, Marshal."

Over the next two weeks, the Stones stayed busy readying themselves for the move to Texas.

Former Senator Aaron Hill felt that he had made an enormous mistake. Why, he asked himself repeatedly, had he allowed the big-money special interests to brow beat him into giving up the one thing in life that he enjoyed most, being a member of the exclusive club of

U.S. Senators. He had enjoyed the power that he held as a senator. Once elected, he didn't have to do anything. He didn't even have to vote on congressional bills if he chose not to. The job paid him to do whatever he wanted, even if what he wanted to do was nothing.

He hated being part of the private sector. Technically, he worked for the National Development and Research Organization, a private sector organization little known to anyone except Hill and the big-money special interests that paid to have the organization deal with public officials at the local, state, and federal levels at their behest. They needed him, especially the railroad robber barons. It was his contacts in the Senate and the House who had passed the law giving the National Railroad Development Coordinator the power of eminent domain—the taking of private property for public or civic use—including use for economic development. And Aaron Hill was the designated National Railroad Development Coordinator.

Technically, he had enormous power. Only he could determine how much property would be required for the development and building of a national railroad. Instead of taking fifty or one hundred feet for a right-of-way, he generally took all of a landowner's property, citing the future use of the land on which to construct railroad buildings, including wood and water stops, and future economic development. That was especially true as he worked his way across Texas. Courts upheld his decisions based on the way the law was written and passed.

He learned that the really big-money special interests generally loathed public officials. In their opinion, public officials were merely pawns in the chess game of private enterprise. And now, he too was their paid pawn. As a senator, he dealt primarily with the paid lobbyists, representatives of the men who sat on the top of the nation's most influential and profitable businesses. Now he dealt with the robber barons themselves, and he found them to be small minded and revolting. Their only interests were money and the power that their money bought. The world was their playground and people were their servants—paid or unpaid—to do their bidding.

Before leaving Washington for the West, Hill ran an advertisement in many of the big newspapers of the east: "*Former Bummers Wanted—Experience a Must.*" Initially, he hired only ten men; all former Union soldiers who had been bummers, experienced at raiding and burning people out of their homes. The ten men who he had hired were the worst of the bunch. They were ideally the type of men that Hill intended to use to grab lands that were needed by the railroads to form a national rail system. He called them railroad police, indicating that they had some kind of police powers. In reality, they were hired thugs working as a private company. They were really employees of the National Development and Research Organization, like Aaron Hill.

Hill left New Orleans and started crossing Texas from east to west, buying and seizing property through the condemnation process. If a rancher refused to sell at a price determined by Hill to be appropriate, then he would condemn the land and have the U.S. Marshal forcefully evict the property owner and his family. He could use U.S. Marshals because he had the law passed by Congress to back up his land grab. In more than a few cases, especially in remote areas, he simply had his band of bummers kill the family. Everyone thought the bummers were on the payroll of the railroad, so few people questioned what they were doing or how they went about their business.

Yet, with all his authority, he hated his job. Not because of what he was doing to affected ranchers and farmers, but because he was no longer the ruler of his own life. Now he was ruled by railroad robber barons. He was just a paid employee. He had grown to hate the robber barons because they had taken away the life he wanted to live, all so that they would have even more money, even more land, and even more influence and power.

TOWARD THE END of January, Don Diego Alejandro Flores returned from his three-week trip to Dallas, worn out but happy. He had eaten too much, drank way too much, and enjoyed loose women as a man is want to do from time to time when circumstances permit. He fully expected that his wife and daughter would continue their wrath through silence, but he didn't care. He had been well satiated of female companionship on his trip. He could put up with their antics, he thought to himself. He was unprepared for their greeting.

His wife kissed him and welcomed him to hearth and home, hugging him. His daughter called him "Papa" in little girl fashion. So, he thought, leaving them was just the medicine they needed for them to come to their senses.

"Come, Papa, dinner is on the table waiting for you."

Veronica poured a large goblet of wine and handed it to her father who smiled and languished in the attention that they were lavishing on him. Seated at the table, Diego Flores turned to his wife and asked, "So what have you two been doing in my absence?"

"Oh," she answered, "just womanly things." Diego Flores nodded his head in a knowing fashion.

"Your daughter has chosen a husband," Maria Flores stated softly.

"No caballero has as yet asked me for her hand," Diego Flores replied.

"He soon will, father," Veronica submitted.

"And just who is this caballero who will ask for your hand, Veronica?"

"Andrew Jefferson Davis," she answered.

Diego Flores choked on the wine and threw the glass across the room.

"The gringo?" he asked in astonishment.

"Husband, you will never call him that again. You will think of him as the son that I was unable to give you, Maria Flores stated emphatically.

"Never!" he shouted. "Never in my lifetime will I give my consent to this marriage."

"Well father, he will not marry me without your blessing, so I guess I will have to go live with him out of wedlock. But you will never see your grandchildren. That I promise you," Veronica yelled back.

"You would live outside the church?" Diego asked incredulously.

Without waiting for an answer, Diego Flores slapped his daughter hard across the face, the first time in his life that he had ever done so. Veronica was more surprised than hurt. The hurt came a moment later and her eyes filled with tears.

"Diego Alejandro, stop," yelled Maria.

Veronica left the table and ran to her room. She hastily packed a bag, left through the kitchen door and went to the barn where she readied the one-horse carriage for the trip to town. She drove down the driveway while her father was looking for her in her room. He was fraught with pain for having slapped her. When told that she had left the ranch, he was filled with rage.

"I will kill that gringo before I let him marry my daughter," he yelled. Maria slammed the bedroom door and locked it. It was the first time the door had ever been locked.

Diego Flores got drunk and decided to sleep in the bunkhouse. He passed out in one of the empty bunks. The vaqueros were afraid to make noise, so the nightly card game ended on his arrival, and the lanterns were turned down. Nobody got much sleep that night; not Don Diego Flores who woke up in the middle of the night wondering why he was in the bunkhouse, not the vaqueros who also wondered why their patron was sleeping in the bunkhouse, not Maria who fumed and prayed most of the night in her bedroom, and especially not Veronica who had gotten a room at the hotel in town and cried the night away, rising in the morning with deep swells under her red and swollen eyes.

Diego Flores stumbled out of the bunkhouse rubbing his eyes and making his way to the main house. The front door was bolted from the inside. He pounded on the door to no avail. No one opened the bolted door. He went around to the back door, but that was locked too. He went to his bedroom window. His wife was dressed and was brushing her hair.

"Maria, mi esposa, please let me in."

"No, I don't know you anymore. You don't live here.
You live in the bunkhouse."

By the time Diego Flores got back to the front door, his clothes were sitting on the ground in a pile. He picked them up and carried them to the bunkhouse, yelling profanities.

Three days later, Diego Flores stopped by his bedroom window where his wife was again brushing her hair.

"Maria, please talk with me." "Talk," she said.

"Let me in." "No."

"Well at least open the window so that I can talk with you." "No."

"What would you have me do, Maria?"

"Do whatever you want, Diego. Go back to your loose women in Dallas. I no longer care. You have driven my daughter away, and you have driven me away as well."

"No, that can't be. See what this grin… man has done to us?"

"Diego, my love, he did nothing. You have brought all of this on yourself."

"Maria, please, let me in." "No."

Another day went by, and then Diego Flores rode to the hotel in town and knocked on his daughter's door.

"Is he here? Are you living with him now?"

"No father, he is a man of honor. He will not take me until we are married with your blessing."

In a very hushed voice, Diego Flores said, "You have my blessing, my child. Please forgive me."

Both father and daughter cried hugging each other. "He is a good man, father. You will be proud of him," she sobbed.

"Come child, let's go to him now. I will give him my blessing this very morning."

The two walked to the telegraph office, where Andy was receiving message traffic from the region. He heard the door bell tinkle, but he could not believe his eyes. Both Veronica and her father stood there smiling.

"I understand you have a question for me," Don Diego Flores said.

Without hesitating, Andy blurted out, "Don Diego Alejandro Flores, I ask for your daughter's hand in marriage."

"Will you marry in the Catholic Church?"

"We will."

"Will you raise your children in the Catholic faith?"

"We will."

"Then come to me, my son. You have my blessing."

Andy went to Diego Flores who hugged him and said, "Now I must ask you both to come with me to the ranch where I will beg for my wife's forgiveness."

Veronica packed her bag at the hotel, paid her bill, went to the livery where she paid the livery fee and hitched her horse to the buggy while Andy saddled his horse. They followed Diego Flores back to the ranch.

A vaquero called to Mrs. Flores saying, "Come see; Señor Flores and the Señorita Veronica, they come together."

Maria looked out the window and then opened the front door, rushing to her husband. Diego Flores dismounted and took his wife into his arms.

"Forgive me, Maria. Please forgive me. I have given them my blessing."

"I forgive you my husband. Now let us be joyful and celebrate the marriage of our daughter."

Andy spent the rest of the morning at the ranch, and then he explained that he had duties that required his attention in town. He rode back to town and reopened the telegraph office, where he spent the rest of the day planning.

Early the next morning he rode to the county seat some twenty miles to the southeast. Entering the Land Office, Andy inquired about the land surrounding the Spires. The Land Agent indicated that the Federal government owned it, but that it was for sale. Looking at the plot map, Andy asked the price for five hundred acres in a rectangle around the Spires. At two dollars per acre for undeveloped land, that would be one thousand dollars.

"How about the Spires? Is that land for sale?"

"Well it doesn't say either way. I don't think anybody ever considered the mountain to be sale-worthy," the agent said.

"If it were for sale, how much would it cost?" "I don't know, what would you offer?"

"Would two-hundred and fifty dollars be enough," Andy asked.

"Well, you can't graze on it, you can't farm it, so I guess that's a fair price," the agent said.

"Then I would like to buy the five hundred acres and the mountain known as the Spires," Andy said. "Will you take a check drawn on the Golden Eagle Hot Springs Bank?"

"Certainly," the land agent replied.

Andy wrote a check for twelve hundred and fifty dollars. The land agent signed the deeds and advised Andy to register his deeds at the county records office down the street. Andy walked down the street and registered his deeds with the county clerk and then returned to the street to retrieve his horse and start his trek back to Golden Eagle Hot Springs.

As he approached his horse, an exceptionally fat man stopped him and asked, "Who are you, and what's your business in town?"

"Andy Davis. I had some business with the county clerk. Why do you ask?"

"I'm the county Sheriff. I make it my business to know who the people are in my town."

"Well, Sheriff, I'm just leaving, so you don't have to wonder any longer."

"You can leave when I say you can leave," the sheriff said.

"I beg your pardon, Sheriff?"

"I said, you can leave when I say you can leave."

"Are you arresting me? If so, what's the charge?"

"Littering."

"And how did I do that," Andy asked.

"Well you're southern trash and you are on my street, so you're littering."

"I could say the same of you, Sheriff, except you look more like a bag of horse manure that's about ready to burst."

The sheriff went for his gun but Andy drew his revolver first and jammed it in the sheriff's open mouth.

"If you're looking to die, Sheriff, today's as good as any, I guess."

The sheriff's eyes widened.

"Now, do I have your permission to leave town?"

The sheriff nodded his head up and down. Andy took the sheriff's revolver and removed the cylinder.

"Nice to meet you, Sheriff," Andy said as he mounted his horse and rode out of town.

Four hours later, Andy related his story to the town Marshal.

"Yep that sounds like the Sheriff alright. He tries to bully everybody. But you better watch your back. People who stand up to him have been known to turn up dead with a bullet in their back."

"Thanks for the tip, Marshal. I'll keep an eye out. By the way Marshal, I have another matter that I would like to discuss with you."

The two men talked for over an hour and parted shaking hands. The next morning, Andy and the marshal rode to one of the mines where they discussed matters of importance to Andy, and again the conversation took well over an hour. When they had concluded their business, the miners shook hands with Andy and the marshal who returned to town talking and planning all the way.

The next morning, two miners showed up at the Spires. Shaping numerous dynamite charges, they blew a tunnel through the mountain. They were surprised to find that the seventy-foot long tunnel opened into a valley. The Spires were not part of a solid mountain range. Rather, they surrounded a lush green valley with fresh water cascading down from one of the spires and hot springs bubbling up nearby at ground level.

That afternoon, wagons of lumber arrived. Andy started building his house. But this was like no house anyone had ever before seen. Only the front face of the house was exposed. When the house was finally finished some months later, a row of Grecian columns decorated the front. Part of the dwelling was built into the tunnel. The main part of the house stood in the valley that had been hidden by the Spires. A patio deck, made of two-by- twelve redwood planks, was attached to the house so that they could enjoy the lush valley paradise.

The front of the house contained a fifty-by-fifty foot reception area. A twenty-foot hallway connected the front to the main part of the house: a two-story edifice built along the Grecian lines reminiscent of antebellum plantation houses in the Deep South.

Finding help was not difficult. Out of work craftsmen from Shreveport gladly made the trip to Golden Eagle Hot Springs. When the rough work was finished, Andy ordered oak, which covered the rough pine walls. The smooth lacquered and polished oak gleamed and reflected the light of lanterns that lined the hallway. He had Spanish marble tile placed on the floors. The marble also reflected the light from the lanterns. Instead of a dark and dreary house under the Spires, the rooms were bright, even those that did not have natural light. When he had finished after several months of building, he invited Veronica and the Flores' to view his work. They were flabbergasted.

"You knew the valley was there!" Veronica exclaimed!

"No, but I suspected it was," Andy replied.

Winter was beginning to give way to spring. They would be married in mid-March, two weeks away. The whole town and nearby ranchers were invited. Because the Catholic Church could not accommodate the entire town, a private wedding mass would be celebrated in the church, and the wedding reception was to be held at the hotel. A private reception would later be held in the reception room of the newly built house under the Spires. It would be a long but glorious day. Maria and Veronica rushed from ranch to town and back daily to make final arrangements. Diego Flores wisely stayed out of their way, tending to business on the ranch.

The wedding day arrived with brilliant sunlight, not a cloud in the sky. The temperature promised to be balmy. Andy bathed in the hot springs behind the hotel, dressed in his wedding suit, and went to the office to handle early morning message traffic. The only messages were from Dwayne and Everett, who sent their best wishes. Andy sent return messages thanking them for their good wishes and signed off for the day, telling the telegraph supervisor in Dallas that he was closing the office for his wedding.

A small column of Union cavalry rode into Golden Eagle Hot Springs from Oklahoma. They had been tracking a band of Indians who had left the reservation, killed a rancher and his family, stole horses and other property, and headed into northern Texas. Just as Andy was about to leave the office, a cavalry lieutenant entered.

"You look like you're closing up," said the lieutenant.

"I need to send a telegram to Fort Sill. Can you send it before you close?"

"Sure thing," Andy responded cheerfully.

The lieutenant handed a short message indicating that his column was still trying to locate the band of Indians and that they would head toward Dallas to see if they could pick up any sign of the renegades in the undeveloped area of northern Texas. Andy calculated the line fee, which the lieutenant paid, saying, "You look awfully well dressed for a telegraph operator."

"It's my wedding day. I'm to be married within the hour."

"Well congratulations," the smiling lieutenant said as he turned to exit the office.

"Thanks," said Andy. "I'll get this right out."

With less than an hour until the wedding mass, Andy closed the office door behind him, anticipating the most glorious day of his new life. In less than an hour, he and Veronica would be man and wife.

Chapter Twenty-Two

March 17, 1866

THE STAGE COACH with Frank and Kaitlin Stone arrived in Dallas near noon where they were met by a deputy U.S. Marshal. The threesome introduced themselves, and the deputy welcomed them to Dallas. Stone was tired of sitting and was anxious to walk around to stretch his bunched up muscles.

"You're bigger than I expected," the deputy said. "Yeah, I tend to stick out in a crowd," Frank replied smiling, tired of saying the same thing repeatedly when people referred to his size.

"I know you're probably tired from your trip, but Judge Hastings asked that we stop by his house on the way to the hotel. I hope that's okay with you and Kaitlin."

"Well, we all have to do what we have to do. Let's get it over with," Stone replied.

The luggage was loaded into a wagon where it was transported to the hotel. A carriage was provided for the ride to the judge's home, which was located in an upscale residential area outside of the downtown area, much of which had burned to the ground a few years ago but which had since been rebuilt.

"Welcome to Texas," the judge said while reaching out to shake hands.

Mrs. Hastings poured iced tea as the group sat in the parlor listening to the judge.

"We have too few judges and too few deputy marshals to adequately bring justice and law enforcement to our district, so unless there are extenuating circumstances, prisoners are generally brought to Dallas for trial."

The informal meeting droned on, and Stone started to nod off from time to time.

"Judge, Mrs. Hastings, I thank you for your courtesies, but I must beg your indulgence. My wife and I need to check into a hotel and get situated. I'll get on your calendar for a more detailed briefing, Your Honor."

"Fine, fine," the judge said smiling but feeling a little rebuffed.

The deputy took the Stones to the downtown hotel. "Thanks for picking us up, Deputy. I'll see you Monday morning unless something happens that makes you think that I should be contacted sooner."

"No problem, sir."

Frank and Kaitlin checked into the hotel. He generously tipped the bellman for bringing the extraordinarily large number of suitcases and canvas luggage to their room. Then he hurriedly undressed and went to bed.

"Wake me up in a year or two," he said.

Kaitlin joined him in the king sized bed saying, "You'll have to wake me up first."

Stone was surprised that it was still light when he awoke. They spent the rest of the weekend looking around the city, which was a lot smaller than either of the two imagined. The city had a population of less than a thousand people. It was a frontier town with dusty, unpaved streets.

At eight in the morning on Monday, Stone walked into the Federal Court building on Commerce Street and made his way to the District Marshal's Office. The deputy who had met him at the stage coach jumped up saying, "Good morning, Marshal." Others in the office, realizing that their new boss had arrived, stood and greeted him accordingly.

"Okay, everybody just relax. I want to check on a few things, and then I would like to meet with the chief deputy for awhile. Following that meeting, I would like to meet with each of you individually. There are no changes to be made just yet, so everybody just relax."

Stone went into his new office—the one with District Marshall written on the door—and picked up the badge that was lying on the wooden desk. Pinning the circled star on his shirt, he settled down behind the desk and started reading reports and statistics about the district. He met with the chief deputy, who seemed to have a firm grasp on cases to be worked, and then he met with each employee— law enforcement officers and administrative staff. By the end of the day, he felt like he had a lot to learn about law enforcement in the West, but he was confident that he had a good crew and that in time, he would learn to deal with law enforcement on a federal level.

Before returning to the hotel for the evening, Stone stopped by the telegraph office and sent a wire to Pinkerton, asking him to send Hermes, the Percheron geldings, and his tack as soon as possible. Kaitlin had been busy, too. She and Mrs. Hastings had found a suitable house on the edge of town with sufficient property for a garden. She and Frank met the land agent at the house where Frank signed the papers securing the sale. They were now officially Texas landowners.

❦

ANDY WALKED OUT of his office and turned toward the church, which was only a couple of blocks away. The column of soldiers, followed by their supply wagon, was slowly making their way out of town. As Andy stepped out into the street, the column turned in front of him, blocking him from crossing the intersection. He was looking down the barrels of twelve rifles held by the uniformed soldiers.

"Do you recognize this man?" the lieutenant asked, pointing to a mounted private.

Andy studied the man's features. It was the private he had allowed to go free at Turner's Corner. The surprise registered on Andy's face.

"Yes, I recognize him. He was one of five soldiers who tried to hang a civilian because the man was a Southerner from Texas."

"Well, that's not the way he tells the story. He says you and another man opened fire on the five soldiers for no apparent reason. He says that you killed four soldiers, but that he was able to get away. I'm going to have to take you into custody. You can explain your story to a federal judge in Dallas."

"I told you, I'm getting married this morning."

"Not this morning, you're not. Sergeant, place him in shackles and load him in the supply wagon."

The sergeant dismounted and took a pair of shackles and leg irons from the supply wagon. Two privates dismounted and grabbed Andy so that they could shackle him.

Andy didn't resist. But then the sergeant said, "Ah Lieutenant..."

The lieutenant turned toward his sergeant, noticing that the column had been surrounded by townspeople who were pointing rifles, shotguns, and revolvers at the outnumbered soldiers. The town marshal stepped forward saying, "What's going on here, Andy?"

"It seems that I've been taken into custody. They say that they're taking me to Dallas to stand trial for the murder of four soldiers killed back in Georgia.

"Did you kill them?"

"Yes, I killed them, but I didn't murder them. They were about to hang a man simply because he was from Texas, and they wouldn't back off."

The Marshal looked at the lieutenant and said, "Well, soldier boy, we're all from Texas, and we don't take to being hanged because we're Texans. Now you soldier boys, drop your weapons."

The lieutenant looked at the townspeople and told his men to drop their rifles. They did.

"Now, Lieutenant, how do you propose that we proceed?"

"Well, if you kill us, the army will come and burn your town to the ground. There will be a lot of bloodshed. If you don't kill us, the army will come looking for us, and your town will still be burned to the ground because the army doesn't like its soldiers held captive."

"Or, we could release you without your weapons and we could just keep Andy here in town," the marshal injected.

"Yes, but we would still come back with a whole lot more soldiers and there would still be a lot of bloodshed. Anyway you look at it, you lose."

Twenty vaqueros rode up with weapons at the ready. Don Diego Flores stepped up by the marshal and said, "You can at least wait until after the wedding."

"No I can't," the lieutenant said. "I have my orders. We are tracking a band of Indians that have already killed at least one family. We don't want to waste time and allow them to kill others."

Andy spoke up saying, "I will go with them, but I will ride my horse. I'm not riding shackled in the back of the supply wagon."

Mr. Flores spoke in Spanish. Two vaqueros rode away and returned shortly with a horse for Mr. Flores. Then in English, Mr. Flores said, "We will ride with you to Dallas. We wouldn't want you to shoot Andy in the back before he got to trial."

"Fair enough." the lieutenant said.

The privates took the leg irons off but left Andy's wrists shackled. Andy walked to the church and talked privately with Veronica who was already dressed in her wedding gown. She broke out in tears, but Andy promised that he would return and that they would be married.

Escorted by soldiers and vaqueros, Andy walked to the hotel stable where he saddled his horse and returned to the column of soldiers and vaqueros. Looking at Mr. Flores, Andy said, "This sure isn't the way I envisioned spending my wedding day." Mr. Flores scowled and remained silent.

Once again, the column moved toward the edge of town, this time followed by the supply wagon, Andy, Mr. Flores, and four vaqueros. By noon, two other vaqueros rode up with supplies for the trip. It took a week of travel, but the column arrived in Dallas at midmorning. Andy was placed in the federal jail. Mr. Flores and the vaqueros went to the hotel and registered for a week's stay.

Stone, who had been meeting with Judge Hastings, returned to the office after lunch and was told of the prisoner who had been brought in by the army on charges of murder.

"Please let me see the reports when they are ready." "Yes sir," the deputy said, "However, we're taking the accused upstairs to Judge Hastings court for a preliminary hearing."

"Okay, just let me know when the reports are available."

"Yes sir."

Andy was led into the upstairs courtroom where a prosecutor was talking with the army lieutenant and the private who had accused Andy of murdering the four Union soldiers at Turner's Corner in Georgia. Mr. Flores and the six vaqueros were also in the court.

Judge Hastings entered the court and took his position on the bench about three feet above the floor.

"Okay Mr. Prosecutor, what have we got?"

"Your Honor, this is a preliminary hearing in the case of Andrew Jefferson Davis who is accused of murdering four Union soldiers in cold blood."

"Mr. Davis," the judge said, "The purpose of a preliminary hearing is to determine whether there is probable cause to detain you until you can be brought to trial for the charges that have been filed against you. This is not a trial. It is a hearing to determine whether there is sufficient evidence to believe that a crime was committed and that you committed that crime. If there is, you will be bound over for trial, and you will be remanded to the custody of the U.S. Marshal until that trial takes place. Do you understand the purpose of these proceedings?"

"Yes, Your Honor."

"Mr. Prosecutor?"

"Your Honor, the government alleges that Mr. Davis shot and killed four Union soldiers at Turner's Corner in Georgia. A witness, who is in the court, and who was himself in danger of being killed, will testify both to the murders and to the identity of Mr. Davis, along with another man who is now reportedly dead as a result of a separate shooting. Another witness, the lieutenant, will testify that Mr. Davis admitted to killing the soldiers at the time of his arrest."

"Mr. Davis?"

"Your Honor, I did not murder those men."

"Well there does appear to be sufficient evidence to bind you over for trial. Until then, you will be held in the custody of the District Marshal. Do you have an attorney, Mr. Davis?"

"No, Your Honor. I don't know any attorneys here in Dallas. I will act as my own attorney."

"Are you a lawyer, Mr. Davis?"

"I'm not a practicing attorney, Your Honor, but I am trained in the law."

"Well if you are foolish enough to represent yourself, then I certainly have no objection."

Turning to the prosecutor, the judge continued saying, "Mr. Prosecutor, are you ready for trial?"

"The prosecution is ready, your honor."

"Mr. Davis?"

"Your Honor, I have had no time to formulate a defense."

"How long will you need, Mr. Davis?" "About a month, I would think."

"You have two weeks. Trial is set for April tenth.

Marshal, please take custody of the prisoner."

"Your Honor, how can I form a defense if I'm sitting in a jail cell?"

"That's your problem, Mr. Davis. Perhaps you should reconsider and hire a local attorney for your defense."

"Your Honor, it's my life on the line here. Keeping me in a jail cell is prejudicial in favor of the prosecution. I need to be able to use the resources outside of jail to put together a defense."

"Okay, Mr. Davis. You will be allowed to conduct the business of formulating your defense during normal business hours on weekdays, but only while under escort of a Deputy U.S. marshal. Will that satisfy you?"

"Yes, Your Honor. Thank you."

Andy knew that he had only one chance. If that didn't work out, he would almost certainly be hanged or shot to death by an army firing squad.

Pursuant to the judge's order, Andy was escorted to the telegraph office where he composed a message to his brother Dwayne. When he went to pay the telegraph fee, the supervisor came out of his office saying that there would be no charge. The two men talked awhile and then it was time to return to jail.

Stone read the reports about the murderer who was sitting in his jail waiting for trial. The name Andrew Jefferson Davis kept nagging at his brain. Somehow, he knew that name. Stretching as he stood up from behind his desk, Stone went to the basement where he immediately recognized Andy as the man who had saved his life, and who had stood guard outside his house after Stone had been shot on a lonely dark night in Maryland.

"My God, Andy, how did you get in this mess?" Stone asked.

It took a moment before Andy recognized Stone. "Well it looks like you survived," Andy replied.

"Thanks to you."

"Deputy, release this man," Stone said.

"I can't. Judge Hastings remanded him to jail. He can only leave under escort and then only during normal business hours."

"Release him to my custody, now."

"Yes sir," the deputy replied as he hurriedly unlocked the jail cell.

"You're coming with me, Andy. You can stay with me and Kaitlin until your trial."

"Won't you get in trouble with the judge?" asked Andy.

"I don't work for the judge. I work for the same guy he does, the President of the United States."

"I don't want you to get into trouble on my account." "You let me worry about that, Andy."

The two men met behind closed doors in Stone's office. Deputies and staff were left to wonder at the strange behavior of their new boss.

Following their meeting, Frank Stone and Andy left the marshal's office for Stone's new home. Stone rented a two-horse carriage at the public livery.

"I don't know where we will sleep," Stone said. "We just bought the house yesterday. We don't even have any furniture."

"Maybe you should join me in jail." Said Andy laughing.

As they pulled up to the house, a wagon was just leaving. Kaitlin was sweeping the front porch. She looked quizzically at the visitor who rode in with her husband.

When she recognized Andy, she dropped her broom and ran to him, hugging him.

"Well isn't that something. I married her, but you get the greeting," Stone said laughing.

"Oh, hush," Kaitlin said as she kissed her husband. "I take it that you bought some furniture."

"Oh yes, I spent your money lavishly," Kaitlin said smiling.

"Well I hope you bought a spare bed for our guest." "Not only a bed but a dresser, chair, table, and bedding," she answered.

"You really have been spending money. Did you buy us a bedroom set too?" he asked.

"You may have to sleep on the sofa tonight if you keep needling me, but yes, I bought us a bed too."

Everyone laughed and entered the home. The parlor and the dining room were not only furnished, they were already decorated. Kaitlin had obviously been very busy.

"I'm afraid I didn't have time to buy food. You will just have to take us out for dinner, Franklin."

"Anything to keep from cooking, huh Kaitlin?"

"I deserve a night out, Mr. Stone. I have furnished your home in a manner that is befitting your station in life, and I am ready for a night of relaxation and intelligent conversation."

"See Andy, not only does she spend my money lavishly, she wants to be rewarded for having done so."

"You are indeed fortunate to have such a good woman, Frank."

"Indeed I am, Andy. Indeed I am," Stone laughed.

DWAYNE RECEIVED THE telegraph message and realized that there was no time to be wasted. Every passing moment drew Andy closer to the gallows. Telling Everett of Andy's predicament, Dwayne saddled a horse, withdrew a thousand dollars from the bank, assembled a bedroll, and headed for the store at Turner's Corner. Even riding hard, it took three days to get there.

Mr. Turner, the store owner who had witnessed the killings, was adamant that he would not leave his wife or Georgia. After a day of pleading, and then only after Mrs. Turner had assured her husband that she could manage without him, the two men headed for the train depot in Atlanta as fast as they could. It took three days to get to Atlanta, another five days to get to Shreveport, Louisiana, and three days to get to Dallas on horseback, arriving at ten-thirty in the morning. The trial had started at ten o'clock.

The courtroom was attended by Mr. Flores, four of the six vaqueros, Franklin Stone, Rob Lowe, a news reporter from the *Dallas Times*, the prosecutor, the two soldiers, and the court staff.

The prosecution started by putting private Billings on the stand.

"Private Billings, please tell the court what happened on the day that four of your comrades were brutally shot and killed at Turner's Corner in Georgia."

"Well I had only been with the unit a few days before we left Atlanta for Tennessee. We got to Turner's Corner, where the sergeant decided to reprovision for the rest of the trip. As we entered the store, I noticed two men, one of which was Mr. Davis, drinking at the bar that was adjacent to the store. They were talking loudly and appeared to me to be drunk. The other man, not Mr. Davis, entered the store where we were and started yelling about damn Yankees being in the South. The sergeant ordered everyone to go outside and mount up. We did that. When the sergeant mounted his horse after paying for the supplies, we were just leaving the area when the two men from the bar came outside and shot my comrades in the back. But I was able to get away."

"You saw Mr. Davis shoot the soldiers?"

"Yes, in the back. They had no chance whatsoever." "Thank you. Your Honor, I have no further questions for this witness," the prosecutor intoned. "Mr. Davis?"

"Yes, Your Honor, a couple of questions." "Private, you just rode off in full uniform?" "Yes, I was able to ride off without getting shot."

"Your Honor, as you will see during argument for the defense, this private did not ride off. Rather he walked away from Turner's Corner without boots or socks. With a nearly one hundred mile walk without shoes or boots, he would likely have cut the bottom of his feet. Your Honor, I would ask you to order the private to remove his boots and socks so that we can inspect the bottoms of his feet."

"Objection—Irrelevant," the prosecutor railed.

"Mr. Davis?"

"Your Honor, both items, the question as to whether the private rode off in full uniform, and the examination of the bottom of the private's feet deal with the credibility of the witness."

"That's a little unusual, but it's so ordered. Remove your boots and socks, Private."

"No."

"Are you refusing to obey a court order?" the judge asked.

"No need, sir. My feet are scared, but that happened at a later time."

"Remove your boots, Private, or I will have the marshal remove them for you."

The private removed his boots and socks. The bottoms of his feet were indeed scared from cuts that were likely the result of walking a long way without protection.

"Your Honor," the prosecutor said, "Those scars prove nothing. First there was no foundation for the question, and as the private said, those cuts happened well after the killings."

"Mr. Davis?"

"Your Honor, the foundation for removing the boots came when the witness stated for the record that he left Turner's Corner in full uniform."

"I will allow the demonstration and the question as to whether the witness left the area in full uniform."

The prosecutor called Lieutenant Brown to the stand. "Lieutenant, please tell the court what Mr. Davis said on the day he was taken into custody regarding the killings."

"Mr. Davis said he killed the soldiers."

"I have no further questions for this witness, your honor."

"Mr. Davis?"

"Lieutenant, what exactly did the accused say?" "He said, "I killed them, but I didn't murder them." "No further questions, Your Honor."

"Mr. Prosecutor?"

"Prosecution rests, your honor."

"Mr. Davis?"

"Your Honor, I was expecting a witness for the defense. I would like a ten minute recess to see if I can locate that witness."

"No, Mr. Davis, there will be no recess. I told you before the trial started that by defending yourself, you would be held to the same standards of any other practicing attorney. You were required to be ready for trial at ten this morning. It is now ten-thirty-five."

"Your Honor, this is a capital case. Surely you can afford a ten minute recess."

"As a matter of fact, Mr. Davis, I can't. If you have no witnesses, then I expect you to summarize your case in your closing argument."

The courtroom door noisily burst open. Dwayne and Mr. Turner entered the court.

"What the hell," Judge Hastings blurted.

"Dwayne Davis, co-counsel for the defense, your honor."

"Are you a practicing attorney?"

"I am, your honor. I have been a practicing attorney in and for the State of Georgia for the past ten or more years."

"Mr. Andrew Davis is this attorney a relative, and if so, is he acting on your behalf?"

"He is Your Honor." "Proceed."

"The defense calls Mr. Turner of Turner's Corner, Georgia," Dwayne stated.

"Objection," called the prosecutor. "I was not made aware that there was a witness for the defense."

"Mr. Andrew Davis?"

The prosecutor was told that there was a witness several times, both by the army and by the accused. The defense, like the prosecutor, did not know the whereabouts of the witness until he came through the courtroom door, your honor."

Overruled, continue with your questions Mr. Dwayne Davis.

"Thank you, your honor."

Mr. Turner took the stand where he was sworn in by the Court Clerk.

"Mr. Turner, do you recall the events of the day when four Union soldiers were killed in front of your store?"

"I do. I was standing out front when it happened." "Please tell us what happened."

"I was working in the hardware store. I had served a drink to one man, Jeb something or other in the bar. The soldiers—all five of them—came into the hardware store. Then they went into the bar where they remained drinking for nearly two hours. Collectively, they drank three bottles of whiskey."

"One of the soldiers got into an argument with Jeb, calling him Confederate trash. The soldier said that all Texans are southern trash and that Lincoln should have put out a bounty on all Southerners. The rest of the soldiers joined in. One soldier got a rope and fashioned a noose. They tied Jeb's hands and placed him on his horse where they threw the loose end of the rope over a tree limb. It was then that Mr. Davis showed up and asked why they were hanging Jeb. The sergeant answered, "Because he's a Southerner."

Mr. Davis asked them to stop several times. He gave them an opportunity to stop the hanging but they kept on insisting that they had the legal authority to conduct the hanging. As the sergeant gave the order to hang Jeb, Mr. Davis opened fire with a shotgun, shooting the sergeant first and then the soldier that was doing the hanging. Two other soldiers went for their revolvers. Mr. Davis shot them with a rifle. The fifth soldier, that private there, threw up his hands, and begged for mercy."

"What happened next, Mr. Turner?"

"Mr. Davis had the private dig a common grave for the soldiers. When the private had finished digging the grave, Mr. Davis said prayers over the dead soldiers and had the private close the gravesite. Mr. Davis then had the private take off his boots and socks. Davis gave the private a canteen and told him to leave and never come back. The private left on foot."

"No further questions, your honor," said Dwayne.

"Mr. Prosecutor?'

"No questions, Your Honor."

"Well I have a question," the judge said. "Mr. Turner, have you talked with the accused at any time since the day in question at your store?"

"No judge. I never saw him again until the moment we entered this courtroom today."

"Did Mr. Dwayne Davis coach you about your testimony?"

"No, your honor. He did say that he would pay my trip expenses to Dallas and back to Georgia, but that was the only conversation that we had about the trial. He said he didn't want to jeopardize the case by talking about it before I got to court."

"Thank you, Mr. Turner. Are you ready to close Mr. Prosecutor?

"Yes sir."

"Please proceed with your summation."

"Your honor, Mr. Andrew Davis demonstrated that he is a rabid Southerner who could not, or would not, coexist with members of the Union Army who were in lawful performance of their duties when they went to Turner's Corner. According to the witness, who himself was in danger of being killed, Mr. Davis came out of the store as the soldiers were leaving and shot them in the back, killing four of them and leaving them in the street for the buzzards. The fifth man, Private Billings, was able to get away while Davis was shooting the other soldiers. Your honor, that completes my summation."

"Mr. Andrew Davis?"

"Your Honor, the private has continuously lied throughout this trial. First, he lied about how the soldiers came to be killed. They were not in performance of their duties. They were drunk. Secondly, the soldiers attempted, unlawfully, to kill a civilian by hanging him until dead, merely because he was a Texan. Third, the private lied about leaving Turner's Corner in full uniform."

"However, the defense also provided a witness; a witness who has nothing to gain, no matter which way you decide. He has indicated that everything the private said was an outright lie, and he has verified the testimony of the accused."

"Your honor, if this was a simple case of one man's testimony against another, then the Trier of Fact would have to determine whether the evidence was of such a clear and convincing nature as to be beyond reasonable doubt. No one hearing the testimony that was presented by the prosecution today could possibly be convinced that the testimony of Private Billings was truthful. The defense asks that at the very least, you acknowledge reasonable doubt and find the defendant not guilty."

"Rebuttal, Mr. Prosecutor."

"No rebuttal, your honor."

The judge looked down from the bench and began to render his decision.

"Mr. Andrew Jefferson Davis, please rise for the court's ruling in this matter."

Before the judge could continue, Marshal Stone stood and said, "Your honor. I would like to address the court as amicus curiae."

"Proceed, Marshal, although I have to admit that this is a bit of a surprise."

"Your honor, the prosecution would have you believe that Andrew Davis is a rabid Southerner who would go to any lengths to kill Yankees. During the war, Mr. Davis, a Captain in the Confederate Army, saved my life when I, a colonel in the U.S. Army, was shot by parties as yet unknown. Not only did he save my life, but he also stood guard over my wife and me while I was being treated by a medical doctor, placing himself at risk of detection and capture. I know this man to be one of the most honorable men I have ever met."

"Anything else, Marshal?"

"No Your Honor, but I do thank you for allowing me to act in the capacity of friend of the court."

"If there are no further interruptions, I will render my verdict. Mr. Davis, it is the determination of this court that the killing of the four soldiers was justified; done in the defense of another human being who the soldiers were about to willfully and unlawfully kill by hanging. It is the determination of this court that you are innocent of wrongdoing. You are hereby found to be not guilty."

"Lieutenant, I have no idea what the army will do with that private of yours, but it cannot be enough to right the wrong that he brought upon Mr. Davis.

Mr. Prosecutor, the outcome of this case should not be viewed as a case upon which the verdict was based solely on reasonable doubt. It wasn't even close. Your witness is a liar of the worst kind. Had he prevailed, Mr. Davis would likely have been hanged. Case dismissed.

Mr. Davis, you are free to go." Judge Hastings slammed the gavel with disgust.

Dwayne leaned over and whispered to Andy, "Not bad for your first case, Attorney Andrew Davis."

"Thanks Dwayne. I owe you my life."

Andy thanked Mr. Turner and said goodbye as the store owner left on the noon stage on his return trip to Georgia. Dwayne slipped Mr. Turner a few hundred dollars for expenses.

Andy introduced his older brother to Mr. Flores and the six vaqueros who had protected him from potentially overzealous soldiers during the trip to Dallas. That night, Mr. Flores, Andy, Dwayne, the six vaqueros and Frank and Kaitlin Stone had a gala dinner at the hotel where they got drunk while celebrating Andy's release from custody. The next morning they all awoke with headaches, even Kaitlin.

Andy never did read the story that broke in the *Dallas Times* that morning. The reporter told of the courtroom drama, how the final witness appeared at the last possible second. He told the story of how Andy saved the life of the new District Marshal, who was then a high-ranking U.S. Army officer. The story was sent by telegraph to the nation's major news outlets that reprinted the story, making Andy a kind of western folk hero to both Northerners and Southerners alike.

By noon Mr. Flores, the vaqueros, Andy, and Dwayne Davis left Dallas for Golden Eagle Hot Springs. Stone talked with the chief deputy, indicating that he was going north to see some of the district for which he was responsible. Kaitlin and Frank Stone had rented horses and tack for the trip because Hermes and the Percherons had not yet arrived in Dallas. Unofficially, they were going to attend a wedding.

Three days later, the group approached Golden Eagle Hot Springs. The whole town turned out to welcome Andy back home. Papers from Shreveport and Dallas had preceded Andy's arrival by a day on the stage coach. Everyone knew of the trial and its outcome.

On Saturday, the town turned out for the wedding. Following a day of festivities, the Flores family, the Stones, and the Davises went to the Spires where they marveled at Andy and Veronica's new home. The party lasted late into the night and on into the early morning, but Mr. and Mrs. Davis disappeared about midnight. The other guests stayed in spacious guest bedrooms overlooking the valley in the Spires.

As Mr. Flores lay besides his wife Maria he thought, *I really am proud of my new son.* He smiled, placed his arm around Maria, and fell soundly asleep, so soundly that the newlyweds could hear his snoring in the next room. They softly laughed.

Chapter Twenty-Three

Mid-April 1866

Kaitlin, Maria, and Veronica cooked breakfast at ten in the morning after the wedding day. Sleepy guests were unable to resist the smell of strong coffee, pancakes, bacon and fried potatoes, which were served on the patio in the valley in the Spires.

"What are you going to do with the valley?" Dwayne asked.

"Originally, I thought I would use it to plant vegetables, but I have since changed my mind. I think I will plant flowers, and bring in some baby deer and some small animals so that they will have an area that is protected from both man and beast. I may even add to the trees that are already there by planting some hardwoods."

"Your own Garden of Eden," Stone surmised. "Why not?" Veronica replied.

"Why not indeed," Dwayne said. "It's a wonderful idea."

"So what will you do with the rest of the land?" Diego Flores asked.

"I thought that I would grow cotton on part of the land and vegetables on about a third of the acreage. I've already talked with the stores in the shanty towns at the lumber mill, the cement plant, and the mining operation. They have all indicated a willingness to buy. And Shreveport isn't that far on the Red River. I'm considering growing hay and sorghum on part of the land to feed livestock.

I guess I'll play it by ear for the first few years to see what the market wants."

"I think that I have a buyer for the other half of the plantation," Dwayne indicated. "If so, we will send you some money to carry you over for a few years while you get started."

"That would really be helpful."

Conversation turned to the economy, which was weak, almost dire, following the war.

"Residents of Golden Eagle Hot Springs have had to go to the county seat to see a doctor, a trip of about forty miles round trip, so Veronica is going to open a practice in town," Andy said.

"Veronica, do you really think that men will want a woman to doctor them?" her father asked.

"Some won't, but those same men won't care if I'm a man or a woman when they are seriously injured. I saw a lot of that in the war. But if the women and children come to me for their medical needs, I'll be happy. But you Papa, you'll come, won't you?" Veronica asked smiling an evil smile.

"No! I don't want my daughter examining my body, he replied angrily."

"I know, Papa. I was just teasing you."

Conversation had turned to lighter subjects when Andy said, "I'll have to go into the office for awhile this morning to deliver some incoming messages."

"Good," said Dwayne. "I need to send a message to Everett."

Stone joined in saying, "I need to send some messages too." "Since the train doesn't go to Dallas yet, I need to find out where my horses are."

"Well I have a ranch to run," said Diego Flores. "Maria and I will head home when you leave."

Kaitlin said, "I'll remain here with Veronica and help her pick up the house."

Stone answered, "Well for heaven's sake, please put it back when you're finished."

"What?"

"Put the house back on its foundation after you pick it up," Stone laughed.

Kaitlin slapped Stone with a tea towel.

"See what I have to put up with?" Stone asked. "No sense of humor at all."

They all laughed and went to their separate bedrooms to prepare to leave.

"Don't be gone all day Andy," Veronica said with a sly smile.

"I won't. I should be home by three this afternoon." Andy, Dwayne, and Frank Stone rode off to town.

Diego and Maria Flores returned to their ranch, while Kaitlin and Veronica poured another cup of coffee and sat while talking on the patio.

Arriving at the telegraph office, Andy checked the battery beakers, hooked up the wires, and checked in with the Dallas office. "We have one message for Marshal Stone," the sounder clicked."

"Send your traffic."

"Telegram received last Wednesday. STOP. Your horses are at the freight depot in Shreveport awaiting pick up. STOP. Please advise, Edwards, Chief Deputy. STOP."

"Well that answers that question," Stone said.

"Andy, I think Kaitlin and I will leave for Shreveport tomorrow morning to pick up the horses on the way back to Dallas."

"Tell that big galoot, Hermes, I said hello," Andy said laughing.

"You never know about Hermes, he might just remember you. After all this time, I just hope he remembers me," Stone laughed.

Stone penciled a reply to the chief deputy. Dwayne wrote a message to Everett saying that he should be home within ten days or two weeks at the latest.

Dwayne and Frank Stone decided to take advantage of the public baths in the hot spring behind the hotel while Andy finished his business.

With no other messages to be sent or received, Andy asked to talk with the telegraph supervisor, who got on the line saying, "So how's married life?"

Andy sent back, "After one day, it's still good."

The sounder clicked off the words, "Hi Hi," which to telegraph operators means the sound of laughter (as in ha ha).

"I have a suggestion," Andy sent.

"What would that be?" the supervisor asked.

"The telegraph line runs along the road that passes my house. If you would send a few hundred feet of cable, some batteries, a key and sounder, I could set up a station at my home. I could provide better service until you find another telegrapher to staff the office here in Golden Eagle Hot Springs."

"Consider it done, Andy. We will have the equipment sent with the next line crew that inspects lines in your area in a few weeks."

"Thanks, for your help and friendship, AJ/SK."

Andy was entering information into the station log when he heard the tinkling of the door bell. Thinking that Stone and Dwayne had returned, Andy looked up from his desk, into the barrel of a twelve-gauge shotgun.

"So now you're some kind of hero, huh," the sheriff said with a sneer.

"I don't think you're a hero. You're just so much Southern trash. Stand up," the sheriff ordered.

Andy stood.

"What? Mr. Hero isn't wearing a gun? Well, that doesn't change anything. I'm still going to kill you."

The sheriff didn't see Andy shift the position of the pencil that he had been using. From a writing position, the pencil was now being held between the second and third fingers, and his hand was balled up into a fist.

The sheriff continued, "I've done some checking on you, and I know something that you don't.

"While you were a prisoner of war, I was one of the Union soldiers who burned your plantation to the ground. And even better than that, Mr. Hero, I'm the one who killed your young son who wouldn't stop screaming. How do you like that? I want you to go to your death knowing I killed your son. And now I'm going to kill you the same way you killed that Union army sergeant, with a shotgun."

The telegraph sounder clicked causing the sheriff to momentarily look toward the sound. Andy grabbed the barrel of the shotgun with his left hand and pushed it away from his body. Simultaneously, his right hand shot up jabbing the pencil deep into the sheriff's throat. The shotgun roared; however, the shot harmlessly hit the wall. Andy immediately removed the pencil and thrust it into each of the sheriff's eyes, instantly blinding the man. Blood and clear liquid squirted out of both eye sockets and more blood spurted out of the hole in the man's throat. Then Andy jammed the pencil as deep as he could in the sheriff's sternum. He broke off the part of the pencil that was protruding from the sheriff's chest so that the pencil couldn't be removed. With each movement, the pencil worked itself deeper and deeper into the sheriff's chest. The sheriff let go of the shotgun and tried to remove the pencil from his chest while running around the office screaming. The screams were eventually choked off as blood, bubbling up in his throat, leaving only intermittent sounds, gurgling, and the hissing of air as it was pushed out of the small hole in the sheriff's throat.

Stone and the town marshal pushed open the door, guns drawn.

"What the hell happened?" Stone asked. "The sheriff tried to shoot me."

"Why?"

"He took exception to my having killed that sergeant back in Georgia."

"We don't have a doctor here in the Hot Springs," the marshal said.

The three men watched for the nearly twenty minutes that it took for the sheriff to expire."

Townspeople gathered outside the telegraph office. The undertaker pushed his way through the crowd, took one look at the dead sheriff and said, "It's going to take a mighty big box to bury him."

"He was an animal," Andy replied. "He doesn't deserve to be buried like a human being. He should be hung in the trees for the birds to pick off his flesh."

No one added anything to those final words.

Several men in the group outside helped the undertaker carry the dead body back to the mortuary. By nightfall, the sheriff was buried without anyone in attendance except those who shoveled dirt into the deep pit that served as an unmarked grave. He was buried in the pit without a casket.

"I'll ride over to the county seat tomorrow and let them know that the sheriff is dead. Not that anyone will miss him," the marshal announced.

Andy, Stone, and Dwayne returned to the house under the Spires, but nothing was mentioned about the sheriff. Veronica could tell that something was bothering Andy, but she wisely remained silent, waiting for him to volunteer the information later. That night, after everyone had gone to bed, Andy and Dwayne sat on the steps in front of the house. Andy told Dwayne what the sheriff had said about his son Toby and the plantation.

"Where did you learn how to use a pencil in that way?" Dwayne asked.

"During the war, a guy by the name of Jubal McGraw trained me to use common implements as weapons."

"Well I guess the pen really can be more powerful than a sword," Dwayne laughed.

"More than you realize," said Andy, with a serious look on his face.

The two men talked for another half hour then went to turn in for the night.

The night ended on a somber note that carried over into the post-wedding bedroom. Andy held his new wife, but made no mention of the killing.

Following breakfast the next morning, Frank and Kaitlin Stone headed out for Shreveport along with Dwayne who would catch the first available train for Atlanta.

"Are you going to tell me what happened in town, now that everyone's gone?"

Andy gave her a short synopsis of the incident, but left out the part about his son.

Man and wife held each other in silence, Veronica thought about how close Andy had come to making her a widow. After nearly an hour of silence, Veronica pleaded with Andy to walk with her through the valley in the Spires. They walked hand in hand until Andy's mood changed so that they could talk about the future.

The future, Andy thought to himself. *Twice, we came close to not having one.*

Chapter Twenty-Four

Early May, 1866

Dwayne, Frank and Kaitlin Stone arrived in Shreveport early in the afternoon. Dwayne caught an evening train headed east. Frank and Kaitlin checked into the Crossroads Hotel, after which, Franklin went to see the freight agent. On the way, he stopped by the grocery store.

"I need some carrots," Stone said.

"You're fortunate. Just got some in yesterday," the grocer responded.

"I just need four."

"That'll be twenty-five cents." "For just four carrots?"

"Yep, we haven't had any all winter. This is the first of the crop."

Grumbling, Stone gave the grocer a quarter and walked to the freight office.

"Man, am I glad you're finally here Marshal. That big stallion of yours is a handful," the freight agent said.

I hope he's alright.

"Oh he's fine, but the two wranglers who have been taking care of him aren't so good."

"What happened?" Stone asked.

"Well they each one tried to ride him, to give him some exercise." Stone smiled a knowing smile.

"Where is he?"

"He's in the barn. Stall number three on the right. Your Percherons are in the next two stalls."

Stone entered the barn and started talking softly as he approached the stall. The stallion let Stone enter before head butting him, slamming him into the wall.

"Easy Hermes," Stone said quietly. Hermes slammed him into the wall again.

"Okay, I get it. You're not all that happy about the train ride or about being cooped up in the barn. I get it, okay?"

Hermes slammed Stone into the wall a third time.

Stone took the bridle and showed it to Hermes. "Are you ready to go for a walk?"

Hermes snorted and pawed at the dirt, but he didn't slam Stone into the wall again.

"Maybe you would like a carrot?" Stone asked.

Hermes smelled the left coat pocket and then the right pocket where Stone's hand was tightly holding one of the morsels. Hermes whinnied and shook his head. Stone pulled the carrot out of his pocket and Hermes' powerful teeth chomped the exposed end, nearly taking Stone's hand with it. Stone gave the big horse the second carrot, carefully watching to see if he was going to bite the hand that was feeding him. He didn't, but he sure came close. Stone rolled his eyes. He gave the remaining carrots to the Percherons.

Stone bridled Hermes and led him out of the stall. Then he put a lead rope on the two Percherons and led the three horses outside where he closely examined them. After he was satisfied, he signed papers acknowledging receipt and releasing the railroad of further obligation or liability. Stone saddled the stallion and, leading the two draft horses, rode out of the city where the horses were allowed to nibble on fresh grass and to drink cold fresh water from a stream. Stone talked with Hermes, and Hermes seemed to respond. *Apparently, we are on good terms again,* Stone thought to himself.

Stone put his three horses up at the public livery and returned to the hotel to find his wife trying on a new dress.

"I see you have been busy," he said.

"I needed something other than trail clothes for the fine dinner you are going to take me to this evening," Kaitlin responded.

"Am I taking you to dinner?"

"Yes, you are, Mr. Stone, and you are taking me to the theater too."

"I am?"

Kaitlin batted her eye lashes.

"I am," he said, and the two laughed and hugged. "Oh Franklin, thank you."

"For what?"

"For following me all the way to Ireland."

"And I thank you Kaitlin, for becoming my wife."

Kaitlin placed her head on his chest and held him close.

The following morning, Stone selected and purchased a carriage that was sturdy, yet comfortable for Kaitlin. Mr. and Mrs. Stone went shopping for supplies, both for the trip and for those things that Dallas, which was still a small town, didn't have. By noon, they were on the road home to Dallas. The Percherons were hitched to the carriage, and Hermes was tied to a steel o-ring on the back of the carriage, a position that Hermes did not like. But Stone, knowing Hermes moods, took to riding him or walking with him every couple of hours.

Because the road to Dallas was a main road from Shreveport, there were inns along the way, so there was no need to camp out at night. The horses were kept at a public livery or in a corral behind the inn. All-in-all, it was an easy and pleasant journey of a few days. After arriving in Dallas, Frank carried the supplies into the house, kissed his wife, and went to the office downtown.

"So, did you have a good vacation?" asked the chief deputy smiling widely.

"Actually it was a good trip. I met many of the sheriffs and marshals in several counties and towns. I even got to know some townspeople. However, on the road from Shreveport, I did notice with some concern that there were a number of deserted ranches along the way. Some of the ranch houses had even been burned to the ground."

"That would be the result of the railroad people. They're buying up land to lay track and to establish the wood and water stops that the railroad needs to fuel their trains. They have a congressionally mandated power of eminent domain, so if the ranchers refuse to sell for pennies on the dollar, the railroad people have been condemning the land and removing the ranchers and their families forcefully. They have even involved us on occasion. Although I disagree with their methods, they do have the legal right to the land, and we have had to enforce their property rights."

"What happens to the ranchers and their families?" "Most of them move on to other places and try to start up a new life. Others, those who chose to fight instead of leaving, have allegedly been killed by the railroad police who were enforcing the condemnation order. But there have never been any witnesses left alive."

"Who's in charge of these railroad police?"

"Well the guy who represents the railroad is some ex- senator named Hill. He's the one who has been designated as the coordinator for acquiring land for the railroad."

"Is he here in Dallas?"

"He was until a few days ago, but he has gone back east. He is supposed to be back in Dallas next month."

"I think that I would like to meet with him when he gets back. There must be a more equitable solution to getting the land the railroad needs while at the same time allowing ranchers to retain their livelihood."

"Yeah, well good luck with that," said the chief deputy with a look of disgust on his face.

Chief Deputy Edwards returned to his office, and Stone began tackling the large pile of paperwork, including vouchers for his men and the judges that had to be paid. As District U.S. Marshal, Stone was responsible for paying the salaries and expenses of the deputies and even the federal judges.

"You going to work all night?" the chief deputy asked as he was leaving. Stone looked at the Regulator clock on the wall. He was surprised to find that it was already six o'clock.

"I didn't realize it was so late. See you in the morning, Chief."

"See you in the morning, Frank," the chief deputy said as he closed the door behind him.

Stone stretched, closed the office, and walked to the corral where he saddled Hermes and headed home.

— ❧ —

AARON HILL RETURNED to Washington D.C. to move his wife and three daughters back to his New York farm and to sell his Georgetown mansion. His family had steadfastly refused to follow him to Texas. And although he drew a more than modest salary with expenses, he was no longer able to maintain two homes in the east plus the cost of living out of hotels in his travels across Texas. He hated the idea of selling his Georgetown home. It had been a source of great pride for the last fifteen years. The Georgetown house had been a visible indication of his wealth and success in life. Selling the mansion was tantamount to publicly admitting that he was no longer successful.

And even more, he hated the powerful big money businessmen who had placed him in this position. He could have refused to leave the Senate, however the businessmen who had financially supported him throughout his political career said that they would leak his corruptions to the news media. He would not have been able to maintain his senate seat were the media to make a mockery of his tenure in the Senate. And worse, he would have been publicly disgraced and humiliated. He had no choice but to serve the big money interests in any manner that they chose.

He temporarily left the acquisition of Texas railroad lands in the hands of the leader of the railroad police that he had hired months earlier. In truth, he was afraid of the big man. A former Union Army Sergeant, the big man had not been a bummer, but he had risen to the top of the railroad police because he was fearless and had never hesitated to kill those who would fight for their land and homes in opposition to the railroad. He had a penchant for killing and enjoyed watching his victims die: men, women, and children. The head of the railroad police was an evil man, and Hill knew that the big man wouldn't hesitate to kill him, should the occasion arise.

7Mid-July 1872

It had been six years since Hill had returned to Washington to sell his Georgetown home. His three daughters had since married and started families of their own. He failed to attend their weddings because his benefactors regarded his duties in Texas to be more important. His daughters refused to see him when he was in town and refused to write to him when he was in Texas. His wife died of a broken heart three years after returning to the New York farm. Aaron Hill wasn't able to attend the funeral. The New York farm was still in his name, but farming the land had been sublet to a local farmer who sent Hill a decreasing percentage of proceeds each year. Never before had Aaron Hill felt so alone.

Originally, the railroad was to bypass Dallas however, a local rancher gave one railroad company five thousand dollars and free right-of-way across his property if they would reroute the railroad through the Dallas area. Hill's benefactors could not resist such an offer. They rerouted the rails close to the main city but outside the direct control of the Dallas City Council. Another railroad was forced to build through Dallas when the state legislature passed a bill that required rail construction to pass through what would soon fall within the city limits of Dallas. So, with the arrival of trains in Dallas, the city's population grew exponentially. Water and gas lines were installed, and the city became the main hub for men and supplies headed further west. Dallas grew from a small town to a big city in less than two years.

Hill's work for the railroad robber barons was not complete with the coming of trains to Dallas. Rather, the rail system was to continue on across Texas to El Paso and then on to San Diego, California. He was also required to acquire land for the railroad from Dallas, north to Oklahoma. With each passing year, Hill felt that his life was ebbing away in worthless servitude to the big- money railroad interests that he had come to loath.

⤙⤚

FOR SIX YEARS, Andy and Veronica Davis had been deliriously happy. Andy had turned the undeveloped ground into productive farmland, producing cotton, vegetables, and grain, which were shipped to markets along the Red River. On occasion, he worked with his father-in-law, Don Diego Flores, where he learned the cattle-ranching business. The two men grew fond of each other. Where Mr. Flores regarded Andy as the son that he always wanted, Andy regarded Diego as his second father, and Maria as his second mother. In time, the older rancher began to see and respect the wisdom that Andy possessed, both as a farmer and as an innovator.

Probably no innovation drew as much attention as did Andy's installation of running water and indoor plumbing. He hired plumbers from New York who had installed a similar system in a hotel and who had used metal pipe instead of hollowed out wood that was normally used as pipe. His venting system, an apparatus that equalized air pressure in the sewage system with the air pressure outside, kept the stench of sewage out of the house. People came from miles around the county to see and to try the new bathrooms with indoor plumbing. Ladies were particularly impressed with running water in kitchen sinks. But Andy had installed other less spectacular water systems, including a fully functional irrigation system to water the crops during those lean water years when there wasn't enough rain, which wasn't very often.

With a telegraph system now wired into the house, the wire being buried underground to hide the fact that he had a telegraph capability, Andy continued to provide telegraph service to the town. In fact the townspeople had come to trust Andy so much with their personal messages, that they were rumored to have run off other would-be telegraphers who came to check out the town for possible relocation. Andy would check for incoming messages after breakfast, and then take the messages to town where he would deliver inbound messages and send any outbound traffic from the telegraph office, returning home by mid-morning. The townspeople were satisfied with that arrangement. Andy would check for message traffic late in the afternoon and deliver messages even at night, if required. He talked by wire with telegraphers throughout the region and became fast friends with many of the operators.

Veronica had opened a medical practice in the town of Golden Eagle Hot Springs, and as she had predicted, both women and eventually men came to her after they had gotten over the shock of a woman being a physician. After four years, she was able to purchase land for a small hospital. Andy designed the building, which included running water, indoor bathrooms, gas lamps, and heating. It was as modern as any hospital in the east.

The first professional nurse came from Denver, Colorado, but two girls from town took an interest in nursing and studied under the tutelage of the Denver nurse.

The doctor who practiced in the county seat used the new hospital too. Veronica was the more experienced surgeon because of her wartime surgical experience, and he was man enough (or doctor enough) to admit it. The two practitioners became close friends, both professionally and personally. Physicians from other close by counties used the hospital on occasion because there were no hospitals in their counties. Veronica appreciated the fact that she had other doctors with whom to discuss new medical procedures. The hospital thrived as did her practice. Women especially liked the fact that she had set up practice. They came from the closer counties and brought their children too.

It was well after noon when Andy finished serving the town's telegraph needs for the day. Having seen the stage from Dallas make its morning stop on the way north, Andy stopped by the Post Office. He picked up the mail, both his and the mail for his father-in-law.

He noticed that both he and Diego Flores had received letters from the railroad company that was laying track two counties to the south.

"Looks like Don Diego and I have received letters from the rail company," Andy said to the Postmaster.

"You're not the only ones," the Postmaster replied. "Every rancher on the west side the valley got one too."

"That can't be good," Andy remarked.

"I wouldn't think so," the Postmaster agreed.

Andy tore open the envelope and read the letter. When he finished, he reread the letter again to make sure that he understood what was being said. As the Postmaster had indicated, it was bad news. Andy walked to Veronica's office where he was told that his wife had gone to the hospital. Andy walked next door to the hospital where Veronica and the two nurse interns were scrubbing floors in the surgical room.

"Can you take a break?" he asked his wife. "I think you need to read this letter from the railroad."

Veronica wiped a curl of dark hair from her brow, stood up, and removed the gloves that protected her hands from the strong bleach solution that was being used to disinfect the Spanish tile floors. She reached for the letter without saying anything, knowing that the news would not be good.

"So what do we do now?" she asked after reading the letter.

"Don Diego got a similar letter. According to the Postmaster, all the ranchers on the west side of the valley got a similar letter. I think I had better ride out to the ranch and see your father before we decide."

"Okay, I'm about finished here. I'll meet you at home in a couple of hours."

Andy kissed his wife and then saddled his horse for the ride to the Flores ranch. His father-in-law was overjoyed to see Andy as he turned into the driveway for an unexpected visit.

"Hola Andy, what a welcome surprise."

"Hola Don Diego. We need to talk, for I fear that I bring bad news."

Andy dismounted, tying Hermes to the rail in front of the house. Both men walked inside where Maria greeted Andy. The two men went to the parlor where Diego read the letter three times.

"Can they do this?" he asked.

"Apparently they can and have been doing that to other ranchers across the state."

"But they say we must vacate the premises within thirty days. I've put a lifetime of work into this ranch and they say I must leave within thirty days? I won't do it. And they say they will pay us one dollar an acre. Are they crazy?"

"No, they're not crazy. They have the right of eminent domain, meaning that if we don't sell at the price they are offering, they can condemn the land and take it for free."

"But why do they need the whole ranch? I'm willing to give them enough land to lay down track for the trains, but I will not give them my whole ranch. I won't do it," Diego said loudly, the rage within spilling out.

"Other ranchers on the west side of the valley are receiving similar letters, I'm told. They will turn to you as the largest rancher in the area, so we need to consider not just ourselves but the other ranchers as well," Andy responded.

"Yes, we must meet with them before we make any decisions. I will have the vaqueros ride to the other ranchers and set up a meeting here for noon Saturday. That will give them a couple of days to read their letters and to think about what they want to do."

Twenty-two ranchers met at Rancho de los Angeles and the mood was dour. Each of the ranchers brought their letter from the railroad indicating that they had to vacate their lands within thirty days. They were angry men who wanted to lash out at the railroad. Their first thoughts were of violence. Some wanted to dynamite the rails that had already been laid. Others wanted to dynamite the rails and to kill those who were laying rail toward their ranch lands and homes. Andy tried to reason with them saying that the problem was a legal problem and thus should be handled in the courts.

"I have been studying the matter," said Andy. "I think that we have a possible case. The greater problem is getting a hearing within the court system. It may take a long time, well outside the thirty-day limit."

After two hours of arguing, the ranchers decided that Don Diego and Andy should go to Dallas and request an injunction with the District Federal Court. The two men left early the next morning and rode hard, arriving in Dallas near midnight on the second day of travel. They woke up the clerk at a hotel and got rooms for the remainder of the night. Sleeping for a few hours, they arose early and had breakfast.

"Before we go to court, I want to stop by the District Marshal's Office to see if Frank Stone is in town. His counsel would be of great value."

The two men from Golden Eagle Hot Springs walked to the courthouse where they entered the marshal's office. Stone greeted the two men warmly, but they were in no mood for friendly banter. "We represent twenty-two other ranchers in the county near Golden Eagle Hot Springs who have been ordered by the railroad to vacate their properties, including my farm, so that the railroad can lay track and build fuel stops for a rail line leading from Dallas to Oklahoma," said Andy. "The peculiar part of this dilemma is that the ranches are all located on the west side of the valley. The land on the east side of the valley belongs to the federal government. I think that we can make a case for the railroad to build their line on the east side of the valley, so we are looking to get on the court docket to file for an injunction. Any suggestions?"

"Yes. First, I would hire a local lawyer to file your injunction. I'll talk to the court clerk to see if you can get a hearing this afternoon or tomorrow morning. Normally I would advise you to talk with the opposing party before going into court. But there is a long history of the railroad moving in and forcing the ranchers off their property immediately after the property has been condemned. I agree that it would be reasonable for the railroad to build on the east side of the valley, but then I don't know why they chose to build on the west side to begin with."

"Do you have a recommendation for a local lawyer?" Andy asked.

"Let's talk with the chief. He's been here for many years and I trust his judgment implicitly," Stone replied.

After explaining the situation, the chief did recommend a lawyer. Andy and Diego consulted with the lawyer, who drafted an injunction for consideration by the court. He immediately took the written document to the court clerk and was told that the judge was available at three in the afternoon. The clerk suggested that to save time, a copy of the injunction request should be presented to the railroad's representative so that the judge could hear both sides of the case—for and against the injunction. The lawyer took a copy to the railroad's representative, ex-senator Hill, whose office was just down the street from the courthouse.

"You can't do this," Hill said explosively.

"I think that we can. I'll see you in court at three o'clock," said the lawyer as he left the office.

The court clerk ushered all parties into the judge's chambers instead of the courtroom.

"I understand you are requesting an injunction against the railroad," Judge Hastings said to the lawyer for the ranchers.

"Yes, Your Honor. We are seeking a permanent injunction against the railroad from building a rail line on the west side of the valley near Golden Eagle Hot Springs, which would require twenty-three ranchers and one farmer to vacate their lands, their homes, and their livelihoods. A copy of the injunction request has been provided to the railroad's representative."

"Mr. Hill, are you representing the railroad?" the judge asked.

"That's Senator Hill, and yes, I represent the railroad."

"Are you a sitting Senator?" the judge asked.

"No, I have retired from the Congress, but I am entitled to be called Senator by virtue of my long years of service in Congress."

"In this matter before the court, and as a representative of the railroad, you are acting as a businessman and an attorney. I have no objection to calling you by your former title, Senator. However, I do think you are being a little pretentious. Now then, Senator, what is the railroad's position?"

"Your Honor, the railroad has been given the right of eminent domain for the purpose of building a national railroad. It is a matter of national security and national economic necessity."

Hill produced several papers saying, "We have been to court several times regarding the matter of eminent domain and the condemnation of lands and property for the national railroad. In each case, the courts have sided with the railroad, based on the law passed by Congress."

The judge turned to the lawyer and asked, "Do you have a rebuttal?"

"Yes, Your Honor. The ranchers are not opposed to the railroad building the rail line through or near Golden Eagle Hot Springs. The ranchers recognize the economic advantages that they will gain as a result of such a line running from Dallas to Oklahoma. What the injunction requests is that the railroad be stopped from building on the west side of the valley. The Federal government already owns most of the land on the east side of the valley. That's why there are no farms or ranches there. It's a matter of being reasonable."

"Senator Hill?"

"Your Honor, the railroad is working on behalf of the national government. We don't have to be reasonable. We have already done the studies and laid plans to take the lands on the west side of the valley because that's where we want the rail to be laid. The ranchers have already established water lines, which will save the railroad a great deal of money. We need water to run the trains, and we don't want to have to establish a new water infrastructure on the east side of the valley."

"Rebuttal?"

"Your Honor, the Constitution of the United States is supposed to protect the rights of its citizens. I believe that there is an inherent requirement that the government and its contractors act with reasonableness towards its citizens, whenever possible. Clearly in this case, there is an opportunity for the government and the railroad to exercise such reasonableness."

"Senator Hill?"

"Clearly, the law is on the side of the railroad. I expect that you will uphold the law."

"Senator Hill, I am going to grant a temporary injunction for ninety days while I study the legal implications of both sides. You, as the railroad's representative, will notify the company that they are to immediately stop building the railway anywhere in the county in which Golden Eagle Hot Springs and the ranches, farms and businesses therein are located for the next ninety days.

"You damn fool," Hill responded. "You can't just stop hundreds of workers. This will cost the railroad an enormous amount of money," Hill exclaimed with anger.

"Mr. Hill, you made a big deal of calling you Senator. You will address me as Judge or your honor. Yes, this action will cost the company money. But removing people from their ranches and farms will cost them everything they own. They will lose more than just money. However, if you can convince the railroad to be reasonable—to do the right thing—you can save everyone a great deal of grief, and you can continue to work without any great loss of money by simply building on the east side of the valley."

"Damn fool," Hill said as he abruptly stomped out of the judge's office.

"Mr. Davis, I don't know how this will turn out for you. Hopefully the railroad will see the value of building on the east side of the valley and save further court action. I wish you the best of luck, he said as he handed the signed and approved temporary injunction to Andy."

"Thank you, your honor."

Rob Lowe, the newspaper reporter for the *Dallas Times* had been sitting at his desk near the big bay window that looked out on the main street. He had seen Andy Davis, Diego Flores and the marshal go into the lawyer's office, and he saw the lawyer hurriedly enter the courthouse a couple of hours later. At noon, the reporter had lunch with the clerk of the court, a long time friend who kept him advised of legal proceedings, and who told Lowe that Andy would be requesting an injunction against the railroad at three in the afternoon.

The reporter watched as the men climbed the steps to the courthouse a little before three. He waited a few minutes, and then climbed those same steps, turning into the hallway where the courtroom was located. He saw his friend ushering the men into the judge's chambers. He had hoped the hearing would be held in the courtroom, but he didn't mind eavesdropping—taking notes while standing in the hall. Senator Hill's loud booming voice carried into the hall especially well. The lawyer's more subdued voice was a little hard to hear, so the newsman, at times, would have to press his ear to the door. He was almost caught unaware when Senator Hill suddenly opened the door to leave the judge's chambers. That evening, the newsman and the court clerk had a drink in the privacy of the back room of the saloon where the clerk filled in those details that the newsman was unable to hear.

That night, the reporter wrote his story by the light of gas lamps. The reporter somewhat embellished on the known facts. His story clearly made the railroad the villains, suggesting that mysterious deaths and the disappearance of families were likely the work of the railroad police. Little did he know that his embellishments were very accurate. Had he known just how violent the railroad policemen really were, he might have been less energetic in his journalistic storytelling.

His story was published two days later. Because of the sensationalized embellishments, the story was picked up by other newspapers across the country. Andy and Don Diego were still on the road to Golden Eagle Hot Springs when the story broke. Once again, the stage coach delivered the newspaper to the valley, and everyone knew that Andy and Diego had been successful in getting a temporary injunction against the railroad.

In Fork Union, Virginia, Jubal McGraw read the newspaper article with great interest. "There's going to be a fight," he said to himself. "The railroad won't sit idly by and let the courts dictate where the rail company will build. Andy is in real danger and I can't sit here reading about it in newspaper articles," he said out loud to no one. Jubal immediately got up and packed for a train trip to Texas. But first, there were a number of things he would need before he could go. He went to Washington, where he met with a number of soldiers. He loaded heavy wooden crates into a rented wagon and headed to the train station where he shipped the crates to Shreveport, Louisiana. He would rent or buy a wagon and horses for the trip to Golden Eagle Hot Springs.

Don Diego called another meeting of west valley ranchers. He and Andy wanted to coordinate plans with valley ranchers for the protection of their families. Following the meeting, Andy returned home and sent a telegram to Madison, Georgia, which was addressed to his two brothers. The message was short and cryptic, saying only "2 KINGS, 11:11."

Dwayne went to Everett's house where they opened their mother's Bible and read the verse: "And the guard stood, every man with his weapons in his hand…" The verse was a call to arms. Dwayne and Everett packed for the trip to Texas, taking with them their weapons and extra ammunition. They too would buy horses and tack for the trip from Shreveport to the house built into the Spires.

———

SENATOR HILL MET in privacy with the leader of the railroad police.

"It's time to earn your pay again," the ex-senator said unfolding a map that showed the lands that the railroad wanted in the valley near Golden Eagle Hot Springs.

"How many ranchers are there?"

"Twenty-three ranchers and one farmer. I'm going to need more men, the rail police leader said."

"Do what you have to do, but I don't want anyone but us showing up in court in ninety days. This guy Davis seems to be the leader, so make sure he doesn't stir up any more trouble for us."

"What do you know about him?"

"Nothing much, other than what the newspapers say. He supposedly came out from Georgia where he killed some Union soldiers who were trying to hang a Southerner from Texas. He was tried in court several years ago here in Dallas, but he was found not guilty."

"What's his first name?" the railroad police leader asked.

"They call him Andy, so I guess his first name is Andrew. Why?"

"I remember an Andrew Davis, a Confederate officer, who I met during the war. I just can't help but wonder if it's the same guy. If so, I will take great pleasure in killing him and any family he might have. I should have killed him when I had the chance."

"You do what you have to do, but get him out of the valley."

"I plan on *planting* him in the valley—him and his family," the big man laughed.

Hill shuddered and left for his lonely hotel room.

The killer caught the morning train to Shreveport making connections across the country to Washington D.C., where he recruited another thirty men from up and down the eastern seaboard for short-term, high-pay employment in Texas. His recruiting took several weeks. He needed to get the right type of people: all former Union soldiers who would not be squeamish about killing men, women, and children, if necessary. While he was recruiting, he made it a point to enjoy the city and its ample supply of whiskey and loose women. "Life is indeed good," he thought.

EVEN THOUGH THEY had packed lightly, it took a little over two weeks and several different railroads for Dwayne and Everett to get to Golden Eagle Hot Springs with their horses. For Everett, it was a new experience. Dwayne had been to Dallas for Andy's murder trial and had made the trip to the house in the Spires to attend the wedding. When Dwayne returned to Madison, he of course told his brother about Andy's house in the mountain, but even with knowing where the house had been built, Everett wasn't prepared for what he saw. The four marble columns and marble steps leading to the house in the Spires were magnificent. The house itself, from the large reception area, and the twenty-foot-long hallway, both which had been built under the mountain, and the main structure that had been built in the hidden valley were unbelievably beautiful. The interior, like the front, looked very much like the antebellum plantation homes of the Deep South.

"This looks a little like the plantation houses in Madison," said Everett.

"Yes, but I've made a number of improvements," Andy replied.

After showing off the house and its improvements, including running water and indoor plumbing, the three brothers went out on the patio and discussed the situation about the railroad.

"Anybody home?" Veronica called as she walked in from the reception area.

"We're out on the patio," Andy replied. "We?" she asked.

"Dwayne and Everett have arrived. You're home early today," said Andy after he had kissed his wife.

"Dr. Robinson from the county seat has a patient in the hospital, so he's staying in town for a couple of days, and I have no patients this afternoon, so I came home early. You must be Everett," Veronica said as she walked over to greet the one brother she had not yet met.

"What a pleasure to finally meet you. I've heard a lot about you," said Everett.

"And I have heard about you too, Ev. Welcome to the Spires," Veronica replied, smiling as she kissed him on the cheek.

After greeting Dwayne, the foursome went out on the patio to continue the conversation about the railroad.

"Are you sure that the railroad is going to attack the ranchers?" Dwayne asked.

"No," said Andy. "But that seems to be their history as they acquire land across the state. If they can't get the ranchers to leave voluntarily, they condemn the land and move them off forcefully. Several of the ranch families have just disappeared or have been killed. But nobody has been left alive who can identify the railroad police as the killers."

"What about this injunction that I've heard about?" Everett asked.

"It's a temporary injunction that expires in October. At that time, Judge Hastings will render a decision about a permanent injunction. But if no one shows up in court on our behalf, then the railroad wins by default. So we are preparing to defend our homes and our property until the judge renders a final decision."

"Sounds prudent to me," Dwayne interjected. "What can I do to help?"

"You are the more experienced lawyer. Could you prepare a brief in case Judge Hastings asks for final arguments?"

"Okay," said Dwayne as he picked up the temporary injunction for review.

"What do you want me to do Andy?" Everett asked. "Over the next few weeks, we will be meeting with the ranchers who are affected by this land grab. You might start putting together a plan for defending our homes."

"I'll see what I can come up with," Everett said reflecting on a number of scenarios.

"Enough talk of railroads and tactics," said Veronica. "Let's enjoy the rest of the evening."

Six weeks after leaving, the leader of the rail police arrived back in Dallas with his new recruits. It took another week to outfit the so called railroad police with horses, tack, and Union Army uniforms, a tactic that the big former army sergeant enjoyed using to make victims think that the killers were army personnel sent to protect them. The ruse had worked every time. None of the ranchers that they had killed ever suspected that the uniformed soldiers were there to harm them.

Hill was nervous. The final judgment from Judge Hastings would be rendered in less than six weeks. He hadn't consulted with the Board of Directors. He would handle the situation himself as he had all the others who chose to defy him. The ranchers had to be removed before October.

Fifty hard-faced riders dressed in civilian work clothes left Dallas on horseback in the early evening hours on Friday, followed by two men on a heavily laden four-mule team supply wagon and another two men on a chuck wagon that was being pulled by two large draft horses. The leader expected to arrive in the Golden Eagle Valley on or about Wednesday of the following week. Lots of people saw them leave. Everybody who saw them leave Dallas surmised that blood would be spilled in the days that were to follow. But then, the railroad police had the law on their side, they assumed.

Chief Deputy Marshal Edwards and U.S. District Marshal Stone watched them leave.

"What do you think they're up to?" Stone asked. "No good, that's for sure," replied the chief deputy.

"You think that they're headed for Andy's place, don't you?" the chief asked seeing the worried look on Stone's face.

"Yes," replied Stone.

"What will you do?"

"Chief, we're supposed to enforce the laws of the President, the Congress, and the courts. I guess I'll take the night train to Shreveport and ride Hermes down to Golden Eagle Hot Springs from there to enforce the injunction. I should be able to get there a few days before those killers."

"You want me to go with you?"

"No, you have to run this office while I'm gone, Chief. If anything happens to me, take care of my wife and get her back to Maryland. Also notify the president."

"You're expecting this to be end badly, aren't you?" "This is going to be more of a fight than those railroad people realize. Those ranchers aren't going to leave voluntarily, not even if they are coerced. I think this will likely end up being a fight to the death of many people, good and bad, before it's done. I need to try and stop it before it gets started," Stone replied.

Rob Lowe also saw the men leave Dallas on horseback. He surmised that they were headed north to "negotiate" with Andy. Lowe walked over to the telegraph office where he drafted a message, telling Andy that fifty hard case railroad people had left Dallas headed north. The telegraph supervisor who knew and liked the newsman read the telegram and asked, "You think they're headed for Andy's place?"

"Yes, I do."

"I'll get this telegram out personally, Rob. No charge."

"Thanks," The newsman said. "At least he will know what's headed his way."

The supervisor sat at the table and sent the message with an urgent precedence. Andy wasn't on the line when the supervisor called, but every operator on the line would listen for Andy. They would pass the telegram before any other message traffic when he did get on the line. Urgent and emergency traffic always got the highest priority.

Stone rode the train to Shreveport. Hermes was in a section of the baggage car built for livestock. The train ride went without incident, arriving at Shreveport near midnight. Stone checked into the Crossroads Hotel and asked for a six o'clock wakeup call. He awoke at five, shaved, packed his canvas bag, and headed for the corral to get Hermes. As he passed the railroad depot, he saw a large man, larger even than Stone, wrestling crates and loading them into a wagon. Stone stopped and offered to help the man load the heavy crates.

"Looks like you could use a hand," he said.

"I wouldn't turn down help. I guess these crates are heavier than I thought."

After loading the crates into the wagon, the big man turned and offered his massive hand.

"Jubal McGraw of Fork Union, Virginia, and I thank you."

"Frank Stone from Dallas, Texas. Glad to help." Where are you headed?" Stone asked.

"A little town called Golden Eagle Hot Springs. Ever heard of it?"

"Yes, that's where I'm headed," Stone replied suddenly more alert. "What takes you there?"

"Friend of mine from the war may need some help." "Anybody I might know?" Stone asked.

"Dunno, but his name is Davis, Andy Davis. You ever run across him?"

"Yeah, several times," Stone said smiling. "He took care of me in Maryland when I was shot during the war."

"In Maryland? I remember him saying something about a big ugly guy who got shot in Maryland named Stone. Are you that Stone?"

"Yep, that's me alright. Well Mr. McGraw, if you want some company, I'd be happy to ride with you."

"It would be downright good to have someone who actually knows how to get where I'm going, but please, call me Jubal."

"Can do, Jubal. If you're ready, we had better get on the road. Daylight's burning," said Stone.

"I'm ready."

The two men headed out of the city and turned north toward Golden Eagle Hot Springs. They progressed at a moderate clip, stopping only to care for their horses and to relieve themselves. They ate hard tack and drank only water from their canteens on the road, riding throughout the night, Stone slept in the saddle. Jubal stayed awake as his recently purchased horses were a bit skittish on the unfamiliar road. They arrived in Golden Eagle Hot Springs on Sunday, just as it was starting to get dark.

"I had better get a room at the hotel," said Jubal.

"I wouldn't do that if I were you. Andy will have a place for you at his place. It's nearly another hour's ride, so I recommend that we keep moving."

"Well Andy doesn't know that I'm coming. I would hate to impose."

"Jubal, Andy doesn't know that I'm coming either, but I wouldn't want to insult the man who saved my life by staying in town. He would not take kindly to you staying in town either."

"Okay Frank. You're the one that knows the lay of the land, so I'll take your suggestion to heart."

The two men rode in silence to the house in the Spires. Stone didn't tell Jubal anything about the house. He wanted Jubal to get the full effect when they arrived.

"What the hell is that, Frank? It looks like the whole base of that mountain is ablaze."

Frank laughed saying, "That my friend, is Andy's house. It's built into the mountain."

"He lives in a cave?" Jubal asked.

"Some cave, Stone said as he continued laughing. "Wait 'till you see the inside."

Stone and Jubal watered their horses in the trough in front of house while Stone knocked loudly on the front door. It took nearly a minute for Andy to open the door.

"Frank, what a wonderful surprise. Come in, come in."

"Well I have another surprise."

Jubal stepped into the light of the gas lamps in the entryway.

"Jubal McGraw? My God, Jubal, what brings you to Golden Eagle Hot Springs?"

"You do, Andy. I read a newspaper article that made me think that you could use my help."

"My God, come in you two. I have never been so glad to lay my eyes on two such ugly characters," Andy laughed.

Veronica came through the hallway and entered the reception area turning everyone's heads.

"Frank," she said, "What a wonderful surprise. Did you bring Kaitlin?"

"No, this is a business trip, otherwise she would have come. She loves this place."

"Honey, let me introduce you to Jubal McGraw," said Andy. "We were in the war together. Jubal, this is my wife, Veronica."

"Mr. McGraw, please consider this house to be your home while you're in Golden Eagle."

"Jubal took Veronica's hand and kissed her fingers saying, "You are too beautiful for words and certainly too beautiful for Andy. However did he convince you to marry him?"

"Actually, I asked him to marry me," Veronica said, laughing."

"Then he is indeed a fortunate man, for he has made an uncharacteristically wise decision."

"Hey you two," Andy said. "I am standing right here, you know." Everyone laughed.

Dwayne and Everett entered the reception area.

"Hi, Frank," Dwayne called out. Let me introduce you to our brother, Everett."

Stone and Everett shook hands while Andy introduced Jubal McGraw.

Veronica invited everyone to join her in the parlor; however, Frank said that they needed to tend the horses. Andy, Jubal, and Stone took the three horses to the barn where the horses were fed oats and hay. The horses ate hungrily because they had eaten oats only sparingly during the trip.

Andy went over to Hermes saying, "Hey big fella. Do you remember me?"

Hermes whinnied and shook his head up and down, pawing at the dirt floor. Andy rubbed the neck of the big stallion.

Jubal, this is the smartest horse I have ever known.

Meet Hermes."

Jubal, who was larger than the other two men, walked over to Hermes and talked gently saying. "You sure are a big fella, good looking too."

Hermes again whinnied and shook his head as if in agreement.

Stone went over and said good night to the big horse. "See you in the morning. Sleep well, my friend."

Hermes snorted in answer to Stone.

"I swear that Hermes knows what you are saying," said Andy.

"Oh he knows, alright. We have conversations all the time."

Andy turned off the kerosene lantern and the three men returned to the house where Veronica had prepared a large meal.

"She cooks too?" Jubal questioned. "And she is a physician."

"Do you have a sister?" Jubal asked.

"Sorry, Jubal," said Andy. "She's one of a kind."

"She surely is," said Stone.

After dinner, Jubal quietly asked Andy to point the way to the outhouse. Andy led him to the indoor bathroom and explained how to flush the toilet.

"Amazing," Jubal said, and closed the door as he marveled at the marble interior.

"We need to talk," said Jubal.

"Tomorrow," said Andy. "You look like you haven't had a night's sleep in quite awhile."

"Only a couple of days," said Jubal.

"We're not as young as we used to be, Jubal. Get some rest and we'll talk in the morning. That goes for you too, Frank."

"You won't get any arguments from me, Andy."

Andy took Jubal and Frank to their bedrooms, and then he and Veronica turned in too. Dwayne and Everett stayed up and talked a while longer.

The next morning, Veronica got up early and cooked a large breakfast, which she served after daybreak on the patio overlooking the valley in the Spires. The aroma of strong coffee brought the five men to the patio where Jubal got his first real glimpse of the hidden valley.

"My God, Andy," said Jubal. "This truly is the Garden of Eden."

"Well it's our Garden of Eden, anyway."

"Who would have thought that there was such a beautiful valley encircled by a mountain? I've never seen such a sight before," said Jubal in complete awe.

"Andy did," said Veronica. "Actually it was quite a surprise to everyone in the area."

Jubal admired the water cascading down from one of the spires and noted the mist rising from the pools of hot springs. "Is that hot water?" he asked.

"Yes," said Andy. There are several hot springs located in the ground near the house. We use one of the springs to provide hot water in the house. We use the other, cooler hot spring to relax in. It's like a hot outdoor bath, which feels great after a hard day's work."

"It's actually very therapeutic," said Veronica.

Following breakfast, Andy hitched the two Percherons to the carriage, and Veronica made her way to her office and to the hospital in town. The five men went out on the patio to discuss the large force of men headed toward the valley.

"Before we get started," said Jubal, "I come bearing gifts. The first one is in this package."

Jubal handed a six by nine inch package wrapped in waxed butcher paper and tied from top to bottom and from side to side with twine.

"I've been holding that since you were captured, but until a few days ago, I had no way of knowing how to get it to you."

"What's in it?" Andy asked. "Open it," Jubal responded.

Andy withdrew a pocket knife and cut the twine. He carefully undid the wax paper and unwrapped the present.

"My journal!" Andy exclaimed. "What a wonderful surprise."

"I rescued it from your room after you were captured," said Jubal. "The rest of your gear was sent over to the Army Supply Warehouse. I'm afraid its gone forever."

"I didn't expect to see this again," said Andy.

"Thanks."

"I have other presents too," said Jubal. "But those can wait until later."

Andy started the meeting by saying, "I received a telegram the other day from Rob Lowe, that newspaper reporter down in Dallas, saying that there is a band of railroad police headed this way."

"He's right. I saw them too. That's why I came," said Stone.

"How big of a force?" Andy asked.

"About fifty men, not counting the two men on the supply wagon and two on the chuck wagon."

"That sounds more like a military force geared up for a campaign," Andy remarked.

"About thirty new men showed up in town about a week before they left. Obviously they were gearing up for something more than for one or two ranchers," Stone replied.

"We have twenty-three ranchers, their families, and Veronica and me who they would like to see gone," Andy said more for Jubal's information than for Stone.

"We got a temporary injunction a few weeks ago, but we have to return to court in October to see if the judge will grant a permanent injunction."

"I know," said Jubal. "I read about it in the papers." "Sorry, Jubal. I didn't realize that the news story got all the way to Fork Union."

Andy continued by saying, "Well, there are more people to consider than just us. I guess we should meet with the ranchers again. Any idea how long we have until they get here?" asked Andy.

"Well their wagons will slow them down. The supply wagon especially looked awful heavy. They had a four- mule team pulling it. I would guess they will be in the area not later than Wednesday. That only gives us three days to prepare for their arrival," Stone replied.

"I have to go into town for a couple of hours, then I think I'll go to my father-in-law's ranch and see if he wants to set up another meeting with the rest of the ranchers for tomorrow morning."

"Is there a livery in town?" asked Jubal. "Yes, a very good one," Andy replied.

"Well then, I would like to ride in with you and see if I can trade in my wagon and the two draft horses that I bought in Shreveport for a couple of riding horses."

"I think I'll ride over and see the new sheriff at the county seat," Stone added. I'll be back in a couple of hours, so I'll see you all this afternoon.

"Looks like we all have a full morning. I'll see everyone back here this afternoon."

Dwayne and Everett, who weren't going anywhere, helped Jubal unload the crates into the reception area.

"What's in those crates?" Jubal, asked Dwayne. "They're heavy!"

"I'll show you later, Jubal replied.

Andy delivered a couple of telegrams to the bank, had a cup of coffee with the town marshal, checked with Veronica to see if there was anything she needed while he was in town. Andy prepared to close the telegraph office as Jubal rode up to the front of the office riding a large bay and leading a slightly smaller sorrel.

"I see you found some riding stock, Jubal."

"Yep, the livery owner was quite generous when he heard that I was staying with you and Veronica."

"He's a good man. We have a lot of good people in Golden Eagle Hot Springs."

"Sounds like you found a good place to settle down, Andy."

"We did. I just hope we can keep it, and stay alive to enjoy it."

Chapter Twenty-Five

Tuesday, September 17, 1872

ALL TWENTY-THREE RANCHERS met in the early evening hours on Tuesday after having put in a full day of work in a light rain that had been falling all day. They were wet and cold, and they were in a foul mood. After introducing the ranchers to Frank Stone, Jubal McGraw, Dwayne, and Everett Davis, Don Diego asked Marshal Stone to address the ranchers. Stone told the group about the large force of railroad police that he had observed leaving Dallas, and said that he believed were headed for the valley of Golden Eagle.

"I expect that they will arrive in this area sometime tomorrow. Jubal McGraw and I will scout the area tomorrow to see if we can confirm their arrival. Our primary objective is to safeguard you and your families. To do that, we need to work together. No one rancher can fight a force of that size with expectations of winning. Jubal and Everett have been doing some planning, so I would ask you to listen to what they have come up with to safeguard your families."

"We don't have enough men to protect the ranches, so our plan is to draw the railroad men to the Spires, which is the most defensible area in Golden Eagle," Everett explained.

"Let me see a show of hands if you fought in the war," he said. Most of the men raised their hands.

"How many of you were cavalry," he asked. Over half of the group raised their hands.

"First, we are going to ask you to move your families to town. The town marshal will take responsibility for safeguarding your families while you are protecting your homes. The hotel will put up most of your families, and some of the townspeople have indicated that they will put up those that the hotel can't handle. We have no reason to believe that the railroad police will attack the town, but if they do, the marshal and the townspeople will protect their town and your families."

"When should we move our families to town?" a rancher asked.

"I don't know. It depends on which tactic the railroad men choose. I'm guessing that the railroad men will take a few days to reconnoiter the area. That means that they would likely attack those ranches that are closest to the main road on Saturday or on Sunday when many of you would normally be in church. If they attack sooner, we will deploy riders to let you know to evacuate your families immediately. I would suggest that you pack your valuables tomorrow. You should have everything ready to go just in case an attack comes before Sunday. The five southernmost ranchers should consider moving their families to town tomorrow morning."

The ranchers shook their heads in understanding and agreement.

"Each of you has a remuda, said Diego. It will be necessary to have your fastest riding stock ready for our riders who will confront the railroad men on the road."

"We have to wait until the railroad men attack ranch property or people before we swing into action against them. Marshal Stone will be the first to make contact with the railroad men in an effort to stop them."

"This is vitally important," Stone explained. "We cannot be seen as the aggressors because sooner or later, any action that we take will end up being reviewed in a court of law. You can't afford to win a battle here and lose the war in court."

Everett continued explaining the plan by saying, "Those of you with cavalry experience will be formed into two groups. Your job is not to fight a battle. Rather, you are to hit and run. You are to get the railroad men to follow you through the county to the

Spires—to bypass the ranches. The first group of raiders will form near the southernmost ranch. The next group will form up at the next ranch to the north. Following a feint attack, the first group will ride to the third ranch and mount fresh horses from the remuda at that location. The second group will attack as the railroad men reach the second ranch and then ride to the fourth ranch to mount fresh horses and to press the attack in a hopscotch fashion on up the valley."

Don Diego took over the explanation saying, "It is very important that your fastest horses be available and ready in front of your house. We will try to wear down the railroad men and their horses. We must have fresh horses so that we can outrun them. You must remove the rest of your horses to an area well away from your ranch so that the railroad men can't use them. Any questions?"

The ranchers talked and argued for nearly three hours. When they finally came to a consensus, the meeting ended with a shaking of hands. The ranchers returned to their homes near midnight, but they were eager to start preparations very early in the morning.

Just after dawn, Frank Stone and Jubal McGraw prepared for the ride south. They joined the rest of the group for breakfast then stood to leave while the others remained at the table.

"Before we go, I think it's time to open the crates so that you can see what I've brought," said Jubal. Andy got a pry bar from the barn and loosened the nails in the boards covering the wooden crates. Jubal opened the first crate exposing twenty-four brand new Henry repeating rifles. The second box was even more of a surprise. It contained a never before used Gatling gun.

"My God," exclaimed Stone. "I've been escorting stolen army weapons."

"No," said Jubal. "Not stolen. Let's just call them army surplus." Jubal was smiling a sly grin.

"We need high ground for the Gatling gun to be fully effective," Jubal said. "Any idea where we should place it?"

"The musician's loft," Andy and Everett said in unison.

"Where's that?" Jubal asked.

Andy pointed to the eight by ten-foot platform with a railing situated above the entryway with stairs ascending from both sides of the reception area.

"We built it for use by musicians so that we could hold dances in the reception area without the dancers getting in the way of the musicians. There's a large removable window under the apex of the roof that provides ventilation for the musicians," said Andy.

Jubal went up the stairs and looked out the octagon- shaped window,

"Perfect," he exclaimed as he returned to the floor of the reception area.

"But there's more," he said as he flipped open the cover of the third crate.

"These are hand propelled bombs, what some people call grenades," he said.

Stone laughed.

"What's so funny," Jubal asked, glowering.

"My wife's first husband invented those. I used them a few years ago, and they can be very effective," said Stone.

The two remaining crates contained ammunition for the rifles and the Gatling gun, however, one small compartmented area in the last crate contained something that Andy had not seen since he had been captured: two Caton telegraph keys and sounders with several hundred feet of thin silk covered wire.

"Where did you get these?" asked Andy with surprise in his voice.

"I took them from the Confederate War Department's telegraph room. They used to belong to C. A. Gaston. After you were captured, I had to learn code and fill the void that you left. C. A. gave these to me when the capitol fell."

"You know how to send and receive code?" Andy asked astonished.

"I'm not as fast as you are, but I can handle about ten words per minute," Jubal responded with a broad smile.

"Well Jubal, they just might come in handy, especially now that you can send and receive code," said Andy.

"Any other surprises?" Stone asked.

"No, that's about it. There are several thousand rounds of ammunition, so we should be able to put up a fight," Jubal replied.

"No wonder those damn crates were so heavy," Stone remarked shaking his head. "And all this time, I've been escorting stolen army weapons."

"No, not stolen. I told you, they are army surplus." "Yeah, right," said Stone.

Everyone laughed.

Jubal turned to Stone and said, "You ought to stay here and let me go check out the whereabouts of the railroad men by myself."

"Why?"

"Because they might recognize you, and they don't know me. But more importantly, sneaking and peeking is my business, or at least it was in the war. Frankly, Marshal, I work better when I'm alone."

"So you're saying that I would slow you down?" "No Frank, but you might get us killed." "Ouch!"

"Frank, don't take this personally, but I'm pretty good at this sort of thing and I do work better when I don't have to worry about someone else. Besides, you will have the opportunity to get yourself killed when you confront those killers during first contact."

"Gee, thanks for the vote of confidence, Jubal."

"Frank, it's going to be close, very close. And remember, you also have a wife to go home to."

"Okay, Jubal. Go with my blessing, but come back in one piece, please."

"Andy, you should periodically check the telegraph system for messages. I will likely send messages and stay with the railroad people until they show some indication how they are going to move on the ranchers," Jubal said.

"Okay, Jubal. Be careful out there."

"I will," said Jubal as he packed a Caton lineman's key and cable into his saddlebag.

Everyone watched grimly as Jubal rode down the driveway leaving the Spires.

"It's really happening. God help us all," thought Andy.

Few people took notice of Rob Lowe, who came in on the Wednesday stage coach. He went to the hotel and waited for the rest of the story that he expected would unfold over the next few days. *It will be worth the wait,* he thought.

Jubal was riding down the main road, thinking to himself; *Remember the lessons learned during the war. Being invisible is a matter of being where you're not expected to be and by blending in so that they don't see you, even when you are right in front of them.*

He had studied the county maps at Andy's house and figured that the railroad men wouldn't be looking for someone who was watching them. They would likely put out a point guard, but they wouldn't look in the foothills above the valley. As he neared the southern limit of the county, Jubal dismounted and walked, sometimes crawled, up a mountainous rock face where he could examine the road with binoculars from the higher elevation but never from on top of the foothills. He didn't want to present a silhouette by being at the very top.

Near dusk, he finally saw what he expected to find at that time of day: smoke from a campfire. He took his time, not hurrying his approach on foot. By the looks of the camp, the railroad men had been at the campsite only for an hour or so; they were still putting up the last of some tents and they were unloading food from the chuck wagon.

The campsite was located on a burned out ranch at the north end of the county that was just south of Golden Eagle County. The few scrub oak trees and brush near an outhouse were not sufficient to be used as an observation post during daylight hours, but they might be good enough at night. Jubal waited patiently, watching as the men formed up at the chuck wagon and drew their rations that two cooks had hurriedly cooked over an open flame. Following dinner, the men passed around a few bottles of whiskey until well into the night, after which they went into their tents for a night's sleep. Jubal saw that guards had been established a few hundred yards in front of, and behind the campsite. He would have to be careful as he made his way around the outskirts of the camp.

As midnight approached, when most of the men had turned in, Jubal made his way to the outhouse, which was close enough to overhear some of the conversation of a small group of men who were talking around the campfire. He listened carefully, not only to the conversation, but also for someone approaching. He had been in the outhouse for nearly a half hour when he heard the locked door rattle.

"Be right out," Jubal said in a slightly distorted voice, acting as if he had been drinking.

He purposely waited a little over a minute so that the man waiting would be more interested in using the facility than getting a good look at Jubal as he exited. Jubal pulled his hat down low and exited the outhouse while looking at the ground to reduce face exposure. He walked toward one of the tents until he heard the outhouse lock.

Must be one of the new guys, the man thought as he locked the outhouse door, impatient to use the facility.

Jubal dropped down to reduce his silhouette until he felt he could safely return to the tree line. He made his way out of the camp and continued working his way toward his horse, which was a mile or more away. Jubal circled around to ensure that no one was following him. After waiting and watching for a half hour, he finished making his way to his horse and walked the horse out of the area.

Jubal rode for about two hours before finding a suitable place to camp in the trees well away from the road. He didn't start a fire. Rather, he broke out some hard tack and drank water from his canteen. He poured oats into his hat and fed and watered his horse, then took his blanket roll and slept for a few hours, waking just before dawn.

After daybreak, Jubal returned to the road where he tapped into a telegraph line and sent Andy a message saying, UOC BIVOUACKED FIVE MILES SOFO, JUBAL. Andy was not on the line, but an operator in another town assured Jubal that he would pass the message as soon as Andy checked in for messages.

Andy picked up his messages about an hour later. Dwayne looked at the telegram and asked, "What did he say?"

Andy laughed and replied, "Well it just proves that you can take the soldier out of the army, but you can't take the army out of the soldier. The message says that the unit of concern is camped five miles south of their first objective, the southernmost ranch."

Jubal disconnected his equipment from the telegraph line and rode to the southernmost ranch where he retreated to a secluded position inside the tree line near the main road. Two hours later, he saw two railroad men stop at the entrance to the ranch. There wasn't much for the two men to see as the rancher had moved his family off the ranch just after dawn. However, a couple of cowboys were moving cattle away from the ranch house toward a pasture further west. The railroad men were joined a few minutes later by two others who rode in from the north. They had evidently passed Jubal before dawn. The four men talked for a few minutes and then turned south and rode together toward their camp.

Jubal returned to the Spires to report what little he had overheard. Arriving near noon, Jubal was surprised to see that rifle pits had already been dug in the shape of an arrowhead that spanned the entire width of the front of the house. Tree-sized logs had been brought in from the lumber mill. They were mounted on huge triangular braces angled upward between the rifle pits and the front of the house. Only the very top part of the house could be seen from the road or the driveway. The window just under the apex of the house was open, and Jubal supposed that the Gatling gun was already mounted on the platform inside, even though he couldn't see it. The centerline of the rifle pits passed under the log barrier so that shooters could come and go through the front door without becoming targets.

Pretty impressive, Jubal thought.

Jubal unsaddled and turned his horse loose in the corral before heading inside through the rifle pits.

"Looks like you have been busy," he said as he was greeted at the front door by Andy and Stone, both of whom wore sweat-stained shirts, evidence that they had been among those who had dug the rifle pits and erected the log barrier.

"Yes, Don Diego's vaqueros came and helped us so that we were able to complete the task this morning. Come in, and get some lunch on the patio."

Veronica and her mother, Maria, had set a table on the patio to feed the twenty-some odd men who had worked all morning digging rifle pits and installing the log barrier in front of the house. After lunch, the men gathered to listen to Jubal

"I came back because I think that we are going to have to change our plans. What little I overheard leads me to believe that the railroad police will attack the Flores Ranch and this farm simultaneously tomorrow afternoon. I overheard them say that they want to get rid of the largest rancher, Mr. Flores, first, and then burn out the smaller ranchers on Saturday and Sunday. Andy, your farm seemed to be a special case. The leader, a big man that they called Sarge, said that you and Flores were to be killed, but the others would simply be burned out. They didn't care if they lived or died."

"Probably because it was Don Diego and I who filed the injunction," Andy surmised.

"The ranchers should move their families to town today, Don Diego announced.

"I will have the vaqueros warn the ranchers this afternoon."

Speaking to the vaqueros in rapid fire Spanish, Don Diego gave his vaqueros instructions to ride to the different ranches, and warn the ranchers to move their families immediately. He instructed two of his most trusted men to move the women on his ranch to town too. "Maria, you and Veronica should ride to town this afternoon too."

"No Papa," I will stay here. Veronica said firmly.

"The hell you will," said Andy. "Do as your father says, and take care of your mother in town."

"Do you expect the railroad thugs to attack the town?"

"No, of course not," Andy replied.

"Then where will a physician be needed?

Andy felt trapped by his own words. He remained silent.

"I have seen as much maiming and killing during the war as anyone here," Veronica continued. "So I will remain here. However, I will ride to town today to pick up some medical supplies so that I will be ready when I'm needed."

Andy turned to Don Diego for verbal help. He got none. Don Diego shrugged his shoulders and said, "She does make a good point, Andy."

"I too will remain here," said Maria.

Diego Flores turned toward his wife and raised his right hand to demand her obedience. Before he could say what was on his mind, Maria interjected, "I will help Veronica with the wounded."

Seeing the determination in his wife's eyes, Diego remained silent and returned his hand to his side. There was a moment of silence as everybody watched the senior rancher. Diego pointed toward a small group of his men and then said quietly, "Vaqueros, ride swiftly and warn the ranchers to move their families now. Go with God."

Instantly, he was again the boss, and six vaqueros quickly ran through the house to their horses in the corral. He was about to give instructions to the rest of his vaqueros, when Jubal McGraw interrupted him.

"Andy, I think they could use some of the repeating rifles."

"I agree," said Andy.

"Don Diego, let us give your men a dozen of the new repeating rifles. Also, we need to show your vaqueros how to use these new weapons before you send them off."

"Repeating rifles?" asked Diego.

"Yes, I feel sure that the railroad men will have repeating rifles, so it is important that your men have weapons that are at least equal to theirs."

"Show me, please," said the old rancher who had never seen such a weapon.

Jubal demonstrated how to load the Henry rifle with fifteen cartridges and how to eject a spent shell. Then he led them out through the front door, into the rifle pits, and demonstrated how to use the weapon. Each vaquero took a rifle and a hundred rounds of ammunition. They all fired fifteen additional rounds, while Jubal, Andy, and Everett instructed them how to properly aim the weapons in the standing, kneeling, and prone positions.

Following the brief but effective training period, Diego sent the rest of his newly armed vaqueros back to the ranch to transport the women and children to town, and to dig new rifle pits that would be needed the following day. Diego stayed behind to help plan for the defense of his ranch and for the defense of the house in the Spires.

Andy hitched the two Percherons for Veronica's trip to town to fetch medical supplies and to ensure that the hospital was ready in case it was needed. Maria cleared the table and washed the dishes while the men met in the reception room to make additional plans for the coming battles.

Andy looked to Everett saying, "Well Ev, have you come up with something that we can use?"

"Well, I haven't seen the Flores ranch, but according to Mr. Flores, the area is wide open from the road to the ranch house, the bunk house, and the barns. So we have to prepare for two different types of battles: one that is in the open, and another here, which is more of a fortress."

"Mr. Flores will need the most men because his ranch is in the open. Here at the Spires, we will need fewer men, but we will have greater firepower because of the Gatling gun. Mr. Flores has indicated that he will dig rifle pits staggered along the sides of the driveway at his ranch so that if anyone gets caught in the open, he has a place to quickly go that offers some degree of protection from cavalry or infantry rifle fire. Also, there are very few trees along the driveway. Because the Flores ranch is so open, he will need the greater supply of grenades. They will be placed in the rifle pits and therefore within throwing distance along the driveway. They should create havoc on the bulk of the attackers, whether they are on foot or on horseback. Others will use the structures as shooting platforms."

Everett continued by saying, "The attacking force will have the advantage of superior manpower. We don't know what they have in the wagon. We only know that it is inordinately heavy. So we should anticipate that they have some type of artillery. Based on what Jubal said, I think it's reasonable to believe that they have already seen the layout of both the Flores ranch and the Spires. We can only hope they saw the Spires before we dug rifle pits and erected the barrier. But in any case, I think they would plan to use the artillery here at the Spires. I wish there was more, but that's all I have been able to come up with, given the number of people we have," Everett said.

There was a silence as everyone listened to Everett's concluding remark.

"Well, I have a lot to accomplish in a short period of time, so I had better get moving." Diego kissed his wife, Maria, hugging her for a full minute, and then he left the house in the Spires with a worried look on his face.

"I guess we had better take a look at our positions too," said Andy.

The five men moved to the front of the house.

"Jubal, you're the only one that has actually fired a Gatling gun, so I imagine that's the best place for you."

"I'll need help loading the gun," said Jubal.

"That will leave us short in the rifle pits," said Everett.

"I can help load the gun," Maria said from the hallway. "Show me what I need to know."

The men looked at each other in silence. Jubal pointed to the musician's loft. He and Maria climbed the steps from different directions. Jubal explained how the gun worked and how it was to be reloaded. Where the original Gatling gun was sometimes prone to jamming, this gun had been redesigned after the war by the inventor, Dr. Richard Gatling, and it was near flawless in its deadly precision. The modified weapon fired a fifty-caliber metal jacket cartridge that was fed by a vertical magazine or drum. Maria's job would be to keep the drums and magazines loaded so that they could be quickly inserted in the gun for continuous firing. Hand-cranked, the gun fired as much as two hundred rounds per minute. Maria loaded three of the unloaded drums and magazines. She would have to work quickly and continuously.

"I can do this," she said.

Looking at her with sad eyes, Jubal said, "Thank you, Maria."

"Since there are no windows in the front of the house, other than the one that Jubal will use for the Gatling gun, we will have to use the rifle pits throughout the battle," said Everett. There is no fallback position other than inside the house or in the valley inside the Spires.

Each of us will have two fully loaded rifles. Let's hope the initial thirty rounds per man will be enough, however, each man will have five hundred rounds staged at his position in the pits in case he does have to reload."

Stone stood next to a tree. In a blurred motion, he jumped into the pit at the very end of the left side of the arrowhead. This would be his position as he would be the first to make contact with the railroad men. He needed a quick avenue of escape in the event the railroad police suddenly opened fire. His was the most exposed position; however, it was necessary to establish that the railroad men were there to unlawfully take the land. He had argued that as a U.S. Marshal, it was rightfully his job to make that determination.

With nothing left to say or do, the men took turns standing watch throughout the night in case the attack came sooner than expected. Maria cooked dinner for the men and cleaned up after them. Veronica returned well after dark. Most of the men had already turned in. Andy helped her unload the medical supplies, unhitched the Percherons, and rolled the carriage into the barn. Veronica ate the meal that her mother had kept hot for her and then, with Andy, retired to the master bedroom. Maria went to her bedroom and prayed to the Virgin Mary for an hour before finally falling asleep.

The next morning arrived cool and dry. The sun rose, but the air temperature remained cool all morning. On the Flores ranch, the men took their predetermined positions and awaited their fate. Near eleven, a column of soldiers three abreast rode north on the main road in front of the ranch. The column was divided into two platoons of twenty-five men. The heavy wagon with its two drivers was positioned between the two platoons. The first platoon and the wagon passed the Flores ranch. The second platoon turned into the ranch.

A corporal, who was at the head of the platoon, rode to the main house where Mr. Flores was standing in the doorway.

"How can I help you, soldier?" Mr. Flores asked. "We're here to protect you," the corporal said. "Protect us from what?" Don Diego said, unmoving. "From the railroad men," the corporal said.

"You are the railroad men, Diego replied. "I recognize you from Dallas."

"Too bad for you," the corporal said as he went for his sidearm.

Diego Flores reached inside the doorway and picked up his Henry rifle. He didn't bother shouldering the weapon, but fired it at waist level, hitting the corporal in the chest. He levered another round into the chamber and fired again. Diego closed the door and crawled on his belly to the back of the house as the remaining soldiers pulled their rifles out of scabbards and began firing at the front of the house thinking that Flores was alone. The still mounted soldiers moved toward the front of the house pumping it with several fusillades of bullets.

Four vaqueros, two on either side of the driveway, flipped back the canvas covers under which they had been hiding ever since the columns had first been sighted. They lit the fuses on hand grenades from the fiery end of cigars and lofted the grenades into the midst of the rear echelons of the columns. The four grenades went off almost simultaneously. Shrapnel hit horses and men when another four grenades went off deeper into the formation. Horses fell squealing, and men yelled, but even then, the trap was yet to be closed. Vaqueros began firing from the loft in the barn and from the bunk house. The railroad men were trapped in a murderous crossfire. More grenades went off. Shrapnel tore into the remaining horses and men. Those who were still mounted pulled their horses to the ground and returned fire using the carcasses of their horses as cover. The vaqueros pumped round after round into the circle of cavalry until no gunfire was returned.

After a few minutes of silence, the vaqueros moved toward the uniformed attackers checking for wounded. A uniformed killer who had no desire to be taken captive— wounded or not—fired his Dragoon into the stomach of a vaquero. And because they did not have the training and discipline of soldiers, the vaqueros again opened fire with their Henry repeating rifles, sending bullets into each and every uniformed body. When they were sure that the killers were dead, they pulled their bodies into a pile and doused them thoroughly with kerosene, which they lit on fire. Black smoke billowed up over the horizon. Men from the first columns who were headed for the Spires looked back and saw the black smoke. They mistakenly thought that the Flores ranch house was on fire. They menacingly laughed, hooted, and hollered.

A solitary figure dressed in civilian clothes came out of the woods and crossed the road into the driveway of the Flores ranch. He held his hands high above his head and called to the vaqueros who pointed their weapons at him.

"I'm not with them," he yelled as loud as he could.

As he walked up the driveway, he was met by Don Diego who asked, "Who are you?"

"Rob Lowe from Dallas. I'm a reporter for the *Dallas Times*. I saw what they did and I came to write the story. I know they were railroad police because I recognized some of them when they passed me on the road. They didn't see me behind the trees because they were looking at the ranch."

"I don't have time to talk with you. The rest of those killers are going to attack my family at the Spires." Vaqueros led saddled horses out of the barn. There was nothing they could do for the dead vaquero, the only casualty they had suffered. They laid him on the porch of the bunkhouse and covered him with a tarp until they could bury him. And then they mounted their horses and headed at a gallop toward the Spires with Don Diego in the lead. Even at a fast pace, the trip would take about a half hour and the odds at the Spires were five to one in favor of the railroad men.

The column of uniformed railroad men stopped at a small rise about a thousand yards from the driveway to the Spires. They aimed a three-inch Ordnance Rifle mounted on the wagon at the wooden barrier.

"Looks like you were right about them bringing artillery," Everett called up to Jubal.

"What type of ordnance is it, Jubal?"

"Looks like a three-inch wrought iron rifle," Jubal called back. "That will be my first target."

"What can that thing do?" asked Dwayne.

Everett replied, "Well an Ordnance Rifle can shoot a projectile about two thousand yards with a one pound charge of gunpowder. Our wooden barrier will be no match for that."

When the work on the wagon was finished, the column started moving toward the entryway. The first shot of artillery came as the column turned into the driveway. The projectile hit high above the wooden barrier sending a cascade of falling rock from the mountain onto the steps of the house. Stone, who had been standing in the open, jumped into the rifle pit. The second shot from the Ordinance Rifle hit the wooden barrier, sending shards of splintered wood down into the rifle pits. But the lashings held, and the logs stayed in place on the braces.

As soon as the artillery had started shooting projectiles toward the house, the column galloped up the driveway. The killers fanned out, pulling their horses down to the ground for cover, and started shooting their Henry repeating rifles. There was about fifty yards between the combatants. The distinctive whine of the artillery shell added an eerie sound while it was in flight before the shells hit the barrier. Letting out a loud rebel yell, Jubal opened up on the wagon from the octagon shaped window, sending a steady stream of fifty-caliber bullets into the wagon. The bullets must have hit one of the bags of gunpowder because the wagon suddenly exploded, sending a plume of smoke, wood, steel, and bodies high into the air. The Ordnance Rifle was silenced. Then Jubal sounded another rebel yell and turned the Gatling gun on targets in the driveway.

Horses screamed and tried to get up and run away as bullets from the Gatling gun penetrated their bodies and pockmarked the ground around them. The killers scurried from their positions behind the horses to new positions behind the trees that lined the driveway. Several bodies lay dead or wounded in the driveway. A few of the horses were able to get away, but most of them lay dead or wounded, writhing and screaming in pain.

The railroad men concentrated their fire on the octagon window. Jubal maintained his position and sprayed the tree line with fifty-caliber bullets. Wood around the octagon window splintered as rifle bullets penetrated the wall and entered a double row of stacked sandbags that had been placed around the inside of the window and down the stairs. As the Gatling gun emptied, Maria and Veronica jammed bullets into the empty drums while lying prone on the platform behind the sandbags that had been placed there for their protection.

The rifle fire forced Jubal to duck down on the floor. When he returned to the Gatling's hand crank, it wouldn't shoot. The rifle barrage had silenced the Gatling gun. Jubal grabbed his rifle and started shooting at targets in the tree line.

Every time that Jubal would sound a rebel yell, the four men in the rifle pits also yelled, and then they concentrated their rifle fire on the tree line. Using the trees as cover, the former Union soldiers advanced on the rifle pits as they had when they fought in the war. The killers realized that a single rush on the rifle pits would mark the end for Stone and the Davis brothers. There was only fifty feet separating them from the cover of the trees to the depths of the rifle pits. It would only take one charge to kill the defenders. With the silencing of the Gatling gun, the sergeant ordered the charge.

The killers advanced on the rifle pits, repeatedly firing one shot after the other, more or less in unison, as they moved forward, they crouched to reduce exposure to those who were defending the house in the Spires. Two other railroad men remained in the trees and maintained a fusillade of cover fire at the octagon window, thereby pinning down rifle fire from above. The killers could taste victory. The whole thing would be finished within a couple of minutes.

The railroad men heard the horses galloping up the driveway. Thinking that it was the second column, arriving after having torched the Flores ranch, they didn't bother to turn around. They kept advancing on the four men in the trenches. Suddenly, rifle fire erupted from behind them and the uniformed killers began falling. The men in the pits ducked down because some of the rifle fire was coming in over their heads. The two men in the trees were also caught unaware. They were shot by two vaqueros who had dismounted and quickly made their way through the trees until they were behind the railroad men.

The uniformed railroad men had been right. The whole thing was over in just a couple of minutes. The men dressed in Union Army uniforms lay dead or wounded after having been caught in the open.

Andy ducked under the wooden barrier and made his way into the house where he yelled for Veronica, Maria, and Jubal.

"We're okay," Jubal yelled back.

Veronica made her way down the stairs on wobbly legs. Andy reached out and helped her down the last few stairs and then held her tightly.

"I was so worried about you," he said emotionally.

Diego rushed into the house and held his wife, who had made her way down the stairs from the platform above.

"What, nobody wants to hug me?" Jubal asked with a grin.

"I'll hug you," said Everett "Thanks," Jubal responded.

Veronica wiggled free of Andy's grasp saying, "I've got to tend to the wounded."

She grabbed her medical bag and went outside. Andy and Dwayne went with her to help.

Veronica started triage using blood to mark the foreheads of the wounded—those who were most likely to survive with medical attention. As she was kneeling over one of the wounded men, the sergeant rose up with a Dragoon in hand. Pulling back the hammer, he aimed the revolver first at Veronica's head and then at Andy. As he pulled the trigger, Dwayne jumped in the path of the bullet, while simultaneously firing his rifle into the sergeant's chest. Dwayne fell at Andy's feet, and Andy emptied his rifle into the sergeant's body.

Veronica immediately went to Dwayne, but there was little that she could do. Andy held Dwayne in his arms.

"Once again you saved my life," Andy said with tears rolling down his face.

Dwayne looked up with glassy eyes and whispered, "I didn't fight in the war, but I fought in the last Confederate battle." With those words, Dwayne died.

Andy continued to hold his older brother to his chest, his tears falling uncontrollably, not unlike the time when Andy had shed tears in front of the burned out plantation house where his first family had been so brutally murdered.

"God, let this be the end of it," he pleaded.

Andy stood and stepped over to the body of the bullet riddled sergeant, removing the dead man's hat to get a better look at his lifeless face. It was only then that he actually recognized the features of the dead man. There, lying at his feet was the body of the man he had sworn to kill so many years earlier. It was the Swede.

"I fulfilled my vow, but oh God, it wasn't worth the cost," he said out loud, as he looked down at the body of his dead brother.

Of the twenty-five men who came to kill, three survived with the quick medical attention that Veronica was able to provide. They were recuperating after surgery in the hospital, guarded night and day by deputized angry townspeople. Stone would take the survivors to Dallas on the southbound stage when they were fit to travel. There they would be tried for murder and failure to obey the judge's injunction: after which, if they were found guilty, they would likely be hanged.

Rob Lowe arrived within a few minutes after Dwayne had been killed. He took notes, sketched the battle scene, and quietly talked with those who would talk with him. When told of Dwayne's last words, the reporter decided to use them for the title of his story. The headline read, **"He died in the Last Confederate Battle."** The news article, a highly exaggerated version, told how five Texas men and two women held off twenty-five killers, all former Union soldiers who were wearing Union Army uniforms when they attacked the home in the Spires. Lowe attributed the attacks to the railroad in violation of the temporary injunction, about which he had reported a couple of months earlier. The story was published after Lowe returned to Dallas by stage coach; a story that was picked up by major newspapers across the nation, but which reverberated mainly throughout the South.

Chapter Twenty-Six

October 22, 1872

JUDGE HASTINGS LOOKED out of the window of his chambers at the growing crowd that was gathering in front of the Federal Courthouse. There was a great interest in his decision regarding the Flores-Davis request for a permanent injunction against the railroad; not only locally and regionally, but nationally as well. Newspaper articles regarding the battle in the valley of Golden Eagle had stirred up a furor against the railroad owners. Newspapermen from the east had made the trip across the country to hear his decision and to record the reaction of the people.

"I'll render my decision in open court," he said to the clerk. "Please ask Marshal Stone to have deputies in court before ten o'clock to maintain order."

The court clerk rushed down the corridor to the marshal's office with the judge's request. Marshal Stone was talking with Don Diego and Andy in the privacy of his office, so the clerk passed the judge's request to Edwards, the chief deputy.

Soon after his arrival in Dallas, Stone had implemented a policy of no guns in the courts. To that end, he had a reinforced closet built in the hallway to the courtrooms. The walls of the closet were ringed with pegs on which to hold gun belts. The owner was given a tag that corresponded with the number on a peg in the closet. The system worked well; however, it required two Marshals to enforce the gun policy in the corridor, and a couple of clerks to handle the push of people who wanted to get a seat in court.

The courtroom quickly filled to capacity. The overflow crowd had to stand outside the building, where city police maintained order in the chill of a gray fall morning that felt more like winter. Inside, Judge Hastings entered the courtroom, causing everyone to stand, more from custom than from respect for the court or the judge.

"Please be seated," the judge said.

"As you are aware," the judge continued, "The purpose of this proceeding today is to render a decision regarding an injunction that was filed on behalf of ranchers in Golden Eagle County. This is not a trial."

"For the record," the judge continued, "Are the parties to the injunction request in court?"

"James Andrews, Attorney-at-Law for the plaintiffs, your honor."

"Aaron Hill, for the national railroad, your honor."

Three men in dark eastern-styled suits pushed their way through the crowd that was standing at the rear of the room.

"Your honor, Mr. Hill does not represent the railroad," said one of the three men."

Everyone turned, craning to look at the three strangers who were making their way to the front of the spectator's gallery.

"And who are you?" the judge asked.

"Barney, Margot, and Jones, Attorneys for the railroad, your honor. May we approach?"

"Please do," answered the judge.

Mr. Barney, the senior partner in the New York law firm, walked to the judge's bench where he was met by Hill and Andrews.

"Your honor, I am James Barney, Attorney at Law, practicing in New York State and representing the railroad, a New York corporation. We also represent its Chief Executive Officer and the Board of Directors."

Mr. Barney gave the judge a copy of a contract between his law firm and the railroad dated three years earlier that did indeed show that his firm represented the railroad for all matters legal. He also gave copies to Andrews and Hill.

"I thought Mr. Hill represented the railroad," the perplexed judge said.

"Mr. Hill has never represented the railroad, Your Honor. He was a…"

"Balderdash!" Hill interrupted.

"Mr. Hill, you will have an opportunity to talk when I give you permission. Until then, please remain silent."

"Mr. Barney, please continue."

"Your honor, as I was saying before I was interrupted, Mr. Hill was an employee of the National Development and Research Organization. He was never an employee of the railroad."

"I…" Hill started to say, before he was cut off by a gesture from the judge.

Mr. Barney presented a copy of Hill's employment agreement with the development company. He also gave copies to Hill and to Andrews.

"The development company was a contractor that the railroad used from time to time to do consulting work. They never actually represented the railroad, which is a separate, wholly owned New York corporation," Barney continued.

"Investigation now reveals that the development company illegally acquired lands by using the name of the rail company, which it then sold at a profit to the railroad."

Barney produced papers showing that the development company had in fact sold lands to the railway.

"Your honor," Hill started.

"Mr. Hill, you will remain silent or I will have you removed," Judge Hastings reprimanded.

"Mr. Barney, please continue."

"Furthermore, your honor, there was never a railroad police. Those men appear to have been hired by Mr. Hill as a way to acquire privately held lands for resale to the railway. Those so-called railway police were not in any way attached to the rail company. In fact, they had no police powers whatsoever; they had never been deputized by any agency of government.

Barney continued by saying, "When the railroad learned what the development company was doing, it immediately severed relations nearly three months ago." Barney handed copies of a notarized termination of services letter to the judge and to Andrews and Hill.

"The development company has since declared bankruptcy," said Barney as he handed copies of a final resolution for bankruptcy signed by a New York judge dated September 15th. The company has closed, and it is being investigated by New York State for fraud."

"Is there a federal interest in the case?" asked Judge Hastings.

"No, Your Honor, the U.S. Attorney General has deferred to the State of New York," said Mr. Barney as he provided copies of a letter from the Office of the U.S. Attorney General.

"So as you can see, your honor, Mr. Hill does not represent the railroad company or any other company. He is in fact, unemployed."

"Mr. Hill," the judge started, as he looked down from the bench.

Hill interrupted by saying, "Your Honor, I know nothing of any of this."

"Mr. Hill, I was not giving you permission to speak. To the contrary, I was about to admonish you to refrain from further dialogue in this matter. As the overwhelming evidence clearly indicates, you have no standing in this court. You may remain in court as an observer, but you will have to return to the spectator's gallery."

"You damn fool! Can't you see that I'm being set up?" Hill exclaimed.

"Marshal, please remove Mr. Hill from the building," the judge demanded, straining hard not to smile.

A deputy grabbed Hill's arm, which Hill shook off. The deputy simultaneously grabbed the seat of Hill's pants and his suit collar, forcing the screaming man out of the building amid hoots and hollers from the people in the gallery. The deputy threw Hill down the steps like he would a bale of hay. Onlookers scattered and Hill landed on the sidewalk skinning his head and hands on the cement.

Judge Hastings restored order in the court.

"Your Honor, "I think we can clear up this whole mess without any further need for an injunction."

The two remaining New York lawyers, Margot, and Jones, who had been standing in the gallery, moved to the defendant's table where they seated themselves.

"Your Honor," Barney continued, "Had the railroad known about the situation in Golden Eagle County, it would have been more than willing to negotiate in good faith with the ranchers."

That was a lie, of course. But only the railroad executives and their attorneys knew that it was a lie.

"As you can see," said Barney, handing the judge and Andrews a copy of a letter dated two weeks earlier, "The Department of Interior has granted the railroad the land it needs to build its connection from the City of Dallas to point's north in Oklahoma. There is no need for an injunction as we will not be acquiring any land on the west side of the valley."

"Mr. Andrews?"

After a quick whispered conversation with Andy and Diego, the attorney spoke saying, "Your honor, if we can get a letter from the railroad promising that it will not seek lands on the west side of the valley, and if it will absolve the plaintiffs of any legal actions that may arise from this matter, and if the railroad corporation is willing to compensate the plaintiffs for their time, travel, and legal costs, the plaintiffs would be willing to withdraw its request for a permanent injunction."

"Mr. Barney?" the judge asked.

The railway accepts those terms and thanks the court for its patience in this matter, your honor."

"Then since the injunction request has been withdrawn pending the receipt of a letter of agreement between the two parties, this petition is dismissed," said the judge as he slammed down the gavel, thereby ending the session.

Mr. Barney crossed the courtroom and approached Andy, Diego and Andrews with a copy of a previously prepared letter that promised not to intrude on lands on the west side of Golden Eagle valley.

The letter included a paragraph absolving the plaintiffs of any claims arising from the incident, while claiming that the railway company had no knowledge of, or participation in, the events that had transpired there. Attached to the letter was a check for ten thousand dollars to reimburse the plaintiffs for any pain and suffering that may have occurred as well as for legal fees. Giving a copy of the letter to the court clerk, the matter was legally and officially ended.

Meeting privately in the law office of their attorney, Andy Davis and Diego Flores decided that the five hundred dollar attorney's fee that they had agreed upon was insufficient based on the results that had been obtained. They paid their lawyer a one thousand dollar bonus. Mr. Andrews, who was not used to clients giving him more than the agreed upon amount, was ecstatic.

"Call on me anytime," Andrews said as his looked at the check.

The men shook hands. Andy and Diego headed back to the hotel to pack for the trip north. As they neared the hotel, Rob Lowe, the reporter from the *Dallas Times*, approached along with a number of reporters from the east. Rob asked for a comment for his next article.

"There are those who would say that we got a lot of money from the railroad today. But no amount of money will replace my brother Dwayne or the vaquero who was shot and killed defending our homes."

"What will you do with the money?" Rob asked.

"We will give it to the family of the vaquero who was killed. He had a wife and three children. The wife lost her husband, and the kids lost their father. He was taken from them in a sudden and violent way."

"What will you do now?" Rob persisted.

"We will go home and try to put our lives back together," said Diego.

That being said, the two men turned to enter the hotel while the pack of reporters pressed in trying to get more comments. Andy and Diego pushed their way through the group of reporters. Going up stairs, the two men packed and left Dallas for their homes and loved ones.

Hill sat in his room in that very same hotel. He was angry, and he was bitter. He had not been paid in nearly three months and he was running low on money. Furthermore, if what the New York lawyers had said was true, he didn't dare go back to his New York farm for fear of being arrested. Not having any plans to offset this latest turn of events in his life's journey, Hill got drunk.

After three days of heavy drinking, Hill staggered down to the hotel restaurant, got something to eat and returned to his room where he drank some more and passed out on his bed, throwing up on the sheets in his sleep. Days went by and the nearly three thousand dollars that he had in the bank was fast being spent. He needed money, and he had no way of getting any, other than by selling his farm in New York.

Wiring a former friend and neighbor, Hill indicated that he was considering selling his farm and asked if the friend would handle the details and mail a bank draft to his hotel in Dallas. The friend responded by offering Hill twenty-five thousand dollars for the land, the home, and its furnishings. That was less than half its true value. The furnishings alone were worth that much. But Hill needed money fast, so he accepted the offer. The draft came in the mail two weeks later and cleared the Dallas bank after another three weeks. Other than the cash in the bank, Hill had nothing: no farm, no home, and no family. He was a very bitter man.

———— ✦ ————

PRESIDENT GRANT WAS in the last year of his second term. He had replaced President Andrew Johnson in March of 1869, and had retained Stone as the District Marshal for northern Texas throughout his presidency.

Chapter Twenty-Seven

March 1876

Kaitlin had been periodically dropping hints over the last few months that she was ready to return to her Maryland home. After ten years as District Marshal, Stone had to admit that he was ready to retire from law enforcement. The world was fast changing and Stone was ready to find new avenues for his life with Kaitlin.

Stone wrote a private letter to President Grant asking to be relieved as District Marshal before the coming election. Furthermore, he recommended that Chief Deputy Edwards be appointed to replace him. Stone was delighted when he received a letter in mid-May that appointed Edwards as District Marshal. The appointment was to take effect on the first of June.

The staff had already gone home for the night when Edwards stopped by. Stone handed him the presidential letter of appointment. Edwards, who had absolutely no knowledge that Stone had requested to be relieved, or that Stone had recommended him for the position of District Marshal, was momentarily stunned.

"How could you do this to me, Frank?" Edwards asked. "I am comfortable being the Chief Deputy."

"And now you can be comfortable being the boss," Stone said with a big smile.

Stone called an early morning staff meeting, during which he announced that Edwards would be taking over as District Marshall in June. Following congratulations by the staff, Stone let Edwards know that he would step aside and let Edwards handle all of the day to day responsibilities while he and Kaitlin prepared for the trip back to Maryland. Then Stone abruptly left the office and surprised Kaitlin by announcing that she had better start packing.

Over the next six weeks, the Stone's sold their house in Dallas, shipped the furnishings that they wanted to keep, and moved into a hotel during Frank's last days in office. Kaitlin asked Frank if they could travel to Golden Eagle Hot Springs. She said that she wanted to spend the Fourth of July with Andy and Veronica. Frank sent a telegram asking Andy if he and Veronica could stand having company for a few weeks. The return telegram assured Frank that they would be most welcome at the home in the Spires.

Frank and Kaitlin made the trip from Dallas to Golden Eagle Hot Springs on the recently completed rail system in just one day, arriving early in the evening. They were met by Andy, who had a horse-drawn wagon for luggage, and by Veronica, who had her carriage for her two guest passengers. Frank felt a little guilty at having to send Hermes and the two Percherons by train to be cared for by Allan Pinkerton until they returned to Washington; however, he was not about to abandon Hermes or the Percherons in Texas.

The Stones enjoyed their stay with Andy and Veronica. They slept late, ate ravenously, and drank and danced the night away in the reception area on the Fourth of July with many of the towns-people and ranchers they had come to know over the years. They danced to mariachi music played by vaqueros on the musician's loft. Don Diego and Maria brought fireworks, which some vaqueros set off in front of the house so as not to frighten animals in the valley behind the house.

On the morning that the Stone's were scheduled to leave, Kaitlin and Veronica were seated on the patio.

Frank walked outside and noticed that the two women were seated next to each other with their heads almost touching in some-what of a conspiratorial manner. They were giggling.

"What's so funny?" Frank asked.

"Oh, woman stuff," Kaitlin answered as the two women began openly laughing.

"What could possibly be that funny?" Frank asked. "Men," Veronica answered, with tears running down both sides of her face in laughter.

"Well," said Frank, "I hate to break up this gabfest, but we do have to get to the train station."

Andy drove the wagon with the luggage. Frank decided to ride on the wagon with Andy rather than to have to put up with the womanly conversations that were sure to continue in the carriage. Kaitlin drove the carriage and the two women did continue their conversation. They laughed openly. Frank looked at Andy and shrugged.

"Women sure can be strange," said Frank.

"Can't live with them and can't live without them," Andy replied. Stone nodded in agreement.

Upon arriving at the train station, Andy helped load the luggage onto the train and said goodbye to Frank and Kaitlin. Veronica, who had already said goodbye, drove on to the hospital. Andy stopped by the telegraph office, but since there were no incoming messages, he went on to the hotel where he sat on the street-side patio with a hot cup of coffee and the newspaper that had been brought in by train from Dallas.

The front page stories talked mainly about the state's economy, which had been severely affected by the stock market crash of 1873. The depression that followed was expected to last another seven years, according to eastern economists. That was bad news for Texas, which had been hit hard by the depression. Cattle production was particularly hard hit. Cotton, which Andy was growing, had become a major Texas export along with wool from the increasing number of herds of sheep that were being raised in the cattle-dominant state. Even Don Diego had taken to raising hay to feed his stock and cotton to offset the financial losses being felt by a depressed cattle market.

On the political front, President Grant was being castigated by a number of heavyweight news organizations for corruption within his administration, as well as for alleged personal corruption. The new elections were warming up, and they promised to be extremely contentious.

On the science front, the paper went on to describe new technologies, such as the telephone that had been made public in March, and the first public exhibition of the electric light in San Francisco.

On the back page of the newspaper, in the obituaries, there was a small article about the death of ex-senator Aaron Hill. He had been found hanging from the rafters in a rundown hotel room on the outskirts of Dallas on the Fourth of July. He died a pauper and was buried in a common grave in Boot Hill, thereby ignominiously ending the 1800's saga of railroad expansion in Texas. Continued development dreams of rail expansion in Texas became another victim of the depression. Considering that the story had not been picked up by eastern newspapers, his three daughters knew nothing of his death. Nobody would miss him, especially not his former colleagues in Congress. Concerning the demise of Aaron Hill, nobody cared.

Chapter Twenty-Eight

July 16, 1876

Arriving at the train depot in Washington, Frank and Kaitlin got help with the luggage from a station attendant. The luggage was loaded into one carriage, while a second carriage had to be hired for their short trip to the Pinkertons. Hermes and the Percherons had arrived safely two weeks earlier. And although Frank was in a hurry to get home, neither Allan nor Joan would hear of it. They insisted that the Stones remain overnight at the Pinkerton house and that they celebrate their arrival by having dinner at a fancy new restaurant within the district. There was no arguing with the Scotsman, so they stayed the night as requested.

Frank and Allan took the opportunity to go to the men's club for a bath and a haircut followed by a couple of stout drinks before heading home. Entering the house, Stone noticed that the two women were in the parlor, where they were talking in hushed tones. As soon as the women saw Frank and Allan, they broke out in laughter.

"What's so funny?" Frank growled.

"Oh, just woman talk, Frank," said Joan. Then both women broke out in even more laughter.

"Okay, just what is going on with you women? First it was Kaitlin and Veronica, and now it's Kaitlin and Joan. Just what is going on?" Frank demanded.

"Growl all you want, Franklin Stone. It will do you no good whatsoever," Kaitlin responded.

And to make matters worse, the women broke out in laughter again.

"Women," Frank grumbled as he walked out to the paddock to check on Hermes.

"Women," Allan agreed as he joined Frank outside to ready a carriage for a trip into town.

While the foursome was enjoying dinner at a local restaurant, Kaitlin quietly asked Frank if he thought they should move his mother to the farm in Maryland.

"Why would we want to do that?" Stone asked.

"Well Mother Stone is reaching an advanced age. I'm sure she would enjoy the rural Maryland area much better than being cooped up in a New York City apartment," Kaitlin argued.

"I doubt that you could pry her out of the city with dynamite," Frank replied.

"I think we should at least ask her, Franklin," Kaitlin continued.

"I can't think of a single reason that would cause her to want to move to Maryland," Frank said, somewhat irritated.

"Well for one, she wouldn't have to walk up all those stairs to her apartment in the city. You could build a ground floor apartment as an addition to the side of our house. And secondly, she could help me with the children."

"Whose children?" Stone asked suspiciously.

"Your children," answered Kaitlin. "Veronica said twins, and she's guessing that they will be girls."

"What?"

"I'm pregnant, silly."

Frank Stone looked as if had been hit in the head with a two by four.

"How did that happen?" he asked.

"Do I really have to explain?" Kaitlin asked impishly.

"No, I just meant that we've been married for years. Why now?"

"Well, congratulations, Papa," Pinkerton teased.

"You keep out of this, you big ugly Scotsman," Stone growled.

"Couldn't you have informed me earlier?" Stone questioned.

"I waited for the right time, Franklin, and the right time is now." Kaitlin laughed.

"Women," said Stone rising from his chair. "I'm going to the Men's Bar for a few minutes."

Both women roared with laughter.

"I can't wait to tell Veronica about Franklin's reaction to the news," Kaitlin said.

"Oh, that's just great!" Stone replied as he moved toward the Men's Bar with Allan by his side.

January 12, 1877

Kaitlin gave birth to twin girls, Erin and Megan. When Frank was finally allowed to see his two daughters, he fell deeply in love again. He had only held the girls for a couple of minutes when Mother Stone whooshed him out of the bedroom saying that they and their mother needed to rest. "There will be time enough for you later," Mother Stone said sternly.

Frank felt rejected to the point that he was about to say something, but thought better of it. He never could win an argument with either his mother or with Kaitlin. Suddenly, Frank realized that as his daughters grew, he would likely never win another argument ever again.

"My God," he thought, "I'm completely surrounded by females." He smiled a broad smile.

June 10, 1877

With his mother now firmly ensconced in the new ground level apartment that Stone had built onto the side of the house, and with Kaitlin tending to the baby girls, Frank began to pay attention to farming. He consulted with Kaitlin every day. He had come to realize that he knew nothing about farming. But the bulk of the work was done by day laborers who had worked the farm for years and who needed no direction from Frank Stone. Clearly, Frank was in their way, so he watched from the sidelines.

By mid-July, mother and grandmother had browbeaten Franklin into buying a larger carriage with two benches in an enclosed cabin, along with stronger horses to replace the aging Percherons for the weekly trip to church. Today was a special day; the twins were to be baptized. The Pinkerton's joined the celebration.

Frank washed the new carriage and hitched the two Shire geldings to the coach, which he drove to the front of the house, waiting for the rest of the family. As Kaitlin and Mother Stone climbed into the carriage, Stone took the two baby girls, one in each arm, to the paddock where Hermes was watching at the fence. Frank hefted the two girls so that Hermes could get a better look. Hermes eyed the two wiggling bundles and whinnied.

"That's okay, Hermes. I can't tell which one is which either. But soon we will be able to distinguish one from the other."

Hermes shook his head up and down. One of the two babies touched Hermes nose. Hermes whinnied again and pawed the ground. For the briefest moment, as Stone turned toward the coach, he could have sworn that he saw Hermes smile.

"Horses don't smile," he mumbled as he looked squarely at Hermes.

Hermes reared up on his hind legs and whinnied again, then ran to the gate side of the paddock. He wanted to go too.

"Not this time, Hermes," Stone said as he walked back to the carriage, handing the girls to Kaitlin and his mother.

Joan climbed into the coach, sitting on the front seat of the enclosed cabin, while Allan joined Frank outside on the driver's bench. Frank guided the geldings to the main road and headed toward town.

"So," Allan asked, "what will you do with yourself, now that you are unemployed?"

"Well, between the farm and my pension from the city, I think we will be okay."

"You could come to work for my agency, you know."

"Allan, I've had all the excitement that I can handle for one lifetime. Besides, I may have found my calling, after all."

"What's that?" Allan asked. "I'll let you know if it pans out."

The two men turned the conversation to other matters until they arrived at the church. Erin and Megan slept through the baptismal ceremony, during which the Stones beamed with pride. As the family was boarding the carriage, Frank stopped a moment to talk with the old priest.

"Would it be okay if I drop by tomorrow morning, Padre? I'd like to talk with you about something that's been on my mind lately."

"Sure, Frank. I'll look for you in the morning."

The next morning, Frank kissed his wife, saying that he was taking Hermes for a ride. He guessed that they would be gone most of the day. Kaitlin didn't really pay attention to what her husband was saying. She was busy with the babies.

Stone saddled Hermes, and they turned down the road toward town. The pace was relaxed as the two entered into their usual conversation. Stone rode for a half hour, and then walked beside Hermes for the rest of the trip. Stone continued talking, and Hermes would answer with an occasional whiney or snort. Stone stopped at a stream and offered the horse a carrot, which Hermes immediately consumed, following which, he drank cool stream water. Then the two walked the rest of the way to the rundown old church.

Stone didn't bother tying Hermes to the rail in front of the church. He knew that the big horse would be there when he had finished talking with the priest.

Father John met Stone on the front steps. The two men shook hands, whereupon the priest invited Stone to sit on the steps saying, "Welcome to my office, Frank. What's on your mind?"

The two men talked for nearly an hour. Stone helped the old Padre to his feet, and the two men shook hands as they walked to where Hermes was patiently waiting.

"You know, Frank, I knew you were the one the very first time that I saw you."

"The one what, Padre?"

"The one who would come in answer to my years of prayers, Frank. I knew," the priest said again smiling.

"Well I have no idea how you knew. I just decided yesterday."

"I knew, Frank. God does in fact work in mysterious ways."

Frank rode to town and talked with the owner of the hardware store and lumber yard. The next morning, Tuesday, Frank met a wagon that was delivering lumber to rebuild the church. He spent the morning stacking the lumber and covering it so that it would not get wet in a summer storm. He spent the afternoon taking notes and measurements.

During dinner, he talked with Kaitlin saying, "There was a time when I thought that I had been called to the priesthood. Now I know that I was just being prepared for the task of rebuilding and maintaining the church in Ellsworth."

"That's nice," said Kaitlin, ignoring him so that she could pay attention to feeding the babies.

Stone stepped outside and looked up into the starry sky asking, "Lord, is there any man more blessed than am I?"

Stone figured that it would take about five years to finish the exterior of the church. By then his girls would be of an age to go to Sunday school and then on to Confirmation. He smiled, relishing the thought of his two girls growing up in a world at peace. "I am indeed an extremely fortunate man," he said out loud.

MEANWHILE IN TEXAS, while Veronica was busy washing the dinner dishes and cleaning the kitchen and the dining room, Andy walked out to the final resting place of his oldest brother, Dwayne. Everett and Andy had decided to bury Dwayne in a thinly wooded area within the valley of the Spires. They designated that area as a family cemetery plot. Dwayne was buried in the land that he helped defend.

A white picket fence with a large vine-covered cottage fence gate surrounded the cemetery plot. A wooden bench was situated next to Dwayne's grave.

Andy sat on the bench and thought about his oldest brother. He remembered him as a youth and later as a successful lawyer and state senator. Tears came to Andy's eyes and he began to talk to the spirit that had once been Dwayne.

"You taught me to appreciate freedom and to fight injustice. You said that it is easy to blame the president for all of the nation's ills. But that when it comes to squandering tax dollars, the blame must be placed squarely at the feet of Congress, because no legislative bill may be passed into law unless it has first been passed by both houses."

Andy was distraught as he continued. "We have seen the Congress, one after another, squander the people's money for political, special interest, and personal gain. To those elected elitists, power and the political party have become more important than the country or the American people whom they deceitfully profess to serve. I fear that we as a nation have exchanged the despotism of a monarch for the repression of professional politicians and a corruptible Congress."

"Increasingly, professional politicians are compelling aggrieved Americans to assume the mantle of a new confederacy, one that is willing to fight political corruption. I see now, that the battle for justice and freedom is a never-ending individual battle."

Andy dried his eyes and started to return to his wife in the comfort of their home in the Spires: His home and his family that were made safe mainly because of the sacrifices of what Dwayne had called, "The Last Confederate Battle."

Looking up at the stars, Andy thought, *Jesus Christ died for our salvation, but it is the soldier who protects our freedom. And only through freedom can we experience the bounty of its handmaidens: peace, prosperity, and happiness.*

Andy crossed the patio and entered the house where he wrapped Veronica in a long and tender embrace.

"I love you without reservation," he said.

Now this is what freedom—real freedom feels like, he thought to himself as he kissed his wife.

And then Andy said a silent prayer as he continued to hold her.

Oh God, I thank you for leading me to green pastures, and I pray that you will always bless this country. Allow us to return to peace and prosperity and to remain one nation under you, Oh God, Amen.

ABOUT THE IDAHO AUTHOR

RECIPIENT OF THE Idaho "Governor's Award in the Arts" for 2012 and named as one of Idaho's Top Fifty authors in 2011, John J. Cline is the author of several books and numerous short stories.

Following a twenty five year career in both the enlisted ranks (Master Chief Petty Officer) and officer corps, John retired from the U.S. Navy as a Limited Duty Officer (Mustang) in July 1993 with the rank of Lieutenant Commander.

Following retirement from the Navy, he was appointed to the position of director of the Idaho Bureau of Disaster Services where he directed disaster mitigation and preparedness programs, and coordinated response and recovery operations for the State of Idaho, leading to the physical and economic recovery of Idaho communities that were seriously affected by natural and man-caused disasters.

He has a Bachelor of Science degree in Workforce Education and Curriculum Development from the University of Southern Illinois at Carbondale, and a Master's Degree in National Security Studies; Homeland Security and Defense, from Naval Postgraduate School, Monterey, California.

He is a graduate of the FBI National Academy (140th Session), and was nationally certified by the International Association of Emergency Managers and the National Coordinating Council on Emergency Management.

An avid Ham Radio Operator with the call sign W5USN, John recently returned to San Diego, California, to be near family while he writes his next book titled, "Rebuilding American Dreams", a sequel to The Last Confederate Battle.